finale

ALSO BY BECCA FITZPATRICK

Hush, Hush

Crescendo

Silence

finale

BECCA FITZPATRICK

THE CONCLUSION TO THE *NEW YORK TIMES*

BESTSELLING  SAGA

SIMON & SCHUSTER BFYR

NEW YORK LONDON TORONTO SYDNEY NEW DELHI

SIMON & SCHUSTER BFYR

An imprint of Simon & Schuster Children's Publishing Division

1230 Avenue of the Americas, New York, New York 10020

SIMON & SCHUSTER BFYR is a trademark of Simon & Schuster, Inc.

For information about special discounts for bulk purchases, please contact Simon & Schuster Special Sales at 1-866-506-1949 or business@simonandschuster.com.

The Simon & Schuster Speakers Bureau can bring authors to your live event. For more information or to book an event, contact the Simon & Schuster Speakers Bureau at 1-866-248-3049 or visit our website at www.simonspeakers.com.

Book design by Lucy Ruth Cummins

The text for this book is set in Seria.

Manufactured in the United States of America

2 4 6 8 10 9 7 5 3 1

CIP data for this book is available from the Library of Congress.

ISBN 978-1-4424-2667-2 (hardcover)

ISBN 978-1-4424-2669-6 (eBook)

ISBN 978-1-4424-8123-7 (Walmart proprietary edition)

For my mom, whom I've always been able to hear
cheering from the sidelines (Run, child, run!)

finale

EARLIER TODAY

SCOTT DIDN'T BELIEVE IN GHOSTS. DEAD MEN stayed in the grave. But the tunnels crisscrossing under Delphic Amusement Park, echoing with rustling, whispered sounds, made him rethink. He didn't like that his mind traveled to Harrison Grey. He didn't want to be reminded of his role in a man's murder. Moisture dripped from the low ceiling. Scott thought of blood. The fire from his torch cast skittish shadows on walls that smelled of cold, fresh earth. He thought of graves.

An icy current tickled the back of his neck. Over his shoulder, he gave the darkness a long, distrustful look.

Nobody knew he'd sworn an oath to Harrison Grey to protect Nora. Since he couldn't say, "Hey, man, sorry for getting you killed," in person, he'd defaulted to vowing to watch over Harrison's daughter. When it came to decent apologies, it didn't make the cut, not really, but it was the best he could think of. Scott wasn't even sure an oath to a dead man held any weight.

But the hollow sounds behind him made him think it did.

"You coming?"

Scott could just make out the dark outline of Dante's shoulders ahead. "How much longer?"

"Five minutes." Dante chuckled. "Scared?"

"Stiff." Scott jogged to catch up. "What happens at the meeting? I've never done this before," he added, hoping he didn't sound as stupid as he felt.

"Higher-ups want to meet Nora. She's their leader now."

"So the Nephilim have accepted that the Black Hand is dead?" Scott didn't fully believe it himself. The Black Hand was supposed to be immortal. All Nephilim were. So who'd found a way to kill him?

Scott didn't like the answer he kept going back to. If Nora had done this— If Patch had helped her—

It didn't matter how carefully they'd covered their tracks. They'd miss something. Everyone always did. It was only a matter of time.

If Nora had murdered the Black Hand, she was in danger.

"They've seen my ring," Dante answered.

Scott had seen it too. Earlier. The enchanted ring had sizzled like it had blue fire trapped under the crown. Even now it glowed a cold, dying blue. According to Dante, the Black Hand had prophesied it would be the sign of his death.

"Have they found a body?"

"No."

"And they're cool with Nora leading them?" Scott pressed. "She's nothing like the Black Hand."

"She swore a blood oath to him last night. It kicked in the moment he died. She's their leader, even if they don't like it. They can replace her, but they'll test her out first and try to figure out why Hank chose her."

Scott didn't like the sound of that. "And if they replace her?"

Dante flashed a dark gaze over his shoulder. "She dies. Terms of the oath."

"We're not going to let that happen."

"No."

"So everything's cool." Scott needed confirmation that Nora was safe.

"As long as she plays along."

Scott recalled Nora's argument from earlier in the day. *I'll meet the Nephilim. And I'll make my position clear: Hank may have started this war, but I'm finishing it. And this war is ending in ceasefire. I don't* care *if that's not what they want to hear.* He squeezed the bridge of his nose—he had a lot of work to do.

He trudged forward, keeping his eyes out for puddles. They rippled like oily kaleidoscopes, and the last one he'd accidentally stepped in had soaked him up to the ankle. "I told Patch I wouldn't let her out of my sight."

Dante grunted. "Scared of him, too?"

"No." But he was. Dante would be too, if he knew Patch at all. "Why couldn't she come with us to the meeting?" The decision to separate from Nora made him uneasy. He cursed himself for not arguing against it earlier.

"I don't know why we do half the things we do. We're soldiers. We take orders."

Scott remembered Patch's parting words to him. *She's on your watch. Don't screw up.* The threat dug under his skin. Patch thought he was the only one who cared about Nora, but he wasn't. Nora was the closest thing to a sister Scott had. She'd stood by him when no one else would, and had talked him down off the ledge. Literally.

They had a bond, and not *that* kind of bond. He cared about Nora more than any girl he'd ever known. She was his responsibility. If it mattered, he'd vowed as much to her dead father.

He and Dante pressed deeper into the tunnels, the walls tightening around their shoulders. Scott turned sideways to squeeze into the next passageway. Clumps of earth broke loose from the

BECCA FITZPATRICK

walls, and he held his breath, half expecting the ceiling to crumble in one great heave and bury them.

At last Dante tugged on a ring pull, and a door materialized out of the wall.

Scott surveyed the cavernous room inside. Same dirt walls, stone floor. Empty.

"Look down. Trapdoor," Dante said.

Scott stepped off the hatch door concealed in the stonework and yanked on the handle. Heated voices carried up through the opening. Bypassing the ladder, he dropped through the hole, landing ten feet below.

He assessed the cramped, cavelike room in an instant. Nephilim men and women wearing hooded black robes formed a tight circle around two figures he couldn't see clearly. A fire roared off to the side. A branding iron plunged into the coals glowed orange with heat.

"Answer me," a wiry old voice at the center of the circle snapped. "What is the state of your relationship with the fallen angel they call Patch? Are you prepared to lead the Nephilim? We need to know we have your full allegiance."

"I don't have to answer," Nora, the other figure, fired back. "My personal life isn't your business."

Scott stepped up to the circle, improving his view.

"You don't have a personal life," the old, white-haired woman with the wiry voice hissed, jabbing a frail finger at Nora, her sagging jowls trembling with rage. "Your sole purpose now is to lead your people to freedom from fallen angels. You're the Black Hand's heir, and while I don't desire to go against his wishes, I will vote you out if I must."

Scott glanced uneasily at the robed Nephilim. Several nodded in agreement.

Nora, he called to her in mind-speak. What are you doing? The blood oath. You have to stay in power. Say whatever you have to. Just calm them down.

Nora glared around with blind hostility until her eyes found his. *Scott?*

He nodded encouragingly. *I'm here. Don't freak them out. Keep them happy. And then I'll get you out of here.*

She swallowed, visibly trying to collect herself, but her cheeks still burned with outraged color. "Last night the Black Hand died. Since then I've been named his heir, thrust into leadership, whisked away from one meeting to the next, forced to greet people I don't know, ordered to wear this suffocating robe, interrogated on a myriad of personal subjects, poked and prodded, sized up and judged, and all this without a moment to catch my breath. So excuse me if I'm still reeling."

The old woman's lips pinched into a thinner line, but she didn't argue back.

"I'm the Black Hand's heir. He chose me. Don't forget," Nora said, and while Scott couldn't tell if she spoke with conviction or derision, the effect was silencing.

"Answer me one thing," the old woman said shrewdly after a heavy pause. "What has become of Patch?"

Before Nora could respond, Dante stepped forward. "She's not with Patch anymore."

Nora and Scott looked sharply at each other, then at Dante. *What was that?* Nora demanded of Dante in mind-speak, including Scott in the three-way conversation.

If they don't let you lead right now, you'll drop dead from the blood oath, Dante answered. *Let me handle this.*

By lying?

Got a better idea?

"Nora wants to lead the Nephilim," Dante spoke up. "She'll do whatever it takes. Finishing her father's work means everything to her. Give her a day to grieve, and then she'll dive in, fully committed. I'll train her. She can do this. Give her a chance."

"You'll train her?" the old woman asked Dante with a piercing gaze.

"This will work. Trust me."

The elderly woman pondered a long moment. "Brand her with the Black Hand's mark," she commanded at last.

The wild, terrified look in Nora's eyes nearly made Scott double over and vomit.

The nightmares. They shot out of nowhere, dancing in his head. Faster. Dizzy. Then came the voice. The Black Hand's voice. Scott flattened his hands to his ears, wincing. The maniacal voice cackled and hissed until the words all ran together to sound like a kicked hive of bees. The Black Hand's mark, seared into his chest, throbbed. Fresh pain. He couldn't differentiate between yesterday and now.

His throat choked out a command. "Stop."

The room seemed to halt. Bodies shifted, and suddenly Scott felt crushed by their hostile stares.

He blinked, hard. He couldn't think. He had to save her. No one had been around to stop the Black Hand from branding him. Scott wouldn't let the same thing happen to Nora.

The old woman walked over to Scott, her heels clicking on the floor in a slow, deliberate cadence. Deep grooves cut her skin. Watery green eyes peered out from sunken sockets. "You don't think she should show allegiance by example?" A faint, challenging smile curved her lips.

Scott's heart hammered. "Make her show it through action." The words just came out.

The woman tilted her head to one side. "What do you mean?"

At the same time, Nora's voice slipped into his head. Scott? she said nervously.

He prayed he wasn't making things worse. He licked his lips. "If the Black Hand had wanted her branded, he would have done it himself. He trusted her enough to give her this job. That's good enough for me. We can spend the rest of the day testing her, or we can get this war started already. Not one hundred feet over our heads lives a city of fallen angels. Bring one down here. I'll do it myself. Brand him. If you want fallen angels to know we're serious about war, let's send them a message." He could hear his own ragged breathing.

A slow smile warmed the old woman's face. "Oh, I like that. Very much. And who are you, dear boy?"

"Scott Parnell." He edged down the collar of his T-shirt. His thumb brushed the warped skin that formed his brand—a clenched fist. "Long live the Black Hand's vision." The words tasted like bile in his mouth.

Placing her spindly fingers on Scott's shoulders, the woman leaned in and kissed each of his cheeks in turn. Her skin was damp and cold as snow. "And I am Lisa Martin. I knew the Black Hand well. Long live his spirit, in all of us. Bring me a fallen angel, young man, and let us send a message to our enemy."

It was over soon.

Scott had helped chain down the fallen angel, a skinny kid named Baruch who looked about fifteen in human years. Scott's greatest fear had been that they would expect Nora to brand the fallen angel, but Lisa Martin had swept her into a private antechamber.

A robed Nephil had placed the branding iron in Scott's hands. He'd gazed down at the marble slab and the fallen angel manacled to it. Ignoring Baruch's cursing vows of revenge, Scott repeated the words the robed Nephil at his side murmured in his ear—a load of crap that compared the Black Hand to a deity—and pressed the hot iron onto the fallen angel's bare chest.

Now Scott leaned back against the tunnel wall outside the antechamber, waiting for Nora. If she stayed in there more than five minutes, he was going in after her. He didn't trust Lisa Martin. He didn't trust any of the robed Nephilim. It was clear they'd formed a secret society, and Scott had learned the hard way that nothing good came of secrets.

The door creaked open. Nora walked out, then threw her arms around his neck and held on tightly. *Thank you.*

He held her until she stopped trembling.

All in a day's work, he teased, trying to soothe her in the best way he knew how. *I'll put the U.O.ME in the mail.*

She sniffled a laugh. "You can tell they're really excited to have me as their new leader."

"They're in shock."

"Shocked that the Black Hand left their future up to me. Did you see their faces? I thought they were going to start weeping. Either that, or throw vegetables at me."

"So what are you going to do?"

"Hank is dead, Scott." She looked at him straight on, then dried her eyes by running her fingers under them, and he saw a flash of something in her expression he couldn't nail down. Assurance? Confidence? Or maybe, outright confession. "I'm going to celebrate."

I'M NOT A PARTY GIRL. THE EARSPLITTING MUSIC, THE gyrating bodies, the inebriated smiles—not my thing. My ideal Saturday night would be at home, snuggling on the sofa and watching a rom-com with my boyfriend, Patch. Predictable, low-key . . . normal. My name is Nora Grey, and while I used to be an average American teen, buying my clothes at the J. Crew outlet and spending my babysitting money on iTunes, normal and I have recently become perfect strangers. As in, I wouldn't know normal if it marched up and poked me in the eye.

Normal and I parted ways when Patch strolled into my life. Patch has seven inches on me, operates on cold, hard logic, moves like smoke, and lives alone in a supersecret, superswanky studio beneath Delphic Amusement Park. The sound of his voice, low and sexy, can melt my heart in three seconds flat. He's also a fallen angel, kicked out of heaven for his flexibility when it comes to following rules. I personally believe Patch scared the pants off normal, and it took off running for the far side of the world.

I might not have normalcy, but I do have stability. Namely, in the form of my best friend of twelve years, Vee Sky. Vee and I have an unshakable bond that even a laundry list of differences can't break. They say opposites attract, and Vee and I are proof of the validity of the statement. I am slender and tallish—by human standards—with big curly hair that tests my patience, and I'm a type A personality. Vee is even taller, with ash-blond hair, serpentine-green eyes, and more curves than a roller coaster track. Almost always, Vee's wishes trump mine. And unlike me, Vee lives for a good party.

Tonight Vee's wish to seek out a good time took us across town to a four-story brick warehouse throbbing with club music, swimming with fake IDs, and jam-packed with bodies producing enough sweat to take greenhouse gases to a whole new level. The layout inside was standard: a dance floor sandwiched between a stage and a bar. Rumor had it that a secret door behind the bar led to the basement, and the basement led to a man named Storky, who operated a thriving pirated *anything* business. Community religious leaders kept threatening to board up Coldwater's hot-bed of iniquity for disorderly teens . . . also known as the Devil's Handbag.

"Groove it, baby," Vee yelled at me over the mindless *thump, thump, thump* of music, lacing her fingers through mine and sway-ing our hands over our heads. We were at the center of the dance floor, being jostled and bumped on every side. "This is how Satur-day night's supposed to be. You and me gettin' down, letting loose, working up good ol'-fashioned girl-sweat."

I did my best to give an enthusiastic nod, but the guy behind me kept stepping on the heel of my ballet flat, and at five-second intervals, I had to shove my foot back into it. The girl to my right was dancing with her elbows out, and if I wasn't careful, I knew I'd get clipped.

"Maybe we should get drinks," I called to Vee. "Feels like Florida in here."

"That's 'cause you and me are burning up the place. Check out the guy at the bar. He can't take his eyes off your smokin' moves." She licked her finger and pressed it to my bare shoulder, making a sizzling noise.

I followed her gaze . . . and my heart lurched.

Dante Matterazzi lifted his chin in acknowledgment. His next gesture was a little more subtle.

Wouldn't have pegged you for a dancer, he spoke to my mind.

Funny, I would have pegged you for a stalker, I shot back.

Dante Matterazzi and I both belonged to the Nephilim race, hence the innate ability to mind-speak, but the similarities stopped there. Dante didn't know how to give it a rest, and I didn't know how much longer I could dodge him. I'd met him for the first time just this morning, when he'd come to my house to announce that fallen angels and Nephilim were on the brink of war and I was in charge of leading the latter, but now I needed a break from war talk. It was overwhelming. Or maybe I was in denial. Either way, I wished he'd disappear.

Left a message on your cell phone, he said.

Gee, I must have missed it. More like I deleted it.

We need to talk.

Kind of busy. To emphasize my point, I rolled my hips and swung my arms side to side, doing my best to imitate Vee, whose favorite television network was BET, and it showed. She had hip-hop stamped on her soul.

A faint smile quirked Dante's mouth. While you're at it, get your friend to give you some pointers. You're floundering. Meet me out back in two.

I glared at him. Busy, remember?

This can't wait. With a meaningful arch of his eyebrows, he disappeared into the crowd.

"His loss," Vee said. "He can't handle the heat, that's all."

"About those drinks," I said. "Can I bring you a Coke?" Vee

didn't look ready to give up dancing anytime soon, and as much as I wanted to avoid Dante, I figured it was best to just get this over with. Suck it up and talk to him. The alternative was having him shadow me all night.

"Coke with lime," Vee said.

I edged my way off the dance floor and, after making sure Vee wasn't watching, ducked down a side hallway and out the back door. The alley was bathed in blue moonlight. A red Porsche Panamera was parked in front of me, and Dante leaned against it, arms folded loosely over his chest.

Dante is six feet nine with the physique of a soldier fresh out of boot camp. Case in point: He has more muscle tone in his neck than I have in my entire body. Tonight he was wearing baggy khakis and a white linen shirt unbuttoned halfway down his chest, revealing a deep V of smooth, hairless skin.

"Nice car," I said.

"It gets the job done."

"So does my Volkswagen, and it cost considerably less."

"Takes more than four wheels to be a car."

Ugh.

"So," I said, tapping my foot. "What's so urgent?"

"You still dating that fallen angel?"

It was only the third time in as many hours that he'd asked. Twice by text messaging, and now face-to-face. My relationship with Patch had gone through a lot of ups and downs, but the current trend was

finale   15

upward. We weren't without our issues, however. In a world where Nephilim and fallen angels would rather die than smile at each other, dating a fallen angel was a definite no-no.

I stood a little taller. "You know it."

"Being careful?"

"Discreet is the watchword." Patch and I didn't need Dante to tell us it was wise not to make a lot of public appearances together. Nephilim and fallen angels never needed an excuse to teach each other a lesson, and racial tensions between the two groups were getting hotter with each passing day. It was autumn, October to be exact, and the Jewish month of Cheshvan was just days away.

Every year during Cheshvan, fallen angels possess Nephilim bodies by the droves. Fallen angels have free rein to do as they please, and since it's the only time during the year they can actually feel physical sensation, their creativity knows no bounds. They chase after pleasure, pain, and everything in between, playing parasites to their Nephilim hosts. For Nephilim, Cheshvan is a hellish prison.

If Patch and I were so much as seen holding hands by the wrong individuals, we'd pay, one way or another.

"Let's talk about your image," Dante said. "We need to generate some positive media around your name. Boost Nephilim confidence in you."

I gave a theatrical snap of my fingers. "Don't you just hate it when your approval ratings are low?"

Dante frowned. "This isn't a joke, Nora. Cheshvan starts in just over seventy-two hours, and that means war. Fallen angels on one side, us on the other. Everything rides on your shoulders—you're the new leader of the Nephilim army. The blood oath you swore to Hank is in effect, and I don't think I have to remind you that the consequences of breaking it are very, very real."

Queasiness pinched my stomach. I hadn't exactly applied for the job. Thanks to my deceased biological father, a truly twisted man named Hank Millar, I'd been forced to inherit the position. With the help of an otherworldly blood transfusion, he'd coerced me into transforming myself from mere human into purebred Nephil so I could take over his army. I'd sworn an oath to lead his army, it had gone into effect upon his death, and if I failed to do that, my mom and I would die. Terms of the oath. No pressure.

"Despite every cautious measure I intend to implement, we can't completely erase your past. The Nephilim are digging around. There are rumors you're dating a fallen angel, and that your loyalties are split."

"I *am* dating a fallen angel."

Dante rolled his eyes. "Could you say it any louder?"

I shrugged. *If that's what you really want.* Then I opened my mouth, but Dante was beside me in an instant, covering it with his hand. "I know it kills you, but could you make my job easy just this once?" he murmured in my ear, glancing around at the shadows with obvious uneasiness, even though I was positive we were alone. I'd only been a purebred Nephil for twenty-four hours, but I trusted my new, sharper sixth sense. If there were eavesdroppers lurking, I'd know.

"Look, I know when we first met this morning I carelessly said the Nephilim would just have to deal with me dating a fallen angel," I said when he lowered his hand, "but I wasn't thinking. I was angry. I've spent the day giving this a lot of thought. I've talked to Patch. We're being careful, Dante. Really careful."

"Nice to know. But I still need you to do something for me."

"Like what?"

"Date a Nephil. Date Scott Parnell."

Scott was the first Nephil I'd ever befriended, at the tender age of five. I hadn't known about his true heritage back then, but in recent months he'd taken on the roles of first my tormentor, then my partner in crime, and eventually my friend. There were no secrets between us. Likewise, there was no romantic chemistry.

I laughed. "You're killing me, Dante."

"It would be for show. For the sake of appearances," he explained. "Just until our race warms to you. You've only been a Nephil one day. Nobody knows you. People need a reason to like you. We have to make them feel comfortable trusting you. Dating a Nephil is a good step in the right direction."

"I can't date Scott," I told Dante. "Vee likes him."

To say Vee had been unlucky in love was putting it optimistically. In the past six months she'd fallen for a narcissistic predator and a backstabbing slimeball. Not surprisingly, both relationships made her seriously doubt her instincts in love. Lately, she had unequivocally refused to so much as smile at the opposite sex . . . until Scott came along. Early last night, just hours before my biological father had compelled me to transform myself into a purebred Nephil, Vee and I had come to the Devil's Handbag to watch Scott play bass for his new band, Serpentine, and she hadn't stopped talking about him since. To sweep in and steal Scott now, even if it was a ruse, would be the ultimate low blow.

"It wouldn't be real," Dante repeated, as if that made everything just peachy.

"Would Vee know that?"

"Not exactly. You and Scott would have to be convincing together. A leak would be disastrous, so I'd want to limit the truth to the two of us."

Meaning Scott would also be a casualty of the ruse. I did the hands-on-hips thing, going for firm and immovable. "Then you're going to have to come up with someone else." I wasn't enamored with the idea of fake-dating a Nephil to boost my popularity. In fact, it seemed like a disaster in the making, but I wanted this mess behind me. If Dante thought a Nephilim boyfriend would give me more street cred, so be it. It wouldn't be real. Obviously Patch wouldn't be thrilled, but tackle one problem at a time, right?

Dante's mouth compressed into a line, and he shut his eyes

briefly. Summoning patience. It was an expression I'd grown quite accustomed to over the course of the day.

"He'd need to be revered in the Nephilim community," Dante said thoughtfully at last. "Someone Nephilim would admire and approve of."

I made an impatient gesture. "Fine. Just throw someone other than Scott at me."

"Me."

I flinched. "Sorry. What? You?" I was too stunned to burst into laughter.

"Why not?" Dante asked.

"Do you really want me to start listing reasons? Because I'll keep you here all night. You've got to be at least five years older than me in human years—total scandal fodder—you don't have a sense of humor, and—oh yeah. We can't stand each other."

"It's a natural connection. I'm your first lieutenant—"

"Because Hank gave you the position. I had no say in that."

Dante didn't seem to hear me, charging ahead with his make-believe version of events. "We met and felt an instant and mutual attraction. I comforted you after your father's death. It's a believable story." He smiled. "Lots of good publicity."

"If you say the P word one more time, I'm going to . . . do something drastic." Like smack him. And then smack myself for even considering this plan.

"Sleep on it," Dante said. "Mull it over."

"Mulling it over." I counted to three on my fingers. "Okay, done. Bad idea. Really bad idea. My answer is no."

"You have a better idea?"

"Yes, but I'll need time to think it up."

"Sure. No problem, Nora." He counted to three on his fingers. "Okay, time's up. I needed a name first thing this morning. In case it isn't painfully obvious, your image is headed down the tubes. Word of your father's death, and subsequently your new leadership position, is spreading like wildfire. People are talking, and the talk isn't good. We need the Nephilim to believe in you. We need them to trust that you have their best interests in mind, and that you can finish your father's work and bring us out of bondage from fallen angels. We need them to rally behind you, and we're going to give them one good reason after another. Starting with a respected Nephilim boyfriend."

"Hey, babe, everything okay back here?"

Dante and I swung around. Vee stood in the doorway, eyeing us with equal parts wariness and curiosity.

"Hey! Everything's fine," I said a little too enthusiastically.

"You never came back with our drinks, and I started to worry," Vee said. Her gaze shifted from me to Dante. Recognition sparked in her eyes, and I knew she remembered him from the bar. "Who are you?" she asked him.

"Him?" I cut in. "Oh. Uh. Well, he's just some random guy—"

Dante stepped forward, hand extended. "Dante Matterazzi.

I'm a new friend of Nora's. We met earlier today when our mutual acquaintance, Scott Parnell, introduced us."

Just like that, Vee's face lit up. "You know Scott?"

"Good friend of mine, actually."

"Any friend of Scott's is a friend of mine."

Inwardly, I gouged my eyes out.

"So what are you two doing back here?" Vee asked us.

"Dante just picked out a new car," I said, stepping aside to give her an unobstructed view of the Porsche. "He couldn't resist showing it off. Don't look too closely, though. I think the VIN number is missing. Poor Dante had to resort to theft, since he used up all his money getting his chest waxed, and boy, does it gleam."

"Funny," Dante said. I thought maybe he'd self-consciously fasten at least one more shirt button, but he didn't.

"If I had a car like that, I'd show it off too," Vee said.

Dante said, "I tried talking Nora into a ride, but she keeps blowing me off."

"That's because she has a hard-A boyfriend. He must have been homeschooled, because he missed all those valuable lessons we learned in kindergarten, like sharing. He finds out you took Nora for a ride, he'll wrap this shiny new Porsche around the nearest tree."

"Gee," I said, "look at the time. Don't you have somewhere to be, Dante?"

"Turns out my night's open." He smiled, slow and easy, and I knew he was relishing every moment of intruding on my private life. I'd made it clear right off the bat this morning that any contact between us had to be done in private, and he was showing me what he thought of my "rules." In a lame attempt at evening the score, I glared my meanest, coldest look at him.

"You're in luck," Vee said. "We know just the thing to fill up your night. You're gonna hang with two of the coolest girls in all of Coldwater, Mr. Dante Matterazzi."

"Dante doesn't dance," I quickly interjected.

"I'll make an exception, just this once," he answered, opening the door for us.

Vee clapped her hands, jumping up and down. "I just knew this night was gonna rock!" she squealed, ducking under Dante's arm.

"After you," Dante said, placing his palm on the small of my back and guiding me inside. I batted his hand away, but to my aggravation, he leaned close and murmured, "Glad we had this little chat."

We haven't resolved anything, I spoke to his mind. *This whole boyfriend-girlfriend thing? Nothing is settled. Just a little something to bear in mind. And for the record, my best friend isn't supposed to know you exist.*

Your best friend thinks I should give your boyfriend a run for his money, he said, sounding amused.

She thinks anything with a beating heart should replace Patch. They have unresolved issues.

finale

Sounds promising.

He followed me down the short hall leading to the dance floor, and I felt his haughty, goading smile the whole way.

The loud monotone beat of the music drove into my skull like a hammer. I pinched the bridge of my nose, cringing against a swelling headache. I had one elbow perched on the bar, and I used my free hand to press a glass of ice water against my forehead.

"Tired already?" Dante asked, leaving Vee on the dance floor to slide onto a bar stool beside me.

"Any idea how much longer she's going to last?" I asked wearily.

"Looks to me like she's caught her second wind."

"Next time I'm in the market for a best friend, remind me to shy away from the Energizer Bunny. She keeps going and going. . . ."

"You look like you could use a ride home."

I shook my head. "I drove, but I can't leave Vee here. Seriously, how much longer can she possibly last?" Of course, I'd been asking myself the same question for the past hour.

"Tell you what. Go home. I'll stay with Vee. When she finally drops, I'll give her a ride."

"I thought you weren't supposed to get mixed up in my personal life." I tried to sound surly, but I was exhausted, and the conviction just wasn't there.

"Your rule, not mine."

I chewed my lip. "Maybe just this once. After all, Vee likes you. And you actually have the stamina to keep dancing with her. I mean, this is a good thing, right?"

He nudged my leg. "Quit rationalizing and get out of here already."

To my surprise, I sighed with relief. "Thanks, Dante. I owe you."

"You can pay me back tomorrow. We need to finish our earlier conversation."

And just like that, any benevolent feelings washed away. Once again, Dante was the thorn in my foot, relentless in his pestering. "If anything happens to Vee, I'm holding you personally responsible."

"She'll be fine, and you know it."

I might not like Dante, but I did trust he'd do what he said. After all, he reported to me now. He'd sworn allegiance to me. Maybe my role as leader of all Nephilim would have a few perks after all. On that note, I left.

It was a cloudless night, the moon a haunting blue against the black of night. As I walked to my car, the music from the Devil's Handbag echoed like a distant rumble. I inhaled the chilly October air. Already my headache ebbed.

The untraceable cell phone Patch had given me rang in my handbag.

finale

"How was girls' night out?" Patch asked.

"If Vee had her way, we'd be here all night." I stepped out of my shoes and slung them on my finger. "All I can think about is bed."

"We're sharing the same thought."

"You're thinking about bed too?" But Patch had told me that he rarely slept.

"I'm thinking about you in my bed."

My stomach did one of those flutter things. I'd stayed the night at Patch's place for the first time last night, and while the attraction and temptation had definitely been there, we'd managed to sleep in different rooms. I wasn't sure how far I wanted to take our relationship, but instinct told me Patch wasn't quite so indecisive.

"My mom's waiting up," I said. "Bad timing." Speaking of bad timing, I unwillingly recalled my most recent conversation with Dante. I needed to bring Patch up to speed. "Can we meet tomorrow? We need to talk."

"That doesn't sound good."

I smacked a kiss into the phone. "I missed you tonight."

"The night's not over. After I finish up here, I could swing by your place. Leave your bedroom window unlocked."

"What are you working on?"

"Surveillance."

I frowned. "Sounds vague."

"My target's on the move. I have to roll," he said. "I'll be there as soon as I can."

And he hung up.

I padded down the sidewalk, wondering who Patch was keeping an eye on, and why—the whole thing sounded a little ominous—when my car, a white 1984 Volkswagen Cabriolet, came into view. I threw my shoes into the backseat and dropped behind the wheel. I stuck the key in the ignition, but the engine didn't roll over. It repeatedly made a strained, chugging sound, and I took the opportunity to think a few choice and inventive words at the worthless piece of scrap metal.

The car had fallen into my lap as a donation from Scott, and had given me more hours of grief than actual miles on the road. I hopped out and propped the hood, glaring speculatively at the greasy labyrinth of hoses and containers. I'd already dealt with the alternator, the carburetor, and the spark plugs. What was left?

"Car trouble?"

I flipped around, surprised by the sound of a nasally male voice behind me. I hadn't heard anyone approach. More perplexing, I hadn't sensed him.

"It would appear so," I said.

"Need some help?"

"Pretty much I just need a new car."

He had a greasy, nervous smile. "Why don't I give you a lift? You look like a nice girl. We could have a nice talk while we drive."

I kept my distance, my mind spinning wildly as I tried to place him. Instinct told me he wasn't human. Nor was he Nephilim.

Funny thing was, I didn't think he was a fallen angel, either. He had a round, cherubic face topped with a thatch of yellow-blond hair, and floppy Dumbo ears. He looked so harmless, in fact, that it made me instantly suspicious. Instantly uneasy.

"Thanks for the offer, but I'll catch a ride with my friend."

His smile vanished and he lunged for my sleeve. "Don't go." His voice rose to a whine of desperation.

I took several startled steps back.

"That is— I mean— I was trying to say—" He gulped, then hardened his eyes into glittering beads. "I need to talk to your boyfriend."

My heart beat faster and a panicky thought seized me. What if he was Nephilim and I couldn't detect it? What if he really did know about me and Patch? What if he'd found me tonight to get a message across—that Nephilim and fallen angels don't mix? I was a brand-new Nephil, no match for him if it came to a physical confrontation.

"I don't have a boyfriend." I tried to stay calm as I turned back toward the Devil's Handbag.

"Put me in touch with Patch," the man called after me, that same desperate squeak pinching his voice. "He's avoiding me."

I picked up my pace.

"Tell him if he doesn't come out of hiding, I'll—I'll—smoke him out. I'll burn down the whole of Delphic Amusement Park if I have to!"

I glanced over my shoulder warily. I didn't know what Patch had gotten himself mixed up in, but I had an uncomfortable feeling swelling in my stomach. Whoever this man was, cherubic features aside, he meant business.

"He can't avoid me forever!" He scurried away on his stumpy legs until he blended into the shadows, whistling a tune that sent a jitter down my spine.

CHAPTER

A HALF HOUR LATER, I PULLED INTO MY DRIVE-
way. I live with my mom in a quintessential Maine
farmhouse, complete with white paint, blue shutters,
and a shroud of ever-present fog. This time of year, the trees blazed
fiery shades of red and gold, and the air held the crisp smells of
pine sap, burning wood, and damp leaves. I jogged up the porch
steps, where five portly pumpkins watched me like sentinels, and
let myself in.

"I'm home!" I called to my mom, the light in the living room giving away her location. I dropped my keys on the sideboard and went back to find her.

She dog-eared her page, rose from the sofa, and squeezed me in a hug. "How did your night go?"

"I am officially drained of every last ounce of energy." I pointed upstairs. "If I make it up to bed, it will be by sheer mental power alone."

"While you were out, a man stopped by looking for you."

I frowned. What man?

"He wouldn't leave his name, and he wouldn't tell me how he knew you," my mom continued. "Should I be worried?"

"What did he look like?"

"Round face, ruddy complexion, blond hair."

Him, then. The man who had a bone to pick with Patch. I fabricated a smile. "Oh, right. He's a salesman. Keeps trying to get me to commit to senior pictures with his studio. Next thing you know, he'll want to sell me graduation announcements too. Would it be completely disgusting if I skipped washing my face tonight? Staying awake an extra two minutes at this point is pushing it."

Mom kissed my forehead. "Sweet dreams."

I climbed to my bedroom, shut the door, and flopped spread-eagled on my bed. The music from the Devil's Handbag still pulsed at the back of my head, but I was too tired to care. My eyes were halfway shut when I remembered the window. On a groan, I staggered over and unlatched the lock. Patch could get inside, but I wished him luck trying to keep me awake long enough to elicit a response.

I pulled my blankets up to my chin, felt the soft, blissful tug of a dream beckoning me closer, let it drag me under—

And then the mattress sank with the weight of another body.

"Not sure why you're so enamored with this bed," Patch said. "It's twelve inches too short, four feet too narrow, and the purple sheets aren't doing it for me. My bed, on the other hand . . ."

I opened one eye and found him stretched out beside me, hands clasped loosely behind his neck. His dark eyes watched mine, and he smelled clean and sexy. Most of all, he felt warm pressed up against me. Despite my best intentions, the close proximity was making it increasingly difficult to concentrate on sleep.

"Ha," I said. "I know you don't care how comfortable my bed is. You'd be fine on a pallet of bricks." One of the downsides of Patch being a fallen angel was that he couldn't feel physical sensation. No pain, but no pleasure either. I had to be content knowing that when I kissed him, he felt it on an emotional level only. I tried to pretend it didn't matter, but I wanted him to feel electrified by my touch.

He kissed me lightly on the mouth. "What did you want to talk about?"

I couldn't remember. Something about Dante. Whatever it was, it seemed unimportant. Talking in general seemed unimportant. I snuggled in closer, and Patch stroked his hand down my bare arm, making a warm tingly sensation shoot all the way to my toes.

"When do I get to see these dance moves of yours?" he asked. "We've never gone dancing at the Devil's Handbag together."

"You aren't missing much. I was told tonight I'm definite fish-out-of-water material on the dance floor."

"Vee needs to be nicer to you," he murmured, pressing a kiss to my ear.

"Vee doesn't get credit for that line. That would go to Dante Matterazzi," I confessed absentmindedly, Patch's kisses lulling me into a happy place that didn't require a lot of reasoning or fore-thought.

"Dante?" Patch repeated, something unpleasant creeping into his tone.

Shoot.

"Did I forget to mention Dante was there?" I asked. Patch had also met Dante for the first time this morning, and for most of the tense meeting, I feared one would drag the other into a fistfight. Needless to say, it wasn't love at first sight. Patch didn't like Dante acting like he was my political adviser and pressuring me into war with fallen angels, and Dante . . . well, Dante hated fallen angels on principle.

Patch's eyes cooled. "What did he want?"

"Ah, now I remember what I wanted to talk to you about." I cracked my knuckles. "Dante's trying to sell me to the Nephilim race. I'm their leader now. Trouble is, they don't trust me. They don't know me. And Dante's made it his mission to change that."

"'Tell me something I don't know."

"Dante thinks it might be a good idea for me to, ah, date him. Don't worry!" I rushed on. "It's all for show. Got to keep the Nephilim thinking their leader is invested. We're going to squash these rumors that I'm dating a fallen angel. Nothing says solidarity like hooking up with one of your own, you know? It makes for good press. They might even call us Norante. Or Danta. Do you like the sound of that?" I asked, trying to keep the mood light.

Patch's mouth turned grim. "Actually, I don't like the sound of that."

"If it's any consolation, I can't stand Dante. Don't sweat this."

"My girlfriend wants to date another guy, no sweat."

"It's for appearances. Look on the bright side—"

Patch laughed, but the humor was lacking. "There's a bright side?"

"It's only through Cheshvan. Hank got Nephilim everywhere all worked up over this one moment. He promised them salvation, and they still think they're going to get it. When Cheshvan comes, and ends up being like any other Cheshvan on record, they'll realize it was a crapshoot, and little by little, things will go back to normal. In the meantime, while tempers are running hot and the hopes and dreams of Nephilim are hanging on the false belief that I can free them from fallen angels, we have to keep them happy."

"Has it occurred to you that the Nephilim might blame you

when their salvation doesn't come? Hank made a lot of promises, and when they aren't fulfilled, no one's going to point fingers at him. You're their leader now. You're the face on this campaign, Angel," he said solemnly.

I stared at the ceiling. Yes, I'd thought of it. More times today than I wanted to sanely contemplate.

One forever night ago, the archangels had made me the deal of a lifetime. They'd promised to give me the power to kill Hank—if I quashed the Nephilim rebellion. At first, I hadn't planned on taking the deal, but Hank had forced my hand. He'd tried to burn Patch's feather and send him to hell. So I shot him.

Hank was dead, and the archangels were expecting me to stop the Nephilim from going to war.

This was where things got tricky. Just hours before I shot Hank, I'd sworn an oath to him, vowing to lead his Nephilim army. Failure to comply would result in my death, and my mom's.

How to fulfill my promise to the archangels and my oath to Hank? I saw only one option. I would lead Hank's army. To peace. Probably not what he had pictured while forcing me to swear the oath, but he wasn't around now to argue the details. It didn't slip my mind, however, that in turning my back on the rebellion, I was also allowing the Nephilim to remain in bondage to fallen angels. It didn't seem right, but life was paved with difficult decisions. As I was learning all too well. Right now, I was more concerned with keeping the archangels happy than the Nephilim.

finale

"What do we know about my oath?" I asked Patch. "Dante said it went into effect when Hank died, but who determines if I keep it or not? Who determines what I can and can't do in terms of carrying out my oath? Take you, for instance. I'm confiding in you, a fallen angel and the sworn enemy of Nephilim. Won't the oath strike me dead for treason?"

"The oath you swore was about as vague as you could have made it. Luckily," Patch said with obvious relief.

Oh, it had been vague all right. And to the point. *If you die, Hank, I'll lead your army.* Not a word more.

"As long as you stay in power and lead the Nephilim, I think you're within the terms of the oath," Patch said. "You never promised Hank you'd go to war."

"In other words, the plan is to stay out of war and keep the archangels happy."

Patch sighed, almost to himself. "Some things never change."

"After Cheshvan, after the Nephilim give up on freedom, and *after* we've put a big, fat smile of contentment on the archangels' faces, we can put this behind us." I kissed him. "It'll just be you and me."

Patch groaned. "It can't come fast enough."

"Hey, listen," I told him, anxious to move on to *any* topic other than war, "I was approached by a man tonight. A man who wants a word with you."

Patch gave a nod. "Pepper Friberg."

"Does Pepper have a face as round as a basketball?"

Another nod. "He's tailing me because he thinks I went back on an agreement we had. He doesn't want a word with me. He wants to chain me in hell and dust his hands of me."

"Is it just me, or does that sound kind of serious?"

"Pepper Friberg is an archangel, but he's got his hand in more than one pot. He's leading a double life, spending half his time as an archangel, and the other half moonlighting as a human. Up until now, he's been living the best of both worlds. He has the power of an archangel, which he doesn't always use for good while indulging in human vices."

So Pepper was an archangel. No wonder I hadn't been able to identify him. I hadn't had a lot of experience dealing with archangels.

Patch went on, "Someone has figured out his crooked game, and word has it they're blackmailing him. If Pepper doesn't pay up soon, his vacation time on Earth is going to become a lot more permanent. The archangels will strip his power and tear out his wings if they find out what he's been up to. He'll be stuck down here for good."

The pieces clicked together. "He thinks you're blackmailing him."

"A while back I figured out what he was up to. I agreed to keep his secret, and in return he agreed to help me get my hands on a copy of the Book of Enoch. He hasn't delivered on his promise, and it seems logical that he thinks I'm feeling hung out to dry. But I think he must have been careless and there's another fallen angel out there looking to benefit off his misdeeds."

"Did you tell Pepper that?"

Patch smiled. "Working on it. He's not feeling very talkative."

"He said he'll burn down all of Delphic if that's what it takes to smoke you out." I knew archangels didn't dare set foot inside Delphic Amusement Park, fearing for their safety in a place built by and highly populated with fallen angels, so the threat made sense.

"His neck's on the line and he's getting desperate. I might have to go under."

"Go under?"

"Lie low. Keep my head down."

I pushed myself up on one elbow and stared at Patch. "How do I fit into this picture?"

"He thinks you're his one-way ticket to me. He's going to be sticking to you like spandex. He's parked down the street as we speak, eyes peeled for my car." Patch stroked his thumb across my cheek. "He's good, but not good enough to keep me from having quality time with my girl."

"Promise me you're always going to be two steps ahead." The thought of Pepper catching Patch and putting him on the fast track to hell didn't exactly give me a warm, fuzzy feeling.

Patch hooked a finger in my neckline and pulled me into a kiss. "Don't worry, Angel. I've been doing this sneaky stuff longer."

· · ·

When I woke, the bed next to me was cold. I smiled at the memory of falling asleep curled in Patch's arms, concentrating on that rather than the probability that Pepper Friberg, aka Mr. Archangel with a Dirty Secret, had sat outside my house all night, playing spy.

I thought back to a year ago, to the fall of my sophomore year. Back then, I hadn't so much as kissed a guy. Never could I have imagined what lay in store. Patch meant more to me than I could put into words. His love and faith in me took the sting out of the hard decisions I'd been forced to make recently. Whenever doubt and regret crept into my conscience, all I had to do was think of Patch. I wasn't sure I'd made the right choice every time, but I knew one thing for certain. I'd made the right choice in Patch. I couldn't give him up. Ever.

At noon, Vee called.

"How about me and you go running?" she said. "I just got a new pair of tennis shoes, and I need to break these bad boys in."

"Vee, I have blisters from dancing last night. And hold on. Since when do you like running?"

"It's no secret I'm carrying around a few extra pounds," she said. "I'm big-boned, but that's no excuse for letting a little flab hold me back. There's a guy out there named Scott Parnell, and if shedding some extra weight is what it's gonna take for me to get up the courage to go after him, then that's what I'm going to do. I want Scott to look at me the way Patch looks at you. I wasn't serious about this diet and exercise stuff before, but I'm turning over a new leaf. Starting today, I love exercise. It's my new BFF."

"Oh? And what about me?"

"Soon as I lose this weight, you'll be my number one girl again. I'll pick you up in twenty. Don't forget a sweatband. Your hair does scary stuff when it gets damp."

I hung up, stretched a tank over my head, followed it up with a sweatshirt, and laced myself into tennis shoes.

Right on time, Vee picked me up. And right away, it became apparent we weren't driving to the high school track. She steered her purple Neon across town, in the opposite direction from school, humming to herself.

I said, "Where are we going?"

"I was thinking we should run hills. Hills are good for the glutes." She turned the Neon onto Deacon Road, and a light popped on in my head.

"Hang on. Scott lives on Deacon Road."

"Come to think of it, he does."

"We're running by Scott's house? Isn't that kind of . . . I don't know . . . stalkerish?"

"That's a real sad-hat way of looking at it, Nora. Why not think of it as motivation? Eye on the prize."

"What if he sees us?"

"You're friends with Scott. If he sees us, he'll probably come out and talk to us. And it would be rude not to stop and give him a couple minutes of our time."

"In other words, this isn't about running. This is a pickup."

Vee wagged her head. "You're no fun at all."

She cruised up Deacon, a winding stretch of scenic road bordered on both sides by dense evergreens. In another couple of weeks, they'd be frosted with snow.

Scott lived with his mom, Lynn Parnell, in an apartment complex that came into view around the next bend. Over the summer, Scott had moved out and gone into hiding. He'd deserted Hank Millar's Nephilim army, and Hank had searched tirelessly for him, hoping to make an example of him. After I killed Hank, Scott had been free to move home.

A cement fence caged the property, and while I was certain privacy had been the intent, it gave the place the feel of a compound. Vee pulled into the entrance, and I had a flashback to the time she had helped me snoop in Scott's bedroom. Back when I thought he was an up-to-no-good jerk. Boy, had things changed. Vee parked near the tennis courts. The nets were long gone, and someone had decorated the turf with graffiti.

We got out and stretched for a couple of minutes.

Vee said, "I don't feel safe leaving the Neon unattended for long in this neighborhood. Maybe we should do laps around the complex. That way I can keep my eye on my baby."

"Uh-huh. It also gives Scott more opportunities to see us."

Vee had on pink sweatpants with DIVA stamped across the butt in gold glitter, and a pink fleece jacket. She also had on full makeup, diamond studs in her ears, and a ruby cocktail ring, and she smelled like Pure Poison by Dior. Just your average day out running.

We picked up our feet and started a slow jog along the dirt trail circling the complex. The sun was out, and after three laps, I stripped off my sweatshirt, tying it around my waist. Vee beelined to a weathered park bench and plunked down, sucking air.

"That had to be about five miles," she said.

I surveyed the trail. Sure . . . give or take four miles.

"Maybe we should peek in Scott's windows," Vee suggested. "It's Sunday. He might be oversleeping and need a friendly wake-up call."

"Scott lives on the third floor. Unless you have a forty-foot ladder stashed in the trunk of the Neon, window peeping is probably out."

"We could try something more direct. Like knocking on his door."

Just then an orange Plymouth Barracuda, circa 1970, vroomed into the parking lot. It pulled under the carport, and Scott swung out. Like most Nephilim men, Scott has the body of someone seemingly well acquainted with a weight room. He's also unusually tall, pushing six feet six. He keeps his hair cropped as short as a prison inmate's, and he's good-looking—in a tough, hardened way. Today he was wearing mesh basketball shorts and a T-shirt with the sleeves ripped off.

Vee fanned herself. "Yowza."

I stuck my hand in the air, intending to call out to Scott and flag his attention, when the Barracuda's passenger door opened and Dante emerged.

"Check it out," Vee said. "It's Dante. Do the math. Two of them, and two of us. I knew I'd like running."

"I'm feeling the sudden urge to keep running," I muttered. And not stop until I'd put a lot of ground between me and Dante. I wasn't in the mood to follow up last night's conversation. Likewise, I wasn't in the mood for Vee to play matchmaker. She was too aggravatingly good at it.

"Too late. We've been made." Vee whipped her arm over her head like a helicopter propeller.

Sure enough, Scott and Dante leaned back against the Barracuda, shaking their heads and grinning at us.

"You stalking me, Grey?" Scott hollered.

"He's all yours," I told Vee. "I'm going to finish running."

"What about Dante? He'll feel like the third wheel," she said.

"It'll be good for him, trust me."

"Where's the fire, Grey?" Scott called out, and to my dismay, he and Dante started jogging over.

"I'm training," I shot back. "I'm thinking about . . . trying out for track."

"Track doesn't start until spring," Vee reminded me.

Hang it all.

finale   43

"Uh-oh, heart rate's dropping," I yelled at Scott. And on that note, I took off running in the opposite direction.

I heard Scott on the trail behind me. A minute later, he snagged the strap of my tank top, tugging on it playfully. "Want to tell me what's going on?"

I turned to face him. "What does it look like?"

"It looks like you and Vee came over to see me under the pretense of running."

I gave his shoulder a congratulatory pat. "Good work, ace."

"So why are you running away? And why does Vee smell like a perfume factory?"

I stayed quiet, letting him figure it out.

"Ah," he said at last.

I spread my hands. "My work here is done."

"Don't take this the wrong way, but I'm not sure I'm ready to hang out with Vee all day. She's pretty . . . intense."

Before I could give him the sage advice, "Fake it till you make it," Dante pulled up beside me.

"A word with you?" he asked.

"Oh boy," I said under my breath.

"That's my cue to go," Scott said, and to my discouragement, he trotted away, leaving me alone with Dante.

"Can you run and talk at the same time?" I asked Dante, thinking I'd prefer not to have to look him in the eye while he rehashed his thoughts on our jury-rigged relationship. Plus, it spoke volumes about just how into this conversation I was.

By way of answer, Dante picked up his pace, jogging beside me.

"Glad to see you out running," he said.

"And why's that?" I panted, shoving some loose hairs off my sweat-soaked face. "You get a thrill out of seeing me a complete mess?"

"That, and it's good training for what I have in store for you."

"You have something in store for me? Why do I get the feeling I don't want to hear more?"

"You may be Nephilim now, Nora, but you're at a disadvantage. Unlike naturally conceived Nephilim, you don't have the advantage of extreme height, and you aren't as physically powerful."

"I'm a lot stronger than you think," I argued.

"Stronger than you *were*. But not as strong as a female Nephil. You have the same body you did when you were human, and while it was adequate back then, it's not enough to compete now. Your frame is too slender. Compared to me, you're abysmally short. And your muscle tone is pathetic."

"Now that's flattery."

"I could tell you what I think you want to hear, instead of what you need to hear, but would I really be your friend then?"

"Why do you think you need to tell me any of this?"

"You're not prepared to fight. You don't stand a chance against a fallen angel. It's as simple as that."

"I'm confused. Why do I need to fight? I thought I made it clear repeatedly yesterday that there isn't going to be a war. I'm leading the Nephilim to peace." And keeping the archangels off my back. Patch and I had decided unequivocally that enraged Nephilim made a better enemy than the all-powerful archangels. It was evident that Dante wanted to go into battle, but we disagreed. And as leader of the Nephilim army, the decision was ultimately mine. I felt like Dante was undermining me, and I didn't like it one bit.

He stopped, catching me by the wrist so he could look straight at me. "You can't control everything that happens from here on out," he said quietly, and a chill of foreboding slipped through me like I'd swallowed an ice cube. "I know you think I've got it out for you, but I promised Hank I'd look after you. I'll tell you one thing. If war breaks out, or even a riot, you won't make it. Not in your current state. If something happens to you and you're unable to lead the army, you'll have broken your oath, and you know what that means."

Oh, I knew what it meant, all right. Jumping into my own grave. And dragging my mom in behind me.

"I want to teach you enough skills to get by, as a precaution," Dante said. "That's all I'm suggesting."

I swallowed. "You think if I train with you, I can get to the point where I'll be strong enough to handle myself." Against fallen angels, sure. But what about the archangels? I'd promised to halt the rebellion. Training for battle wasn't aligned with that goal.

"I think it's worth a shot."

The idea of war turned my stomach into a bundle of knots, but I didn't want to show fear in front of Dante. He already thought I couldn't handle myself. "So which is it? Are you my pseudo boyfriend or my personal trainer?"

His mouth twitched. "Both."

3

WHEN VEE DROPPED ME OFF AFTER RUN-ning, there were two missed calls on my cell phone. The first was from Marcie Millar, my sometimes arch-nemesis and, as fate would have it, my half sister by blood, but not by love. I'd spent the past seventeen years having no knowledge that the girl who stole my chocolate milk in elementary school and adhered feminine pads to my school locker in junior high shared my DNA. Marcie had figured out the truth first, and flung it in my face. We had an unspoken contract not to discuss our relationship publicly, and for the most part, the knowledge hadn't changed us any. Marcie was still a spoiled anorexic airhead, and I still spent a good portion of my waking hours watching my back, wondering what humiliation scheme she'd launch at me next.

Marcie hadn't left a message, and I couldn't guess what she'd want from me, so I moved to the next missed call. Unknown number. The voice mail consisted of controlled breathing, low and masculine, but no actual words. Maybe Dante, maybe Patch. Maybe Pepper Friberg. My personal number was listed, and with a little investigative spirit, Pepper could have tracked it down. Not the most reassuring of thoughts.

I hauled out my piggy bank from under my bed, removed the rubber cheat plug, and shook out seventy-five dollars. Dante was picking me up at five tomorrow morning for wind sprints and weight lifting, and after one disgusted glance at my current tennis shoes, he'd remarked, "Those won't make it through a day of training." So here I was, using my allowance to buy cross-trainers.

I didn't think the threat of war was as serious as Dante had made it sound, especially since Patch and I secretly had plans to pull the Nephilim out of the doomed uprising, but his words on my size, speed, and agility had struck a chord. I *was* smaller than every other Nephil I knew. Unlike them, I had been born into a human body—average weight, average muscle tone, average in every single aspect—and it had taken a blood transfusion and the

finale

swearing of a Changeover Vow to turn me into a Nephil. I was one of them in theory, but not in practice. I didn't want the discrepancy to paint a target on my back, but a little voice at the back of my mind whispered it might.

And I had to do whatever it took to stay in power.

"Why do we have to start so early?" should have been my first question to Dante, but I suspected I knew the answer. The world's fastest humans would appear as though out for a leisurely stroll if racing beside Nephilim. At top speed, I suspected that Nephilim in their prime could run upward of fifty miles per hour. If Dante and I were seen using that speed on the high school track, it would draw a lot of unwanted attention. But in the predawn hours of Monday morning most humans were fast asleep, giving Dante and me the perfect opportunity to have a worry-free workout.

I tucked the money in my pocket and headed downstairs. "I'll be back in a few hours!" I called to my mom.

"Pot roast comes out at six, so don't be late," she returned from the kitchen.

Twenty minutes later I strolled through the doors of Pete's Locker Room and headed toward the shoe department. I tried on a few pairs of cross-trainers, settling on a pair from the clearance rack. Dante might have my Monday morning—a day off school, due to a district-wide teacher in-service day—but I wasn't going to give him the sum total of my allowance, too.

I paid for the shoes and checked the time on my cell. Not even four yet. As a precaution, Patch and I had agreed to keep calls in public to a minimum, but a hasty look both ways down the sidewalk outside confirmed I was alone. I dug the untraceable phone Patch had given me out of my handbag and dialed his number.

"I have a free couple of hours," I told him, walking toward my car, which was parked on the next block. "There's a very private, very secluded barn in Lookout Hill Park behind the carousel. I could be there in fifteen minutes."

I heard the smile in his voice. "You want me bad."

"I need an endorphin boost."

"And making out in an abandoned barn with me will give you one?"

"No, it will probably put me in an endorphin coma, and I'm more than happy to test the theory. I'm leaving Pete's Locker Room now. If the stoplights are in my favor, I might even make it in ten—"

I didn't get to finish. A cloth bag dropped over my head, and I was wrestled into a bear hug from behind. In my surprise, I dropped the cell phone. I screamed and tried to swing my arms free, but the hands shoving me forward and into the street were too strong. I heard a large vehicle rumble down the street, then come to a screeching halt beside me.

A door opened, and I was thrust inside.

The air inside the van held the tang of sweat masked by lemon air freshener. The heat was cranked up to high, blasting through vents

finale

at the front, making me sweat. Maybe that was the intent.

"What's going on? What do you want?" I demanded angrily. The full weight of what was going on hadn't hit yet, leaving me more outraged than frightened. No answer came, but I heard the steady breathing of two nearby individuals. Those two, plus the driver, meant three of them. Against one of me.

My arms had been twisted behind my back, pinned together by what felt like a tow chain. My ankles were secured by a similar heavy-duty chain. I was stretched out on my stomach, the bag still over my head, my nose pushed into the roomy floor of the van. I tried to rock onto my side but felt as though my shoulder joint would tear from its socket. I screamed out in frustration and received a swift kick in the thigh.

"Keep it down," a male voice growled.

We drove for a long time. Forty-five minutes, maybe. My mind jumped in too many directions to keep track accurately. Could I escape? How? Outrun them? No. Outwit them? Maybe. And then there was Patch. He would know I'd been taken. He'd track my cell phone to the street outside Pete's Locker Room, but how would he know where to go from there?

At first the van stopped repeatedly for stoplights, but eventually the road cleared. The van climbed higher, weaving back and forth on switchbacks, which made me believe we were moving into the remote, hilly areas far outside of town. Sweat trickled beneath my shirt, and I couldn't seem to force a single deep breath. Each inhalation came shallow, panic clamping my chest.

The tires popped over gravel, steadily rolling uphill, until at last the engine died. My captors unchained my feet, dragged me outside and through a door, and yanked the bag off my head.

I was right; there were three of them. Two males, one female. They'd brought me to a log cabin, and they rechained my arms to a decorative wooden post that ran from the main level up to the tie beams at the ceiling. No lights, but that may have well been because the power had been shut off. Furniture was sparse, and covered in white sheets. The air couldn't have been more than a degree or two warmer than outside, telling me the furnace wasn't on. Whoever the cabin belonged to had closed up for winter.

"Don't bother screaming," the bulkiest of them told me. "There isn't another warm body around for miles." He hid behind a cowboy hat and sunglasses, but his precaution was unnecessary; I was positive I'd never seen him before. My heightened sixth sense identified all three as Nephilim. But what they wanted from me . . . I didn't have a clue.

I jerked against the chains, but other than producing a weak grinding sound, they didn't budge.

"If you were a *real* Nephil, you'd be able to break out of the chains," the Nephil in the cowboy hat snarled. He seemed to be the spokesman for the other two, who hung back, limiting their communication with me to glares of disgust.

"What do you want?" I repeated icily.

finale

Cowboy Hat's mouth curled into a sneer. "I want to know how a little princess like yourself thinks she can pull off a Nephilim revolution."

I held his hateful gaze, wishing I could fling the truth in his face. There wasn't going to be a revolution. Once Cheshvan started in less than two days, he and his friends would be possessed by fallen angels. Hank Millar had had the easy part: filling their heads with notions of rebellion and freedom. And now I was left to work the actual miracle.

And I wasn't going to.

"I looked into you," Cowboy Hat said, pacing in front of me. "I asked around and found out you're dating Patch Cipriano, a fallen angel. How's that relationship working out for you?"

I swallowed discreetly. "I don't know who you've been talking to." I knew the danger I faced if my relationship with Patch were found out. I'd been careful, but it was starting to look like not careful enough. "But I ended things with Patch," I lied. "Whatever we had is in the past. I know where my loyalties lie. As soon as I became a Nephil—"

He thrust his face in mine. "You aren't Nephilim!" His eyes raked over me with contempt. "Look at you. You're pathetic. You don't get the right to call yourself Nephilim. When I look at you, I see human. I see a weak, sniveling, entitled little girl."

"You're angry because I'm not as physically strong as you," I stated calmly.

"Who said anything about strength! You don't have pride.

There's no sense of loyalty inside you. I respected the Black Hand as a leader because he earned that respect. He had a vision. He took action. He named you his successor, but that means nothing to me. You want my respect? Make me give it to you." He snapped his fingers savagely in my face. "Earn it, princess."

Earn his respect? So I could be like Hank? Hank was a cheat and a liar. He'd promised his people the impossible with smooth words and flattery. He'd used and deceived my mom and turned me into a pawn in his agenda. The more I thought about the position he'd put me in, leaving me to carry out his demented vision, the more maddened I grew.

I met Cowboy Hat's eyes coldly . . . then bucked my foot up with all the force I had and planted it squarely in his chest. He sailed backward into the wall and crumpled on the floor.

The other two rushed forward, but my anger had started a fire inside me. A foreign and violent power swelled in me, and I strained against the chains, hearing the metal creak as the links snapped apart. The chains dropped to the floor, and I didn't waste a minute before lashing out with my fists. I pummeled the nearest Nephil in the ribs and gave the female a roundhouse kick. My foot collided with her thigh, and I was amazed by the solid mass of muscle I found there. Never before in my life had I encountered a woman of such strength and durability.

Dante was right; I didn't know how to fight. A moment too late, I realized I should have followed through, mercilessly attacking while they were down. But I was too stunned by what I'd done to do more than hunch in a defensive position, waiting to see what their response would be.

Cowboy Hat charged at me, thrusting me backward into the post. The impact knocked all air from my lungs and I doubled over, trying but failing to draw oxygen.

"I'm not done with you, princess. This was your warning. If I find out you're still running with fallen angels, it won't be pretty." He patted my cheek. "Use this time to reconsider your loyalties. Next time we meet, for your sake, I hope they've shifted."

He signaled the others with a jerk of his chin, and they all filed out the door.

I gulped air, taking a few minutes to recover, then staggered to the door. They were already gone. Road dust sifted through the air, and dusk crept across the skyline, a smattering of stars glittering like tiny shards of broken glass.

4

I STEPPED OUT ON THE CABIN'S SMALL STOOP, WONDER-
ing how I'd navigate my way home, when the sound of an
engine roared up the long gravel driveway ahead. I braced
myself for the return of Cowboy Hat and friends, but it was a
Harley Sportster motorcycle that tore into view, carrying a single
rider.

Patch.

He swung off and crossed to me in three quick strides. "Are

you hurt?" he asked, taking my face between his hands and look-ing me over for any sign of injury. A mix of relief, worry, and rage blazed in his eyes. "Where are they?" he asked, his tone as hardened as I'd ever heard it.

"There were three of them, all Nephilim," I said, my voice still shaky from fright and the whiplash of having my breath knocked out of me. "They left about five minutes ago. How did you find me?"

"I activated your tracking device."

"You put a tracking device on me?"

"Sewn into the pocket of your jean jacket. Cheshvan starts with Tuesday's new moon, and you're an unsworn Nephil. You're also the Black Hand's daughter. You've got a premium on your head, and that makes you pretty damn appealing to just about every fallen angel out there. You're not swearing fealty, Angel, end of story. If that means I have to cut into your privacy, deal with it."

"Deal with it? Excuse me?" I wasn't sure if I should hug him or shove him.

Patch ignored my indignation. "Tell me everything you can about them. Physical descriptions, make and model of the car, any-thing that will help me track them down." His eyes sizzled with vengeance. "And make them pay."

"Did you also bug my phone?" I wanted to know, still not over the idea that Patch had invaded my privacy without telling me.

He didn't hesitate. "Yes."

"In other words, I have no secrets."

His expression softened and he looked as though, had the mood not been so tense, he might have considered smiling. "There are still a few things you've managed to keep secret from me, Angel."

Okay, I walked right into that.

I said, "The ringleader hid behind sunglasses and a cowboy hat, but I'm positive I've never seen him before. The other two—a male and a female—wore nondescript clothing."

"Car?"

"I had a bag over my head, but I'm positive it was a van. Two of them sat in the back with me, and the door sounded like it slid open sideways when they forced me out."

"Anything else stand out?"

I told Patch the ringleader had threatened to uncover our secret relationship.

Patch said, "If word of us gets out, things could get ugly fast." His brows pulled together, and his eyes darkened with uncertainty. "Are you sure you want to continue trying to keep our relationship off the radar? I don't want to lose you, but I'd rather do it on our terms than theirs."

I slipped my hand in his, noting how cold his skin felt. He'd grown still, too, as if bracing for the worst. "I'm either in this with you, or I'm out," I told him, and I meant every word. I'd lost Patch once before, and not to be melodramatic, but death was preferable. Patch was in my life for a reason. I needed him. We were two halves of the same whole.

finale

Patch gathered me against him, holding me with a certain possessive ferocity. "I know you're not going to like this, but we might want to think about staging a public fight to send a clear message that our relationship is over. If these guys are serious about digging up secrets, we can't control what they find. This is starting to feel like a witch hunt, and we might be better off making the first move."

"Stage a fight?" I echoed, dread trickling through me like a winter chill.

"We'd know the truth," Patch murmured in my ear, running his hands briskly over my arms to warm them. "I'm not going to lose you."

"Who else would know the truth? Vee? My mom?"

"The less they know, the safer they are."

I let go of a conflicted sigh. "Lying to Vee is getting really old. I don't think I can do it anymore. I feel guilty every time I'm around her. I want to come clean. Especially about something as important as you and me."

"It's your call," Patch said gently. "But they won't hurt her if they think she has nothing to tell."

I knew he was right. Which didn't leave me a choice in the matter, did it? Who was I to put my best friend in harm's way for the sake of appeasing my conscience?

"We probably won't be able to fool Dante—you work too closely with him," Patch said. "And it might even work out better if he knows. He can back up your story when he talks with influential

Nephilim." Patch shrugged out of his leather jacket and slipped it over my shoulders. "Let's get you home."

"Can we make a quick stop by Pete's Locker Room first? I need to pick up my cell phone, and the untraceable one you gave me. I dropped one during the attack, and the other got left behind in my handbag. If we're lucky, my new shoes are still on the sidewalk too."

Patch kissed the top of my head. "Both phones need to be put out of service. They left your possession, and if we assume the worst, your Nephilim abductors put their own tracking or listening devices on them. Best to get new phones."

One thing was sure. If I'd been unmotivated to train with Dante before, all that had changed. I needed to learn to fight, and fast. Between dodging Pepper Friberg and advising me on my new role as Nephilim leader, Patch had enough to worry about without needing to rush in from the sidelines every time I got in over my head. I was immensely grateful for his protection, but it was time I learned to take care of myself.

It was full dark by the time I got home. I walked through the door, and my mom hurried out of the kitchen, looking both worried and aggravated.

"Nora! Where have you been? I called but kept getting your voice mail."

I could have slapped my forehead. Dinner. At six. I'd completely missed it.

"I am so sorry," I said. "I misplaced my phone in one of the stores. By the time I realized I'd lost it, it was almost dinnertime, and I had to backtrack all over town. I never found it, so now I'm not only out a phone, but I blew you off. I am so sorry. I didn't have a way to call." I hated that I was forced to lie to her again. I'd done it so many times it seemed like once more shouldn't hurt, but it did. It made me feel less and less like her daughter, and more and more like Hank's. My biological father had been an expert and unrivaled liar. And I was hardly in a position to be critical.

"You couldn't stop and find some way to call me?" she said, not sounding for one minute like she believed my story.

"It won't happen again. I promise."

"I don't suppose you were with Patch?" I didn't miss the cynical emphasis on his name. My mother regarded Patch with as much affection as the raccoons that often wreaked havoc on our property. I didn't doubt she fantasized about standing on the porch with a rifle perched on her shoulder, watching for him to show his face.

I inhaled, swearing this would be the last lie. If Patch and I were really going through with the staged fight, it was best to start planting seeds now. I told myself that once I took care of Mom and Vee, everything else would be downhill. "I wasn't with Patch, Mom. We broke up."

She raised her eyebrows, still not looking convinced.

"It just happened, and no, I don't want to talk about it." I started for the stairs.

"Nora—"

I turned back, and there were tears in my eyes. They were unexpected and not part of the act. I merely remembered the last time Patch and I had broken up for real, and a viselike sensation squeezed me, stealing my breath. The memory would forever haunt me. Patch had taken the best parts of me with him, leaving a lost and hollow girl behind. I didn't want to be that girl again. Ever.

Mom's expression eased up. She met me on the stairs, rubbed my back soothingly, and whispered in my ear, "I love you. If you change your mind and want to talk . . ."

I nodded, then went to my bedroom.

There, I told myself, trying hard to sound optimistic. *One down, one to go.* I wasn't exactly lying to my mom and Vee about the breakup; I was merely doing what had to be done to keep them safe. Honesty was the best policy, most of the time. But sometimes safety trumped all, right? It seemed like a valid argument, but the thought soured in my stomach.

There was another worrisome thought scratching at the back of my mind. How long could Patch and I live a lie . . . and not let it become the truth?

Five o'clock Monday morning arrived all too soon. I smacked my alarm, cutting it off mid-beep. Then I rolled over and told myself, *Two more minutes.* I closed my eyes, let my mind float, saw a new dream start to take shape—and the next thing I knew, I caught a handful of clothes in the face.

"Rise and shine," Dante said, standing over my bed in the dark.

"What are you doing in here?" I shrieked groggily, snatching my blanket and tugging it higher.

"Doing what any decent personal trainer would. Get your butt out of bed and get dressed. If you're not in the driveway in three minutes, I'll come back with a bucket of cold water."

"How did you get in?"

"You left your window unlocked. Might want to break that habit. Hard to control what comes in when you give the world a free pass."

He strolled toward my bedroom door just as I stumbled out of bed.

"Are you crazy? Don't use the hall! My mom might hear you. A guy doing what appears to be the walk of shame out my bedroom door? I'll be grounded for life!"

He looked amused. "For the record, I wouldn't be ashamed."

I stood in place a whole ten seconds after he left, wondering if I was supposed to read deeper into his words. Of course not. His line might have felt flirtatious, but it wasn't. End of story.

I tugged on black track pants and a stretchy microfiber shirt, and slicked my hair into a ponytail. If nothing else, I'd look good while Dante ran me into the ground.

Exactly three minutes later, I met him in the driveway. I looked around, sensing the absence of something important. "Where's your car?"

Dante punched me lightly in the shoulder. "Feeling lazy? Tsk, tsk. I thought we'd warm up with a brisk ten-mile run." He pointed toward the densely wooded area across the street. As kids Vee and I had explored the woods, and even built a fort one summer, but I'd never taken the time to wonder how far they stretched. Apparently, at least ten miles. "After you."

I hesitated. I didn't feel great about running off into the wilderness with Dante. He'd been one of Hank's top men— reason enough not to like or trust him. In hindsight, I never should have agreed to train alone with him, especially if our training arena was remote.

"After training, we should probably review the feedback I'm getting from various Nephilim groups about morale, expectations, and you," Dante added.

After training. Meaning he didn't intend to discard me at the bottom of an abandoned well in the next hour. Besides, Dante answered to me now. He'd sworn loyalty. No longer Hank's lieu-tenant, he was now mine. He wouldn't dare harm me.

Allowing myself the luxury of one final thought of blissful sleep, I shrugged off the fantasy and darted into the tree line. The branches stretched like a canopy overhead, shutting out what little trace of light the early sky might have had to offer. Relying on my heightened Nephilim vision, I ran hard, vaulting over fallen trees, dodging low-hanging branches, and keeping my eyes sharp for sunken rocks and other camouflaged debris. The ground was treacherously uneven, and at the speed I was traveling, one missed step could be disastrous.

"Faster!" Dante barked behind me. "Run lighter on your feet. You sound like a stampeding rhinoceros. I could find and catch you with my eyes closed!"

I took his words to heart, lifting my feet the moment they hit ground, repeating this process with every step, concentrating on making myself as noiseless and undetectable as possible. Dante raced ahead, blowing past me with ease.

"Catch me," he ordered.

Chasing after him, I marveled at the strength and agility of my new Nephilim body. I was amazed by how clunky, slow, and uncoordinated my human body had been in comparison. My athleticism wasn't merely improved, it was superior.

I dipped under branches, jumped over potholes, and darted around boulders as though I were on an obstacle course I'd long ago memorized. And while I felt like I was running fast enough to lift off and soar into the sky at any moment, my pace lagged behind Dante's. He moved like an animal, gaining the momentum of a predator chasing down its next meal. Soon I'd lost track of him altogether.

I slowed, straining my ears. Nothing. A moment later he bounded out of the darkness ahead.

"That was pathetic," he criticized. "Again."

I spent the next two hours sprinting after him and hearing that same directive repeated over and over: *Again*. And again. Still not right—do it *again*.

I was about to call it quits—my leg muscles trembled with exhaustion and my lungs felt scraped raw—when Dante circled back. He gave me a congratulatory pat on the back. "Good work. Tomorrow we'll move to strength training."

"Oh? By lifting boulders?" I managed cynically, still huffing and puffing.

"By uprooting trees."

I stared at him.

"Pushing them over," he elaborated cheerfully. "Get a full night's sleep—you're going to need it."

"Hey!" I called after him. "Aren't we still miles from my house?"

"Five, actually. Consider it your cooldown jog."

finale

CHAPTER

5

TWELVE HOURS LATER I WAS STIFF AND SORE FROM
this morning's workout, edging my way gingerly up and
down the stairs, which seemed to give my muscles the
most grief. But any R & R would have to wait; Vee was picking me
up in ten minutes, and I still hadn't changed out of the sweats I'd
spent the day lounging in.

Patch and I had decided to stage our fight publicly tonight, so
there'd be no question about the state of our relationship: We had

split ways and were staunchly on opposite sides in this brewing war. We'd also opted to make our scene at the Devil's Handbag, knowing it was a popular Nephilim hangout. While we didn't know the identities of the Nephilim who'd attacked me, or if they'd be there tonight, Patch and I were certain that news of our split would travel fast. Finally, the bartender scheduled to work the night shift, Patch had learned, was a quick-tempered Nephilim supremacist. Vital, Patch had assured me, to our plan.

I shucked out of my sweats and slipped into a chunky cable-knit sweaterdress, tights, and ankle boots. I twisted my hair into a low bun, shaking a few pieces loose to frame my face. Exhaling, I stared at my reflection in the mirror and manufactured a smile. All in all, I didn't look too bad for a girl about to engage in a devastating fight with the love of her life.

The consequences of tonight's fight only have to last a couple weeks, I told myself. Just until this whole Cheshvan mess blows over.

Besides, the fight wasn't real. Patch had promised we'd find ways to meet. In secret moments and stolen glances. We'd just have to be extra careful.

"Nora!" my mom called up the stairs. "Vee's here."

"Wish me luck," I murmured to my reflection, then grabbed my coat and scarf and flicked off the bedroom light.

"I want you home by nine," my mom told me when I descended to the foyer. "No exceptions. It's a school night."

I kissed her on the cheek and hustled out the door.

Vee had the Neon's windows rolled down, and her stereo was cranking out Rihanna. I dropped into the passenger seat and called over the music, "I'm surprised your mom let you out on a school night."

"She had to fly to Nebraska last night. Her uncle Marvin died, and they're divvying up his estate. Aunt Henny is watching me." Vee looked sideways, and her grin hinted at mischief.

"Wasn't your Aunt Henny in rehab a couple years ago?"

"That would be the one. Too bad it didn't work out for her. She's got a gallon of apple juice in the fridge, but it's the most fermented apple juice I've ever taken a swig of."

"And your mom deemed her responsible enough to watch you?"

"Guess the prospect of getting some of Uncle Marvin's money softened her up."

We roared down Hawthorne, belting out the lyrics and dancing in our seats. I was antsy and nervous but thought it best to act like nothing was out of the ordinary.

The Devil's Handbag was only moderately busy tonight, a decent crowd, but not standing room only. Vee and I slid into a booth, unloaded our coats and handbags, and ordered Cokes from a waitress who swept past. I surreptitiously glanced around for Patch, but he hadn't surfaced. I'd rehearsed my lines too many times to count, but my palms were still slick with sweat. I wiped them on my thighs, wishing I were a better performer. Wishing I liked drama and attention.

BECCA FITZPATRICK

"You don't look so good," Vee said.

I was about to quip that I was probably carsick from her lack of finesse at driving, when Vee's eyes swiveled past me and her expression soured. "Oh heck no. Tell me that isn't Marcie Millar flirting with my man."

I craned my neck toward the stage. Scott and the other members of Serpentine were onstage warming up for the show, while Marcie propped her elbows prettily on the stage, singling out Scott for conversation.

"Your man?" I asked Vee.

"Soon to be. Same difference."

"Marcie flirts with everyone. I wouldn't worry about it."

Vee did some deep breathing that actually made her nostrils flare. Marcie, as if sensing Vee's negative vibe like voodoo, looked our way. She gave us her best beauty pageant wave.

"Do something," Vee told me. "Get her away from him. Now."

I jumped up and strolled over to Marcie. On the way over, I worked up a smile. By the time I reached her, I was pretty sure it looked almost genuine. "Hey," I told her.

"Oh, hey, Nora. I was just telling Scott how much I love indie music. Nobody in this town ever amounts to anything. I think it's cool he's trying to make it big."

Scott winked at me. I had to shut my eyes briefly to keep from rolling them.

"So . . . ," I drew out, struggling to fill the lapse in conversation.

finale

At Vee's command, I'd come over here, but now what? I couldn't just drag Marcie away from Scott. And why was *I* the one over here playing referee? This was Vee's business, not mine.

"Can we talk?" Marcie asked me, saving me from having to come up with a tactic on my own.

"Sure, I have a minute," I said. "Why don't we go somewhere more quiet?"

As if reading my mind, Marcie grabbed my wrist and propelled me out the back door and into the alley. After glancing both ways to make sure we were alone, she said, "Did my dad tell you anything about me?" She dropped her voice further. "About being Nephilim, I mean. I've been feeling funny lately. Tired and crampy. Is this some kind of weird Nephilim menstruation thing? Because I thought I already went through that."

How was I supposed to tell Marcie that purebred Nephilim, like her parents, rarely mated together successfully, and when they did, the offspring were weak and sickly, and that some of Hank's final words to me included the somber truth that Marcie would in all likelihood not live much longer?

In short, I couldn't.

"Sometimes I feel tired and crampy too," I said. "I think it's normal—"

"Yeah, but did my dad *say* anything about it?" she pressed. "What to expect, how to cope, that kind of thing."

"I think your dad loved you and would want you to keep living

BECCA FITZPATRICK

your life, not stressing about the whole Nephilim thing. He'd want you to be happy."

Marcie looked at me incredulously. "Happy? I'm a freak. I'm not even human. And don't think for one minute I've forgotten you aren't either. We're in this together." She jabbed her finger accusingly at me.

Oh boy. Just what I needed. Solidarity . . . with Marcie Millar.

"What do you really want from me, Marcie?" I asked.

"I want to make sure you understand that if you so much as hint to anyone that I'm not human, I will burn you. I will bury you alive."

I was running out of patience. "First off, if I wanted to announce to the world that you're Nephilim, I already would have. And second, who would believe me? Think about it. 'Nephilim' isn't an everyday word in the vocabulary of most people we know."

"Fine," Marcie huffed, apparently satisfied.

"Are we done here?"

"What if I need someone to talk to?" she persisted. "It's not like I can dump this on my psychiatrist."

"Um, your mom?" I suggested. "She's a Nephil too, remember?"

"Ever since my dad disappeared, she's refused to accept the truth about him. Big-time denial issues going on there. She's convinced he's coming back, that he still loves her, that he'll annul the divorce, and our lives will go back to being peachy keen."

Denial issues, maybe. But I wouldn't put Hank above mind-tricking his ex-wife with a memory-altering enchantment so powerful that its effects lasted beyond his death. Hank and vanity went together like matching socks. He wouldn't have wanted anyone speaking ill of his memory. And as far as I knew, no one in Coldwater had. It was as if a numbing fog had settled over the community, keeping human and Nephilim residents alike from asking the big question of what had happened to him. There wasn't a single story going around town. People, when they spoke of him, simply murmured, "What a shock. Rest his soul. Poor family, ought to ask how I can help . . ."

Marcie continued, "But he's not coming back. He's dead. I don't know how or why or who did it, but there is no way my dad would drop off the grid unless something happened. He's dead. I know it."

I tried to keep my expression sympathetic, but my palms started to sweat again. Patch was the only other person on Earth who knew I'd sent Hank to the grave. I had no intention of adding Marcie's name to the insider list.

"You don't sound too broken up about it," I said.

"My dad was messed up in some pretty bad stuff. He deserved what he got."

I could have opened up to Marcie then and there, but something didn't feel right. Her cynical gaze never wavered from my face, and I got the feeling she suspected I knew vital information about her father's death, and her indifference was an act to get me to divulge.

I wasn't going to walk into a trap, if that's what this was.

"It's not easy losing your dad, believe me," I said. "The pain never really goes away, but it does eventually become bearable. And somehow, life moves on."

"I'm not looking for a sympathy card, Nora."

"Okay," I said with a reluctant shrug. "If you ever need to talk, I guess you can call me."

"I won't have to. I'm moving in with you," Marcie announced. "I'll bring my stuff over later this week. My mom is driving me crazy, and we both agree I need somewhere else to crash for a while. Your place is as good as any. Well, I for one am so glad we had this talk. If there's one thing my dad taught me, it's that Nephilim stick together."

CHAPTER

6

No," I BLURTED AUTOMATICALLY. "NO, NO, NO. YOU can't just—move in with me." A feeling of pure panic escalated from my toes to the tips of my ears, blowing up faster than I could contain it. I needed an argument. Now. But my brain kept spitting out the same frantic and completely unhelpful thought—No.

"I've made up my mind," Marcie said, and disappeared inside.

"What about me?" I called out. I kicked the door, but what I really felt like doing was kicking myself around for an hour or two. I'd done Vee a favor and look where it had gotten me.

I flung open the door and marched inside. I found Vee at our booth.

"Which way did she go?" I demanded.

"Who?"

"Marcie!"

"I thought she was with you."

I shot Vee my best bristled look. "This is all your fault! I have to find her."

Without further explanation, I pushed through the crowd, eyes alert and attentive for any sign of Marcie. I needed to sort this out before it got wildly out of hand. *She's testing you*, I told myself. *Putting feelers out. Nothing is set in stone.* Besides, my mom had final say in this. And she wouldn't let Marcie move in with us. Marcie had her own family. She was short one parent, sure, but I was a living testament that family was about more than numbers. Buoyed by this line of thinking, I felt my breathing start to relax.

The lights dimmed and the lead singer for Serpentine grabbed the mic, pounding his head in a silent cadence. Taking the cue, the drummer hammered out an intro, and Scott and the other guitarist joined in, kicking off the show with a violent and angsty number. The crowd went wild, head-banging and chanting the lyrics.

I gave one last frustrated glance around for Marcie, then dropped it. I'd have to sort things out with her later. The start of the show was my signal to meet Patch at the bar, and just like that, my heart was back to lurching in my chest.

I made my way over to the bar and took the first bar stool I saw. I sat down a little too hard, losing my balance at the last second. My legs felt like they were made of rubber, and my fingers shook. I didn't know how I was going to get through this.

"ID, sweetheart?" the bartender asked. An electric-like current vibrated off him, alerting me that he was Nephilim. Just as Patch had said he'd be.

I shook my head. "Just a Sprite, please."

Not a moment later, I felt Patch move behind me. The energy radiating off him was far stronger than the bartender's, skimming like heat under my skin. He always had that effect on me, but unlike usual, tonight the sizzling current made me sick with anxiety. It meant Patch had arrived, and I was out of time. I didn't want to go through with this, but I understood that I didn't really have a choice. I had to play this smart and factor in my safety, and that of those I loved most dearly.

Ready? Patch asked me in the privacy of our thoughts.

If feeling like I'll throw up at any minute constitutes ready, sure.

I'll come over to your place later and we'll talk it over. Right now, let's just get through this.

I nodded.

Just like we rehearsed, he spoke calmly to my mind.

Patch? Whatever happens, I love you. I wanted to say more, those three words pitifully inadequate for the way I felt about him. And at the same time, so simple and accurate, nothing else would do.

No regrets, Angel.

None, I returned solemnly.

The bartender finished up with a customer and walked over to take Patch's order. His eyes raked over Patch, and by the scowl that immediately appeared on his face, it was obvious he'd discerned that Patch was a fallen angel. "What'll it be?" he asked, his tone clipped, as he wiped his hands on a dish towel.

Patch slurred in an unmistakably inebriated voice, "One beautiful redhead, preferably tall and slim, with legs a man can't seem to find the end of." He traced his finger down my cheekbone, and I tensed and pulled away.

"Not interested," I said, taking a sip of Sprite and keeping my eyes steadfastly on the mirrored wall behind the bar. I let just enough anxiety leak into my words to pique the bartender's attention.

He leaned across the bar, resting his massive forearms on the slab of granite, and stared Patch down. "Next time review the menu before you waste my time. We don't offer disinterested females, red hair or otherwise." He paused with menacing effect, then started toward the next waiting customer.

"And if she's Nephilim, all the better," Patch announced drunkenly.

The bartender stopped, eyes glittering with malice. "Mind

keeping your voice down, pal? We're in mixed company. This place is open to humans, too."

Patch brushed this off with an uncoordinated wave of his arm. "Sweet of you to worry about the humans, but one quick mind-trick later, and they won't remember a word I've said. Done the trick so many times I can do it in my sleep," he said, letting a bit of swagger creep into his tone.

"You want this lowlife gone?" the bartender asked me. "Say the word and I'll get the bouncer."

"I appreciate the offer, but I can handle myself," I told him. "You'll have to excuse my ex for being a total jerk-off."

Patch laughed. "Jerk-off? That's not what you called me last time we were together," he implied suggestively.

I just stared at him, disgusted.

"She wasn't always Nephilim, you know," Patch informed the bartender with wistful nostalgia. "Maybe you've heard of her. The Black Hand's heir. Liked her better when she was human, but there's a certain cachet in running around with the most famous Nephil on Earth."

The bartender eyed me speculatively. "You're the Black Hand's kid?"

I glared at Patch. "Thanks for that."

"Is it true the Black Hand is dead?" the bartender asked. "Can't hardly comprehend it. A great man, rest his soul. My respects to your family." He paused, bewildered. "But dead as in . . . *dead*?"

"Word has it," I murmured quietly. I couldn't quite bring myself to shed a tear for Hank, but I did speak with a melancholic reverence that seemed to satisfy the bartender.

"A free round of drinks to the fallen angel who got him," Patch interrupted, raising my glass in a toast. "I think we can all agree that's what happened. Immortal just doesn't have the same ring anymore." He laughed, banging his fist on the bar in high spirits.

"And you used to date this pig?" the bartender asked me.

I flicked my eyes to Patch and frowned. "A repressed memory."

"You know he's a"—the bartender lowered his voice—"fallen angel, right?"

Another sip and a hard swallow. "Don't remind me. I've made amends—my new boyfriend is Dante Matterazzi, one hundred percent Nephilim. Maybe you've heard of him?" No time like the present to start a rumor.

His eyes lit up, impressed. "Sure, sure. Great guy. Everyone knows Dante."

Patch closed his hand over my wrist too firmly to be affectionate. "She's got it all wrong. We're still together. What do you say we get out of here, sugar?"

I jumped at his touch, as if shocked. "Get your hands off me."

"I've got my bike out back. Let me take you for a ride. For old time's sake." He stood, then dragged me off my barstool so roughly it toppled.

finale

"Get the bouncer," I ordered the bartender, letting full-fledged anxiety flood my voice. "Now."

Patch hauled me toward the front doors, and while I put on a convincing show of trying to wrench free, I knew the worst was still to come.

The club's bouncer, a Nephil who had the advantage not only of several inches over Patch, but also a hundred pounds, elbowed his way toward us. He grabbed Patch by the collar, tearing him off me and sending him flying into the wall. Serpentine had worked up to a fever pitch, drowning out the scuffle, but those in the immediate vicinity parted, forming a semicircle of curious onlookers around the two men.

Patch raised his hands level with his shoulders. He flashed a brief, intoxicated smile. "I don't want any trouble."

"Too late," the bouncer said, and smashed his fist into Patch's face. The skin above Patch's eyebrow split, seeping blood, and I forced myself not to wince or reach for him.

The bouncer jerked his head at the doors. "If you ever show your face here again, you and trouble gonna be fast friends. You understand?"

Patch stumbled toward the door, giving a sloppy salute to the bouncer. "Aye, aye, sir."

The bouncer planted his foot in the crook of Patch's knee, sending him tripping down the cement stoop. "Would you look at that. My foot slipped."

A man just inside the door laughed, low and harsh, and the sound snatched my attention. This wasn't the first time I'd heard the laugh. When I was human, I wouldn't have recognized it, but all my senses were heightened now. I squinted through the darkness, trying to match the rankling laugh to a face.

There.

Cowboy Hat. He wasn't wearing a hat or sunglasses tonight, but I could place those hunched shoulders and that caustic smile anywhere.

Patch! I shouted, unable to see whether he was still within hearing range as the crowd closed around me, filling in the empty spaces now that the fight was over. *One of the Nephilim from the cabin. He's here! He's just inside the doorway, wearing a red-and-black flannel shirt, jeans, and cowboy boots.*

I waited, but there was no response.

Patch! I tried again, using all the mental power I possessed. I couldn't follow him outside—not if I wanted to keep my cover.

Vee appeared at my side. "What's going on here? Everyone's talking about a fight. I can't believe I missed it. Did you see any of it?"

I pulled her aside. "I need you to do something for me. See the guy just inside the doors, in the hick flannel shirt? I need you to find out his name."

Vee frowned. "What's this all about?"

"I'll explain later. Flirt, steal his wallet, whatever it takes. Just don't mention my name, okay?"

finale

"If I do this, I want a favor in return. A double date. You and your whack-job boyfriend, and me and Scott."

With no time to explain that Patch and I were finished, I said, "Yes. Now hurry before we lose him in the crowd."

Vee cracked her knuckles and sashayed off. I didn't hang around to see how she fared. I threaded my way through the crowd, ducking out the back door and jogging to the top of the alley. I rounded the building, looking both ways for Patch.

Patch! I cried out to the shadows.

Angel? What are you doing? It's not safe for us to be seen together.

I spun around, but Patch wasn't there. Where are you?

Across the street. In the van.

I looked across the street, and sure enough, there was a rusty brown Chevy van parked at the curb. It blended into the backdrop of dilapidated buildings. The windows were tinted, shielding the inner cab from prying eyes.

One of the Nephilim from the cabin is inside the Devil's Handbag! A thick beat of silence.

Did he see the fight? Patch asked after a moment.

Yes.

What does he look like?

He's wearing a black-and-red flannel shirt and cowboy boots.

Get him to leave the building. If the others from the cabin are with him, get them out too. I want to talk to them.

Coming from Patch it sounded ominous, but then again,

they had it coming. They'd lost my sympathies the moment they'd stuffed me inside their van.

I jogged back inside the Devil's Handbag and worked my way into the thick crowd packed around the stage. Serpentine was still going strong, rocking out a ballad that had everyone riled up. I didn't know how to get Cowboy Hat to leave the premises, but I knew one person who could help me clear the whole place.

Scott! I yelled. But it was useless. He couldn't hear me over the thunderous music. It probably didn't help that he was deep in concentration.

I rose up on my tiptoes and looked for Vee. She was heading this way.

"I put the ol' Vee charm on him, but he wasn't having any of it," she told me. "Maybe I need a new haircut." She sniffed her underarms. "Far as I can tell, deodorant's still working."

"He blew you off?"

"Yup, and I didn't get his name, either. Does this mean our double date is off?"

"I'll be right back," I said, and fought my way to the alley once again. I had every intention of getting close enough to Patch to mind-speak to him that forcing our Nephil friend out of the Devil's Handbag was going to be harder than I anticipated, when two shadowy figures standing on the back stoop of the next building down, and conversing in hushed tones, brought me to an abrupt stop.

finale

Pepper Friberg and . . . Dabria.

Dabria used to be an angel of death, and dated Patch before both were banished from heaven. Patch had sworn up and down that the relationship was boring, chaste, and more of a convenience than anything. Still. After deciding I was a threat to her plans to rekindle their relationship here on Earth, Dabria had tried to kill me. She was cool, blond, and sophisticated. I'd never seen her have a bad hair day, and her smile had a way of filling my veins with ice. Now a fallen angel, she made her living swindling victims on the false pretense of having the gift of foresight. She was one of the most dangerous fallen angels I knew, and I had no doubt I was right at the top of her hate list.

Instantly I drew back against the Devil's Handbag. I held my breath for five seconds, but neither Pepper nor Dabria seemed to have noticed me. I inched closer but didn't dare press my luck. By the time I'd get close enough to hear what they were saying, one or both would have sensed my presence.

Pepper and Dabria talked a few minutes longer before Dabria turned on her heel and strolled away down the alley. Pepper made an obscene gesture at her back. Was it just me, or did he look especially disgruntled?

I waited until Pepper left too before I stepped out of the shadows. I went directly inside the Devil's Handbag. I found Vee at our booth and slid in beside her.

"I need to clear this place out right now," I said.

BECCA FITZPATRICK

Vee blinked. "Come again?"

"What if I shout 'fire'? Will that work?"

"Shouting 'fire' seems a little old-school to me. You could try shouting 'police,' but that falls into the same category. Not that I have anything against old-school. But what's the big rush? I didn't think Serpentine sucked that bad."

"I'll explain—"

"Later." Vee nodded. "Saw that coming from a mile away. If it were me, I'd go with shouting 'police.' Bound to be more than a few someones doing illegal activity in this place. Scream 'cops!' and you'll see movement."

I gnawed nervously at my lip, debating. "Are you sure?" This seemed like a plan with high potential for blowing up in my face. Then again, I was out of options. Patch wanted to have a chat with Cowboy Hat, and that's what I wanted too. I also wanted to get the interrogation wrapped up quickly so I could tell Patch about Dabria and Pepper.

Vee said, "Thirty-five percent sure . . ."

Her voice trailed off as cold air blasted the room. At first I couldn't tell if the sudden temperature drop came from the doors, which had been kicked open, or my own physical response to intuitively sensing trouble—of the worst kind.

Fallen angels flooded into the Devil's Handbag. I lost count of them at ten, with no sign to an end in their numbers. They moved so fast, I saw only blurs of motion. They'd come prepared to fight, swinging knives and knuckles bearing steel hardware at anything standing in their path. Among the fray, I stared helplessly as two Nephil boys sank to their knees, futilely resisting the fallen angels who stood over them, clearly demanding their oaths of fealty.

One fallen angel, bony and pale as the moon, chopped his arm so viciously at a Nephil girl's neck, he broke it in the middle of her scream.

He inspected the girl's face, which eerily resembled my own face from this distance. Same long, curly hair. She was also about my height and build.

He studied her face and growled impatiently. His cold eyes scanned the crowd, and I got the feeling he was hunting for his next victim.

"We need to get out of here," Vee said urgently, gripping my hand tightly. "This way."

Before I could wonder if Vee, too, had seen the fallen angel break the girl's neck, and if she had, how she was possibly remaining so calm, she shoved me forward into the crowd.

"Don't look back," she yelled in my ear. "And hurry."

Hurry. Right. Trouble was, we were fighting at least a hundred other people to the doors. In a matter of seconds, the crowd had turned into a frantic mob, shoving and scrambling to reach an exit. Serpentine had stopped mid-song. There was no time to go back for Scott. I could only hope he'd escaped through the stage doors.

Vee stayed on my heels, bumping me from behind so often, I

had to wonder if she was trying to shield my body. Little did she know, *I* would be trying to protect *her* if the fallen angels caught up to us. And despite my single yet grueling training session with Dante this morning, I didn't think I stood a chance at succeeding.

The temptation to turn back and fight ballooned suddenly inside me. Nephilim had rights. *I* had rights. Our bodies didn't belong to fallen angels. They had no just cause to possess us. I'd hastily promised the archangels I would stop the war, but I had a personal stake in the outcome. I wanted war, and I wanted freedom, so that I would never, ever have to bend on one knee and swear my body over to anyone else.

But how could I get what I wanted, and appease the archangels?

At last Vee and I plunged into the cold night air. The crowd fled into the darkness both ways down the street. Without stopping to catch our breath, we raced toward the Neon.

CHAPTER

V EE BOUNCED THE NEON INTO THE DRIVEWAY OF
the farmhouse and punched the stereo off.

"Well, that was enough crazy for one night," she said.
"What was that? Greasers verses Socs?"

I'd been holding my breath, but I exhaled softly in relief. No
hyperventilating. No hysterical hand gestures. No mention of
necks snapping. Luckily, Vee hadn't seen the worst of it. "You're
one to talk. You never read *The Outsiders*."

"I saw the movie. Matt Dillon was hot before he got old."

A thick, expectant silence filled the car.

"Okay, cut the crap," Vee said. "Small talk's over. Spill." When I hesitated, she added, "That was some crazy business back there, but something was wrong way before that. You were acting funny all night. I saw you running in and out of the Devil's Handbag. And then, suddenly, you want to clear out the place. I gotta tell you, babe. I need an explanation."

This was where things got tricky. I wanted to tell Vee the whole truth, but it was also vital to her safety that she believe the lies I was about to tell her. If Cowboy Hat and his friends were serious about digging around in my personal life, sooner or later they'd learn Vee was my best friend. I couldn't stand the idea of them threatening or questioning her, but if they did, I wanted every answer she gave them to sound convincing. Most important, I wanted her to tell them, without any hesitation, that all my ties to Patch had been severed. I intended to throw water on this fire before it raged out of hand.

"While I was at the bar tonight, Patch came over, and it wasn't pretty," I began quietly. "He was—wasted. He said some stupid things, I refused to leave with him, and he got physical."

"Holy shiz," Vee muttered under her breath.

"The bouncer kicked Patch out."

"Wow. I'm speechless. What do you make of all this?"

I flexed my hands opened and closed in my lap. "Patch and I are over."

finale

"Over over?"

"As over as they come."

Vee leaned across the console and gave me a hug. She opened her mouth, saw my expression, and thought better of it. "I won't say it, but you know I'm thinking it."

A tear wobbled at the edge of my eye. Vee's evident relief only made the lie feel that much uglier inside me. I was an awful friend. I knew it, but I didn't know how to set it right. I refused to put Vee in harm's way.

"What's the story with the dude in the flannel shirt?"

What she doesn't know can't hurt her. "Before Patch got kicked out, he warned me to stay away from the guy in the flannel shirt. Patch said he knew him, and he was trouble. That's why I asked you to find out his name. I kept catching him watching me, and it made me nervous. I didn't want him to follow me home, if that's what he planned on doing, so I decided to cause mass chaos. I wanted us to be able to leave the Devil's Handbag without making it easy for him to pick us out and follow us."

Vee exhaled, long and slow. "I believe you broke up with Patch. But I don't believe for one minute the other story."

I flinched. "Vee—"

She put her hand up. "I get it. You've got your secrets, and one of these days you'll tell me what's going on. And I'll tell you." She arched her eyebrows knowingly. "That's right. You aren't the only one with secrets. I'll spill when the time is right, and I figure you will too."

I stared at her. This wasn't how I'd expected our conversation to go. "You have secrets? What secrets?"

"Juicy secrets."

"Tell me!"

"Would you look at that," Vee said, tapping the clock on the dash. "I believe it's your curfew."

I sat openmouthed. "I can't believe you're keeping secrets from me."

"I can't believe you're being such a hypocrite."

"This conversation isn't over," I said, opening the door reluctantly.

"Not easy on the other side, is it?"

I said good night to my mom, then locked myself in my bedroom and called Patch. When Vee and I fled the Devil's Handbag, the brown Chevy van had no longer been parked at the curb. It was my guess that Patch had left before the fallen angels' surprise invasion, since he would have stormed inside the club if he'd believed I was in danger, but I was more curious to know if he'd picked up Cowboy Hat. For all I knew, they were having a conversation right now. I wondered if Patch was asking questions or making threats. Probably both.

Patch's voice mail kicked on, and I hung up. Leaving a message seemed too risky. Besides, he'd see the missed call and know it was from me. I hoped he still planned on coming over tonight.

I knew our messy confrontation had been staged, but I wanted the reassurance that nothing had changed. I was rattled, and needed to know we were still at the same place emotionally that we'd been before the fight.

I dialed Patch's cell once more for good measure, then went to bed feeling restless.

Tomorrow was Tuesday. Cheshvan began with the rise of the new moon.

Based on tonight's grisly free-for-all, I had a feeling fallen angels were counting down the hours until they could unleash their wrath in full.

I awoke to the sound of floorboards creaking. My vision adjusted to the darkness, and I found myself staring at two rather large, muscled legs clad in white track pants.

"Dante?" I said, flailing an arm toward the nightstand, hunting for the clock. "Uuhn. What time is it? What day is it?"

"Tuesday morning," he said. "You know what that means." A ball of workout clothes landed in my face. "Meet me in the driveway at your convenience."

"Really?"

In the dark, his teeth gleamed with a smile. "Can't believe you fell for that. Your butt better be outside in T-minus five minutes."

Five minutes later I trudged outside, shivering against the chill of mid-October. A light wind stripped leaves off the trees and creaked their branches. I stretched my legs and jumped up and down to get the blood flowing.

"Keep up," Dante instructed, and he took off sprinting into the woods.

I still wasn't wild about traipsing through the woods alone with Dante, but I rationalized that if he was going to hurt me, he'd had plenty of opportunities yesterday. So I raced after him, looking for the occasional streak of white that alerted me to his presence. His eyesight must have put mine to shame, because while every now and then I tripped over logs, lost my footing in natural potholes, and smacked my head on low-hanging branches, he navigated the terrain with flawless accuracy. Each and every time I heard his taunting chuckle of amusement, I jumped back on my feet, determined to shove him off a steep slope the first chance I got. There were plenty of ravines around; I just needed to get close enough to him to do the job.

At last Dante stopped, and by the time I caught up, he was stretched out on a large boulder with his hands clasped loosely behind his neck. He'd peeled out of his track pants and Windbreaker, leaving him in knee-length shorts and a fitted T-shirt. Other than a slight rise and fall of his chest, I never could have guessed he'd just sprinted what must have been about ten miles gradually uphill.

I crawled onto the boulder and flopped next to him. "Water," I said, gasping for breath.

Dante rose up on an elbow and smiled down at me. "Not happening. I'm going to wring you dry. Water makes tears, and tears are one thing I can't stand. And once you see what I've got planned next, you're going to want to cry. Lucky for me, you won't be able to."

He hooked me under the armpits and dragged me to standing. Dawn was just beginning to light the horizon, coloring the sky an icy pink. Standing side by side on the boulder, we could see for miles. The evergreen trees, spruces and cedars, spread like a towering carpet in every direction, rolling over hills and into the basin of a deep ravine that cut through the scenery.

"Pick one," Dante instructed.

"Pick one what?"

"A tree. After you've uprooted it, you get to go home."

I blinked at the trees, at least a hundred years old and as thick around as three telephone poles, and felt my jaw drop slightly. "Dante . . ."

"Strength Training 101." He gave me a slap on the back by way of encouragement, then settled back into a relaxed recline on the boulder. "This is going to be better than watching the Today show."

"I hate you."

He laughed. "Not yet, you don't. But an hour from now . . ."

An hour later I had deposited every ounce of energy—and maybe my soul, too—into the uprooting of one very stubborn and unaccommodating white cedar. Other than making it slant slightly, it was a perfect specimen of a thriving tree. I had tried pushing it over, digging it out, kicking it into submission, and futilely beating my fists against it. To say the tree had won was an understatement. And all the while, Dante had sat perched on his boulder, snorting, laughing, and hollering carping remarks. Glad one of us found this entertaining.

He sauntered over, a slight but very obnoxious smile tugging at his mouth. He scratched his elbow. "Well, Commander of the Great and Mighty Nephilim Army, any luck?"

Sweat ran in rivulets down my face, dripping off my nose and chin. My palms were scraped raw, my knees were scuffed, my ankle was sprained, and every muscle in my body cried out in agony. I grabbed the front of Dante's shirt and used it to wipe my face. And then I blew my nose in it.

Dante stepped back, palms raised. "Whoa."

I flung an arm in the direction of my chosen tree. "I can't do it," I admitted on a sob. "I'm not cut out for this. I'll never be as strong as you, or any other Nephil." I felt my lip quiver in disappointment and shame.

His expression softened. "Take a deep breath, Nora. I knew you wouldn't be able to do it. That was the point. I wanted to give you an impossible challenge so later, when you finally *can* do it, you'll look back and see how far you've come."

I stared at him, feeling my temper boil.

"What?" he asked.

"What? What? Are you crazy? I have school today. I have a test to study for! And I thought I was giving it up for something worthwhile, but now I find out this was all just to make a point? Well, here's me making a point! I'm throwing in the towel. I'm done! I didn't ask for this. Training was your idea. You've called all the shots, but this time it's my turn. I QUIT!" I knew I was dehydrated and probably not thinking rationally, but I'd had enough. Yes, I'd wanted to boost my endurance and strength and learn how to defend myself. But this was ridiculous. Uproot a tree? I'd given it my best shot, and he'd sat back and laughed, knowing full well I'd never be able to do it.

"You look really pissed," he said, frowning and stroking his chin in a perplexed manner.

"You think?"

"Consider it an object lesson. A benchmark of sorts."

"Yeah? Benchmark this." And I gave him a stiff middle finger.

"You're blowing this out of proportion. You see that, right?"

Sure, two hours from now maybe I'd see it. After I'd showered, rehydrated, and zonked out in bed. Which, as much as I wanted it, wasn't going to happen because I had school.

Dante said, "You're commander of this army. You're also a Nephil trapped in a human body. You have to train harder than the rest of us, because you're starting with a serious disadvantage. I'm not doing you any favors by going easy."

With sweat running into my eyes, I glared at him. "Did it ever occur to you that maybe I don't want this job? Maybe I don't want to be commander?"

He shrugged. "Doesn't matter. It's done. No use fantasizing other scenarios."

My tone turned despondent. "Why don't you stage a coup and steal my job?" I muttered, only half joking. Far as I could tell, Dante had no reason to keep me in power and keep me alive. "You'd be a million times better at it. You actually care."

More chin stroking. "Well, now that you've put the idea into my head . . ."

"This isn't funny, Dante."

His smile vanished. "No, it's not. For what it's worth, I swore an oath to Hank that I'd help you succeed. My neck is on the line just as much as yours. I'm not out here every morning to earn a few extra karma points. I'm here because I need you to win. My life is riding on your shoulders."

His words sank in. "Are you saying if I don't go to war, and win, you'll die? Is that the oath you swore?"

He exhaled, long and slow, before answering. "Yes."

I closed my eyes, kneading my temples. "I really wish you hadn't told me."

"Stressed?"

Leaning back against the boulder, I let the breeze blow across my skin. *Deep breaths.* Not only could I potentially kill my mom and myself if I failed to lead Hank's army, but now I'd kill Dante, too, if I didn't lead it to victory. But what about peace? What about my deal with the archangels?

Damn Hank. This was his fault. If he'd gone anywhere but straight to hell upon his death, there was no justice in—or out of—the world.

"Lisa Martin and the Nephilim higher-ups want to meet with you again," Dante said. "I've been stalling, because I know you're not sold on war, and I'm worried how they'll react. We need them to keep you in power. In order to do that, we need them to think your desires are aligned with theirs."

"I don't want to meet them yet," I said automatically. "Keep stalling." I needed time to think. Time to decide on a course of action. Who was my greatest threat—displeased archangels, or rebellious Nephilim?

"Do you want me to tell them that for now, you want every-thing to go through me?"

"Yes," I said gratefully. "Do whatever it takes to buy me a little more time."

"By the way, I heard about your faux breakup last night. You must have put on quite a show. The Nephilim are buying it."

"But not you."

"Patch gave me the heads-up." He winked. "I wouldn't have bought it anyway. I've seen the two of you together. What you have doesn't die just like that. Here," Dante said, handing me a chilled bottle of Cool Blue Gatorade. "Drink up. You've lost a lot of fluid."

Twisting off the cap, I gave a nod of gratitude and drank deeply. The liquid poured down my throat, instantly thickening to clog my esophagus. Heat clawed at my throat, broke through, and swarmed the rest of my body. I bent forward, coughing and wheezing.

"What is this stuff?" I gagged.

"Post-workout hydration," he said, but he wouldn't look me in the eye.

I continued to choke, my lungs rioting in spasms. "I thought— it was Gatorade—that's what—the bottle says!"

All emotion vanished off his face. "It's for your own good," he said dully. Then he darted off in a blur of speed.

I was still bent at the waist, feeling as though my insides were slowly liquefying. Specks of electric blue burst across my eyes. The world swayed left . . . then right. Clutching my throat, I trudged forward, fearing that if I passed out here, I'd never be found.

CHAPTER

8

ONE STAGGERING STEP AFTER ANOTHER, I
made it out of the woods. By the time I reached the
farmhouse, most of the fire-in-my-bones feeling had
dissipated. My breathing was back to normal, but my alarm was
still front and center. What had Dante given me? And—*why*?

I had a key on a chain around my neck, and I let myself in.
Taking off my shoes, I crept upstairs and padded quietly past my
mom's bedroom. The clock on my nightstand read ten minutes

till seven. Before Dante came into my life, this would have been a normal, if not slightly early, hour to rise. Most days I woke up feeling refreshed, but this morning I felt exhausted and worried. Grabbing clean clothes, I headed to the bathroom to shower and get ready for school.

At ten before eight, I pulled the Volkswagen into the student parking lot and hiked up to the school, a towering gray building that resembled an old Protestant church. Inside, I crammed my belongings into my locker, grabbed my first- and second-period textbooks, and headed to class. My stomach clenched with hunger, but I was too rattled to eat. The blue drink still swam uneasily in my stomach.

First up, AP U.S. History. I took my seat and scanned my new cell phone for messages. Still no word from Patch. *It's cool,* I told myself. *Something probably came up.* But I couldn't ignore the feeling that something wasn't right. Patch had told me he'd come over last night, and it wasn't like him to break a promise. Especially since he knew how upset I'd been over the breakup.

I was about to tuck my cell away when it chimed with a text.

MEET ME BY THE WENTWORTH RIVER IN 30, Patch's text read.

ARE YOU OKAY? I immediately texted back.

YES. I'LL BE AT THE BOAT DOCKS. MAKE SURE YOU AREN'T FOLLOWED.

The timing wasn't great, but I wasn't going to not meet Patch. He said he was fine, but I wasn't convinced. If he was fine, why was he calling me out of class, and why were we meeting all the way out at the boat docks?

I approached Mrs. Warnock's desk. "Excuse me, Mrs. Warnock? I'm not feeling well. Can I go lie down in the nurse's office?"

Mrs. Warnock removed her glasses and studied me. "Is everything all right, Nora?"

"It's that time of the month," I whispered. Could I be any less creative?

She sighed. "If I had a nickel for every time a student said that . . ."

"I wouldn't ask if my cramps weren't absolutely killing me." I considered rubbing my stomach, but decided it might be too much.

At last she said, "Ask the nurse for acetaminophen. But the minute you're feeling better, I want you back in class. We're starting our unit on Jeffersonian republicanism today. If you don't have someone reliable to borrow notes from, you're going to spend the next two weeks playing catch-up."

I nodded vigorously. "Thank you. I really do appreciate it."

I scuttled out the door, jogged down a flight of stairs, and, after looking both ways down the hall to make sure the vice principal wasn't making rounds, fled through a side door.

I threw myself into the Volkswagen and made a break for it. Of course, that was the easy part. Getting back into class without a signed permission slip from the nurse was going to require nothing short of magic. No *sweat*, I thought. Worse-case scenario, I'd get caught ditching and spend the next week in early-morning detention.

If I needed an excuse to stay away from Dante, whom I no longer trusted, it was as good as any.

The sun was out, the sky a hazy fall blue, but the crisp air cut through my puffer vest with the relentless foreboding of winter. The parking lot upriver from the boat docks was empty. No recreational fishermen out today. After parking, I crouched in the vegetation at the edge of the parking lot a few minutes, waiting to see if anyone followed me. Then I took the paved walkway leading down to the docks. I quickly realized why Patch had selected the spot: Other than a few chirping birds, we were completely alone.

Three boat ramps stretched into the wide river, but no boats. I walked to the end of the first ramp, shielded my eyes from the glare of the sun, and looked around. No Patch.

My cell phone chimed.

I'M IN THE THICKET OF TREES AT THE END OF THE WALKWAY, Patch texted.

I followed the walkway past the docks to the thicket, and that was when Pepper Friberg stepped out from behind a tree. He had Patch's cell phone in one hand and a gun in the other. My eyes fixed on the gun, and I took an involuntary step back.

"It won't kill you, but a gunshot can be excruciatingly painful," he said. His polyester pants rode high on his waist, and his shirt hung at an ill-fitting angle—he hadn't lined up the buttons properly. However, despite his goofy, bumbling appearance, I felt his power ripple over me like the sun's hottest rays. He was far more dangerous than he appeared.

"Am I supposed to take it from someone who knows?" I returned.

His eyes darted both ways down the path. He sponged his forehead with a white handkerchief, further proof of his anxiety. His fingernails had been chewed to stubs. "If you know what I am, and I'm betting Patch told you, then you know I can't feel pain."

"I know you're an archangel, and I know you haven't been playing by the rules. Patch told me you've been living a double life, Pepper. A powerful archangel moonlighting as a human? With your powers, you could really work the system. Are you after money? Power? A good time?"

"I already told you what I'm after: Patch," he said, a fresh sheen of sweat breaking across his forehead. He couldn't seem to mop it up fast enough. "Why won't he meet me?"

Uh, because you want to chain him in hell. I jerked my chin at the cell phone in Pepper's hand. "Nice trick, luring me here with his phone. How did you get it?"

"I took it from him last night at the Devil's Handbag. I found him hiding out in a brown van parked across the street from the entrance. He bolted before I got my hands on him, but in his hurry, he missed grabbing his belongings, including his phone with all his contacts. I've been dialing and texting numbers all morning, trying to reach you."

Secretly, I breathed in relief. Patch had escaped. "If you brought me here to interrogate me, you're out of luck. I don't know where Patch is. I haven't talked to him since yesterday. In fact, it sounds like you were the last to see him."

"Interrogate?" The tips of his Dumbo ears glowed pink. "Golly, that sounds ominous. What do I look like? A common criminal?"

"If you don't want to question me, why lure me all the way out here?" So far, we'd kept our conversation light, but I was growing increasingly nervous. I didn't trust Pepper's bungling, inept antics. They had to be a ploy.

"See that boat over there?"

I followed Pepper's gaze to the river's edge. A gleaming white motorboat bobbed on the water's surface. Sleek, expensive, and probably very fast. "Nice boat. Going on a trip?" I asked, trying not to sound worried.

"Yes. And you're coming with me."

I GAVE YOU A CHANCE TO DO THIS THE EASY WAY, but I'm running out of patience," Pepper said. He stuffed the gun into the waistband of his pants, freeing up both hands to wipe his gleaming brow. "If I can't get to Patch, I'll make him come to me."

I saw where this was going. "This is a kidnapping? You're most definitely not a common criminal, Pepper. Felon, sociopath, and nefarious evildoer all sound a bit closer to the mark."

He loosened his collar and grimaced. "I need Patch to do something for me. A little . . . favor. That's all. Harmless, really."

I had a feeling that "favor" included following Pepper down to hell, just before he jumped clear and slammed the gates shut on Patch. It was one way to take care of a blackmailer.

"I'm one of the good guys," Pepper said. "An archangel. He can trust me. You should have told him to trust me."

"The fastest way to break his trust would be to kidnap me. Think this through, Pepper. Taking me isn't going to make Patch cooperate with you."

He tugged harder at his collar. His face had flushed to the point that he resembled a sweaty pink pig. "There's a lot more going on here than meets the eye. I'm out of options, can't you see that?"

"You're an archangel, Pepper. And yet here you are, strolling around on Earth, carrying a gun and threatening me. I don't believe you're harmless, just like I don't believe you mean no ill will toward Patch. Archangels don't hang around on Earth for extended periods of time, and they don't take hostages. You know what I think? You've turned bad."

"I'm down here on assignment. I'm not bad, but I do have to take certain . . . liberties."

"Gee, I'm almost tempted to believe you."

"I have a job for your boyfriend that only he can do. I don't want to kidnap you, but you've forced my hand. I need Patch's help, and I need it now. Walk toward the boat, nice and easy. Any sudden movements and I shoot."

Pepper made a summoning gesture, the boat glided obediently through the water, moving toward the closest boat ramp. Patch hadn't told me archangels could command objects. I didn't like the surprise, and I wondered how much this would complicate my attempt at escape.

"Didn't you hear? He's not my boyfriend anymore," I told Pepper. "I'm dating Dante Matterazzi. Surely you've heard of him? Everyone has. Patch is one hundred percent in my past."

"Guess we'll find out, won't we? If I have to ask you to start walking again, I'll put a hole in your foot."

I raised my arms level with my shoulders and walked to the boat ramp. A little late, I wished I'd worn my jean jacket with the tracking device. If Patch knew where I was, he'd come for me. Maybe he'd sewn a device into my puffer vest too, but I couldn't count on it. And since I didn't know where Patch was, or if he was even okay, I couldn't count on him, either.

"Climb into the boat," Pepper ordered me. "Take the rope on the seat and tie your hands to the guardrails."

"You're serious about this," I said, stalling. I glanced at the trees framing the river. If I could get to them, I could hide. Pepper's bullets would have more success hitting trees than me.

"Thirty miles from here, I have a nice roomy storage room with your name on it. Once we get there, I'll give your boyfriend a ring." He made a fist, extending his thumb and pinkie finger, and placed the hand-phone near his ear. "We'll see if we can't come to an agreement. If he swears an oath to handle a personal matter for me, you just might get to see him, and your friends and family, again."

"How are you going to call him? You have his cell phone."

Pepper frowned. He hadn't thought this through. *Maybe I could use his disorganization to my advantage.* "Then we'll just have to wait for him to call us. For your sake, I hope he doesn't dawdle."

Reluctantly, I climbed inside the boat. I picked up the rope and started looping it into a knot. I couldn't believe Pepper was this stupid. *Did he honestly think a run-of-the-mill rope would contain me?*

Pepper answered my question. "In case you're having any escape-type thoughts, you should know that rope has been enchanted. It looks harmless, but it's stronger than structural steel. Oh, and once you've secured your wrists, I'll enchant it again. If you so much as tug against the rope to break free, it will pump two hundred volts of electricity into your body."

I tried to keep my composure. "Special trick of archangels?"

"Let's just say I'm more powerful than you think."

Pepper swung one short leg over the boat, balancing his foot on the driver's seat. Before he could bring his other leg over, I slammed my body against the side of the boat, rocking it forcefully away from the ramp. Pepper stood one foot in, one foot out, with the gap of air between his legs widening.

He reacted instantly. He shot into the air, hovering several feet above the boat. Flying. In my split-second decision to unbalance him, I'd forgotten he had wings. And not only that, but now he was clearly furious.

I dove overboard, swimming hard for the center of the river, hearing shots being fired into the water from above.

A splash sounded behind me, and I knew Pepper had dived in after me. In a matter of seconds he would catch me and fulfill that promise to put a hole in my foot—and probably a lot worse. I wasn't as strong as an archangel, but I was Nephilim now, and I'd trained with Dante . . . twice. I decided to do something either incredibly stupid, or incredibly brave.

Planting my feet firmly on the sandy riverbed, I pushed up with all my strength, vaulting straight out of the water. To my surprise I overshot, soaring above the treetops crowding the riverbanks. I could see for miles and miles, past the factories and fields, to the highway strung out with tiny cars and tractor-trailers. Beyond that, I saw Coldwater itself, a cluster of homes, shops, and green-lawned parks.

Just as quickly, I lost velocity. My stomach flip-flopped, air skidding over my body as my direction reversed. The river rushed up at me. I had the urge to pinwheel my arms frantically, but it was as if my body wouldn't stand for it. It refused to be anything less than graceful and efficient, tucking into a tight missile. My feet crashed into the boat ramp, smashing through the planks of wood, plunging me back into the water.

More bullets whizzed past my ears. I scrabbled out of the debris, lunged up the riverbank, and took off sprinting for the trees. Two mornings of running in the dark had given me some preparation, but it didn't explain why I was suddenly running at speeds that rivaled Dante's. The trees passed in a dizzying blur, but my feet leaped and bounded with ease, almost as if they could anticipate the necessary steps a half second before my mind.

I raced at top speed up the walkway, flung myself inside the Volkswagen, and floored it out of the parking lot. To my amazement, I wasn't even out of breath.

Adrenaline? Maybe. But I didn't think so.

I drove to Allen's Drug and Pharmacy and slid the Volkswagen into a parking space nestled between two trucks that hid me from the street. Then I slouched in my seat, trying to make myself invisible. I was pretty sure I'd lost Pepper at the river, but it didn't hurt to be cautious. I needed time to think. I couldn't go home. I couldn't go back to school. What I really needed was to find Patch, but I didn't know where to start.

My cell phone rang, startling me out of my reverie.

"Yo, Grey," Scott said. "Vee and I are on our way to Taco Hut for lunch, but the big question of the day is, where are you? Now

finale

that you (a) can drive, and (b) have wheels—ahem, thanks to me—you don't have to eat in the school cafeteria. FYI."

I ignored his jesting tone. "I need Dante's number. Text it to me and make it fast," I told Scott. I'd had Dante's number stored on my old phone, but not this one.

"Uh, *please?*"

"What is this? Double-standard Tuesday?"

"What do you need his number for? I thought Dante was your boy—"

I hung up and tried to think things through. What did I know for certain? That an archangel leading a double life wanted to kidnap me and use me as incentive to get Patch to do him a favor. Or to quit blackmailing him. Or both. I also knew Patch wasn't the blackmailer.

What information was I low on? Mostly Patch's whereabouts. Was he safe? Would he contact me? Did he need my help?

Where are you, Patch? I shouted into the universe.

My cell phone chimed.

HERE'S DANTE'S NUMBER. ALSO, I HEAR CHOCOLATE WORKS WELL FOR PMS, Scott texted.

"Funny," I said out loud, punching in Dante's number. He answered on the third ring.

"We need to meet," I said with an edge.

"Listen, if it's about this morning—"

"Of course it's about this morning! What did you give me? I

drank an unknown liquid, and suddenly I can run as fast as you and soar fifty feet into the air, and I'm pretty sure my vision is better than twenty-twenty."

"It'll wear off. To sustain those speeds, you'd need to drink the blue stuff daily."

"Does the blue stuff have a name?"

"Not over the phone."

"Fine. Meet me in person."

"Be at Rollerland in thirty."

I blinked. "You want to meet at the roller-skating rink?"

"It's noon on a weekday. Nobody there but moms and toddlers. Makes it easy to spot potential spies."

I wasn't sure who Dante thought might be spying on us, but I had an uneasy feeling fluttering around in my stomach that whatever the blue stuff was, Dante wasn't the only one who wanted it. My best guess, it was a drug of some sort. I'd witnessed its enhancement properties firsthand. The powers it gave me were surreal. It was as if I had no boundaries, and the extent of my own physical prowess was . . . limitless. The feeling was exhilarating and unnatural. It was the latter that had me worried.

When Hank was alive, he'd experimented with devilcraft, summoning the powers of hell to his advantage. The objects he'd enchanted had always cast an eerie blue hue. Up until now I'd believed that the knowledge of devilcraft had died with Hank, but I

finale

was beginning to have doubts. I hoped Dante's blue mystery drink was a coincidence, but instinct told me otherwise.

I got out of the car and walked the last few blocks to Rollerland, checking over my shoulder often for signs that I was being followed. No strange men in dark trench coats and sunglasses. No overly tall people, a dead giveaway of Nephilim, either.

I swung through Rollerland's doors, rented a pair of size-eight roller skates, and sat down on a bench just outside the rink. The lights were low and a disco ball scattered shades of bright, saturated light across the polished wood floor. Old-school Britney Spears played through the speakers. As Dante had predicted, only small children and their moms were skating at this hour.

A shift in the air, snapping with voltage, alerted me to Dante's presence. He lowered himself onto the bench beside me, dressed in dark tailored jeans and a fitted navy polo. He hadn't bothered to remove his sunglasses, making it impossible to see his eyes. I wondered if he regretted giving me the drink and was experiencing some degree of moral conflict. I hoped so.

"Going skating?" he asked with a nod at my feet.

I noticed he wasn't carting skates. "The sign said you have to rent skates to go beyond the lobby."

"You could have mind-tricked the counter attendant."

I felt my mood darken. "That's not really how I play."

Dante shrugged. "Then you're missing out on a lot of the perks of being Nephilim."

"Tell me about the blue drink."

"It's an enhancement drink."

"So I gathered. What's it enhanced with?"

Dante leaned his head toward mine and spoke in a whisper. "Devilcraft. It's not as bad as it sounds," he assured me.

My spine stiffened, and the hairs at the back of my neck tingled. No, no, no. Devilcraft was supposed to be eradicated from Earth. It had disappeared with Hank. "I know what devilcraft is. And I thought it was destroyed."

Dante's dark eyebrows furrowed. "How do you know about devilcraft?"

"Hank used it. So did his accomplice, Chauncey Langeais. But when Hank died—" I caught myself. Dante didn't know I'd killed Hank, and to say that it wasn't going to help my rapport with the Nephilim, Dante included, if my secret got out, was the understatement of the year. "Patch used to spy for Hank."

A nod. "I know. They had a deal. Patch fed us information on fallen angels."

I didn't know whether Dante intentionally left out that Patch had agreed to spy for Hank on one condition: that he preserve my life, or if Hank had kept those details private.

"Hank told Patch about devilcraft," I lied, covering my tracks. "But Patch told me that when Hank died, devilcraft went with him. Patch was under the impression that Hank was the only one who knew how to manipulate it."

Dante shook his head. "Hank put his right-hand man, Blakely, in charge of developing devilcraft prototypes. Blakely knows more about devilcraft than Hank ever did. Blakely has spent the past several months holed up in a lab, enchanting knives, whips, and studded rings with devilcraft, transforming them into deadly weapons. Most recently, he's formulated a drink that will elevate Nephilim powers. We're evenly matched, Nora," he said with an excited glint in his eyes. "Used to be it took ten Nephilim to every fallen angel. Not so anymore. I've been testing the drink for Blakely, and when I take the enhanced drink, the playing field consistently tilts to my advantage. I can go up against a single fallen angel without any fear that he's stronger."

My thoughts spun wildly. Devilcraft was thriving on Earth? The Nephilim had a secret weapon, being fabricated in a secret lab? I had to tell Patch. "Is the drink you gave me the same one you've been testing for Blakely?"

"Yes." A crafty smile. "Now you understand what I'm talking about."

If he wanted accolades, he wasn't getting them from me. "How many Nephilim know about the drink or have ingested it?"

Dante leaned back on the bench and sighed. "Are you asking for yourself?" He paused with meaning. "Or to share our secret with Patch?"

I hesitated, and Dante's face fell.

"You have to choose, Nora. You can't be loyal to us and Patch.

You're making an admirable go of it, but in the end, loyalty is about taking a side. You're either with the Nephilim or against us."

The worst part of this conversation was that Dante was right. Deep down, I knew it. Patch and I had agreed that our endgame in the war was to come out of it safely together, but if I still maintained that that was my only goal, where did it leave the Nephilim? I was supposedly their leader, asking them to believe I was going to help them, but I really wasn't.

"If you tell Patch about devilcraft, he won't sit on the information," Dante said. "He'll go after Blakely and try to destroy the lab. Not out of a lofty sense of moral duty, but out of self-preservation. This isn't just about Cheshvan anymore," he explained. "My goal isn't to push fallen angels back behind some arbitrary line, such as stopping them from possessing us. My goal is to annihilate the entire fallen angel race using devilcraft. And if they don't already know it, they're going to figure it out soon."

I sputtered. "What?"

"Hank had a plan. This was it. The extinction of their race. Blakely believes that with a little more time, he can develop a prototype of a weapon strong enough to kill a fallen angel, something that was never even considered possible. Until now."

I jumped off the bench and began pacing the floor. "Why are you telling me this?"

"It's time to make your choice. Are you with us or not?"

"Patch isn't the problem. He isn't working with fallen angels.

He doesn't want war." Patch's only goal was making sure I stayed in power, fulfilled my oath, and came out alive. But if I told him about devilcraft, Dante was right: Patch would do everything he could to destroy it.

"If you tell him about devilcraft, it's over for us," Dante said.

He was asking me to either betray him, Scott, and thousands of innocent Nephilim . . . or Patch. A heavy weight roiled my stomach. The pain was so sharp, I nearly doubled over.

"Take the afternoon to think about it," Dante said, rising to his feet. "Unless I hear otherwise, I'll expect you to be ready to train first thing tomorrow." He watched me a moment, his brown eyes steady but holding a shade of doubt. "I hope we're still on the same side, Nora," he said quietly, then walked out.

I stayed in the building several minutes, sitting in the semi-darkness, surrounded by the bizarrely cheerful squeals and laughter of children trying to do the Hokey Pokey in roller skates. I bowed my head and hid my face in my hands. This wasn't how things were supposed to happen. I was supposed to call off the war, declare a cease-fire, and walk away from it all to be with Patch.

Instead Dante and Blakely had plowed ahead, picked up right where Hank had left off, and raised the stakes to all or nothing. Stupid, stupid, stupid.

Under normal circumstances, I wouldn't think Dante and Blakely, and all Nephilim for that matter, stood a chance at anni-hilating fallen angels, but I suspected that devilcraft changed everything. And what did it mean for my half of the deal? If the Nephilim waged war without me, would the archangels still hold me accountable?

Yes. Yes, they would.

Wherever Blakely was holed up, undoubtedly guarded by his own small and vigilant Nephilim security detail, it was clear he was experimenting with more powerful and more dangerous proto-types. He was the root of the problem.

Which put finding him, and his secret lab, at the top of my priority list.

Right after I found Patch. My stomach somersaulted with worry, and I sent up yet another silent prayer for him.

CHAPTER

I WAS A SHORT DISTANCE FROM THE VOLKSWAGEN WHEN I saw a shadowy figure taking up space in the driver's seat. I stopped, my thoughts taking an initial dive into Cowboy-Hat-back-for-round-two territory. I held my breath, debating the wisdom of running. But the longer I debated, the more my overactive imagination waned, and the figure took its true form. Patch crooked his finger, beckoning me inside. I broke into a grin, my worry dissolving instantaneously.

"Skipping school for roller-skating?" he asked as I dropped inside the car.

"You know me. Purple wheels are my weakness."

Patch smiled. "I didn't see your car at school. I've been looking for you. Can you spare a few minutes?"

I handed him my keys. "You drive."

Patch drove us to a gorgeous luxury townhouse complex overlooking Casco Bay. The building's historic charm—deep red brick mixed with stone from a local quarry—placed it well over a hundred years old, but it had been completely renovated with gleaming windows, black marble columns, and a doorman. Patch pulled into a single-car garage and lowered the door, leaving us in cool darkness.

"New place?" I asked.

"Pepper hired a few Nephilim thugs to redecorate my studio beneath Delphic. I needed a place on short notice with upgraded security."

We exited the Volkswagen, climbed a narrow set of stairs, walked through a door, and came out in Patch's new kitchen. Wall-to-wall windows offered stunning views of the bay. A few white sailboats dotted the water, and a picturesque blue fog shrouded the surrounding cliffs. Autumn foliage ringed the bay, burning in vibrant shades of red that seemed to set the landscape to flame. The dock at the base of the townhomes appeared to be valet-access.

"Swanky," I told Patch.

He handed me a mug of hot cocoa from behind and kissed the back of my neck. "It's more exposed than I'd like, and that's not something you'll hear me say often."

I leaned back against him, sipping my drink. "I was worried about you."

"Pepper surprised me outside the Devil's Handbag last night. Meaning I didn't get a chance to talk to our Nephilim friend, Cowboy Hat. But I made a few calls and did some legwork, starting with looking into the cabin he took you to. He's not very smart. He took you to his grandparents' cabin. Cowboy Hat's real name is Shaun Corbridge, and he's two years old by Nephilim count. He swore fealty two Christmases ago and willingly enlisted in the Black Hand's army. He has a short temper and a history of drug abuse. He's looking for a way to make a name for himself and thinks you're his ticket. His proclivity for stupidity goes without saying." Patch kissed my neck again, this time letting his mouth linger. "I missed you, too. What have you got for me?"

Hmm, where to start.

"I could tell you how Pepper tried to kidnap me this morning and hold me hostage, or maybe you'd like to hear how Dante secretly fed me a drink enhanced with devilcraft? Turns out Blakely, Hank's right-hand man, has been tinkering with devilcraft for months and has developed a high-performance drug for Nephilim."

"They did *what?*" he growled in a voice that couldn't have been more enraged. "Did Pepper hurt you? And I'm going to rip Dante to pieces!"

I shook my head no, but was surprised when tears sprang to my eyes. I knew why Dante had done it—he needed me strong enough physically to lead the Nephilim to victory—but I resented his approach. He'd lied to me. He'd tricked me into consuming a substance that was not only forbidden on Earth, but potentially dangerous. I wasn't naive enough to think devilcraft didn't have negative side effects. The powers might wear off, but a seed of evil had been embedded inside me.

I said, "Dante said the effects of the drink fade after a day. That's the good news. The bad news is I think he's planning to introduce it to countless other Nephilim soon. It will give them . . . superpowers. That's the only way I can describe it. When I took it, I ran faster and jumped higher, and it sharpened my senses. Dante said that one-on-one, a Nephil could outfight a fallen angel. I believe him, Patch. I got away from Pepper. An *archangel.* Without the drink, he'd have me under lock and key right now."

Cold fury burned in Patch's eyes. "Tell me where I can find Dante," he said crisply.

I hadn't expected Patch to get so angry—a major oversight, in retrospect. Of course he was seething. Trouble was, if he went to find Dante now, Dante would know I'd told Patch about devil-craft. I needed to play my hand carefully. "What he did was wrong, but he thought he had my best interests in mind," I offered.

A harsh laugh. "Do you really believe that?"

"I think he's desperate. He doesn't see a lot of other options."

"Then he's not looking for them."

"He also gave me an ultimatum. Either I'm with him and the Nephilim, or I'm with you. He told me about devilcraft to test me. To see if I'd tell you." I tossed my hands up and let them drop. "I'd never keep that information from you. We're a team. But we need to think how we're going to play this."

"I'm going to kill him."

I sighed, pressing my fingertips into my temples. "You're not seeing beyond your own personal distaste of Dante—that, and your rage."

"Rage?" Patch chuckled, but it was undeniably menacing. "Oh, Angel. That's a bit tame for what I'm feeling. I've just learned that a Nephil forced devilcraft into your body. I don't care if he wasn't thinking, and I don't care if he was desperate. It's one mistake he's not making again. And before you're tempted to feel sorry for him, know this. He saw it coming. I warned him if you so much as got a scratch while under his watch, I'd hold him accountable."

"Under his watch?" I echoed slowly, trying to connect the dots.

"I know you're training with him," Patch announced bluntly.

"You know?"

"You're a big girl. You can make your own decisions. You obviously had your reasons for wanting to learn self-defense from

BECCA FITZPATRICK

Dante, and I wasn't going to stop you. I trusted you; it was him I worried about, and it looks like I had every reason to be. I'll ask once more. Where is he hiding?" he nearly growled, his face darkening.

"What makes you think he's hiding?" I said miserably, upset that once again I felt caught between Patch and Dante. Between fallen angels and Nephilim. I hadn't intentionally meant to keep our training sessions from Patch; I'd simply thought it would be better not to stir up any more competition between him and Dante.

Patch's icy laugh sent a shiver dancing up my spine. "If he's smart, he's hiding."

"I'm angry too, Patch. Trust me, I wish I could go back and undo this morning. But I hate feeling like you're calling the shots without me. First, you put a tracking device on me. Next, you threatened Dante behind my back. You're operating perpendicular to me. I want to feel like you're on my side. I want to feel like we're working together."

Patch's new cell phone rang, and he glanced at the readout. Unusual behavior for him. These days, he let all calls go to voice mail, then carefully screened which to return.

"Expecting an important call?" I asked.

"Yes, and I have to take care of it now. I am on your side, Angel. I always will be. I'm sorry if you feel like I'm subverting your wishes. That's the last thing I want, believe me." He brushed a kiss across my mouth, but it felt brusque. He was already striding with purpose toward the stairs leading down to the garage. "I need you to do something for me. See if you can dig up anything on Blakely. Where he calls home these days, locations he's visited lately, how many Nephilim bodyguards he has protecting him, any new prototypes he's developing, and when he plans on introducing this super-drink to the mainstream. You're right—I don't think devilcraft has spread beyond Dante and Blakely yet. If it had, the archangels would have jumped on it. Talk soon, Angel."

"So we'll finish this conversation later?" I called after him, still stunned by his rapid departure.

He paused at the top of the stairs. "Dante gave you an ultimatum, but it was coming, with or without him. I can't make the decision for you, but if you want a sounding board, let me know. I'm happy to help. Engage the alarm before you leave. Your personal key is on the counter. You're welcome anytime. I'll be in touch."

"What about Cheshvan?" I said. I hadn't made it through half the things I'd wanted to discuss with him, and now he was running off. "It starts tonight with the rising moon."

Patch gave a brusque nod. "There's a bad feeling in the air. I'll be keeping tabs on you, but I want you to watch your back just the same. Don't be out any later than necessary. Sundown is your curfew tonight."

Since I didn't see the point in going back to school without a valid excuse slip, and since, if I left now, I'd only catch the last hour before the dismissal bell, I decided to stay at Patch's place and do some thinking-slash-soul-searching.

I went to the fridge to hunt down a snack, but it was bare. It was very apparent Patch had moved in quickly and the furnishings had been included. The rooms were immaculate, lacking any personal touches. Stainless-steel appliances, taupe paint, walnut flooring. Modern American furniture in solid colors. Flat-screen TV and leather club chairs facing each other. Masculine, stylish, and lacking warmth.

I replayed my conversation with Patch and decided he hadn't seemed the least bit sympathetic over Dante's ultimatum and my big dilemma. What did that mean? That he thought I could work things out on my own? That choosing between Nephilim and fallen angels was a no-brainer? Because it wasn't. The choice was getting harder with each passing day.

I mulled over what I did know. Namely that Patch wanted me to find out what Blakely was up to. Patch probably thought Dante was my best contact—a middleman between me and Blakely, so to speak. And in order to keep the lines of communication open between us, it was probably best that I keep Dante thinking I was on his side. That I saw eye to eye with the Nephilim.

And I did. In many ways. My sympathy was with them because they weren't fighting for dominion or some other virtue-less ambition—they were fighting for their freedom. I got it. I admired it. I'd do anything to help. But I didn't want Blakely or

Dante putting the fallen angel population at risk. If fallen angels were wiped off the face of the Earth, Patch would go with them. I wasn't willing to lose Patch, and I'd do whatever it took to make sure his species survived.

In other words, I was no closer to answers. I was right back at square one, playing both sides of the field. The irony of it all struck me. I was just like Pepper Friberg. The only difference between me and Pepper was that I *wanted* to take a side. All this sneaking around and lying, and pretending to have allegiances to two opposing sides, was keeping me up at night. Pretty soon my mind would be consumed with memorizing lies so I wouldn't get caught in my own elaborate net.

I heaved a sigh. And double-checked Patch's freezer. No cartons of ice cream had magically appeared since I'd last checked.

11

AT FIVE THE FOLLOWING MORNING MY MAT-tress dipped under the weight of a second body. My eyes sprang open to find Dante seated at the foot of the bed, wearing a somber expression.

"Well?" he asked simply.

I'd spent all of yesterday, into the night, trying to make up my mind, and I'd finally decided on a course of action. Now came the hard part: carrying it out. "Give me five minutes to get dressed, and I'll meet you outside."

His eyebrows lifted slightly in question, his hope visible. "Does that mean what I think it does?"

"I'm not out training with fallen angels, am I?" Not exactly a straight answer, and I hoped Dante didn't press the issue.

He smiled. "Five minutes it is."

"But no more blue stuff," I said, bringing him to a halt at the door. "Just so we're clear."

"Yesterday's sample didn't convince you?" To my dismay, he didn't look remorseful. If anything, his expression revealed disappointment.

"I get the feeling it wouldn't make the FDA's approved list."

"If you change your mind, it's on the house."

I decided to take advantage of the conversation's direction. "Is Blakely developing any other enhancement drinks? And when do you think he'll widen his test group?"

A noncommittal shrug. "I haven't talked to Blakely in a while."

"Really? You're testing devilcraft for him. And you were both close to Hank. I'm surprised you don't keep in touch."

"You know the saying 'don't put all your eggs in one basket'? That's our strategy. Blakely develops the prototypes in his lab, and someone else delivers them to me. If something happens to one of us, the other is safe. I don't know where Blakely is, so if fallen angels grab and torture me, I can't tell them anything useful. Standard procedure. We're starting off with a fifteen-mile run, so make sure you're well hydrated."

"Wait. What about Cheshvan?" I studied his face steadfastly, bracing myself for the worst. I'd lain awake several hours last night, tensely waiting for an outward manifestation that it had arrived. I'd expected a shift in the air, a current of negative energy sizzling over my skin, or some other supernatural sign. Instead Cheshvan had arrived without so much as a whisper. And yet, somewhere out there, I was sure thousands of Nephilim were suffering in ways I couldn't imagine.

"Nothing," Dante said grimly.

"What do you mean nothing?"

"As far as I know, not one fallen angel possessed their vassal last night."

I sat up. "That's a good thing! Isn't it?" I added upon seeing Dante's grave expression.

He was slow to respond. "I don't know what it means. But I don't think it's good. They wouldn't hold off without a reason—a very good one," he added hesitantly.

"I don't understand."

"Welcome to the club."

"Could it be mental warfare? Do you think they're trying to unsettle the Nephilim?"

"I think they know something we don't."

After Dante quietly shut my bedroom door, I dragged on some sweats and mentally stored away this new information. I was dying to get Patch's take on last night's unexpected and anticlimactic start to Cheshvan. Since he was a fallen angel, he'd likely have a more detailed explanation. What did the standoff mean?

Disappointed not to have an answer, but knowing it was a waste of time to speculate, I turned my focus on what else I'd learned. I felt one infinitesimal step closer to tracking devilcraft back to its source. Dante said he and Blakely never met in person, and that a middleman acted as a go-between, passing Blakely's prototypes to Dante. I needed to find the go-between.

Outside, Dante merely had to take off running into the woods, and it was my signal to follow. Right away, I could tell that the blue drink infused with devilcraft had been flushed from my system. Dante zipped between trees at dangerous speeds, while I lagged behind, concentrating on each step to minimize injury. But even though I was relying on my own strengths, and mine alone, I could tell I was improving. Rapidly. A large boulder sat in my path directly ahead, and rather than veer around it, I made the split-second decision to vault it. I planted my foot halfway up the curved surface, propelled myself up, and soared over the boulder. Upon landing, I immediately slid under a brambly tree with low branches, and without missing a beat, sprang to my feet on the other side and kept running.

At the end of the fifteen-mile loop, I was plastered in sweat and breathing hard. I leaned back against a tree and tilted my face up to catch the breeze.

"You're getting better," Dante said, sounding surprised. I

glanced sideways. He, of course, still looked freshly showered, not a hair out of place.

"And without the help of devilcraft," I pointed out.

"You'd see even bigger results if you'd agree to take the super-drink."

I pushed up from the tree and windmilled my arms, stretching my shoulder muscles. "What's on the docket? More strength training?"

"Mind-tricks."

That caught me off guard. "Invading minds?"

"Making people, especially fallen angels, see what isn't really there."

I didn't need a definition. I'd had mind-tricks performed on me, and never once had the experience been enjoyable. The whole point of a mind-trick was to deceive a victim.

"I'm not sure about this," I hedged. "Is it really necessary?"

"It's a powerful weapon. Especially for you. If you can make your faster, stronger, larger opponent believe you're invisible, or that they're about to walk off a cliff, the few extra seconds might be what saves you."

"All right, show me how it's done," I said reluctantly.

"Step one: Invade your opponent's mind. This is just like using mind-speak. Try it on me."

"That's easy," I said, casting my mental nets toward Dante, ensnaring his mind, and pushing words into his conscious thought. *I'm in your mind, having a look around, and it's awfully empty in here.*

Wiseacre, Dante returned.

Nobody says that anymore. Speaking of which, how old are you in Nephilim years? I'd never thought to ask.

I swore fealty during Napoleon's invasion of Italy—my homeland.

And that was in what year . . . ? Help me out. I'm not a history buff.

Dante smiled. 1796.

Wow. You're old.

No, I'm experienced. Next step: Tease apart the threads forming your opponent's thoughts. Break them down, scramble them, snap them in half, whatever works for you. The means of carrying out this step varies among Nephilim. For me, breaking down my victim's thoughts works best. I take the wall in their mind, the one that guards the very center where every thought is formed, and I tear it down. Like this.

Before I even realized what was happening, Dante had me backed up against a tree, gently stroking a few stray hairs off my forehead. He tipped my chin up to look in my eyes, and I couldn't have pulled away from his penetrating gaze if I'd wanted. I drank in his gorgeous features. Deep brown eyes set an even distance from his strong, straight nose. Lush lips that bowed into a confident smile. Thick brown hair that fell over his forehead. His jawline was wide and chiseled, and smooth from a fresh shave. And all this set against a backdrop of creamy, olive-toned skin.

I could think of nothing but how good it would feel to kiss him. Every other thought in my head had been stripped away, and I didn't mind. I was lost in a heavenly dream, and if I never woke up, I wouldn't care. Kiss Dante. Yes, that's exactly what I wanted.

I reached up on my tiptoes, closing the distance between our mouths, a thrilling flutter beating like wings in my chest.

Wings. Angels. Patch.

Impulsively, I threw up a new wall in my head. And suddenly I saw the situation for what it really was. Dante had me backed up against a tree, all right, but I did not want to make out with him.

"Demonstration finished," Dante said, his smile a bit too cocky for my liking.

"Next time choose a more appropriate demonstration," I said tensely. "Patch would kill you if he found out about this."

His smile didn't fade. "That's a figure of speech that doesn't work very well with Nephilim."

I wasn't in the mood for humor. "I know what you're doing. You're trying to set him off. This petty feud between the two of you will blow up to a whole new level if you mess with me. Patch is the last person you want to antagonize. He doesn't hold grudges, because the people who cross him tend to disappear quickly. And what you just did? That was crossing him."

"It was the first idea that came to mind," he said. "It won't happen again." I might have felt better about his apology had he sounded remotely penitent.

"See that it doesn't," I answered in a steely tone.

Dante seemed to shrug off any ill feelings with ease. "Now it's your turn. Get inside my head and break down my thoughts. If you can, replace them with something of your own making. In other words, create an illusion."

Since getting back to work was the fastest way to end the lesson, and end my time with Dante, I shoved my personal irritation aside and concentrated on the task at hand. With my nets still swimming through Dante's mind, I envisioned first ensnaring his thoughts, and then pulling them apart one small thread at a time. The image in my head wasn't all that different from peeling apart string cheese, one thin ribbon after another.

Work faster, Dante ordered. I feel you in my head, but you're not causing any turbulence. Make waves, Nora. Rock the boat. Hit me before I even see it coming. Think of this as an ambush. If I were a real opponent, all this would accomplish is letting me know you're dabbling in my head. And that will put you face-to-face with one very pissed-off fallen angel.

I backed out of Dante's mind, drew a deep breath, and threw my nets again—farther this time. Shutting my eyes to block out any distractions, I created a new image. Scissors. Giant, gleaming scissors. I snipped apart Dante's thoughts—

"Faster," Dante barked. "I can feel your hesitancy. You're so unsure of yourself, I can practically smell your self-doubt. Any fallen angel worth his weight will pounce on that. Take control!"

I retreated again, balling my hands into fists as I grew more frustrated. With Dante, and myself. He pushed too hard and set expectations too high. And I couldn't banish the voices of doubt sniggering in my head. I berated myself for being the very thing Dante believed I was. Weak.

I'd come out this morning to keep up relations with Dante, motivated by using him to get to Blakely and his devilcraft lab, but that meant nothing to me now. I wanted to *own* this. Fury and resentment popped behind my eyes like little red dots. My vision narrowed. I didn't want to be inadequate anymore. I didn't want to be smaller, slower, weaker. Fierce determination seemed to set my blood to boil. My entire body quaked with obstinate resolve as I leveled my gaze on Dante. Everything else dropped away. There was only me, and him.

I cast a mental net into Dante's mind with all the fervor I had. I threw my anger at Hank, my insecurities with myself, and the awful tug-of-war sensation ripping me apart every time I thought about choosing between Patch and the Nephilim into Dante's mind. Instantly I envisioned a massive explosion, clouds of smoke and debris mushrooming higher, endlessly higher. I set off another explosion, and another. I wreaked havoc on any hope he had at keeping his thoughts orderly.

Dante rocked back on his heels, visibly shaken. "How did you do that?" he finally managed to ask. "I—couldn't see. I'm not even sure where I was." He blinked several times in succession, staring at me like he wasn't sure I was real. "It was like—hanging between two moments in time. There was nothing. Nothing. It was like I didn't exist. I've never had anything like that happen before."

"I imagined I was setting off bombs in your head," I confessed.

"Well, it worked."

"So I passed?"

"Yeah, you could say that," Dante told me, shaking his head in disbelief. "I've been doing this a long time, and I've never seen anything like that."

I wasn't sure whether I should feel elated over finally doing something right, or guilty over having been surprisingly good at invading Dante's mind. It wasn't the most honorable talent to excel at. If I could have any trophy displayed on my dresser, I wouldn't voluntarily choose one for corrupting people's minds.

"Then I guess we're done here?" I asked.

"Until tomorrow," Dante said, his expression still dazed. "Good work, Nora."

I jogged the rest of the way home at a normal human pace—an excruciatingly lagging six miles per hour—because the sun had started to rise, and while I didn't sense any humans in the vicinity, it didn't hurt to be prudent. I came out of the woods, crossed the street to the farmhouse, and stopped abruptly at the base of the driveway.

Marcie Millar's red Toyota 4Runner was parked directly ahead.

With an ever-increasing tightening of my stomach, I jogged up the porch. Several moving boxes were stacked by the door. I shoved my way into the house, but before I could get a word out, my mom jumped up from the kitchen table.

"There you are!" she exclaimed impatiently. "Where have you

been? Marcie and I have spent the past half hour trying to figure out where you could have run off to at this hour."

Marcie sat at my kitchen table, hands cupped around a mug of coffee. She gave me an innocent smile.

"I went jogging," I said.

"I can see that," Mom stated. "I just wish you would have told me. You didn't even bother to leave a note."

"It's seven in the morning. You're supposed to be in bed. What is she doing here?"

"I'm right here," Marcie said sweetly. "You can talk to me."

I settled my eyes on her. "Fine. What are you doing here?"

"I told you. I'm not getting along with my mom. We need some breathing room. For the time being, I think it's better if I move in with you guys. My mom doesn't have a problem with it." Not looking the least bit disconcerted, she took a sip of coffee.

"Why would you think that was a good idea, let alone a reasonable one?"

Marcie rolled her eyes. "Hello. We're family."

My jaw fell open, and my eyes immediately cut to my mom. To my disbelief, she didn't look rattled.

"Oh, come on, Nora," she said. "We all knew it, even if no one was willing to say it. Under the circumstances, Hank would want me to take Marcie in with open arms."

I was speechless. How could she be kind to Marcie? Could she not remember our history with the Millars?

finale

This was Hank's fault, I seethed inwardly. I'd hoped his grip on my mom would end with his death, but every time I tried to talk to her about him, she adopted the same serene attitude: Hank was coming back to her, she wanted him to, and she'd wait stalwartly until he did. Her bizarre behavior was further evidence of my theory: Hank had employed some crazy devilcraft mind-trick on her before he died. No amount of arguing on my part would penetrate her picture-perfect recollection of one of the vilest men to ever inhabit our planet.

"Marcie is family, and while the circumstances are a bit sticky, she was right to come to us for help. If you can't count on family, who can you count on?" Mom went on.

I was still staring at my mom, frustrated by her sedate attitude, when a second light went on. Of course. Hank wasn't the only one to blame in this charade. How had it taken me this long to catch on? I swiveled my eyes to Marcie.

Are you mind-tricking her? I said accusingly to her mind. *Is that it? I know you're doing something, because there is no way my mom in her rational mind would let you move in with us.*

Marcie's hand flew to her head, and she yelped. "Ow! How did you do that?"

Don't play dumb with me. I know you're a Nephil, remember? You can perform mind-tricks and you can mind-speak. Whatever this little act is? I see right through it. And there is no way you're moving in.

Fine, Marcie fired back. *I know about mind-speak. And I know about mind-tricks. But I'm not using them on your mom. My mom justi-*

fies all her crazy behavior by saying my dad would have wanted it that way too, you know. He probably mind-tricked both our moms before he died. He wouldn't have wanted our families fighting. Don't blame me just because I'm an available target for your anger.

"Marcie, I'll have the spare bedroom cleared out for you by the time you get home from school this afternoon," Mom said, looking daggers at me. "You'll have to forgive Nora for being so ungracious. She's used to being an only child and getting her way. Maybe this new living arrangement will give her a new outlook."

"I'm used to getting my way?" I challenged. "Marcie's an only child too. If we're going to point fingers, let's be fair about it."

Marcie smiled, clasping her hands together in delight. "Thank you so much, Mrs. Grey. I really appreciate it." She had the audacity to bound over and hug my mom.

"Kill me now," I muttered.

"Careful what you wish for," Marcie crooned in a sugary tone.

"Are you ready for this?" I asked my mom. "Two teenage girls, one ugly rivalry, and most importantly, one shared bathroom?"

To my disgust, Mom smiled. "Family: the latest extreme sport. After school, we'll carry Marcie's boxes upstairs, get her settled in, and then we'll all go out for pizza. Nora, do you think you could ask Scott to help? Some of the boxes might be heavy."

"I think Scott practices with his band on Wednesdays," I lied, knowing full well Vee would throw an epic fit if she discovered I'd knowingly allowed Marcie and Scott in the same room together.

finale

"I'll talk to him," Marcie piped up. "Scott is such a sweetheart. I can convince him to come over after practice. Is it all right if I invite him for pizza, Mrs. Grey?"

Hello? Scott Parnell? A sweetheart? Was I the only one hearing the absurdity in all this?

"Of course," Mom said.

"I have to shower," I said, looking for any excuse to flee the scene. I'd hit my maximum Marcie limit for the day and needed to recuperate. A daunting thought struck me. If Marcie moved in, I'd hit my limit by seven every morning.

"Oh, Nora?" Mom called before I'd reached the stairs. "The school left a message on the phone yesterday afternoon. I think it was the attendance office. Do you know why they'd be calling?"

I froze.

Marcie stood behind my mom, mouthing *Busted* at me, barely able to control her glee.

"Uh, I'll swing by the office today and see what they need," I said. "The call was probably routine."

"Yeah, probably," Marcie echoed, wearing that haughty grin of hers that I hated most of all.

CHAPTER

12

SHORTLY AFTER BREAKFAST, I BUMPED INTO MARCIE ON the front porch. She was on her way out the door, chatting on her cell phone, and I was on my way back inside, looking for her.

"Your 4Runner is blocking my car," I said.

She held up a finger, signaling me to wait. I grabbed her cell phone, ended the call, and repeated more testily, "You're blocking my car."

"Don't blow a gasket. And don't piss me off. If you touch my cell phone again, I'll pee in your Cheerios."

"That's disgusting."

"That was Scott on the phone. He doesn't have practice today, and he wants to help move boxes."

Great. I could look forward to arguing about this with Vee, who wouldn't believe me when I said, "I tried."

"As much as I'd love to sit here and shoot the breeze, I have class. So . . ." I gestured dramatically at Marcie's 4Runner, which was inconveniently boxing in the Volkswagen.

"You know, if you need an excused-absence slip, I have a few extras. I work in the front office, and every now and then they find their way into my purse."

"Why would you think I'd need an excused-absence slip?"

"The attendance office left a message on your phone," Marcie stated, clearly unimpressed by my feigned innocence. "You skipped class, didn't you?" It wasn't really a question.

"Okay, so maybe I need an excused absence from the nurse," I admitted.

Marcie gave me a patronizing look. "Did you use the old 'I have a headache' excuse? Or maybe the classic: PMS. And what did you ditch school for?"

"None of your business. Can I get the excused slip or not?"

She opened her purse, scrounged around, and produced a pink slip of paper bearing the school logo. As far as I could tell, it wasn't a reproduction. "Take it," she said.

I hesitated. "Is this one of those things that's going to come back to haunt me?"

"My, my, aren't we suspicious."

"If it seems too good to be true . . ."

"Take the slip already," she said, waving it in my face.

I had the bad feeling this was a favor with strings attached. "Ten days from now, are you going to need something in return?" I pressed.

"Maybe not ten days from now . . ."

I held up my hand. "Then forget it."

"I'm only kidding! Yeesh. You are no fun. Here's the truth. I was trying to be nice."

"Marcie, you don't know how to be nice."

"Consider this a sincere attempt," she said, and slapped the pink slip into my palm. "Take it, and I'll move my car."

I pocketed the slip and said, "While we're still on speaking terms, I have a question. Your dad was friends with a man named Blakely, and I need to find him. Does his name ring a bell?"

Her face was a mask. Hard to tell if she'd had a reaction. "Depends. Are you going to tell me why you need to find him?"

"I have some questions for him."

"What kind of questions?"

"I'd rather not share."

"Then neither would I."

I swallowed down a few unsavory comments and tried again.

"I'd like to tell you, Marcie, really I would, but there are some things you're better off not knowing."

"That's what my dad always told me. I think he was lying then, and I think you're lying now. If you want my help finding Blakely, I want full disclosure."

"How do I know you even have anything on Blakely?" I protested. Marcie was good at playing games, and I wouldn't put her past bluffing right now.

"My dad took me to Blakely's house once."

I jumped on the information. "Do you have an address? Could you find your way back?"

"Blakely doesn't live there anymore. He was getting divorced at the time, and my dad temporarily put him up in an apartment. But I did see some pictures on the mantel. Blakely has a little brother. You know him, because he goes to school with us. Alex Blakely."

"The football player?"

"The star running back."

I was stunned. Did this mean Alex was Nephilim too? "Are Blakely and his brother close?"

"Blakely bragged about Alex the whole time I was there. Which was, like, stupid because our football team sucks. Blakely said he's never missed a game."

Blakely had a brother. And his brother was Coldwater High's star running back. "When is the next football game?" I asked Marcie, trying to contain my excitement.

"Friday, *duh*. Games are always on Friday."

"Home or away?"

"Home."

A home game! Blakely was presumably working around the clock developing prototypes—all the more reason he'd want to leave his laboratory for a few hours and do something he actually enjoyed. Chances were he'd surface for a few hours this Friday night to watch his little brother play football. Since Blakely was divorced, Alex just might be the only family he had left. Making it to Alex's game would be important to him.

"You think Blakely is going to come to the game," Marcie said.

"It would be really helpful if he did."

"This is the part where you tell me what you're going to ask him."

I met Marcie's eyes and lied to her straight-faced. "I want to know if he has any idea who killed our dad."

Marcie almost flinched, but caught herself at the last moment. Her eyes stared ahead without blinking, giving away nothing to her thoughts. "I want to be there when you ask him."

"Sure," I lied again. "No problem."

I watched Marcie back down the driveway. As soon as she cleared the curb, I shoved the key into the Volkswagen's ignition. Six attempts later, it still hadn't whined to life. I brushed aside my impatience; nothing could sour my mood, not even the Volkswagen. I'd just found the lead I'd so desperately needed.

After school I drove to Patch's. I did the safety-conscious thing and circled the block a few times before parking in the freshly paved lot with extra-wide parking spaces. I didn't like feeling like I constantly had to watch my back, but I liked surprise visits from unfriendly Nephilim and devious archangels even less. And as far as the outside world knew, Patch and I were Splitsville. Using my key, I let myself inside.

"Hello?" I called out. The place felt empty. The couch cushions weren't indented from a recent sitting, and the TV remote hadn't moved since yesterday. Not that I could picture Patch sitting around watching ESPN all afternoon. If I had to guess, he'd probably spent the day trying to find Pepper's real blackmailer or tracking down Cowboy Hat and Co.

I walked deeper into the townhome. Half bath on the right, spare bedroom on the left, master bedroom at the back. Patch's lair.

His bed had a navy duvet with matching navy sheets and decorative pillows that also didn't appear touched. I opened the shutters and drank in the breathtaking panoramic views of Casco Bay and Peaks Island under an overcast sky. If Marcie got to be too much, I could always move in with Patch. My mom would love that.

I sent Patch a text. GUESS WHERE I AM?

I DON'T HAVE TO GUESS. YOU'RE WEARING THE TRACKING DEVICE, he answered.

I looked down. Sure enough, I'd worn the jean jacket today.

GIVE ME 20 AND I'LL BE THERE, Patch texted. WHICH ROOM SPECIFICALLY ARE YOU IN?

YOUR BEDROOM.

MAKE THAT TEN MINUTES.

I smiled and tucked my cell phone inside my purse. Then I flopped back on the king-size bed. The mattress was soft, but not too soft. I imagined Patch lying here, stretched out on this very bed, wearing who knew what. Boxers? Briefs? Nothing at all? I had the means and the method to find out, but going down that route didn't feel like the safest option. Not when I was doing my best to keep my relationship with Patch as uncomplicated as possible. I needed our lives to calm down before I figured out when and if I wanted to take that next big step . . .

Ten minutes later Patch strolled in to find me channel surfing on the couch. I clicked off the TV.

"You moved rooms," he said.

"It's safer this way."

"I'm that scary?"

"No, but the consequences might be." Who was I kidding? Yes, Patch was *that* scary. At six foot two, he was the embodiment of male physical perfection. I had a slim, well-proportioned figure, and I knew I was attractive, but I was no supergoddess. I didn't suffer from low self-esteem, but I was susceptible to intimidation, thank you very much.

finale

"I heard about Cheshvan," I said. "I heard it was a little anti-climactic."

"Don't believe everything you hear. Things are still pretty tense out there."

"Any idea what fallen angels are waiting for?"

"Who wants to know?"

I fought the urge to roll my eyes. "I'm not spying for Dante."

"Happy to hear it." Patch's tone was carefully noncommittal.

I sighed, hating this tension between us. "In case you're wondering, I made my choice. I'm yours," I said softly. "All yours."

Patch tossed his keys in the dish. "But?"

"But this morning, I basically told Dante the same thing. I thought about what you said—that we need to find Blakely and eradicate devilcraft. I decided Dante was probably my best shot at getting anywhere near Blakely, so I sort of . . ." It was hard to say it out loud and not feel like total slime.

"You're playing him."

"It sounds horrible when you put it that way, but yeah. I guess that's what I'm doing." Coming clean didn't make me feel any better. Dante and I didn't always see eye to eye on things, but he didn't deserve to be manipulated, either.

"Is he still pretending to date you?" Patch's tone chilled a degree.

"If I had to guess, he's been planting seeds about our relationship for days now. Either way, it's a hoax, and he knows that better than anyone."

Patch sat down beside me. Unlike usual, he didn't lace his fingers through mine.

I tried not to let it bother me, but a lump caught in my throat. "Cheshvan?" I prompted again.

"I know about as much as you. I've made it clear to fallen angels that I want nothing to do with this war. They resent me and clam up when I'm around. I'm not going to be the best source of information on fallen angel activity anytime soon." He tilted his head back to take advantage of the sofa's headrest and covered his face with his ball cap. I half expected him to start snoring, he looked so tired.

"Long day?" I asked.

He made a grunt of agreement. "I chased around a few leads on Pepper, hoping to shed some light on the identity of his blackmailer, but ended up back at square one. I can handle a lot of things, but an unproductive day isn't one of them."

"This from the guy who's constantly trying to convince me to spend the day in bed with him," I teased, hoping to lighten the mood.

"Angel, that would be a *very* productive day." His words were playful, but his tone sounded more worn out than anything.

"Any chance Dabria is the blackmailer?" I asked. "The other night at the Devil's Handbag, I saw her arguing with Pepper in the alley. He didn't look happy."

Patch grew still, pondering this news.

"Do you think it's possible?" I pressed.

"Dabria isn't blackmailing Pepper."

"How do you know?" I didn't like that he'd taken all of two seconds to make up his mind. Blackmailing seemed to fit Dabria to a T.

"I just do. How was your day?" he asked, clearly not going to elaborate.

I told him about Marcie's executive decision to move in, and about my mom's compliance. The more I talked, the more worked up I got. "She has an agenda in this," I told Patch. "I have this nagging feeling that Marcie suspects I know who killed her dad. And moving in is a ploy to spy on me."

Patch rested his hand on my thigh, and I felt a surge of hope. I hated feeling like there was a divide between us. "There are only two people in the world who know you killed Hank, and it's a secret I'll carry to hell and back if I have to. No one will find out."

"Thank you, Patch," I told him sincerely. "I'm sorry if I hurt your feelings earlier. I'm sorry about Dante, and about this whole mess. I just want to feel close to you again."

Patch kissed the palm of my hand. Then he laid it on his heart, holding it there. I want you close too, Angel, he murmured to my mind.

I snuggled in beside him, resting my head on his shoulder. Just touching him made the string of knots inside me loosen. I'd been waiting all day for this moment. I could stand tension between us about as well as I could tolerate being away from him. *Someday it will just be you and Patch*, I told myself. *Someday you'll escape Cheshvan, war, fallen angels, and Nephilim. Someday . . . just the two.*

"I found out something interesting," I said, and I told Patch about Blakely's football-star little brother, and Blakely's perfect home game attendance record.

Patch tipped his hat up and looked into my eyes. "Good work, Angel," he said, clearly impressed.

"What now?" I asked.

"Friday night, we show up at the game."

"Do you think we'll spook Blakely if he spots us?"

"He won't think it's strange if you're at the game, and I'll be in disguise. I'll grab him and drive him to some property I own near Sebago Lake. It's empty up there this time of year. Bad for Blakely, good for us. I'll get him to tell me about the prototypes, where he's fabricating them, and we'll find a way to deactivate them. Then I'll keep him permanently under my watch. It'll be the end of his days working with devilcraft."

"I should warn you that Marcie thinks she's going to be involved in interrogating him."

Patch lifted his eyebrows.

"It was the price I had to pay for getting this information," I explained.

"Did you swear an oath to let her tag along?" Patch asked.

"No."

finale

"Do you have a conscience?"

"No." I bit my lip. "Maybe." A pause. "Fine. Yes! Yes, I have a conscience. If we ditch Marcie, I'll spend the whole night feeling guilty. I lied to her face this morning, and it has haunted me all day. I live with her now, Patch. I have to face her. Maybe we can use this to our advantage. If we show her she can trust us, she just might give us more info."

"There are easier ways to get info, babe."

"I say we let her tag along. What's the worst that could happen?"

"She could figure out we didn't really break up and tell the Nephilim."

I hadn't thought of that.

"Or we can let her tag along, and I can erase her memory later." He shrugged. "No guilt here."

I mulled this over. It seemed like a viable plan. It also pretty much made me a hypocrite.

A hint of a smile crept to Patch's mouth. "Are you going to take point on this operation, or are you going to babysit Marcie?"

I shook my head. "You do the dirty work, and I'll keep tabs on Marcie."

Patch leaned sideways and kissed me. "As much as I'm going to enjoy questioning Blakely, I'm disappointed I won't get to watch you battle it out with Marcie."

"There's not going to be a battle. I'm going to calmly explain to her that she can come along for the ride, but that she'll have to wait with me in the car while you face off with Blakely. That's our final offer. She can take it or leave it." As I said it, I realized just how stupid I sounded for believing it would actually be that easy. Marcie hated taking orders. In her book, the only thing worse than taking orders was taking them from me. On the other hand, she might very well come in useful in the future. She was Hank's legal daughter, after all. If Patch and I were going to build an alliance, now was the time.

"I'll be firm," I promised Patch, adopting a no-nonsense expression. "No backing down."

By now Patch was full-on grinning. He kissed me again, and I felt my mouth soften its resolve. "You look cute when you're trying to be tough," he said.

Trying? I could be tough. I could! And Friday night, I'd prove it.

Watch out, Marcie.

I was a few miles from home when I passed a police car tucked out of sight on a side street. I hadn't gotten fifty feet beyond the intersection when the cop switched on his siren and wailed after me.

"Great," I muttered. "Just great!"

While I waited for the officer to approach the window, I mentally added up my babysitting money, wondering if I'd have enough to pay off the ticket.

finale

He rapped his pen on my window and motioned for me to lower it. I glanced through the glass at his face—and stared. Not just any cop, but my least favorite one. Detective Basso and I had a long-standing history of mutual suspicion and strong dislike.

I lowered my window. "I was only going three over!" I argued before he got a word out.

He was chewing on a toothpick. "I didn't pull you over for speeding. Left taillight is broken. That's a fifty-dollar fine."

"You've got to be kidding."

He scribbled on his pad and passed my ticket through the window. "Safety hazard. Nothing to joke about."

"Do you follow me around looking for ways to bust me?" I asked, half sarcastically, half under my breath.

"You wish." With that, he sauntered back to his patrol car. I watched him steer onto the road and cruise past. He waved as he did, but I couldn't bring myself to make a rude gesture in response. Something wasn't right.

My spine tingled, and my hands felt like I'd plunged them into ice water. I'd felt a cold vibe rolling off Detective Basso, chilly as a blast of winter air, but I had to have imagined it. I was getting paranoid. Because—

Because I only felt that way around nonhumans.

13

FRIDAY NIGHT I TRADED OUT MY SCHOOL CLOTHES FOR cords, my warmest merino wool sweater, a coat, hat, and mittens. The football game wouldn't start until dusk, and by then the outside temperature would have plunged. As I tugged the sweater over my head, I caught a flash of muscle in the mirror. Halting, I took a closer look. Sure enough, there was definition in both my biceps and triceps. Unbelievable. I'd trained one week, and it was already showing. It seemed my Nephil body developed muscle at a much faster rate than I ever could have hoped for as a human.

Loping down the stairs, I kissed my mom on the cheek and hurried out. The Volkswagen's engine protested against the cold, but eventually turned over. "You think this is bad? Wait until February," I told it.

I drove to the high school, parked on a side road just south of the football stadium, and called Patch.

"I'm here," I said. "Are we still going with plan A?"

"Unless you hear from me, yes. I'm in the crowd. No sign of Blakely yet. Have you heard from Marcie?"

I glanced at my watch—the one I'd synchronized to Patch's earlier tonight. "She's meeting me by the concession stand in ten."

"Do you want to go over the plan one last time?"

"If I see Blakely, I call you right away. I don't approach him, but I don't let him out of my sight, either." At first I'd been a little disgruntled that Patch wanted me to stay a safe distance from the action, but the truth was, I didn't want to take Blakely down on my own. I didn't know how strong he was, and let's face it, I didn't even know my own strength. It seemed like letting Patch, who was far more experienced in this kind of tactic, handle the take-down was the smartest move.

"And Marcie?"

"I stick to her all night. After you grab Blakely, I drive her to your cabin near Sebago Lake. I've got the directions right here. I

BECCA FITZPATRICK

take the long route, giving you time to question and incapacitate Blakely before we get there. That's everything, right?"

"One more thing," Patch said. "Be careful."

"Always," I said, and pushed out of the car.

I flashed my student ID at the ticket booth, bought a ticket, and meandered toward the concession stand, eyes alert for Blakely. Patch had given me a thorough description, but as soon as I was inside the stadium, mingling with the crowd, half the men in sight could have passed for Blakely. Tall and distinguished-looking with gray hair, a wiry build, and the intelligent but slightly nerdy appearance of a stereotypical chemistry professor. I wondered if, like Patch, he'd be in disguise, which would only make picking him out of the crowd that much more challenging. Would he be dressed in lumberjack clothes? Standard CHS Razorbills garb? Would he go so far as to dye his hair? If nothing else, he would be in the top percentile when it came to height. I'd start with that.

I found Marcie at the concession stand, shivering in pink jeans, a white turtleneck, and a matching pink puffer vest. Seeing her dressed this way made something in my brain click.

"Where's your cheerleading costume? Don't you have to cheer tonight?" I asked.

"It's a uniform, not a costume. And I quit."

"You quit the team?"

"I quit the squad."

"Wow."

finale

"I have bigger things to worry about. Everything else kind of pales in comparison to finding out that you're"—she glanced around uneasily—"Nephilim."

Quite unexpectedly, I felt a strange sense of kinship with Marcie. The moment quickly dissolved when I ran down the list of various ways Marcie had made my life miserable in the past year alone. We might both be Nephilim, but any similarities ended there. And I'd be smart to remember it.

"Do you think you'll recognize Blakely if you see him?" I asked her, keeping my voice down.

She shot me a look of irritation. "I said I know him, didn't I? Right now I'm your best shot at finding him. Don't question me."

"When and if you see him, keep it discreet. Patch will grab Blakely, and we'll follow him up to his cabin, where we can all question Blakely together." Except by that point, Blakely would be passed out and no good to Marcie. Minor detail.

"I thought you broke up with Patch."

"I did," I lied, trying to ignore the guilt twisting my stomach. "But I also don't trust anyone else to help me deal with Blakely. Just because Patch and I aren't together doesn't mean I can't call in a favor." If she didn't buy my explanation, I wasn't too worried. Patch would erase her memory of this conversation shortly.

"I want to question Blakely before Patch does," Marcie said.

"You can't. We have a plan and we have to stick to it."

Marcie hitched her shoulder in a really snooty way. "We'll see."

Mentally, I did some deep breathing. And quashed the urge to grind my teeth. Time to show Marcie she wasn't running the show. "If you mess this up, I will make you regret it." I put all my warning behind it, but right away I knew I needed to work on issuing threats. Maybe I could recruit Dante's help. Even better—get Patch to teach me the finer points.

"Do you really think Blakely has information about who killed my dad?" Marcie asked, fixing her eyes on me in a calculating, almost perceptive way.

My heart stumbled, but I held my expression in check. "Hopefully tonight we'll find out."

"What now?" Marcie said.

"Now we walk around and try not to draw attention."

"Speak for yourself," Marcie said with a snort.

Okay, so maybe she was right. Marcie did look fantastic. She was cute and annoyingly confident. She had money, and it showed in everything from her tanning-salon glow, to her so-natural-they-passed-as-real highlights, to her push-up bra. A mirage of perfection. As we marched up the bleachers, eyes flicked in our direction, and they weren't looking at me.

Think about Blakely, I directed myself. You've got bigger things to worry about than energy-sucking envy.

We strode along the bleachers, past the restrooms, and cut across the track circling the football field, heading toward the visitors' section. Much to my chagrin, I saw Detective Basso in uniform

finale

standing on the top row of the bleachers, gazing down at the rowdy visiting crowd with hard, skeptical eyes. His gaze shifted to me, and the doubt in his expression deepened. Remembering the strange feeling he'd given me two nights ago, I grabbed Marcie's elbow and forced her to walk away with me. I couldn't accuse Basso of following me—he was clearly on the clock—but that didn't mean I wanted to remain the subject of his scrutiny any longer.

Back and forth along the track Marcie and I walked. The stands were crowded, night had settled in, the game had started, and other than Marcie's throngs of male admirers, I didn't think we drew any unwanted attention, despite the fact that we hadn't taken a seat in over thirty minutes.

"This is getting old," Marcie complained. "I'm tired of walking. In case you didn't notice, I'm wearing wedge boots."

Not my problem! I wanted to scream. Instead I said, "Do you want to find Blakely or not?"

She huffed, and the sound scraped my nerves. "One more walk-through, and then I'm done."

Good riddance! I thought.

On our way back to the student section, I felt an eerie tingle slink over my skin. Automatically I turned, following the sensation to its origin. A few men loitered in the darkness outside the high fence surrounding the stadium, hanging their fingers on chain links. Men who hadn't bought tickets but still wanted to watch the game. Men who preferred sticking to the shadows rather than showing their faces under the stadium lights. One man in particular, lean and tall despite the way he slumped his shoulders, caught my attention. A vibe of nonhuman energy whipped off him, sending my sixth sense into overdrive.

I kept walking, but I said to Marcie, "Look over by the fence. Do any of the men over there look like Blakely?"

To her credit, Marcie limited her glance to a surreptitious flick of her eyes. "I think so. In the middle. The guy who's hunching his shoulders. That could be him."

It was all the confirmation I needed. Continuing to walk along the curve of the track, I pulled out my phone and placed a call.

"We found him," I told Patch. "He's on the north side of the stadium, outside the fence. He's wearing jeans and a gray Razorbill sweatshirt. There are a few other men hanging around, but I don't think they're with him. I only sense one Nephil, and that's Blakely himself."

"On my way," Patch said.

"We'll meet you at the cabin."

"Drive slow. I've got a lot of questions for Blakely," he said.

I'd stopped listening. Marcie was no longer by my side.

"Oh no," I whispered, suddenly feeling a shade paler. "Marcie! She's running over to Blakely! I have to go." I charged after Marcie.

Marcie was almost to the fence, and I heard her high-pitched voice screech, "Do you know who killed my dad? Tell me what you know!"

finale

A slew of curse words followed her question, and Blakely instantly turned and bolted.

In an impressive display of pure determination, Marcie scrabbled over the fence, slipping and struggling before she swung her legs over, and took off after Blakely into the unlit breezeway tunneling between the stadium and the high school.

I reached the fence a moment later, shoved my shoe into a chain link and, without breaking speed, vaulted over. I barely registered the shocked expressions of the men milling about. I would have attempted erasing their memories, but I didn't have time. I tore after Blakely and Marcie, surveying the darkness as I sprinted ahead, glad my night vision was much sharper than it had been when I was human.

I sensed Blakely ahead. Marcie, too, although her power was considerably weaker. Since both her parents were purebred Nephilim, she was lucky she'd been conceived, let alone born alive. She may have been Nephilim by definition, but I'd possessed more strength than her as a human.

Marcie! I hissed in mind-speak. *Get back here now!*

Suddenly Blakely went off my radar. I couldn't detect him at all. I stopped in my tracks, mentally feeling my way through the dark breezeway, trying to pick up his trail. Had he run so far and so fast he'd vanished off my grid completely? *Marcie!* I hissed again.

And then I saw her. Standing at the far end of the breezeway, the moonlight illuminating her silhouette. I jogged over, trying to

BECCA FITZPATRICK

keep my anger under control. She'd ruined everything. We'd lost Blakely, and worse, he now knew we were onto him. I couldn't imagine him surfacing at another football game after tonight. He'd probably retreat into his current secret hideout entirely. Our one chance . . . blown.

"What was that?" I demanded, stalking up to Marcie. "You were supposed to let Patch go after Blakely. . . ." My last few words came out slow and hoarse. I swallowed. I was looking at Marcie, but something about her was horribly, terribly wrong.

"Patch is here?" Marcie asked, only it wasn't her voice. It was low, masculine, and sourly amused. "I haven't been as careful as I thought."

"Blakely?" I asked, my mouth running dry. "Where's Marcie?"

"Oh, she's here. Right here. I'm possessing her body."

"How?" But I already knew. Devilcraft. It was the only explanation. That, and it was Cheshvan. The only month when possession of another body was possible.

Footsteps rang out behind us, and even in the darkness, I saw Blakely's eyes harden. He lunged for me without warning. He moved so fast, I didn't have time to react. He spun me against him, holding me to his chest. Patch appeared ahead, but slowed when he saw me standing backed up against Marcie.

"What's going on, Angel?" he asked, low and uncertain.

"Don't say a word," Blakely hissed in my ear.

Tears glistened in my eyes. Blakely was using one arm to pin me, but the other held a blade, and I felt it bite into my skin, a few inches above my hip.

"Not a single word," Blakely repeated, his breath ruffling my hair.

Patch came to a stop, and I could see confusion written all over his face. He knew something was wrong, but he couldn't figure out what. He knew I was stronger than Marcie and could break free if I wanted.

"Let Nora go," Patch told Marcie, his voice quiet, wary.

"Don't come another step," Blakely commanded Patch, only this time he made his voice sound like Marcie's. High and quivering. "I have a knife, and I'll use it if I have to." Blakely waved the knife to make his point.

Devilcraft, Patch spoke to my mind. *I feel it everywhere.*

Be careful! Blakely is possessing Marcie's body, I tried to tell him, but my thoughts were blocked. Somehow Blakely was shielding them. I felt them bounce back, as though I were yelling at a wall. He seemed to have complete and utter control over devilcraft, using it like an unstoppable and highly adaptive weapon.

From the corner of my eye, I saw Blakely hold up the knife. The blade glowed an ethereal shade of blue. Before I could blink, he plunged the knife into my side, and it was as though I'd been pushed into a raging furnace.

I collapsed, trying to howl and scream in pain, but too much in shock to manage a single sound. I writhed on the ground, wanting to pull out the knife, but every muscle in my body was in shock, paralyzed in unspeakable agony.

The next thing I knew, Patch was at my side, uttering a litany of curses, fear sharpening his voice. He tugged out the knife. Now I screamed, the sound shattering out from deep within. I heard Patch shouting directives, but the words snapped in two, insignificant next to the pain torturing every corner of my body. I was on fire, the flames licking me from the inside out. The heat was so intense, great convulsive shudders made me twitch and flail against my will.

Patch scooped me into his arms. I vaguely noted that he was sprinting out of the breezeway. The sound of his footsteps echoing off the walls was the last thing I heard.

CHAPTER

I WOKE WITH A START, INSTANTLY TRYING TO GET MY bearings. I was in a vaguely familiar bed, in a dark room that smelled warm and earthy. A body was stretched out beside mine, and it stirred.

"Angel?"

"I'm awake," I said, a flood of relief welling up inside me now that I knew Patch was close. I didn't know how long I'd been out, but I felt safe here in his home, with him watching over me. "Blakely was possessing Marcie's body. I didn't sense him and walked right up to him without the slightest clue it was a trap. I tried to warn you, but Blakely had me in some kind of bubble—my mind-speak kept bouncing back."

Patch nodded, coaxing a stray curl behind my ear. "I saw him exit Marcie's body and run. Marcie's okay. Shaken up, but fine."

"Why did he have to stab me?" I grimaced in pain as I lifted my sweater to see the wound. My Nephilim blood should have healed me by now, but the stab was still fresh, casting a bluish hue.

"He knew if you were hurt, I'd stay by your side instead of going after him. A move that's going to cost him," Patch said, his jaw rigid. "When I brought you here, your entire body was radiating blue light, head to toe. You appeared to be in a coma. I couldn't reach you, even through mind-speak, and it terrified me." Patch pulled me against him, curling his body protectively around mine, holding me almost too tight, and that's when I knew just how worried he was.

"What does this mean for me?"

"I don't know. It can't be good that you've had devilcraft forced into your body twice now."

"Dante is drinking it daily." If he was okay, I'd be okay too. Wouldn't I? I wanted to believe it.

Patch said nothing, but I had a good idea where his thoughts were going. Like me, he knew there had to be side effects to ingesting devilcraft.

"Where's Marcie?" I asked.

"I altered her memory so she won't remember seeing me tonight, then had Dabria take her home. Don't look at me like that. I was low on options, and I had Dabria's phone number."

"That's what I'm worried about!" I instantly winced when my strong reaction caused my wound to throb.

Patch bent down to kiss my forehead, rolling his eyes as he did. "Don't make me tell you again there's nothing between me and Dabria."

"She's not over you."

"She's pretending to feel something for me to antagonize you. Don't make it easy for her."

"Don't call her up for favors like she's part of the team," I countered. "She tried to kill me, and she'd steal you back in a heartbeat, if you'd let her. I don't care how many times you deny it. I've seen the way she looks at you."

Patch looked like he had a comeback, but he forced it down and rolled agilely out of bed. His black T-shirt was rumpled, his hair mussed, giving him the appearance of a perfect pirate. "Can I get you something to eat? Drink? I feel useless, and it's driving me crazy."

"You could go after Blakely, if you're looking for something to do," I said crisply. What would it take to get rid of Dabria, once and for all?

A smile that was equally devious and truly sinister crept over

Patch's expression. "We don't have to find him. He'll come to us. To get away, he had to leave his knife behind. He knows we have it, and he knows it's evidence I can take to the archangels to prove he's using devilcraft. He's going to come looking for that knife. Soon."

"Let's turn him over to the archangels now. Let them worry about eradicating devilcraft."

Patch breathed a laugh, but it held an edge. "I no longer trust the archangels. Pepper Friberg isn't the only bad egg. If I turn this over to them, I have no guarantee they'll take care of this mess. I used to think the archangels were incorruptible, but they've done a good job of convincing me otherwise. I've seen them tamper with death, look the other way on serious offenses of the law, and punish me for crimes I haven't committed. I've made mistakes, and I've paid for those mistakes, but I suspect they won't give up until they've locked me away in hell. They don't like opposition, and that's the first word that comes to mind when they think of me. This time I'm taking matters into my own hands. Blakely is going to come for his knife, and when he does, I'll be ready."

"I want to help," I said immediately. I wanted to take down the Nephil who'd been foolish enough to stab me. Blakely was aiding the Nephilim army, but *I* was leading it. While I considered his actions gravely disrespectful, there were some who'd consider them treasonous. And I knew for a fact that Nephilim as a race don't look kindly on traitors.

Patch locked eyes with me, studying me wordlessly as though

judging my ability to go up against Blakely. To my deep satisfaction, he gave a nod. "All right, Angel. But first things first. The football game ended two hours ago, and your mom is going to wonder where you are. Time to get you home."

The lights were off at the farmhouse, but I knew my mom wouldn't fall asleep until I'd made it home. I knocked softly on her bedroom door, nudged it open, and whispered into the darkness, "I'm home."

"Did you have a good time?" she asked, yawning.

"The team played really well," I said evasively.

"Marcie came home a few hours ago. She didn't say much, just went straight to her room and shut the door. She seemed . . . quiet. Upset, maybe." There was a hint of inquiry in her tone.

"Probably PMS." Probably she was doing everything in her power not to launch into a full-fledged panic attack. I'd been possessed before, and words couldn't describe how violating it felt. But I wasn't feeling especially sympathetic. If Marcie had done what I'd asked, none of this would have happened.

In my bedroom, I shucked out of my clothes and examined my stab wound once more. The electric blue tint was fading. Slowly, but fading nonetheless. It had to be a good sign.

I'd just crawled into bed when there was a tap at the door. Marcie opened it and stood in the entrance. "I'm freaking out," she said, and she genuinely looked like she meant it.

I motioned for her to come in and shut the door.

"What happened back there?" she demanded, her voice cracking. Tears brimmed in her eyes. "How did he take over my body like that?"

"Blakely possessed you."

"How can you be calm about this?" she shrieked in an undertone. "He was living inside me. Like some kind of . . . *parasite!*"

"If you had let me take down Blakely like we agreed, this wouldn't have happened." As soon as I said it, I regretted sounding so harsh. Marcie had done a stupid thing, but who was I to judge? I'd made my fair share of impulsive decisions. Caught up in the moment, she'd reacted. She wanted to know who killed her father, and who could blame her? Certainly not me.

I sighed. "I'm sorry, I didn't mean it like that."

But it was too late. She gave me a wounded look, and left.

15

I AWOKE WITH A JOLT. DANTE WAS LEANING OVER MY bed, his hands straddling my shoulders. "Good morning, sunshine."

I tried to roll away, but his arms had me pinned in place. "It's Saturday," I protested wearily. Training was all fine and good, but I deserved one day off.

"I've got a surprise for you. A good one."

"The only surprise I want is another two hours of sleep." The window showed that the sky was still full dark, and I doubted it was much later than five thirty.

He flung off my covers and I squealed, grabbing blindly for them. "Do you mind!"

"Cute pj's."

I was wearing a black T-shirt I'd swiped from Patch's closet, and it barely reached mid-thigh.

I simultaneously tugged the shirt down and the sheets higher. "Fine," I relented with a huff. "I'll meet you outside."

After dragging on my running clothes and lacing up my shoes, I trudged outside. Dante wasn't in the driveway, but I sensed him nearby, most likely in the woods across the street. Oddly, I thought I sensed another Nephil with him. Frowning, I walked in that direction.

Sure enough, Dante had brought a friend. Only, by the look of the friend—two black eyes, a cut lip, a swollen jaw, and one painful-looking goose egg on his forehead—the two were on anything but good terms.

"Recognize him?" Dante asked cheerfully, holding the injured Nephil up by the scruff of his neck for my appraisal.

I stepped closer, unsure what kind of game Dante was playing. "No. He's too beat up. Did you do this to him?"

"Sure this handsome mug doesn't ring a bell?" Dante asked again, jerking the Nephil's jaw side to side, clearly enjoying himself. "He was shooting his mouth off last night about you. He bragged about giving you a serious beating. Of course, that's when he caught my interest. I told him he'd never done such a thing. And if he had, well, let's just say I don't take kindly to Nephil underlings disrespecting their leaders, especially the commander of the Black Hand's army." All lightheartedness had faded from Dante's tone, and he eyed the injured Nephil with open contempt.

"It was a prank," the Nephil said sullenly. "Thought we'd see how sincere she is about following through with the Black Hand's vision. She wasn't even born a Nephil. Thought we'd give her a taste of what she's up against—"

"Cowboy Hat?" I blurted aloud. His face was too disfigured to bear any resemblance to the Nephil who'd hauled me to a cabin, tied me to a post, and threatened me, but his voice rang true. He was definitely Cowboy Hat. Shaun Corbridge.

"Prank?" Dante chuckled with venom. "If that's what constitutes a prank in your mind, maybe you'll find something to laugh about in what we're going to do to you." He slugged Cowboy Hat in the head so viciously he collapsed to his knees.

"Can I talk to you?" I asked Dante. "Privately?"

"Of course." He pointed a warning finger at Cowboy Hat. "You budge, you bleed."

After I was sure we had walked out of Cowboy Hat's hearing range, I said, "What's going on?"

"I was at the Devil's Handbag last night, and that numskull buffoon over there was bragging about using you as his personal punching bag. At first I thought I was hearing wrong. But the louder he talked, the more I realized he wasn't, in any way, shape, or form, making up his story. Why didn't you tell me some of our soldiers attacked you?" Dante demanded. His tone wasn't angry. Hurt, maybe, but not angry.

"Are you asking because you're concerned about what this means for my ratings, or are you concerned about me?"

Dante shook his head. "Don't say that. You know I'm not thinking about your numbers. Truth is, I stopped caring about them almost instantly. This is about you. That punk over there laid his hands on you, and I don't like it. Not one bit. Yes, he should show you respect as commander of an army he claims to belong to, but it's more than that. He should respect you because you're a good person, and you're giving this your best shot. I see it, and I want him to see it too."

I was uncomfortable with his honesty and intimacy. Especially after the kiss he'd almost mind-tricked me into. His words seemed to stray beyond professional, and that was what our relationship was. That was what I wanted it to remain.

I said, "I appreciate everything you just said, but exacting revenge isn't going to change his mind. He hates me. Lots of Nephilim do. This might be a good opportunity to show them they just might be wrong about me. I think we should let him go and get on with training."

Dante didn't look swayed. If anything, his face bore disappointment and maybe even impatience. "Compassion isn't the way to go. Not this time. That punk over there is only going to make his case stronger if you let him off easy. He's trying to convince people you aren't fit to lead this army, and if you go easy on him, it only proves his point. Rattle him up a bit. Make him think twice about shooting off his mouth again or touching you."

"Let him go," I said more firmly. I didn't believe violence trumped violence. Not now, not ever.

Dante opened his mouth, going a little red in the face, but I cut him off. "I'm not backing down on this. He didn't hurt me. He took me up to the cabin because he's scared and he didn't know what else to do. Everyone's scared. Cheshvan is here, and our future hangs in the balance. What he did was wrong, but I can't hold it against him for trying to do something to alleviate his fears. Put down your pitchfork and let him go. I mean it, Dante."

Dante exhaled a long, disapproving sigh. I knew he wasn't happy, but I also believed I was making the right decision. I didn't want to fuel the fires of contention any more than I already had. If the Nephilim as a whole were going to get through this, we had to be unified. We had to be willing to display compassion, respect, and civility, even when we didn't see eye to eye.

"So that's it?" Dante asked, clearly not satisfied.

I cupped my hands over my mouth to amplify my voice. "You're free to go," I called to Cowboy Hat. "I apologize for any inconvenience."

Cowboy Hat stared at us, his mouth parted in disbelief, but not wanting to press his luck, he scrabbled out of the woods as if being pursued by bears.

"So," I said to Dante. "What cruel machinations do you have planned for me today? Sprint a marathon? Move mountains? Part the seas?"

An hour later my arm and leg muscles quivered from exhaustion. Dante had pushed me through grueling intervals of calisthenics: push-ups, pull-ups, sit-ups, and flutter kicks. We were on our way out of the woods, when I brought my arm up suddenly, catching Dante across the chest. I held a finger to my lips, gesturing for him not to make a sound.

In the distance, I could just make out the soft crunch of footsteps.

Dante must have heard it too. *Deer?* he asked me.

I squinted into the darkness. The woods were still unlit, and the densely packed trees only added to my decreased visibility.

No. The rhythm's not right.

Dante tapped my shoulder and pointed toward the sky. At first I didn't understand. Then his meaning became clear. He wanted us to climb the trees, giving us an eagle-eye view of trouble, if that was indeed what was headed our way.

Despite my exhaustion, I scaled a white cedar noiselessly with a few expert leaps and quick foot placement. Dante perched in a neighboring tree.

We didn't wait long. Moments after climbing to safety, six fallen angels crept stealthily into the clearing below. Three males and three females. Their bare torsos were marked with strange hieroglyphics that bore a distant resemblance to the paint splatter on Patch's wrist, and their faces were painted a deep bloodred. The effect was chilling, and I couldn't help but think of Pawnee warriors.

I fastened my gaze on one in particular. A lanky boy with black-ringed eyes. His familiar face froze my blood. I remembered his savage march through the Devil's Handbag, and the way his hand had flashed out. I remembered his victim. I remembered how she'd looked just like me.

A vicious snarl hardened his expression, and he stalked through the trees with purpose. His chest bore a recent wound, small and circular, as if a knife had been used to crudely cut out a piece of flesh. Something cold and unforgiving gleamed in his eyes, and I shuddered.

Dante and I stayed in the trees until the party moved on. When we were back on solid ground, I said, "How did they find us?"

His eyes turned on mine, hooded and cold. "They made a big mistake coming after you like this."

"Do you think they've been spying on us?"

"I think someone tipped them off."

"The lanky one. I've seen him before, at the Devil's Handbag. He attacked a Nephilim girl who looked a lot like me. Do you know him?"

"No." But it seemed to me he paused a half moment before answering.

Five hours later I was showered and dressed, I'd eaten a healthy breakfast of Egg Beaters with mushrooms and spinach, and as a bonus, I'd finished all my homework. Not bad, considering it wasn't even noon.

Down the hall, Marcie's bedroom door opened and she emerged. Her hair stuck up all over the place, and there were dark circles under her eyes. I could almost smell her morning breath from here.

"Hey," I said.

"Hey."

"My mom wants us to rake leaves in the yard, so you might want to hold off showering until after we finish."

Marcie's eyebrows pulled together. "Come again?"

"Saturday chores," I explained. I understood that this was probably a new term for Marcie. And I thoroughly enjoyed being the one to teach it to her.

"I don't do chores."

"You do when you live here."

"All right," Marcie said reluctantly. "Let me get breakfast and make a few calls."

On a normal day I didn't think Marcie would be so agreeable, but I was beginning to think her willingness could be an apology for her big screwup last night. Hey, I'd take it any way I could get it.

While Marcie poured cereal for breakfast, I went to the garage

finale

to find rakes. I was halfway done raking the front yard when a car rumbled up the street. Scott parked his Barracuda in the driveway and swung out. His T-shirt hugged every bulge of muscle, and for Vee's sake, I wished I had a camera.

"What's up, Grey?" he said. He pulled leather work gloves out of his back pocket and tugged them on. "I'm here to help. Put me to work. I'm your slave for the day. Never mind your boy Dante should be here, not me." He kept teasing me about Dante, but I couldn't tell if he believed in the relationship. I always detected a slight note of mockery. Of course, I detected that same mockery underscoring one out of every ten words he spoke.

I leaned on my rake. "I don't understand. How did you know I was raking the yard?"

"Your new best friend told me."

I didn't have a new best friend, but I had a perennial archenemy. I narrowed my eyes. "Marcie recruited you?" I guessed.

"Said she needed help with chores. She has allergies and can't work outdoors."

"Total lie!" And I'd been naive enough to think she was actually going to help.

Scott grabbed the extra rake I'd propped against the front porch and came over to help. "Let's make a really big pile and toss you in."

"That defeats the point."

Scott grinned and nudged my shoulder. "But it would be fun."

Marcie opened the front door and came out on the porch. She perched herself on the steps, crossing her legs and leaning forward on them. "Hi, Scott."

"Yo."

"Thanks for coming to my rescue. You're my knight in shining armor."

"Oh, gag," I said, rolling my eyes melodramatically.

"Anytime," Scott told her. "I can't pass up an excuse to torment Grey." He came up behind me and stuffed a fistful of leaves down my shirt.

"Hey!" I shrieked. I picked up my own handful of leaves and flung them in his face.

Scott dropped his shoulder, barreled toward me, and took me down, scattering my tidy pile of leaves everywhere. I was mad that in one moment he'd obliterated my hard work, but at the same time, I couldn't stop laughing. He was on top of me, cramming leaves down my shirt, into my pockets, and up my pant legs. "Scott!" I giggled.

"Get a room," Marcie said in a bored voice, but I could tell she was irritated.

When Scott finally rolled off me, I said to Marcie, "Too bad about those allergies. Raking leaves can be a lot of fun. Did I forget to mention that?"

She nailed me with a look of sheer gall, then marched inside.

finale

AFTER SCOTT AND I HAD SCOOPED ALL THE leaves into orange garbage sacks decorated to look like pumpkins, and placed them decoratively around the yard, he came inside for a glass of milk and my mom's deliciously gooey mint-chocolate-chip cookies. I thought Marcie might have retreated to her room, but instead she was waiting for us in the kitchen.

"I think we should throw a Halloween party here," she announced.

I snorted and set down my milk glass. "No offense, but we're not big into parties in this family."

Mom's whole face lit up. "I think it's a wonderful idea, Marcie. We haven't hosted a party here since Harrison passed. I could swing by the party store later today and see what they have for decorations."

I looked to Scott for help, but he merely shrugged. "Could be cool."

"You have a milk mustache," I told him tartly in return.

He wiped it on the back of his hand . . . then wiped it on my arm.

"Eeew!" I shrieked, giving him a shove to the shoulder.

"I think we should have a theme. Like famous couples through-out history, and tell everyone to come in pairs," Marcie said.

"Hasn't that been done before," I said, "like a million times?"

"The theme should be favorite character from the Halloween movies," Scott said with a sadistic grin.

"Whoa. Back up. Everyone just . . . chill," I said, holding my hands out in a Stop motion. "Mom, you realize we'd have to clean the whole house, right?"

Mom gave an insulted laugh. "The house isn't that dirty, Nora."

"Is it BYOB, or are we providing?" Scott asked.

"No beer," my mom and I chimed in unison.

"Well, I like the famous couples idea," said Marcie, clearly hav-ing made up her mind. "Scott, we should go together."

Scott didn't miss a beat. "Could I be Michael Myers and you be one of the babysitters I mutilate?"

"No," Marcie said. "We're going as Tristan and Isolde."

I stuck my tongue out. "Way to be original."

Scott kicked my leg playfully. "Well, hello there, Little Miss Cheerful."

I think it's pretty frivolous to be planning a Halloween party when we're right in the middle of Cheshvan, I said critically to his thoughts. *Fallen angels might be holding their breath, but not for long. We both know war is brewing, and everyone is expecting me to do something about it. So forgive me if I seem a little cranky!*

Fair enough, Scott returned. *But maybe the party will help take your mind off things.*

Are you seriously considering going with Marcie?

A smile surfaced on his lips. *You think I should go with you instead?*

I think you should go with Vee.

Before I could gauge Scott's reaction, Marcie said, "Let's go to the party store together, Mrs. Grey. And we can stop by the stationery store afterward so I can look for invitations. I want something spooky and festive, but cutesy, too." She bobbed her shoulders and gave a squeal. "This is going to be so much fun!"

"Who are you going to ask to the party, Nora?" my mom asked.

I pursed my lips, unable to come up with the right answer. Scott was taken, Dante wouldn't do—it would help fuel our relationship rumor, but I wasn't in the mood—and my mom detested Patch.

Worse, I was supposed to hate his guts. We were immortal enemies as far as the outside world was concerned.

I didn't want to be included in this party. I had bigger problems. I had a vengeful archangel after me; I was the leader of an army, but lacked direction—despite my pact with the archangels, I was starting to feel like war might not only be inevitable, it just might be the right move; my best friend was keeping secrets, and speculating about their nature was keeping me up at night; and now this. A Halloween party. In my own home. Where I'd be expected to play hostess.

Marcie smirked. "Anthony Amowitz has a crush on you."

"Ooh, tell me more about Anthony," Mom prodded.

Marcie loved a good story, and she launched right into this one. "He was in our PE class last year. Every time we played softball, he played catcher and would gawk at Nora's legs the whole time she was at bat. He couldn't catch a single pitch, he was so distracted."

"Nora does have lovely legs," Mom teased me.

I hitched my thumb at the stairs. "I'm going to my room to bang my head against the wall a few thousand times. Anything has to be better than this."

"You and Anthony could be Scarlett and Rhett," Marcie called after me. "Or Buffy and Angel. What about Tarzan and Jane?"

That night I left my window cracked, and just after midnight, Patch crawled inside. He smelled earthy, like the woods, as he slid quietly into bed beside me. Even though I would have preferred to meet him in the open, there was something undeniably sexy about our secret rendezvous.

"I brought you something," he said, setting a brown paper sack on my tummy.

I sat up and peeked inside. "A caramel apple from Delphic Beach!" I grinned. "No one makes them better. And you even got one dipped in coconut flakes—my favorite."

"It's a get-well present. How's the wound doing?"

I lifted my nightshirt, showing him the good news myself. "All better." The last of the blue discoloration had vanished a few hours ago, and as soon as it had, the wound had healed almost instantly. Only the palest ribbon of a scar remained.

Patch kissed me. "That is good news."

"Any sign of Blakely?"

"No, but it's only a matter of time."

"Have you sensed him following you?"

"No." An edge of frustration crept into his tone. "But I'm sure he's keeping tabs on me. He needs the knife back."

"Devilcraft is changing all the rules, isn't it?"

"It's forcing me to be inventive, I'll give it that."

"Did you bring Blakely's knife with you?" I eyed his pockets, which looked empty.

He lifted his shirt just high enough to reveal the handle sticking out of his leather belt. "Never let it out of my sight."

"Are you sure he'll come for it? Maybe he's calling your bluff. Maybe he knows the archangels aren't as straitlaced as we all thought they were, and he knows he can get away with devilcraft."

"It's a possibility, but I don't think so. The archangels are good at hiding things, particularly from Nephilim. I think Blakely is scared, and I think he's going to make a move soon."

"What if he brings backup? What if it's you and me against twenty of them?"

"He'll come alone," Patch said confidently. "He screwed up, and he's going to try to salvage this mess privately. Knowing how valuable he is to the Nephilim, there's no way he was allowed to attend a football game by himself. I'm betting Blakely sneaked out. Worse, he left behind a knife enchanted with devilcraft. He's sweating this, and he knows he has to fix it before anyone finds out. I'm going to use his fear and desperation to our advantage. He knows we're still together. I'll make him swear an oath not to breathe a word of our relationship, and I'll tell him he won't get the knife back until he does."

I loosened a presliced wedge from the caramel apple and bit it in half. Might as well fake calm.

"Anything else?" Patch asked.

"Hmm . . . yeah. During training this morning, Dante and I were interrupted by a few fallen angel thugs." I shrugged. "We hid until they went away, but you can tell Cheshvan has everyone's blood heated up. You wouldn't happen to know a skinny fallen angel with markings all over his chest, would you? This made the second time I've seen him."

"Doesn't ring a bell. But I'll keep my eyes sharp. You sure you're all right?"

"Positive. In other news, Marcie's throwing a Halloween party here at the farmhouse."

Patch smiled. "Grey-Millar family drama?"

"The theme is famous couples from history. Could she be any less original? Worse, she's roped my mom into this. They went shopping for decorations today. For three whole hours. It's like they're suddenly best friends." I picked up another apple slice and made a face at it. "Marcie is ruining everything. I wanted Scott to go with Vee, but Marcie already convinced him to go with her."

Patch's smile widened.

I aimed my best sulky look at him. "This isn't funny. Marcie is destroying my life. Whose side are you on anyway?"

Patch raised his hands in surrender. "I'm staying out of this."

"I need a date for the stupid thing. I need to upstage Marcie," I added on a spark of inspiration. "I want a hotter guy on my arm, and I want a better costume. I'm going to come up with something a million times better than Tristan and Isolde." I gazed at Patch hopefully.

He merely looked at me. "We can't be seen together."

"You'd be in costume. Think of it as a challenge to be really sneaky. You have to admit, all this sneaking around is kind of hot."

"I don't do costume parties."

"Pretty please with a cherry on top?" I batted my lashes.

"You're killing me."

"I know of only one guy who is better-looking than Scott. . . ." I let the idea tempt his ego.

"Your mom isn't going to let me step foot inside this place. I've seen the gun she keeps on the top shelf of the pantry."

"Again, you'll be in disguise, silly. She won't know it's you."

"You aren't going to let this go, are you?"

"Nope. What do you think of John Lennon and Yoko Ono? Or Samson and Delilah? Robin Hood and Maid Marian?"

He lifted an eyebrow. "Ever consider Patch and Nora?"

I laced my fingers over my stomach and eyed the ceiling deviously. "Marcie is going down."

Patch's cell phone rang, and he looked at the readout. "Unknown number," he murmured, and my blood chilled.

"Do you think it's Blakely?"

"One way to find out." He answered the phone, his voice calm but not inviting. Right away, I felt Patch's body tense beside mine, and I knew it had to be Blakely. The call lasted only a handful of seconds.

"It's our guy," Patch told me. "He wants to meet. Now."

"That's it? It almost feels too easy."

Patch locked eyes with me, and I knew there was more. I couldn't quite interpret his expression, but the way he watched me

finale

made anxiety bubble up inside me. "If we give him the knife, he'll give us the antidote."

"What antidote?" I asked.

"When he stabbed you, he infected you. He didn't say with what. He only said if you don't get the antidote soon—" He broke off, swallowing. "He said you're going to regret it. We both are."

E'S BLUFFING. IT'S A TRAP. HE'S TRYING TO make us panic so we'll be too busy concentrating on whatever fictitious disease he put inside me to play this smart." I jumped out of bed and paced my room. "Oh, he's good. Real good. I say we call him back and tell him he'll get the knife after he swears an oath to stop using devilcraft. That's a trade I'll agree to."

"And if he's not lying?" Patch asked quietly.

I didn't want to think about that. If I did, I'd play right into Blakely's hands. "He is," I said with more conviction. "He was Hank's protégé, and if Hank was good at one thing, it was lying. I'm sure the vice rubbed off. Call him back. Tell him there's no deal. Tell him my wound has healed, and if there was anything wrong with me, we'd know by now."

"This is devilcraft we're talking about. It doesn't play by the rules." There was both worry and frustration behind Patch's words. "I don't think we can make assumptions, and I don't think we can risk underestimating him. If he did anything to hurt you, Angel . . ." A muscle in Patch's jaw contracted with emotion, and I feared he was doing exactly what Blakely wanted. Thinking with his anger and not with his head.

"Let's wait this out. If we're wrong, and I don't think we are, but if that's the case, Blakely is still going to want the knife back two, four, six days from now. We're holding the cards. If we begin to suspect that he really did infect me with something, we'll call him. He'll still meet us, because he needs the knife. We have nothing to lose."

Patch didn't look sold. "He said you'd need the antidote soon."

"Notice how vague soon sounds. If he was telling the truth, he'd have a more specific time frame." My bravery wasn't an act. Not one part of me believed Blakely was being forthright. My wound had healed, and I'd never felt better. He hadn't injected me with a disease. I wasn't going to fall for that. And it frustrated me that Patch was being so cautious, so gullible. I wanted to stick to our original plan: drag Blakely in and curtail the production of devilcraft. "Did he set up a meeting place? Where did he want to make the switch?"

"I'm not going to tell you," Patch answered in a calm, measured tone.

I flinched in confusion. "Sorry. What did you just say?"

Patch walked over and cupped his hands around the back of my neck. His expression was immovable. He was serious—he intended to hold out on me. He might as well have slapped me, the betrayal stung that bad. I couldn't believe he was going against me on this. I started to turn away, too enraged to speak, but he caught me by the wrist.

"I respect your opinion, but I've been doing this a lot longer," he said, his voice low and serious and heartfelt.

"Don't patronize me."

"Blakely isn't a nice guy."

"Thanks for the tip," I said bitingly.

"I wouldn't put it past him to infect you with something. He's been messing around with devilcraft far too long to have any sense of decency or humanity left. It has hardened his heart and put ideas into his mind—crafty, malicious, dishonorable ideas. I don't think he's making blind threats. He sounded sincere. He sounded dead set on carrying out every threat he spoke. If I don't meet him tonight, he'll throw away the antidote. He's not afraid of showing us what kind of man he is."

finale

"Then let's show him who we are. Tell me where he wants to meet. Let's grab him and bring him in for questioning," I challenged. I glanced at the clock. Five minutes had passed since Patch ended the call. Blakely wouldn't wait all night. We had to get going—we were wasting time.

"You're not meeting Blakely tonight, end of story," Patch said.

I hated how infuriatingly *alpha* he was being about this. I deserved an equal say, and he was brushing me aside. He didn't care about my opinion—that was just a thinly veiled platitude. "We're going to miss our chance to catch him!" I argued.

"I'm going to make the trade, and you're staying here."

"How can you say that? You're letting him call the shots! What has happened to you?"

His eyes locked with mine. "I thought it was quite obvious, Angel. Your health is more important than getting answers. There will be another time to get Blakely."

My mouth hung open, and I shook my head from side to side. "If you walk out of here without me, I'll never forgive you." A strong threat, but I believed I meant it. Patch had promised we were a team from now on. If he cut me out now, I'd view it as a betrayal. We'd been through too much for him to coddle me now.

"Blakely is already on edge. If anything feels off, he'll run, and there goes our antidote. He said he wanted to meet me alone, and I'm going to honor his request."

I shook my head fiercely. "Don't make this about Blakely. This is about you and me. You said we'd be a team from now on. This is about what *we* want—not what he wants."

There was a knock at my bedroom door, and I snapped, "What?"

Marcie pushed the door open and stood in the entrance, arms folded snugly over her chest. She was wearing a baggy old tee and boxer shorts. Not what I pictured Marcie wearing to bed. I would have expected more pink, more lace, more skin.

"Who are you talking to?" she wanted to know, rubbing sleep out of her eyes. "I can hear you yapping all the way down the hall."

I swiveled my attention back to Patch, but it was just Marcie and me left in my bedroom. Patch had vanished.

I snatched a pillow off my bed and flung it against the wall.

Sunday morning I woke with a strange, insatiable hunger clawing at my belly. I pushed myself out of bed, skipped the bathroom, and headed straight to the kitchen. I opened the fridge, eyeing the shelves greedily. Milk, fruit, leftover beef stroganoff. Salad, cheese slices, Jell-O salad. None of it looked remotely appealing, and yet my stomach twisted with hunger pangs. I stuck my head in the pantry, raked my eyes up and down the shelves, but every last item had the appeal of chewing polyester. My unaccountable cravings intensified at the lack of food, and I started to feel nauseated.

It was still dark out, a few minutes before five, and I lugged myself back to bed. If I couldn't eat my pains away, I'd sleep them off. Trouble was, my head felt perched on a Tilt-A-Whirl, vertigo reeling me up in its madness. My tongue was dry and swollen with thirst, but the thought of sipping something even as bland as water made my insides threaten to heave in revolt. I briefly wondered if this could be an aftereffect of the stabbing, but I was too uncomfortable to do much thinking.

I spent the next several minutes rolling around, trying to find the coolest part of my sheets for relief, when a silky voice whispered in my ear, "Guess what time it is?"

I let out a genuine groan. "I can't train today, Dante. I'm sick."

"Oldest excuse in the book. Now get out of bed," he said, swatting my leg.

My head hung over the side of the mattress, and I eyed his shoes. "If I throw up on your feet, will you believe me?"

"I'm not that squeamish. I want you outside in five. If you're late, you'll make it up to me. An extra five miles for every tardy minute sounds about fair."

He left, and it took all my motivation and then some to drag myself out of bed. I laced up my shoes slowly, locked in a battle with raging hunger attacking me from one side, and sharp vertigo from the other.

When I made it to the driveway, Dante said, "Before we get started, I have an update on our training efforts. One of my first acts as lieutenant was assigning officers over our troops. I hope you approve. Training of the Nephilim is going well," he went on without waiting for my response. "We've been focusing on anti-possession techniques, mind-tricks as both offensive and defensive strategies, and rigorous physical conditioning. Our biggest area of weakness is spy recruiting. We need to develop good information sources. We need to know what fallen angels are planning, but we've been unsuccessful up to this point." He looked at me expectantly.

"Uh . . . okay. Good to know. I'll be thinking of ideas."

"I'd suggest that you ask Patch."

"To spy for us?"

"Use your relationship to your advantage. He may have information on fallen angels' weak points. He may know of fallen angels who'd be easier to flip."

"I'm not using Patch. And I told you: Patch is staying out of the war. He hasn't sided with fallen angels. I'm not asking him to spy for the Nephilim," I said almost coldly. "He isn't getting involved."

Dante gave a brief nod. "Understood. Forget I asked. Standard warm-up. Ten miles. Push yourself on the back half—I want you sweating."

"Dante—" I protested weakly.

"Those extra miles I warned you about? They go for excuses too."

Just get through this, I tried to encourage myself. You have the rest of the day off to sleep. And eat, and eat, and eat.

Dante worked me hard; after the ten-mile warm-up, I practiced vaulting over boulders twice my height, then sprinting up the steep slopes of a ravine, and we brushed up on the lessons I'd already learned, particularly working mind-tricks.

Finally, at the end of the second hour, he said, "Let's call it a day. Can you find your way home?"

We'd traveled quite far into the woods, but I could tell by the rising sun which way was east, and I felt confident I could make it back alone. "Don't worry about me," I said, and left.

Halfway to the farmhouse I found the boulder we'd deposited our belongings on—the Windbreaker I'd shed after my warm-up, and Dante's navy gym bag. He brought it every day, toting it several miles into the woods, which had to be not only heavy and awkward, but impractical. So far, he'd never once unzipped it. At least, not in my presence. The bag could be stocked with a myriad of torture devices he intended to employ in the name of training me. More likely, it held a change of clothes and spare shoes. Possibly including—I laughed at the thought—a pair of tighty whities or boxers printed with penguins that I could tease him endlessly about. Maybe even hang on a nearby tree. There was no one around to see them, but he'd be embarrassed enough knowing I had.

Smiling sneakily, I pulled the zipper back a few inches. As soon as I saw the glass bottles filled with ice-blue liquid lined up inside, the pangs in my stomach twisted ferociously. Hunger clawed through me like something living.

Unquenchable need threatened to explode inside me. A high-pitched scream roared in my ears. In one overpowering wave, I remembered the potent taste of devilcraft. Awful, but so worth it. I remembered the surge of power it had given me. I could barely keep my balance, I was so consumed by the need to feel that unstoppable high again. The skyrocketing jumps, the unmatched speed, the animal-like agility. My pulse was giddy, beating and fluttering with *need, need, need.* My vision blurred and my knees slackened. I could almost taste the relief and fulfillment that would come with one little sip.

I quickly counted the bottles. Fifteen. No way would Dante notice if one went missing. I knew it was wrong to steal, just as I knew devilcraft wasn't good for me. But those thoughts were dull arguments floating aimlessly at the back of my head. I rationalized that prescription medicine in the wrong doses wasn't good for me either, but sometimes I needed it. Just like I needed a taste of devilcraft.

Devilcraft. I could hardly think, I was so smitten and greedy for the power I knew it would give me. A sudden thought seized me—I might die if I didn't get it, the need was that potent. I would do anything for it. I had to feel that way again. Indestructible. Untouchable.

Before I knew what I'd done, I took a bottle. It felt cool and reassuring in my grip. I hadn't even taken a sip, and already my head was clearing. No more vertigo, and soon, no more cravings.

The bottle fit perfectly in my grip, as if it were meant to be there all along. Dante wanted me to have this bottle. After all, how many times had he tried to get me to drink devilcraft? And hadn't he said my next dose was on the house?

I'd take one bottle, and it would be enough. I'd feel the rush of power once more and I'd be satisfied.

Just once more.

CHAPTER

18

MY EYES OPENED TO A SUDDEN RAP ON THE door. I sat up, disoriented. Sunlight streamed through my bedroom window, indicating that it was late morning. My skin was clammy with sweat, my sheets tangled around my legs. On my nightstand, an empty bottle lay tipped on its side.

The memory stormed back.

I'd barely made it to my bedroom before twisting off the cap, flinging it hastily aside, and draining the devilcraft in seconds. I'd choked and gagged, feeling as though I would suffocate as the liquid clogged my throat, but I knew that the faster I guzzled, the sooner it would be over. A surge of adrenaline unlike anything I'd ever felt had expanded inside me, vaulting my senses to an exhilarating high. I'd had the urge to run outside and push my body to the limit, sprinting and bounding and dodging everything in my path. Like flying. Only better.

And then, just as quickly as the urge had spiked inside me, I'd collapsed. I didn't even remember falling into bed.

"Wake up, sleepyhead," my mom called through the door. "I know it's the weekend, but let's not sleep the whole day away. It's already after eleven."

Eleven? I'd been out cold for four hours?

"I'll be down in a second," I responded, my whole body shaking from what had to be a side effect of the devilcraft. I'd consumed too much, too fast. It explained my body shutting down for hours, and the peculiar, jittery sensation pulsating inside me.

I couldn't believe I'd stolen the devilcraft from Dante. Worse, I couldn't believe I'd drunk it. I was ashamed of myself. I had to find a way to correct it, but I didn't know where to start. How could I tell Dante? He already thought I was as feeble as a human, and if I couldn't control my own appetites, it only proved him right.

I should have just asked him for it. But I was disconcerted to realize that I'd enjoyed stealing it. There had been a certain thrill in doing something bad and getting away with it. Just like there had been a thrill in overindulging in the devilcraft, drinking it all immediately and refusing to ration it.

How could I be having these awful thoughts? How could I have let myself act on them? This wasn't who I was.

Swearing that this morning would be the last time I ever used devilcraft, I buried the bottle at the bottom of the wastebasket and tried to flush the incident from my head.

I assumed that by this hour I'd be eating breakfast alone, but I found Marcie at the kitchen table, crossing off a list of phone numbers. "I've spent all morning inviting people to the Halloween party," she explained. "Feel free to jump in at any time."

"I thought you were mailing invites."

"Not enough time. The party is Thursday."

"A school night? What's wrong with Friday?"

"Football game." My face must have registered confusion, because she elaborated, "All my friends will either be playing in the game or cheering. Plus, it's an away game, so we can't just invite them over after."

"And Saturday?" I asked, incredulous that we were throwing a party during the week. My mom would never go for it. Then again, Marcie had a way of talking her into just about anything these days.

"Saturday was my parents' anniversary. We are not doing it Saturday," she said with a note of finality. She pushed the list of

finale

phone numbers toward me. "I'm doing all the work, and it's really starting to get on my nerves."

"I don't want anything to do with the party," I reminded her.

"You're just huffy because you don't have a date."

She was right. I didn't have a date. I'd talked about bringing Patch, but that would require me to forgive him for meeting Blakely last night. The memory of what had happened came rushing back. Between sleeping last night, training with Dante this morning, and falling unconscious for several hours, I'd completely forgotten to check my phone for messages.

The doorbell chimed, and Marcie jumped up. "I'll get it."

I wanted to yell at her, "Quit acting like you live here!" but instead, I squeezed past her and took the stairs two at a time to my room. My handbag hung over my closet door, and I dug through it until I found my cell phone.

I drew in a sharp breath. No messages. I didn't know what it meant, and I didn't know if I should worry. What if Blakely had ambushed Patch? Or what if his silence was merely because we'd parted on bad terms last night? When I got angry, I wanted space, and Patch knew it.

I fired him a quick text. CAN WE TALK?

Downstairs, I heard Marcie break into a flustered argument. "I said I'll go get her. You have to wait here. Hey! You can't just burst in without being invited!"

"Says who?" Vee shot back, and I heard her bustle up the stairs.

I met them in the hallway outside my bedroom. "What's going on?"

"Your fat friend elbowed her way inside without being invited," Marcie complained.

"This skinny cow is acting like she owns the place," Vee told me. "What is she doing here?"

"I live here now," Marcie said.

Vee barked a laugh. "Always a funny one, you are," she said, wagging her finger at Marcie.

Marcie's chin jutted up. "I do live here. Go 'head. Ask Nora."

Vee looked to me, and I sighed. "It's temporary."

Vee rocked back on her heels as though hit by an invisible punch. "Marcie? Living here? Am I the only one who realizes all logic just got up and walked off?"

"It was my mom's idea," I said.

"It was my idea, and my mom's, but Mrs. Grey agreed it was for the best," Marcie corrected.

Before Vee could ask more questions, I snagged her elbow and dragged her inside my bedroom. Marcie inched forward, but I shut the door on her. I was trying my hardest to be civil, but letting her in on a private conversation with Vee was taking the idea of courtesy too far.

"Why is she really here?" Vee demanded, not bothering to lower her voice.

"It's a long story. The short of it is . . . I don't know what she's doing here." Evasive, yes, but honest, too. I had no clue what Marcie was doing here. My mom had been Hank's mistress, I was their love child, and it stood to reason that Marcie would want nothing to do with us.

"Gee, everything's clear now," Vee said.

Time to hit her with a distraction. "Marcie is throwing a Halloween party here at the farmhouse. Dates are required, ditto on costumes. The theme is famous couples from history."

"And?" Vee said, not warming up at all.

"Marcie's got dibs on Scott."

Vee narrowed her eyes. "Like heck she does."

"Marcie already asked him, but he didn't sound very committed," I offered helpfully.

Vee cracked her knuckles. "Time to work some Vee magic before it's too late."

My cell phone chimed with a text. GOT THE ANTIDOTE. WE NEED TO MEET, Patch's message read.

He was okay. Tension left my shoulders.

Discreetly, I slipped my phone into my pocket and told Vee, "My mom needs me to pick up the dry cleaning and return library books. But I can swing by your place later."

"And then we can plan how I'm going to steal Scott from the ho," Vee said.

I gave Vee a five-minute head start, then backed the Volkswagen down the driveway.

LEAVING THE FARMHOUSE NOW, I texted Patch. WHERE ARE YOU?

HEADING TO THE TOWNHOME, he responded.

MEET YOU THERE.

I drove to Casco Bay, too busy formulating what I'd say to Patch to take in the stunning fall scenery. I was only half-aware of the deep blue water glinting under the sun, and the waves spraying and foaming as they smashed into the craggy cliffs. I parked a few blocks from Patch's place and let myself inside. I was first to arrive, and went out on the balcony to gather my thoughts one final time.

The air was cool and sticky with salt, with just enough breeze to raise goose bumps, and I hoped it would temper my anger and the lingering sting of betrayal. I appreciated that Patch always had my safety in mind, and I was touched by his concern and didn't want to sound ungrateful that I was lucky enough to have a boyfriend who would go to any lengths for me, but a deal was a deal. We'd agreed to work as a team, and he'd broken my trust.

I heard the garage door glide open, followed by Patch's motorcycle pulling in. A moment later he appeared in the living room. He kept his distance, but his eyes were all over me. His hair was wind-blown, and a dark stubble dotted his jawline. He wore the same clothes I'd last seen him in, and I knew he'd been out all night.

"Busy night?" I asked.

"I had a lot on my mind."

finale

"How's Blakely?" I asked with just enough indignation to let Patch know I hadn't forgiven or forgotten.

"He swore an oath to keep our relationship quiet." A pause. "And he gave me the antidote."

"So your text said."

Patch sighed and scrubbed his hand through his hair. "So this is how it's going to be? I get that you're mad, but can you step back a minute and see things from my side? Blakely told me to come alone, and I didn't trust how he'd react if I showed up with you by my side. I'm not opposed to taking risks, but not when the odds are clearly against me. He had the better hand—this time."

"You promised we were a team."

"I also swore to do everything in my power to protect you. I want what's best for you. It's as simple as that, Angel."

"You can't keep taking charge and then claiming that it's for my safety."

"Making sure you're safe is more important to me than your goodwill. I don't want to fight, but if you're set on seeing me as the bad guy, so be it. Better that than lose you." He shrugged.

I gasped at his arrogance, then promptly narrowed my eyes. "Is that really how you feel?"

"Have you ever known me to lie, especially when it comes to my feelings for you?"

I snatched my handbag off the sofa. "Forget this. I'm leaving."

"Suit yourself. But you're not stepping a foot outside until you've taken the antidote." As if to prove his point, he leaned back against the front door, folding his arms over his chest.

Glaring at him, I said, "For all we know, the antidote could be poison."

He shook his head. "Dabria analyzed it. It's clean."

I gritted my teeth. Controlling my temper was officially out of the question now. "You took Dabria, didn't you? I guess this means the two of you are a team now," I snapped.

"She stayed far enough off Blakely's radar not to alert him, but got close enough to read bits and pieces of his future. Nothing there indicated foul play with regard to the antidote. He made a fair trade. The antidote is good."

"Why don't you try seeing things from my side?" I seethed. "I have to put up with my boyfriend choosing to work closely with his ex—she's still in love with you, you know!"

Patch kept his steady gaze glued to me. "And I'm in love with you. Even when you're irrational, jealous, and willful. Dabria has had substantially more practice in mind-tricks, take-downs, and fighting Nephilim in general. Sooner or later you're going to have to start trusting me. We don't have a lot of allies, and we need all the help we can get. As long as Dabria is contributing, I'm willing to keep her on board."

My fists were clenched so hard, I felt my nails threaten to break skin. "In other words, I'm not good enough to be your teammate. Unlike Dabria, I don't have any special powers!"

"That's not it at all. We've been over this: If something were to happen to her, I wouldn't consider it unfortunate. You, on the other hand—"

"Yeah, well, your actions speak for themselves." I was hurt and angry, and determined to show Patch he was underestimating me, and all of the above led to my next startling declaration. "I'm leading the Nephilim to war against fallen angels. It's the right thing to do. I'll deal with the archangels later. I can live in fear of them, or I can get over myself and do what I know is best for the Nephilim. I don't want another Nephil to swear fealty—ever. I've made up my mind, so don't bother talking me out of it," I stated bluntly.

Patch's black eyes watched me, but he said nothing.

"I've been feeling this way for a while," I said, made uncomfortable by his silence and anxious to prove my point of view. "I'm not going to let fallen angels continue to bully Nephilim."

"Are we talking about fallen angels and Nephilim, or you and me?" Patch asked quietly at last.

"I'm tired of playing defense. Yesterday a war party of fallen angels came after me. That was the last straw. Fallen angels need to know we're done being messed with. They've harassed us long enough. And the archangels? I don't think they care. If they did, they'd have stepped in by now and put an end to devilcraft. We have to assume they know and are looking the other way."

"Did Dante have anything to do with your decision?" Patch asked, not a single crack in his quiet composure.

His question irritated me. "I'm the leader of the Nephilim army. I call the shots."

I expected his next question to be, "Where does this leave us?" so his ensuing words took me by surprise. "I want you by my side, Nora. Being with you is my top priority. I've been at war with the Nephilim a long time. It's shaped me in ways I wish I could take back. The deception, the cheap tricks, even the brute force. There are days I wish I could go back and take a different path. I don't want you to have the same regrets. I need to know you're strong enough physically, but I also need to know you're straight up here." He touched my forehead gently. Then he caressed my cheek, holding my face in the palm of his hand. "Do you really understand what you're getting into?"

I pulled away, but not quite so hard as I'd intended. "If you'd quit worrying about me, you'd see I'm up for this." I thought of all the training I'd done with Dante. I thought of how gifted he believed I was at mind-tricks. Patch had no clue how far I'd come. I was stronger, faster, and more powerful than I'd ever imagined possible. I'd also been through enough over the past several months to know I was now firmly in his world. Our world. I knew what I was getting into, even if Patch didn't like it.

"You might have stopped me from meeting Blakely, but you can't stop the war from coming," I pointed out. We were on the brink of a deadly and dangerous conflict. I wasn't going to sugar-coat it, and I wasn't about to look the other way. I was ready to fight. For Nephilim freedom. For mine.

"It's one thing to think you're ready," Patch said quietly. "Jumping into war and seeing it firsthand is a different ball game. I admire your bravery, Angel, but I'm being honest when I say I think you're rushing into this without fully weighing the consequences."

"You think I haven't thought this through? I'm the one who has to lead Hank's army. I've spent many sleepless nights thinking this through."

"Lead the army, yes. But no one ever said anything about fighting. You can fulfill your oath and stay far out of harm's way. Delegate the deadliest tasks. That's what your army is for. That's what I'm here for."

This argument was starting to make me bristle. "You can't constantly protect me, Patch. I appreciate the thought, but I'm Nephilim now. I'm immortal and less in need of your protection. I'm a target of fallen angels, archangels, and other Nephilim, and there's nothing I can do about that. Except learn to fight back."

His eyes were clear, his tone level, but I sensed a certain sadness under his cool exterior. "You're a strong girl, and you're mine. But strength doesn't always mean brute force. You don't have to kick ass to be a fighter. Violence doesn't equal strength. Lead your army by example. There's a better answer to all this. War isn't going to solve anything, but it will tear our two worlds apart, and there will be casualties, including humans. There's nothing heroic about this war. It will lead to a destruction unlike anything you or I have ever seen."

I swallowed. Why did Patch always have to do this? Say things that only made me more conflicted. Was he telling me this because he honestly meant it, or was he trying to sweep me off the battlefield? I wanted to trust his intentions. Violence wasn't always the way. In fact, most of the time it wasn't. I knew that. But I saw Dante's point of view too. I had to fight back. If I came across as weak, it only hung a larger target on my back. I had to show that I was tough and would retaliate. For the foreseeable future, physical strength mattered more than strength of character.

I pressed my fingers into my temples, trying to rub away the worry that echoed like a dull ache. "I don't want to talk about this now. I just need—some quiet time, okay? I had a rough morning, and I'll deal with this when I'm feeling better."

Patch didn't look convinced, but he didn't say anything more on the matter.

"I'll call you later," I said wearily.

He retrieved a vial of milky white liquid from his pocket and handed it to me. "The antidote."

I'd been so caught up in our argument, I'd completely forgotten about it. I scrutinized the vial suspiciously.

"I did manage to get Blakely to tell me that the knife he stabbed you with is the most powerful prototype he's developed yet. It put twenty times the amount of devilcraft into your system than the drink Dante gave you. That's why you need the antidote. Without it, you'll develop an unbreakable addiction to devilcraft. In high enough doses, certain devilcraft prototypes will rot you from the inside out. They will scramble your brains same as any other lethal drug."

Patch's words caught me off guard. I'd woken this morning with an insatiable appetite for devilcraft because Blakely had caused me to crave it more than eating, drinking, or even breathing?

The thought of waking up every day, driven by that hunger, put a red-hot feeling of shame in my veins. I hadn't realized how high the stakes were. Unexpectedly, I found myself grateful to Patch for getting the antidote. I'd do anything to never feel that unconquerable need again.

I unstopped the vial. "Anything I should know before I take this?" I passed the vial under my nose. No odor.

"It won't work if you've had devilcraft introduced into your system in the last twenty-four hours, but that shouldn't be a problem. It's been well over a day since Blakely stabbed you," Patch said.

I had the vial an inch from my lips when I stopped. Just this morning I'd consumed an entire bottle of devilcraft. If I took the antidote now, it wouldn't work. I'd still be addicted.

"Plug your nose and tip it back. It can't taste as bad as devilcraft," Patch said.

I wanted to tell Patch about the bottle I'd stolen from Dante. I wanted to explain myself. He wouldn't blame me. This was Blakely's fault. It was the devilcraft. I'd guzzled a whole bottle of it and I'd hardly had a choice, I was so blinded by need.

I opened my mouth to confess everything, but something stopped me. A dark, foreign voice planted deep inside murmured that I didn't want to be free of devilcraft. Not yet. I couldn't forfeit the power and strength that came with it—not when we were on the brink of war. I had to keep those powers close, just in case. This wasn't about devilcraft. It was about protecting myself.

The cravings started then, licking up my skin, watering my mouth, causing me to shudder with hunger. I pushed the feelings aside, proud of myself when I did. I wouldn't give in the way I had this morning. I would only steal and drink devilcraft when I absolutely needed it. And I'd keep the antidote with me always, so I could break the habit whenever I wanted. I'd do it on my terms. I had a choice in this. I was in control.

Then I did something I never imagined I'd do. The impulse fired into my consciousness, and I acted without thinking. I locked eyes with Patch for the briefest of moments, summoned all my mental energy, feeling it flex inside me like a great, unleashed, and natural power, and mind-tricked him into thinking I'd taken the antidote.

Nora drank it, I whispered deceptively to his mind, planting an image there that backed up my lie. Every last drop.

Then I slipped the vial into my pocket. The whole thing was over in seconds.

CHAPTER

I LEFT PATCH'S PLACE, INTENDING TO DRIVE HOME, all the while combating a violent wrenching in my stomach that felt part guilt, part genuine illness. I couldn't remember a single time in my life when I'd felt more ashamed.

Or more ravenous.

My stomach contracted, spiking with hunger pangs. They were so sharp, they left me doubled over against the steering wheel. It was as though I'd swallowed nails, and they were scraping my insides raw. I had the strangest sensation of feeling my organs shrivel. It was followed by the frightening question of whether my body would eat itself for nourishment.

But it wasn't food I needed.

I pulled over and called Scott. "I need Dante's address."

"You've never been to his place before? Aren't you his girl-friend?"

It irritated me that he was slowing the conversation. I needed Dante's address; I didn't have time to chitchat. "Do you have it or not?"

"I'll text you the address. Something wrong? You sound antsy. Have for a few days now."

"I'm fine," I said, then hung up and slouched in my seat. Sweat beaded my upper lip. I clenched the steering wheel, trying to fend off the cravings that seemed to grip me by the throat and rattle me. My thoughts were glued to one word—devilcraft. I tried to swat the temptation away. I'd just taken devilcraft this morning. A whole bottle. I could beat these cravings. I decided when I needed more devilcraft. I decided when, and how much.

The prickly sweat spread to my back, little rivulets scurrying beneath my shirt. The bottoms of my thighs, hot and moist, seemed to stick to the seat cushions. Even though it was October, I blasted the AC.

I steered back onto the road, but the blare of a passing horn caused me to brake abruptly. A white van sped past, its driver making an obscene gesture through the window.

Get a grip, I told myself. *Pay attention.*

After a few head-clearing breaths, I uploaded the address to Dante's house onto my cell phone. I studied the map, gave an ironic laugh, and flipped a U-turn. Dante, it seemed, lived less than five miles from Patch's townhouse.

Ten minutes later I'd driven under a lush arch of trees canopying the road, crossed a cobblestone bridge, and parked the Volkswagen on a quaint and curving tree-lined street. Houses were predominantly white Victorians with gingerbread detail and steeply pitched roofs. All were flamboyant and excessive. I identified Dante's—a Queen Anne at 12 Shore Drive—that was all spindles and towers and gables. The door was painted red with a big brass knocker. I skipped the knocker and went straight for the bell, pushing it repeatedly. *If he didn't hurry and answer . . .*

Dante cracked the door, his face registering surprise. "How'd you find this place?"

"Scott."

He frowned. "I don't like people showing up at my door unexpectedly. A lot of foot traffic looks suspicious. I've got nosy neighbors."

"It's important."

He jerked his chin back toward the road. "That piece of junk you drive is an eyesore."

I wasn't in the mood to exchange witty insults. If I didn't get devilcraft into my system soon—just a few drops—my heart was going to gallop right out of my chest. Even now my pulse raced and

I was laboring to draw breath. I might as well have spent the past hour running up a steep hill, I was so winded.

I said, "I changed my mind. I want devilcraft. As a backup," I quickly added. "In case I find myself in a situation where I'm outnumbered and I need it." I couldn't focus long enough to tell if my reasoning sounded flimsy. Red spots flashed across my vision. I desperately wanted to wipe my brow, but I didn't want to draw extra attention to how profusely I was sweating.

Dante gave me a questioning look I couldn't quite interpret, then led me inside. I stood in the foyer, darting my eyes over the clean white walls and lush Oriental rugs. A hallway led back to the kitchen. Formal living room on my left, and dining room, painted the same oxblood red as my eye spots, on my right. As far as I could see, every furnishing was antique. A crystal-droplet chandelier hung overhead.

"Nice," I managed to choke out between my skittering pulse and tingling extremities.

"The house belonged to friends. They left it to me in their will."

"Sorry they passed."

He strode into the dining room, tilted a large painting of a haystack to one side, and revealed the time-honored hidden wall safe. He punched in the code and opened the box.

"Here you go. It's a new prototype. Incredibly concentrated, so drink it in low doses," he cautioned. "Two bottles. If you decide to start taking it now, it should last a week."

I nodded, trying to hide my watering mouth as I took the blue-glowing bottles. "There's something I want to tell you, Dante. I'm leading the Nephilim to war. So if you can spare more than two bottles, I could use them." I'd fully intended to tell Dante about my decision to go into battle, but I had not meant to tell him with the intent of hoping to score extra devilcraft. It seemed like a sneaky maneuver, but I was too hungry to feel much more than a pinch of guilt.

"War?" Dante repeated, sounding startled. "Are you sure?"

"You can tell the Nephilim higher-ups that I'm devising plans to go against fallen angels."

"This is—great news," Dante said, still sounding shell-shocked as he stuffed an extra bottle of devilcraft into my hands. "What made you change your mind?"

"A conversion of heart," I said, because I thought it sounded good. "I'm not just leading the Nephilim. I *am* one."

Dante saw me out, and it took every ounce of control to walk calmly to the Volkswagen. I kept our farewell short, then drove around the corner, immediately parked, and twisted the cap off the bottle. I was about to tip it back when the sound of Patch's ringtone caused me to jump, splashing blue liquid on my lap.

It evaporated instantly, rising into the air like smoke from a snuffed match. I cursed under my breath, furious that I'd lost even a few precious drops.

"Hello?" I answered. The red spots streaked my vision.

"I don't like finding you in another man's house, Angel."

Immediately, I looked both ways out the window. I shoved the devilcraft under my seat. "Where are you?"

"Three cars back."

My eyes flew to the rearview mirror. Patch swung off his motorcycle and strolled toward me, phone pressed to his ear. I wiped my face with the neck of my shirt.

I cranked down my window. "Following me?" I asked Patch.

"Tracking device."

I was starting to hate that thing.

Patch leaned a forearm on the roof of my car, bending close. "Who lives on Shore Drive?"

"That tracking device is pretty specific."

"I only buy the best."

"Dante lives at 12 Shore Drive." No use lying when it sounded like he'd already done his research.

"I don't like finding you in another man's home, but I hate finding you in his." His expression was calm enough, but I could tell he wanted an explanation.

"I needed to confirm our workout time for tomorrow morning. I was in the area and figured I might as well stop by." The lie slipped out easy, so easy. All I could think of was getting rid of Patch. My throat filled with the taste of devilcraft. I swallowed impatiently.

Gently, Patch pushed my sunglasses higher on my nose,

then bent through the window and kissed me. "I'm on my way to research a few more leads into Pepper's blackmailer. Need anything before I head out?"

I shook my head no.

"If you need to talk, you know I'm here for you," he added softly.

"Talk about what?" I asked, almost defensively. Could he know about the devilcraft? No. No, he couldn't.

He studied me a moment. "Anything."

I waited until Patch drove off before I drank, one greedy sip at a time, until I was full.

20

THURSDAY EVENING ARRIVED, AND WITH IT, THE complete transformation of the farmhouse. Garlands of autumn leaves in scarlet, gold, and chestnut spilled off the eaves. Bushels of dried cornstalks framed the door. Marcie had purchased what appeared to be every pumpkin and gourd in all of Maine, and lined them up along the sidewalk, the driveway, and every last square inch of porch. Some were carved into jack-o'-lanterns, flickering candlelight in their spooky expressions. A vindictive part of me wanted to tell her it looked like a craft store had thrown up on our lawn, but the truth was, she'd done a nice job.

Inside, haunted music played from the stereo. Skulls, bats, cobwebs, and ghosts cluttered the furniture. Marcie had rented a dry-ice machine—as if we didn't have enough authentic fog in the yard.

I had two paper bags filled with last-minute items in my arms, and I carted them into the kitchen.

"I'm back!" I yelled. "Plastic cups, one bag of spider rings, two bags of ice, and more skeleton confetti—just like you asked. Soda is still in the trunk. Any volunteers to help carry it in?"

Marcie sashayed into the room, and I did a jaw drop. She wore a black vinyl bra and matching leggings. Nothing more. Her ribs poked through her skin, and she had total Popsicle-stick thighs. "Put the soda in the fridge, the ice in the freezer, and sprinkle the skeleton confetti on the dining room table, but don't get any in the food. That's it for now. Stay close in case I need anything else. I have to go finish my costume."

"Well, that's a relief. For a minute there, I thought that was all you planned on wearing," I said, gesturing at the skimpy vinyl.

Marcie glanced down. "It is. I'm Catwoman. I just need to hot-glue black felt ears to my headband."

"You're wearing a bra to the party? Just a bra?"

"A bandeau."

Oh, this was going to be good. I couldn't wait for Vee's commentary. "Who's Batman?"

"Robert Boxler."

"I guess that means Scott bailed?" It was more of a rhetorical question. Just to give the proverbial knife one last twist.

Marcie gave her shoulders a pompous little hike. "Scott who?" she said, and marched upstairs.

"He chose Vee over you!" I called triumphantly after her.

"I don't care," Marcie singsonged back. "You probably made him. It's no secret he does everything you say. Put the soda in the fridge before the turn of the century."

I stuck my tongue out, even though she couldn't see it. "I have to get ready too, you know!"

At seven, the first guests arrived. Romeo and Juliet, Cleopatra and Mark Anthony, Elvis and Priscilla. Even a bottle of ketchup and mustard strolled through the front door. I let Marcie play hostess and moseyed into the kitchen, stacking my plate with deviled eggs, cocktail wieners, and candy corn. I'd been too busy granting Marcie's every pre-party command to eat dinner. That, and the new formula of devilcraft Dante had given me, seemed to curb my appetite for the first several hours after I took it.

I'd done a reasonably good job of rationing it and still had enough to last a few more days. The night sweats, headaches, and strange tingling sensation that would seize me at the oddest moments when I'd first started taking the new formula had gone away. I was sure this meant that the dangers of addiction had passed and I'd learned to use devilcraft safely. Moderation was key. Blakely might have tried to hook me on devilcraft, but I was strong enough to set my own limits.

The effects of devilcraft were unbelievable. I'd never felt so mentally and physically superior. I knew I had to stop taking it eventually, but with the stress and dangers of Cheshvan and war looming, I was glad I was being cautious. If another of my doubting Nephilim soldiers attacked me, this time I'd be ready.

After filling up on appetizers and Sprite served from a black cauldron, I elbowed my way into the living room, looking to see whether Vee and Scott had arrived. The lights were dimmed, everyone was in costume, and I had a hard time picking faces out of the crowd. Plus, I'd peeked at the guest list. It was heavily weighted in favor of Marcie's friends.

"Love the costume, Nora. But you're anything but a devil."

I looked sideways at Morticia Addams. I squinted in confusion, then smiled. "Oh, hey, Bailey. I almost didn't recognize you with black hair." Bailey sat beside me in math, and we'd been friends since junior high. I picked up my devil tail, with the little red spade at the tip, to save it from the guy behind me, who kept accidentally stepping on it, and said, "Thanks for coming tonight."

"Did you finish your math homework? I didn't understand a single thing Mr. Huron tried to teach us today. Every time he started working a problem on the chalkboard, he'd stop halfway through, erase his work, and start over. I don't think *he* knows what he's doing."

"Yeah, I'm probably going to spend hours on it tomorrow."

Her eyes lit up. "We should meet at the library and do it together."

"I promised my mom I'd clean out the cellar after school," I hedged. Truth be told, homework had slipped a few notches on my list of priorities as of late. It was hard to stress about school when I feared that any day now the eerie cease-fire between fallen angels and Nephilim was going to snap. Fallen angels were up to something. And I'd give anything to find out what.

"Oh. Maybe next time," Bailey said, sounding disappointed.

"Have you seen Vee?"

"Not yet. Who is she coming as?"

"A babysitter. Her date is Michael Myers from *Halloween*," I explained. "If you see her, tell her I'm looking for her."

When I made it across the living room, I bumped into Marcie and her date, Robert Boxler.

"Food status?" Marcie asked me authoritatively.

"My mom's handling it."

"Music?"

"Derrick Coleman is DJ."

"Are you working the crowd? Is everyone having fun?"

"I just finished a round." More or less.

Marcie eyed me with criticism. "Where's your date?"

finale

"Does it matter?"

"I heard you're dating some new guy. I heard he doesn't go to school. Who is he?"

"Who'd you hear that from?" Guess word about Dante and me was getting around after all.

"Does it matter?" she echoed snidely. She scrunched her nose in distaste. "What are you dressed up as?"

"She's a devil," Robert said. "Pitchfork, horns, red vamp dress."

"Don't forget the black combat boots," I said, showing them off. I had Vee to thank for them, as well as the red glitter laces.

"I can see that," Marcie said. "But the party's theme is famous couples. A devil doesn't go with anything."

Just then Patch ambled through the front door. I did a double take to make sure it was really him. I hadn't expected him to come. We'd never resolved our fight, and I'd pridefully refused to take the first step, forcing myself to lock my cell phone in a drawer every time I was tempted to call him and apologize, despite my increasing distress that he might never call either. My pride immediately turned to relief at the sight of him. I hated fighting. I hated not having him close. If he was ready to mend this, so was I.

A smile flickered over my face at the sight of his costume: black jeans, black T-shirt, black face mask. The latter concealed all but his cool, assessing gaze.

"There's my date," I said. "Fashionably late."

Marcie and Robert turned. Patch gave me a low wave and handed his leather jacket to some poor freshman Marcie had roped into coat duty. The price some girls would pay to attend an upperclassman party was almost shameful.

"No fair," Robert said, taking off his Batman mask. "The dude didn't dress up."

"Whatever you do, don't call him dude," I told Robert, smiling at Patch as he made his way over.

"Do I know him?" Marcie asked. "Who is he supposed to be?"

"He's an angel," I said. "A fallen angel."

"That isn't what a fallen angel looks like!" Marcie protested.

Shows how much you know, I thought, just as Patch slung his arm around my neck and pulled me into a light kiss.

I've missed you, he spoke to my thoughts.

Same here. Let's not fight anymore. Can we put it behind us?

Consider it done. How's the party going? he asked.

I haven't felt like jumping off the roof yet.

Glad to hear it.

"Hi there," Marcie said to Patch, her tone more flirtatious than I would have thought with her date standing inches away.

"Hey," Patch returned, extending acknowledgment with a brief nod.

"Do I know you?" she asked, tilting her head inquisitively to one side. "Do you go to CHS?"

"No," he said without elaborating.

finale

"Then how do you know Nora?"

"Who doesn't know Nora?" he returned mildly.

"This is my date, Robert Boxler," Marcie told him with an air of superiority. "He plays quarterback for the football team."

"Impressive," Patch answered, his tone just polite enough to scrape by as interested. "How's the season shaping up, Robert?"

"We've had a few rough games, but it's nothing we can't bounce back from," Marcie cut in, patting Robert's chest consolingly.

"What gym do you use?" Robert asked Patch, eyeing his physique with open admiration. And envy.

"Haven't had a lot of time lately for the gym."

"Well, you look great, man. If you ever want to lift weights together, call me."

"Good luck with the rest of the season," Patch told Robert, giving him one of those tricky handshakes all guys seem to know instinctively.

Patch and I wandered deeper into the house, winding through hallways and rooms, trying to find a secluded corner. At last he pulled me inside the powder room, kicked the door shut, and locked it. He leaned me back against the wall and fingered one of my red devil ears, his eyes deep black with desire.

"Nice costume," he said.

"Ditto. I can tell you put a lot of thought into yours."

Amusement curled his mouth. "If you don't like it, I can take it off."

I tapped my chin thoughtfully. "That just might be the best proposal I've had all night."

"My offers are always the best, Angel."

"Before the party started, Marcie asked me to lace up the back of her Catwoman pants." I raised and lowered my hands in a weighing gesture. "Between both offers, it's a tough call."

Patch removed his mask and laughed softly into my neck, brushing my hair back off my shoulders. He smelled incredible. He felt warm and solid and so very close. My heart beat faster, squeezing with guilt. I'd lied to Patch. I couldn't forget. I shut my eyes, letting his mouth explore mine, trying to lose myself in the moment. All the while, the lies beat, beat, beat, in my head. I'd taken devilcraft, and I'd mind-tricked him. I was still taking devilcraft.

"Trouble with your costume is, it doesn't hide your identity very well," I said, pulling back. "And we're not supposed to be seen together in public, remember?"

"Just stopping by for a minute. Couldn't miss my girl's party," he murmured. He lowered his head to kiss me again.

"Vee's still not here," I said. "I tried her cell. And Scott's. I got sent to voice mail both times. Should I worry?"

"Maybe they don't want to be disturbed," he spoke into my ear, his voice deep and gravelly. He pushed my dress higher up my leg, stroking his thumb over my bare thigh. The warmth of his caress overrode my bad conscience. Sensation shivered through me. I shut my eyes again, this time involuntarily. All the knots loosened.

finale

My breath came a little faster. He knew just how to touch me.

Patch lifted me onto the sink's ledge, his hands splayed on my hips. I got warm and woozy inside, and when he put his mouth on mine, I could have sworn sparks went off. His touch seared me with passion. The fluttery, intoxicating liquid heat of being near him never grew old, no matter how many times we touched, flirted, kissed. If anything, that electric jolt intensified. I wanted Patch, and I didn't trust myself when I did.

I don't know how long the bathroom door stood open before I noticed. I jerked away from Patch, mouth gaping. My mom stood in the shadowy entrance, muttering about how the lock had never worked properly, and she'd been meaning to fix it for ages, when her eyes must have adjusted to the dimness, because she stopped mid-apology.

Her mouth snapped shut. Her face blanched . . . then flushed a deep, sizzling red. I'd never seen her look so enraged. "Out!" She flung her finger away. "Out of my house this instant, and don't think of coming back, or touching my daughter again!" she hissed at Patch, livid.

I jumped off the sink. "Mom—"

She turned on me. "Not a word from you!" she sputtered. "You said you broke up with him. You said it—this thing—between you and him—it was over. You lied to me!"

"I can explain," I started, but she'd swiveled back to Patch.

"Is this what you do? Seduce young girls in their own homes,

BECCA FITZPATRICK

with their own mothers standing feet away? You should be ashamed of yourself!"

Patch laced his hand in mine, gripping it tightly. "Quite the opposite, Blythe. Your daughter means everything to me. Completely and wholly. I love her—it's as simple as that." He spoke with calm assurance, but his jaw was as rigid as if cut from stone.

"You destroyed her life! From the moment she met you, everything fell apart. You can deny it all you want, but I know you were involved in her kidnapping. Get out of my house," she snarled.

I clung to Patch's hand fiercely, murmuring, *I'm sorry, so sorry,* over and over in mind-speak. I'd spent the summer locked away against my will in a remote cabin. Hank Millar was the mastermind behind my imprisonment, but my mom didn't know that. Her mind had erected a wall around his memory, trapping in everything good and casting out the rest. I blamed Hank, and I blamed devilcraft. She'd worked it out in her mind that Patch had been responsible for my kidnapping, and it was as much a truth to her as the sun rising each morning.

"I should get going," Patch told me, giving my hand a reassuring squeeze. *I'll call you later,* he added privately to my thoughts.

"I should think so!" my mom snapped, her shoulders rising from the exertion of breathing heavily.

She stepped aside, allowing Patch to exit, but closed off the doorway before I could escape.

"You're grounded," she said in a voice like iron. "Enjoy the party while it lasts, because it's going to be your last social event for a long, long time."

"Are you even interested in hearing me out?" I shot back, enraged by the way she'd treated Patch.

"I need time to cool down. It's in your best interest to give me some space. I might be in the mood to talk tomorrow, but that's the last thing I'm interested in right now. You lied to me. You went behind my back. Worse, I had to find you stripping off your clothes with him in our bathroom. Our bathroom! He wants one thing from you, Nora, and he'll take it wherever he can get it. There's nothing special about losing your virginity over a toilet."

"I wasn't—we weren't—my virginity?" I shook my head and made a disgusted gesture. "Forget it. You're right—you don't want to listen. You never have. Not when it comes to Patch."

"Everything okay here?"

My mom and I turned to find Marcie standing just outside the door. She held an empty cauldron in her arms and hitched her shoulders apologetically. "Sorry to interrupt, but we've run out of monster eyeballs, aka peeled grapes."

My mom shoved some hair off her face, trying to collect herself. "Nora and I were just finishing up. I can make a quick run to the store for grapes. Anything else we're low on?"

"Nacho cheese dip," Marcie said in this timid mouse voice, as if she hated imposing on my mom's kindness. "But it's really no big deal. I mean, it's only nacho dip. There will be nothing to go with the chips, of course, and it is my favorite, but really and truly—no big deal." The tiniest sigh escaped her.

"Fine. Grapes and nacho dip. Anything else?" my mom asked.

Marcie hugged the cauldron and beamed. "Nope. That's it."

My mom fished her keys out of her pocket and walked off, her every movement harsh and stiff. Marcie, however, stayed put.

"You could always mind-trick her, you know. Make her think Patch was never here."

I turned cool eyes on Marcie. "How much did you hear?"

"Enough to know you're in deep crapola."

"I'm not going to mind-trick my own mom."

"If you want, I could talk to her."

I breathed a laugh. "You? My mom doesn't care what you think, Marcie. She took you in under some misguided sense of hospitality. And probably to prove something to your mom. The only reason you're living under this roof is so my mom can throw it in your mom's face: She was the better lover, and now she's the better mother." It was a horrible thing to say. It had sounded better in my head, but Marcie didn't give me time to amend my statement.

"You're trying to make me feel bad, but it won't work. You're not going to ruin my party." But I thought I saw her lip wobble. With an intake of air, she seemed to collect herself.

Suddenly, as if nothing had happened, she said in a bizarrely cheerful voice, "I think it's time to play Bob-for-a-Date."

"Bob-for-a-what?"

finale

"It's like bobbing for apples, except every apple has a name of someone from the party attached. Whoever you draw is your next blind date. We play it every year at my Halloween party."

I frowned. We hadn't gone over this game idea beforehand. "Sounds tacky."

"It's a blind date, Nora. And since you're grounded for eternity, what have you got to lose?" She pushed me into the kitchen, toward the giant tub of water with red and green apples floating in it. "Hey, everyone, listen up!" Marcie called over the music. "Time to play Bob-for-a-Date. Nora Grey goes first."

Applause broke out across the kitchen, along with catcalls and a few shouts and whistles of encouragement. I stood there, mouth moving but emitting no words, cursing Marcie fluently in my mind.

"I don't think I'm the best person for this," I yelled at her over the noise. "Can I pass?"

"Not a chance." She gave me what looked like a playful shove, but it was forceful enough to send me stumbling to my knees in front of the tub of apples.

I shot her a look of pure indignation. *I'll make you pay for this,* I told her.

"Pull your hair back. Nobody wants nasty stray hairs floating in the water," Marcie instructed.

In agreement, the crowd roared a collective "Booo."

"Red apples are matched to boys' names," Marcie added. "Green to girls'."

Fine! Whatever! Just get this over with, I told myself. It wasn't like I had anything to lose: Starting tomorrow, I was grounded. There were no blind dates in my future, game or no.

I dipped my face into the cold water. My nose bumped into one apple after another, but I couldn't sink my teeth into any of them. I came up for air, and my ears rang with boos and jeering hisses.

"Give me a break!" I said. "I haven't done this since I was five. That should say a lot about this game!" I added.

"Nora hasn't had a blind date since she was five," Marcie said, misinterpreting my meaning and adding her own commentary.

"You are so next up," I told Marcie, glaring at her from my knees.

"If there is a next. Looks to me like you might be sucking face with apples all night," she returned sweetly, and the crowd howled with amusement.

I plunged my head into the tub, snapping my teeth at apples. Water sloshed over the rim, drenching the front of my red devil costume. I came this close to grabbing an apple with my hand and pressing it into my mouth, but figured Marcie would disqualify the move. I wasn't in the mood for a do-over. Just as I was about to come up for another breath, my front teeth crunched into a bloodred apple.

I surfaced, shaking water out of my hair to the sounds of cheering and applause. I chucked the apple at Marcie and grabbed a towel, patting my face dry.

"And the lucky guy who gets a blind date with our drowned rat here is . . ." Marcie pulled a sealed tube from the center of the cored apple. She uncurled the scroll of paper inside the tube, and her nose wrinkled. "Baruch? Just Baruch?" She pronounced it like Bar-ooch. "Am I saying that right?" she asked the audience.

No response. Already people were shuffling away now that the immediate entertainment had ended. I was grateful that Bar-ooch, whoever he was, appeared to be a fake entry. Either that, or he was too mortified to own up to a date with me.

Marcie stared me down, as though expecting me to admit I knew the guy.

"He's not one of your friends?" I asked her as I scrunched the tips of my hair in the towel.

"No. I thought he was one of yours."

I was on the verge of wondering whether this was another one of her bizarre games, when the lights in the house flickered. Once, twice, then they shut off completely. The music faded to eerie silence. There was a moment of stupefied confusion, and then the screaming started. Baffled and jumbled at first, rising to a hair-raising note of terror. The screams preceded the unmistakable thud of bodies being thrown against the living room walls.

"Nora!" Marcie cried. "What's going on?"

I didn't have a chance to answer. An invisible force seemed to smack me back a step, rendering me paralyzed. Cold, crisp energy coiled up my body. The air crackled and flexed with the power of multiple fallen angels. Their sudden appearance in the farmhouse was as tangible as a gust of arctic wind. I didn't know how many there were, or what they wanted, but I could feel them move deeper into the house, spreading out to fill every room.

"Nora, Nora. Come out and play," a male voice singsonged. Unfamiliar and eerily falsetto.

I drew two shallow breaths. At least now I knew what they were after.

"I'll find you my sweet, my pet," he continued to croon in chilling tones.

He was close, so close. I crawled behind the family room sofa, but someone had beat me to the hiding place.

"Nora? Is that you? What's going on?" Andy Smith asked me. He sat two chairs behind me in math and was Marcie's friend Addyson's boyfriend. I could feel the heat of his sweat rising off him.

"Quiet," I instructed him softly.

"If you won't come to me, I'll come to you," the fallen angel sang out.

His mental power sliced into me like a hot knife. I gasped as he felt around inside my mind, probing every which way, analyzing my thoughts to determine where I was hiding. I threw up wall after wall to stop him, but he plowed through them like I'd constructed them from dust. I tried to recall every defense mechanism Dante had taught me against mind-invasion, but the fallen angel moved too fast. He was always two—dangerous—steps ahead. I'd never had a fallen angel have this effect on me before. There was only one way to describe it. He was directing all his mental energy at me through a magnifying glass, amplifying the effect.

Without warning, an orange glow flared in my mind. A great furnace of energy blasted across my skin. I felt the heat of it melt my clothes. Flames chewed through the fabric, raking my skin with hot torment. In unimaginable agony, I coiled into a ball. I tucked my head between my knees, grinding my teeth to keep from screaming. The fire wasn't real. It had to be a mind-trick. But I didn't really believe it. The heat was so blistering, I was sure he really had lit me on fire.

"Stop!" I finally cried out, lunging into the open and writhing on the floor—anything to suffocate the flames devouring my flesh.

In that instant, the fiery heat vanished, though I hadn't felt the water that had surely extinguished it. I lay on my back, my face bathed in sweat. It hurt to breathe.

"Everyone out," the fallen angel commanded.

I'd almost forgotten there were others in the room. They would never forget this. How could they? Did they understand what was happening? Did they know this hadn't been staged for the party? I prayed someone would go for help. But the farmhouse was so remote. It would take time to bring help.

And the only person who could help was Patch, and I had no way to reach him.

Legs and feet scrabbled across the floor, darting for the exit. Andy Smith dodged from behind the sofa and plowed frantically through the doorway.

I lifted my head just high enough to look at the fallen angel. It was dark, but I saw a towering, skeletal, half-naked silhouette. And two savage, glittering eyes.

The bare-chested fallen angel from the Devil's Handbag and the woods watched me. His disfiguring hieroglyphics seemed to twitch and flutter over his skin, as though attached to invisible strings. In realty, I was sure they moved with the rise and fall of his breathing. I couldn't peel my eyes away from the small, raw wound on his chest.

"I'm Baruch." He pronounced it Ba-rewk.

I scooted to the corner of the room, wincing in pain.

"Cheshvan has started, and I don't have a Nephil vassal," he said. He kept his tone conversational, but there was no light in his eyes. No light, and no warmth.

Too much adrenaline made my legs feel twitchy and weighted. I didn't have many options. I wasn't strong enough to barrel past him. I couldn't fight him—if I tried, one call to his buddies would leave me outnumbered in seconds. I cursed my mom for kicking Patch out. I needed him. I couldn't do this on my own. If Patch were here, he'd know what to do.

Baruch traced his tongue along the inside of his lip. "The leader of the Black Hand's army, and what am I to do with her?"

He plunged into my mind. I felt him do it, but I was powerless to prevent it. I was too exhausted to fight. The next thing I knew, I had crawled obediently over and lay at his feet like a dog. He kicked me onto my back, gazing predatorily down at me. I wanted to bargain with him, but my teeth were clenched so tightly, it was as if my jaw had been sewn shut.

You can't argue with me, he whispered hypnotically to my mind. *You can't refuse me. Whatever I command, you must do.*

I tried unsuccessfully to shut out his voice. If I could break his control, I could fight back. It was my only shot.

"How does it feel to be a brand-new Nephil?" he murmured in a cold, scornful voice. "The world is no place for a Nephil without a master. I'll protect you from other fallen angels, Nora. From now on, you belong to me."

"I don't belong to anyone," I spat, the words slamming out of me with grueling effort.

He exhaled, slow and deliberate. It came out like a chastising whistle between his teeth. "I'll break you, my pet. Just see if I won't," he growled.

I looked at him square on. "You made a big mistake coming here tonight, Baruch. You made a big mistake coming after me."

He grinned, a flash of sharp white teeth. "I'm going to enjoy this." He took a step closer, power spilling off him. He was almost as strong as Patch, but there was a bloodthirsty edge to his power that I'd never felt with Patch. I didn't know how long ago Baruch had fallen from heaven, but I knew without any doubt that he had given himself over to evil, wholeheartedly.

"Swear your oath of fealty, Nora Grey," he ordered.

CHAPTER

I WOULD NOT SWEAR THE OATH. AND I WOULD NOT allow him to drag the words out of me. No matter how much pain he heaped on me, I had to stay strong. But a resilient defense alone wasn't going to be enough to endure this. I needed an offense, and fast.

Counter his mind-tricks with a few of your own, I commanded myself. Dante had said mind-tricks were my best weapon. He'd said I was better at it than almost any Nephil he knew of. I'd fooled

Patch. And I would fool Baruch now. I'd create my own reality and shove him so hard inside it, he wouldn't know what hit him.

Squeezing my eyes shut to block out Baruch's insidious chant to swear my oath, I catapulted myself inside his head. My greatest confidence came from knowing I'd consumed devilcraft earlier today. I didn't trust my own strength, but the devilcraft made me a more powerful version of myself. It heightened my natural talents, including my aptitude for mind-tricks.

I fled down the dark, twisted corridors of Baruch's mind, planting one explosion after another. I worked as quickly as I could, knowing that if I made one mistake, if I gave him any reason to think I was reconstructing his thoughts, if I left any evidence of my presence . . .

I chose the one thing I knew would alarm Baruch. Nephilim.

The Black Hand's army! I thought explosively at Baruch. I assailed his thoughts with an image of Dante rushing into the room, followed by twenty, thirty, no—forty Nephilim. I leaked pictures of their enraged eyes and hard fists into his subconscious. To make the vision even more convincing, I made Baruch think he was watching his own men being dragged away captive by Nephilim.

Despite all this, I felt Baruch's resistance. He stood nailed to the spot, not reacting as he should have at being surrounded by Nephilim. I feared that he suspected something was off, and plunged ahead.

Mess with our leader, mess with us—all of us. I flung Dante's venomous words into Baruch's mind. Nora isn't going to swear fealty now. Not now, not ever. I created a picture of Dante picking up the poker from the fireplace toolkit and plunging it into Baruch's wing scars. I shoved the vivid image deep inside Baruch's brain.

I heard Baruch fall to his knees before I opened my eyes. He was down on all fours, shoulders hunched. An expression of utter shock seized his features. His eyes glazed, and spittle pooled in the corners of his mouth. His hands reached for his back, grasping at air. He was trying to remove the poker.

I exhaled in weary relief. He'd bought it. He'd bought my mind-trick.

A figure moved near the doorway.

I shot to my feet and snatched the real poker from the fireplace. I raised it off my shoulder, readying to swing, when Dabria stepped into view. In the semidarkness, her hair glowed glacial white. Her mouth was a grim line. "You mind-tricked him?" she guessed. "Nice. But we have to get out of here now," she told me.

I almost laughed, cold and disbelieving. "What are you doing here?"

She stepped over Baruch's unmoving body. "Patch asked me to take you somewhere safe."

I shook my head. "You're lying. Patch didn't send you. He knows you're the last person I'd ever go with." I tightened my grip on the poker. If she came another step closer, I'd gladly shove it in her wing scars. And like Baruch, she'd be in a near-comatose state until she found a way to dislodge it.

"He didn't have much of a choice. Between chasing out the other fallen angels who raided your party, and erasing the minds of your panic-stricken friends who are fleeing down the street as we speak, I'd say he's a little preoccupied. Don't the two of you have a secret code word for situations like this?" Dabria asked without a crack in her icy composure. "When I was with Patch, we had one. I would have trusted anyone Patch gave it to."

I didn't take my eyes off her. Secret code word? My, my, but she was good at worming under my skin.

"In fact, we do have a secret code," I said. "It's 'Dabria's a pathetic leech who doesn't know when to move on.'" I covered my mouth. "Oh. I just realized why Patch probably failed to share our secret code"—scorn dripped from the words—"with you."

Her lips thinned further.

"Either tell me what you really came here for, or I'm going to shove this thing in your scars so deep, it will be your new permanent appendage," I told her.

"I don't have to put up with this," Dabria said, turning on her heel.

I followed her through the vacant house and out to the driveway. "I know you're blackmailing Pepper Friberg," I said. If I'd taken her by surprise, she didn't show it. Her stride never faltered. "He thinks Patch is blackmailing him, and he's doing everything he can to put Patch on the fast track to hell. Credit goes to you, Dabria. You claim you're still in love with Patch, but you have a funny way of showing it. Because of you, he's in danger of exile. Is that your plan? If you can't have him, no one can?"

Dabria beeped her key chain, and taillights flashed on the most exotic sports car I'd ever seen.

"What is that?" I asked.

She shot me a condescending look. "My Bugatti."

A Bugatti. Flashy, sophisticated, and in a class of its own. Just like Dabria. She dropped behind the wheel. "Might want to get that fallen angel out of your living room before your mom gets back." She paused. "And you might want to check the validity of your accusations."

She started to pull her door closed, but I wrenched it back open. "Are you denying blackmailing Pepper?" I asked angrily. "I saw the two of you arguing behind the Devil's Handbag."

Dabria wrapped a silk driving scarf around her head, flinging the ends over her shoulders. "You shouldn't eavesdrop, Nora. And Pepper is one archangel you'd do well to stay away from. He doesn't play nice."

"Neither do I."

She locked eyes with me. "Not that it's any of your business, but Pepper searched me out that night because he knows I have connections to Patch. He's looking for Patch, and mistakenly thought I'd help him." She started the ignition, flooring the gas to drown out my response.

I glared at Dabria, not buying that her interaction with Pepper had been that innocent. Dabria had a solid track record of lying. On top of that, we had bad blood. She stood as an awful reminder that Patch had been with someone before me. It wouldn't have been so nettling if she would stay in his past where she belonged. Instead she kept popping up like the villain with multiple lives in a slasher film.

"You're a poor judge of character," she said, thrusting the Bugatti in gear.

I leaped to the front bumper, slamming my palms on the hood. I wasn't finished with her yet. "When it comes to you, I'm not wrong," I called over the engine. "You're a conniving, backstabbing, selfish, and egotistical narcissist."

Dabria's jaw clenched visibly. She smoothed a few flyaways off her face, shoved out of the car, and stalked over to me. In heels, she matched my height. "I want to clear Patch's name too, you know," she said in her witch-cool voice.

"Now there's an Oscar-worthy line."

She stared at me. "I told Patch you were immature and impulsive and couldn't get over your jealousy of what he and I had long enough to make this work."

My cheeks flushed, and I grabbed her arm before she could avoid me. "Don't talk to Patch about me again. What's more, don't talk to him period."

"Patch trusts me. That should be good enough for you."

"Patch doesn't trust you. He's using you. He'll string you along, but in the end, you're expendable. The minute you're no longer useful, it's over."

Dabria's mouth pinched into something ugly. "Since we're giving each other advice, here's mine. Get off my back." Her eyes raked over me warningly.

She was threatening me.

She had something to hide.

I was going to dig up her secret, and I was going to bring her down.

CHAPTER

TURNING AWAY FROM THE ROAD DUST DABRIA'S
tires kicked up, I jogged back inside. My mom would be
home any minute now, and not only would I have some
serious explaining to do about the party's abrupt ending, but I
needed to dump Baruch's body. If he truly believed I'd rammed a
poker into his wing scars, he'd resign his body to a near-comatose
state for several more hours, making moving it considerably easier.
Finally, a lucky break.

I found Patch in the living room, crouched over Baruch's body. Relief surged through me at the sight of him. "Patch!" I exclaimed, running over.

"Angel." His face was etched with worry. He rose to his feet, opening his arms as I flung myself into them. He squeezed me hard.

I nodded to alleviate any concern he might have over my well-being, and swallowed the lump in my throat. "I'm fine. I'm not hurt. I mind-tricked him into thinking there was a Nephilim raid. And I made him believe I jammed a poker into his scars for good measure." I blew out a shaky sigh. "How did you know fallen angels crashed the party?"

"Your mom kicked me out, but I wasn't going to leave you unprotected. I took up guard down the street. There was a lot of traffic heading toward your place, but I assumed it was for the party. When I saw people running out the front door looking like they'd seen a monster, I came as fast as I could. There was a fallen angel standing guard outside your door who thought I'd shown up to steal his spoils of war. Needless to say, I had to stab him, and a few others, in their wing scars. Hope your mom doesn't notice I pruned a few branches off the tree outside. They made excellent stakes." His mouth twitched mischievously.

"She'll be home any minute."

Patch nodded. "I'll take care of the body. Can you get the electricity running? Fuse box is in the garage. Check to see if any of the switches are tripped. If they cut the wires to the house, we're going to have a lot more work on our hands."

"I'm on it." I stopped halfway to the garage and turned back. "Dabria showed up. She offered me a flimsy story, saying you told her to get me out. Do you think she could have been helping them?"

To my astonishment, he said, "I called her. She was in the area. I went after the fallen angels and told her to get you out."

I was speechless, both from shocked disbelief and irritation. I didn't know if I was angrier that Dabria had been telling the truth, or that she was clearly following Patch, since "in the area" was hard to pull off when you considered my street was one mile long, ours was the only house on it, and it dead-ended into the woods. She probably had a tracking device on him. When he'd called her, she'd probably been parked a hundred feet back, clutching a pair of binoculars.

I didn't doubt Patch was faithful to me. Likewise, I didn't doubt Dabria hoped to change that.

Figuring now wasn't the time to blow this into an argument, I said, "What are we going to tell my mom?"

"I'll—I'll take care of it."

Patch and I turned toward the mouselike squeak coming from the doorway. Marcie stood there, wringing her hands. As if she sensed how weak this made her look, she dropped them to her sides. Flinging her hair off her shoulders, she jutted her chin and said with more self-assurance, "The party was my idea,

finale

which makes this just as much my mess as yours. I'll tell your mom some losers showed up to crash the party and started destroying furniture. We did the only responsible thing: canceled the party." It looked to me like Marcie was working hard to avoid gazing at Baruch's body lying facedown on the rug. If she didn't see it, it couldn't be true.

"Thanks, Marcie," I said, and I sincerely meant it.

"Don't sound so surprised. I'm in this too, you know. I'm not—I mean—I *am* non—" Deep breath. "I *am* one of—you." She opened her mouth to say more, then abruptly shut it. I didn't blame her. "Nonhuman" was a difficult word to think, let alone say aloud.

A knock at the front door caused Marcie and me to jump. We exchanged a brief look of uncertainty before Patch spoke.

"Pretend we were never here," he said, slinging Baruch over his shoulders and hefting him toward the back door. *And Angel?* he added in mind-speak. *Erase Marcie's memory of seeing me here tonight. We need to keep our secret watertight.*

Consider it done, I responded.

Marcie and I went to answer the door. I'd just turned the knob when Vee sashayed inside, pulling Scott with her, their fingers entwined.

"Sorry we're late," Vee announced. "We got a little, ahem . . ." She shared a secret, knowing look with Scott, and they both burst out laughing.

"Distracted," Scott finished for her, grinning.

Vee fanned herself. "You can say that again."

When Marcie and I simply stared at them in somber silence, Vee glanced around, becoming aware of the vacant and trashed house for the first time. "Hold up. Where is everyone? The party can't be over yet."

"We got crashed," Marcie said.

"They were wearing Halloween masks," I explained. "Could have been anyone."

"They started destroying furniture."

"We sent everyone home," I added.

Vee examined the damage in wordless shock.

Crashed? Scott spoke to my mind, clearly not buying my acting skills and sensing there was more to the story.

Fallen angels, I answered. *One in particular tried his best to make me swear fealty. It's okay,* I added quickly when I saw his face contort with anxiety. *He didn't succeed. I need you to get Vee out of here. If she hangs around, she's only going to start asking questions I can't answer. And I need to clean up before my mom gets home.*

When are you going to tell her?

I flinched, Scott's straightforward question catching me off guard. *I can't tell Vee. Not if I want to keep her safe. Advice I'm asking you to heed as well. She's my best friend, Scott. Nothing can happen to her.*

She deserves the truth.

She deserves a lot more, but right now, her safety matters most to me.

finale

What do you think matters most to her? Scott said. *She cares about you and trusts you. Show her the same respect.*

I didn't have time to argue. *Please, Scott,* I begged him.

He gave me a long, considering look. I could tell he wasn't pleased, but I could also tell he was going to let me win this battle—for now.

"Tell you what," he told Vee. "I'll make it up to you. Let's go see a movie. Your choice. Not to sway your opinion, but there's a new superhero movie out. Crappy reviews, which is always a sign it's going to be sweet."

"We should stay and help Nora clean up this mess," Vee said. "I'm going to find out who did this and teach them some manners. Maybe a dead fish will just happen to find its way inside their locker. And they'd better keep an eye on their tires, because I've got a knife just itching to stab rubber."

"Take the night off," I told Vee. "Marcie will help me clean up, won't you, Marcie?" I slung my arm over her shoulder and said it sweetly enough, but there was a note of superciliousness underscoring my words.

Vee caught my gaze, and we shared a moment of understanding.

"Well, isn't that big of you," Vee told Marcie. "Dustpan is under the kitchen sink. Trash bags, too." She gave Marcie's shoulder a slug. "Have fun, and don't break too many fingernails."

After the door shut behind them, Marcie and I slumped against the wall. At the same time, we breathed a sigh of relief.

Marcie smiled first. "Jinx."

I cleared my throat. "Thanks for your help tonight," I said, and I honestly meant it. For once in her life, Marcie had been . . .

Helpful, I realized with a start. And I was going to repay her by erasing her memory.

She pushed up from the wall, dusting her hands. "Night's not over yet. Dustpan is under the sink?"

THE FOLLOWING MORNING CAME EARLY. THE
rap at my bedroom window acted as my alarm, and I
rolled over to see Dante behind the glass, crouched on a
tree branch, beckoning me outside. I held up five fingers, signaling
that I'd be out in as many minutes.

Technically, I was grounded. But I didn't think the excuse
would hold much sway with Dante.

Outside, the dark morning air held the crisp tang of autumn, and I rubbed my hands together briskly to warm them. A slice of the moon still hung overhead. Far away, an owl cried out with a plaintive hoot.

"An unmarked car with radar equipment made several passes by your house this morning," Dante told me, blowing on his hands. "Pretty sure he was a cop. Dark hair and a few years older than me, from what I could see. Any thoughts on that?"

Detective Basso. What had I done to get on his radar this time?

"No," I said, thinking now wasn't the time to reveal my sordid history with local law enforcement. "Probably the end of his shift, looking for busywork. He's not going to catch any speeders down here, that's for sure."

An ironic smile twitched Dante's lips. "Not in cars, anyway, track star. You ready for this?"

"No. Does that count for anything?"

He bent down and knotted a shoelace I'd apparently over-looked. "Warm-up time. You know the drill."

I knew the drill, all right. What Dante didn't know was that my warm-up also consisted of fantasizing I was flinging knives, darts, and other shrapnel at his back as I sprinted across the woodsy terrain, following him deep into our secluded training arena. Whatever it took to get in the mood, right?

When I was thoroughly drenched in sweat, Dante walked me through a series of stretches intended to make me more limber. I'd seen Marcie doing a few of the very same stretches in her

finale

bedroom. She wasn't on the cheerleading squad anymore, but apparently maintaining her ability to do the splits was important to her.

"What's the plan for today?" I asked, sitting on the ground with my legs spread in a wide V. I bent at the waist, resting my forehead on my kneecap, feeling a pull in my hamstring.

"Possession."

"Possession?" I repeated, taken aback.

"If fallen angels can possess us, it's only fair that we learn to possess them. What better warfare than to be able to control your enemy's mind and body?" Dante continued.

"I didn't know possessing fallen angels was even an option."

"It is now—now that we have devilcraft. We were never strong enough before. I've been training a few select Nephilim, including myself, in secret on the process of possession for months now. Mastering this skill is going to be the turning point of the war, Nora. If we can do it successfully, we stand a chance."

"You've been training? How?" Possession was possible only during Cheshvan. How could he have been practicing the technique for months?

"We've been training on fallen angels." A wicked smile sparkled in his eyes. "I told you: We're stronger than we've ever been. One fallen angel wandering around alone can't hold his own against a group of us. We've been picking them up off the streets at night and taking them to the training facility Hank organized."

"Hank was involved in this?" It seemed his skeletons would never stop spilling from the closet.

"We pick the loners, the introverts, the ones we don't think will be missed. We feed them a special devilcraft prototype that makes possession possible for short periods of time, even when it's not Cheshvan. And then we practice on them."

"Where are they now?"

"Detained at the training facility. We keep a metal rod enchanted with devilcraft stabbed in their wing scars when we're not practicing on them. It keeps them completely immobilized. Like lab rats at our disposal."

I was certain Patch knew nothing of this. He would have mentioned something if he had. "How many fallen angels do you have detained? And where is the training facility?"

"I can't tell you the location. When we set up the facility, Hank, Blakely, and I decided it would be safer to keep it top secret. With Hank gone, Blakely and I are the only Nephilim who know where it is. It's better that way. If you relax the rules, you get turncoats. People who'll do anything for a profit, even betray their own race. It's Nephilim nature, just like it's human nature. We're eliminating the temptation."

"Are you going to take me to the training center to practice?" I was sure there would be protocol in that, too. I'd either be blindfolded, or have my memory of the route erased. But maybe I could find a way around it. Maybe Patch and I could retrace our way to the training center together—

"Don't need to. I brought one of the lab rats with me."

My eyes darted to the trees. "Where?"

"Don't worry—the combination of devilcraft and a rod through her wing scars is keeping her cooperative." Dante disappeared behind a boulder, but returned dragging a female fallen angel who didn't look more than thirteen in human years. Her legs, two toothpicks sprouting out from white gym shorts, couldn't have been much thicker than my arms.

Dante threw her down, her limp body settling on the dirt like a sack of trash. I turned away from the rod protruding from her wing scars. I knew she couldn't feel a thing, but the image made the hairs on the back of my neck tingle just the same.

I had to remind myself that she was the enemy. I had a personal stake in the war now: I refused to swear fealty to any fallen angel. They were all dangerous. Every last one of them had to be stopped.

"Once I pull the rod out, you'll only have a couple seconds before she'll start fighting. This particular devilcraft has a short half-life and won't linger in her body. In other words, don't let your guard down."

"Will she know I'm possessing her?"

"Oh, she'll know. She's been through this drill hundreds of times. I want you to possess her and command her actions for a few minutes to get used to the feeling of manipulating her body. Warn me when you're ready to exit her body. I'll have the rod ready."

"How do I get inside her body?" I asked, goose bumps crawling up my arms. I was cold, but not only from the chill in the air. I didn't want to possess the fallen angel, but at the same time, I needed to give Patch as much information as possible about how the process worked. We couldn't solve a problem we didn't understand.

"She'll be weak from the devilcraft, which will help. And we've entered Cheshvan, which means the conduits of possession are wide open. All you have to do is mind-trick her. Take control of her thoughts. Make her think she wants you to possess her. Once she lets her guard down, everything becomes a piece of cake. You'll gravitate toward her naturally. You'll get sucked into her body so fast you'll hardly notice the transition. Next thing you know, you'll be in control."

"She's so young."

"Don't let that fool you. She's as cunning and dangerous as the rest of them. Here—I brought you a special dose of devilcraft that will make your first go at it easier."

I didn't reach for the vial right away. My fingers tingled with desire, but I kept them at my sides. I'd taken so much devilcraft already. I'd promised myself I'd stop, and that I'd come clean with Patch. So far, I'd done neither.

I glanced at the vial of gleaming blue liquid, and a fierce hunger seemed to gnaw through my stomach. I didn't want the devilcraft, and at the same time, I desperately needed it. My head spun, growing dizzy without it. Taking a little more couldn't be that harmful. Before I could stop myself, I reached out and accepted the vial. Already my mouth salivated. "Should I drink the whole thing?"

"Yes."

I tossed the vial back, the devilcraft burning like poison down my throat. I coughed and sputtered, wishing Blakely could devise a way to make it taste better. It would be equally helpful if he could minimize the negative side effects. Immediately after drinking this dose, a headache spiked into my skull. Experience told me it would only worsen as the day wore on.

"Ready?" Dante asked.

I wasn't quick to give my nod of affirmation. To say I had little desire to possess the girl was an understatement. I'd been possessed once before—by Patch, in a desperate move to save me from being slain by Chauncey Langeais, a long-lost relative who had no familial affection for me. While I was glad Patch had tried to protect me, the violation I'd felt while being possessed wasn't something I wanted to experience again. Or put someone else through.

My eyes swept over the girl. She'd suffered through this hundreds of times before. And here I was, about to make her do it all over again.

"Ready," I said heavily at last.

Dante plucked the rod from the girl's wing scars, careful to keep his hands off the blue-glowing lower half. "Any second now," he murmured in warning. "Get ready. Her thoughts will give off magnetic impulses; as soon as you feel mental activity, get inside her head. Don't waste any time convincing her she wants you to possess her."

Silence hung in the woods, thick and tense. I took a step closer to the girl, straining to pick up any mental feedback. Dante's knees were bent, as if he expected to have to jump to action at any moment. A crow's sharp caw carried across the dark expanse above. A faint bleep of energy landed on my radar, and that was all the warning I got before the girl launched herself at me, teeth bared and fingernails scratching like a wild animal.

We smacked back against the dirt together. My reflexes were sharper, and I rolled on top of her. I lunged for her wrists, hoping to pin them above her head, but she bucked me off in a single spurt of athleticism. I skidded over the dirt, hearing her land agilely a few feet away. I looked up just in time to see her spring into the air, soaring toward me.

Tucking into a ball, I rolled out of her range.

"Now!" Dante boomed. From the corner of my eye, I saw him holding the rod up, readying himself to attack the girl if I failed.

I shut my eyes, homing in on her thoughts. I could feel them zooming this way and that, like frantic insects. I dove into her head, shredding everything I came across. I tangled her thoughts into one giant mass and whispered a hypnotic, Let me in, let me in now.

Much faster than I expected, the girl's defenses sagged. Just as Dante had predicted, I felt myself gliding toward her, like my soul was being reeled in by a powerful force field. She offered no resistance. The sensation had a dreamlike quality; woozy and slippery, and blurred at the edges. There was no defining moment when I felt the change; I merely blinked and found myself viewing the world from a different angle.

I was inside her, body, mind, and soul, possessing her.

"Nora?" Dante asked, squinting at me skeptically.

"I'm in." My voice startled me; I'd commanded the response, but it had come out in her voice. Higher and sweeter than I would have expected from a fallen angel. Then again, she was so young. . . .

"Do you feel any resistance? Any backlash from her at all?" Dante asked.

This time I shook my head no. I wasn't ready to hear myself speak in her voice again. As much as Dante wanted me to practice commanding her body, I wanted out.

I hastily completed a short list of drills, commanding the fallen angel's body to run a short distance, hurdle a fallen tree branch with ease, and untie and retie her shoelaces. Dante was right; I had full control. And I knew, somewhere deep inside, that I was dragging her against her will through the motions. I could have commanded her to stab her own wing scars, and she would have had no choice but to comply.

I'm done, I spoke to Dante's mind. I'm coming out.

"A little longer," he argued. "You need more practice. I want this to feel like second nature. Run through the drills again."

Ignoring his request, I commanded her body to expel mine, and again, the transition was as easy as it was abrupt.

Cursing under his breath, Dante rammed the rod back into the fallen angel's wing scars. Her body crumpled as though dead, arms and legs hitting the ground at funny angles. I wanted to look away but couldn't. I kept wondering what her existence on Earth had been like before. If anyone missed her. If she'd ever be free again. And how bleak her outlook must be.

"That wasn't long enough," Dante told me, clearly annoyed. "Didn't you hear me tell you to practice the drills again? I know it's a little uncomfortable at first—"

"How does it work?" I asked. "Two objects can't exist in the same space at the same time. So how does possession work?"

"It all boils down to quantum realm, wave function, and wave-particle duality."

"I haven't taken quantum theory yet," I said with a touch of rancor. "Break it down into something I can actually understand."

"From what I can tell, everything happens at a subatomic level. Two objects *can* exist in the same place at the same time. I'm not sure anyone understands exactly how it works. It's just the way it is."

"That's all you can give me?"

"Have a little faith, Grey."

finale

"Fine. I'll give you faith. But I want something in return," I said, eyeing Dante shrewdly. "You're good at surveillance, right?"

"You could do worse."

"There's a rogue archangel wandering around town named Pepper Friberg. He claims a fallen angel is blackmailing him, and I'm pretty sure I know which one. I want you to get me the evidence I need to nail her."

"Her?"

"Women can be crafty too."

"What does this have to do with leading the Nephilim?"

"This is personal."

"All right," Dante said slowly. "Tell me what I need to know."

"Patch told me that any number of fallen angels out there could be blackmailing Pepper Friberg for numerous things—pages from the Book of Enoch, glimpses into the future, full pardon on a past crime, information deemed both sacred and secret, or even to be elevated to the status of guardian angel—the list of what an archangel could provide could go on and on, I think."

"What else did Patch say?"

"Not much. He wants to find the blackmailer too. I know he's been following leads and tracking at least one suspect. But I'm pretty sure he's looking down the wrong holes. The other night I saw his ex talking to Pepper behind the Devil's Handbag. I couldn't hear what they said, but she looked confident. And Pepper looked furious. Her name is Dabria."

I was surprised to see a shadow of recognition cloud Dante's expression. He crossed his arms over his chest. "Dabria?"

I groaned. "Don't tell me you know her too. I swear, she's *everywhere*. If you tell me you think she's beautiful, I'll kick you off the ledge of the ravine behind you and send this boulder rolling down after you."

"It's not that." Dante shook his head, pity creeping into his countenance. "I didn't want to be the one to tell you."

"Tell me what?"

"I know Dabria. Not personally, but—" The sympathy on his face deepened. He looked at me like he was about to break awful news.

I'd taken a seat on a tree stump to tell my story, but now I jumped to my feet. "Just tell me, Dante."

"I have spies working for me. People I employ to keep an eye on influential fallen angels," Dante confessed, sounding almost guilty. "It's no secret Patch is highly respected in the fallen angel community. He's smart, clever, and resourceful. He's a good leader. Years as a mercenary gave him more experience in battle than most of my men combined."

"You've been spying on Patch," I said. "Why didn't you tell me?"

"I trust you, but I'm not discounting the possibility that he has influence over you."

"Influence? Patch has never made my decisions for me—I'm capable of doing that on my own. I'm in charge of this operation.

finale

If I wanted spies sent out, I would have done it myself," I said, my irritation evident.

"Point taken."

I paced to the nearest tree, facing away from Dante. "Are you going to tell me why you're divulging all this in the first place?"

He expelled a reluctant sigh. "While spying on Patch, Dabria has popped onto our radar more than once."

I shut my eyes, wishing I could tell him to stop there. I didn't want to hear more. Dabria followed Patch everywhere—I knew that. But the tone of Dante's voice suggested he had much more devastating news to deliver than simply telling me that Patch had a stalker who also happened to be his gorgeous ex.

"A couple nights ago, they were together. I have evidence. Multiple photos."

I clenched my jaw and swung around. "I want to see them."

"Nora—"

"I can handle it," I snapped. "I want to see this so-called evidence your men—my men—collected." Patch with Dabria. I spun through my memory, trying to pinpoint which night it could have been. I felt frantic and jealous and unsteady. Patch hadn't done this. There was some explanation. I owed him the benefit of the doubt. We'd been through too much for me to pounce on the first conclusion that flew my way.

I had to stay calm. I'd be foolish to pass judgment this early. Dante had pictures? Fine. I'd analyze them myself.

Dante pressed his lips together, then nodded. "I'll have them delivered to your house later today."

CHAPTER

I WENT THROUGH THE MOTIONS OF GETTING READY for the day, but they felt mechanical. I couldn't flush out the image of Patch and Dabria together. At the time, I hadn't thought to ask Dante for specifics, and now my unanswered questions seemed to burn holes in my brain. *They were together. I have photos.*

What did that mean? Together how? Was I naive for even asking? No. I trusted Patch. I was tempted to call him now, but of course I didn't. I'd wait until I saw the pictures. Whether or not they were condemning . . . I'd know right away.

Marcie strolled into the kitchen and perched herself on the table's edge. "I'm looking for a shopping buddy today after school."

I pushed my now soggy bowl of cereal away. I'd been lost in thought for so long, any chance at salvaging it had expired.

"I always shop on Friday afternoon," Marcie said. "It's, like, a ritual."

"You mean a tradition," I corrected.

"I need a new fall coat. Something warm and wool, but still chic," she said, frowning slightly in contemplation.

"Thanks for the offer, but I have some hardcore trig homework to catch up on."

"Oh, come on. You haven't done homework all week, why start now? And I really need a second opinion. This is an important purchase. And just when you were starting to act normal," she muttered.

I pushed up from my chair and carried my bowl to the sink. "Flattery gets me every time."

"Come on, Nora, I don't want to fight," she complained. "I just want you to come shopping with me."

"And I want to pass trig. Plus, I'm grounded."

"No worries, I already talked to your mom. She's had time to cool off, and to come around. You're not grounded anymore. I'll hang around an extra thirty minutes after school. That should give you plenty of time to finish trig."

I narrowed my eyes speculatively at her. "Are you mind-tricking my mom?"

"You know what I think? You're jealous that she and I have bonded."

Ugh.

"It's not just math, Marcie. I also need to think. About what happened last night, and how to prevent it from happening again. I'm not going to swear fealty," I said with resolve. "And I don't want any more Nephilim to either."

Marcie made a sound of exasperation. "You're just like my dad. For once stop being such a—"

"Nephil?" I supplied. "Hybrid, freak, accident of nature? Target?"

Marcie clenched her hands so tightly they flushed pink with blood. At last she tilted her chin up. Challenge and pride flashed in her eyes. "Yeah. A mutant, a monster, a phenomenon. Just like me."

I raised my eyebrows. "So that's it? You're finally going to accept what you are?"

An almost bashful smile broke across her face. "Hell's bells, yeah."

"I like this version of you better," I said.

"I like this version of you better." Marcie stood, grabbing her handbag off the counter. "Do we have a shopping date or what?"

Not two hours after the final bell dismissed us, Marcie had blown nearly four hundred dollars on a wool coat, jeans, and a few

BECCA FITZPATRICK

accessories. I didn't spend four hundred on my entire wardrobe for the year. It occurred to me that if I'd grown up in Hank's household, I wouldn't think twice about sliding my credit card all afternoon either. In fact, I'd have a credit card.

Marcie drove, since she claimed she didn't want to be seen in my car, and while I didn't blame her, it did drive the message home. She had money and I didn't. Hank had left me his doomed army, and he'd left Marcie his inheritance. Unfair didn't begin to cover it.

"Can we make a quick stop?" I asked Marcie. "It's a little out of the way, but I need to pick up something from my friend Dante." I felt queasy at the thought of seeing the pictures of Patch and Dabria, but I wanted to get the unknown over with. I didn't have the patience to wait for Dante to deliver them. Since I had no way of knowing if he already had, I decided to be proactive.

"Dante? Do I know him?"

"No. He doesn't go to school. Take your next right—he lives close to Casco Bay," I told her.

The irony of this moment didn't slip past me. Over the summer, I'd accused Patch of getting involved with Marcie. Now, just a few months later, I was riding shotgun in her car, on my way to investigate the same story—just with a different girl.

I pressed the heel of my hand between my eyes. Maybe I should let it go. Maybe this said a lot about my insecurities, and I should just trust Patch unconditionally. The thing was, I did trust him.

And then there was Dabria.

Besides, if Patch was innocent, and I hoped with everything I had that he was, there was no harm in looking at the pictures.

Marcie followed my instructions to Dante's house and made an immediate sound of appreciation as she gazed at the architecture. "This Dante friend of yours has style," she said, eyes sweeping over the quintessential Queen Anne house set back from a large apron of lawn.

"His friends left it to him in their will," I said. "Don't bother getting out—I'll just run up to the door and get what I need."

"No way. I have got to see the interior," Marcie said, hopping out before I could stop her. "Does Dante have a girlfriend?" She pushed her sunglasses to the top of her head, blatantly admiring Dante's wealth.

Yeah, me, I thought. And I was clearly doing a stellar job keeping up the charade. Even my half sister who slept down the hall knew nothing of my "boyfriend."

We climbed the porch and rang the bell. I waited, then rang it again. Cupping my hands around my eyes, I peered through the dining room window into shadowy darkness. Just my luck I'd stop by when he wasn't home.

"Yoo-hoo! Are you girls looking for the young man who used to live here?"

Marcie and I turned to find an elderly woman standing on the sidewalk. She had pink slippers on her feet, pink rollers in her hair, and a little black dog at the end of a leash.

"We're looking for Dante," I said. "Are you a neighbor?"

"I moved in with my daughter and her husband at the beginning of summer. Just down the street," she said, gesturing behind her. "My husband, John, is gone now, bless his soul, and it was either a nursing home or my son-in-law's residence. He never puts the toilet seat down," she informed us.

What is she yapping about? Marcie asked my thoughts. *And, hello. That dog needs a bath. I can smell it from here.*

I affected a neighborly smile and walked down the porch steps. "I'm Nora Grey. I'm friends with the guy who lives here, Dante Matterazzi."

"Matterazzi? I knew it! I knew he was Italian. Name like that screams Italian. They're invading our shores," the woman said. "Next thing you know, I'll be sharing a garden wall with Mussolini himself." As if to weigh in, the dog gave a snarling bark of agreement.

Marcie and I shared a look, and Marcie rolled her eyes. I said to the woman, "Have you seen Dante today?"

"Today? Why would I have seen him today? I just told you he moved out. Two days ago. Did it in the middle of the night, just like an Italian would. Sneaky and wily as a Sicilian mobster. Up to no good, I'll tell you what."

"You must be mistaken. Dante still lives here," I said, trying to hold a pleasant tone.

"Ha! That boy is a goner. Always kept to himself and was about as unneighborly as they come. Was from the day he moved in. Wouldn't so much as say hello. Sneaky boy like that in this nice, respectable neighborhood. It just wasn't right. He only lasted a month, and I can't say I'm sad to see him go. Ought to be laws against renters in this neighborhood, dragging down home values like they do."

"Dante wasn't renting. He owns this house. His friends left it to him in their will."

"Is that what he told you?" She wagged her head, staring at me with sharp blue eyes like I was the biggest sucker the world had ever seen. "My son-in-law owns this house. Been in his family for years. Rented it out during the summertime, back before the economy crashed. Back when you could make a buck off tourism. Now we have to rent to Italian mobsters."

"You must be mistaken—" I began a second time.

"Check the county land records! They don't lie. Can't say the same for shady Italians."

The dog was running circles around the woman's legs, tying her up in the leash. Every once in a while he stopped to give Marcie and me a guttural growl of warning. Then he went right back to sniffing and chasing circles. The woman untangled herself and shuffled down the sidewalk.

I stared at her from behind. Dante owned this house. He wasn't renting.

A terrifying sensation vised my chest. If Dante *was* gone, how would I get more devilcraft? I was almost out. I had a day's supply left, two if I cut back.

"Well, someone's lying," Marcie said. "I think it's her. I never trust old women. Especially the cranky ones."

I hardly heard her. I tried Dante's cell, praying he'd pick up, but I got nothing. Not even his voice mail.

I helped Marcie carry her shopping bags inside, and my mom came downstairs to meet us. "One of your friends dropped this off," she said, extending a manila envelope. "He said his name was Dante? Should I know him?" she prodded.

I tried not to look too eager as I snatched the envelope. "He's a friend of Scott's," I explained.

My mom and Marcie kept their eyes on the envelope, watching me expectantly.

"It's probably just something he wants me to pass on to Scott," I lied, not wanting to draw extra attention to the situation.

"He looked older than your friends. I'm not entirely comfortable with the idea of you hanging out with older guys," Mom said doubtfully.

"Like I said, he's Scott's friend," I responded evasively.

In my bedroom I drew a deep breath and broke the envelope's seal. I shook out several blown-up photographs. All black and white.

The first several were taken at night. Patch strolling down a deserted street. Patch doing what appeared to be surveillance from his motorcycle. Patch talking on a pay phone. Nothing new there, since I already knew he was working around the clock to find Pepper's blackmailer.

The next photo was of Patch and Dabria.

They were in Patch's new black Ford F-150 pickup truck. Little needles of rain sliced through the streetlight above them. Dabria had her arms around Patch's neck, a coy smile dancing on her lips. They were locked in an embrace, and Patch didn't appear to be offering resistance.

I flipped through the last three pictures rapidly. My stomach heaved, and I knew I was going to be sick. Kissing.

Dabria kissing Patch. Right there in the photos.

25

I WAS SITTING ON THE BATHROOM FLOOR, MY BACK against the shower door. My knees were drawn up, and even though the space heater was running, I felt cold and clammy. An empty bottle of devilcraft lay beside me. It was the last of my supply. I hardly remembered drinking it. A whole bottle gone, and it had done nothing for me. Even it couldn't make me immune to heart-sickening despair.

I trusted Patch. I loved him too much to believe he'd hurt me this way. There had to be a reason, an explanation.

An *explanation*. The word echoed in my head, empty and taunting.

A knock sounded on the door.

"We have to share this thing, remember? And I have a bladder the size of a squirrel's," Marcie said.

I was slow to climb to my feet. Of all the absurd things to worry about, I wondered if Dabria was a better kisser. If Patch wished I was more like her. Crafty, icy, sophisticated. I wondered the precise moment he'd gone back to her. I wondered whether he hadn't broken things off with me yet because he knew how devastated I'd be.

Yet.

A heavy feeling of uncertainty pressed down on me.

I opened the door and brushed past Marcie. I'd made it five steps down the hall when I felt her eyes on my back.

"Are you okay?" she asked.

"I don't want to talk about it."

"Hey, wait up. Nora? Are you crying?"

I swiped my fingers under my eyes, surprised to find I had been crying. The whole moment felt frozen and distant. As if it were happening far away, in a dream.

Without turning I said, "I'm going out. Can you cover for me? I might not make curfew."

. . .

I stopped once on my way to Patch's place. I veered the Volkswagen sharply to the roadside, swung out, and paced the shoulder. It was full dark, and cold enough that I wished I'd brought my coat. I didn't know what I'd say when I saw him. I didn't want to launch into a raving outburst. I didn't want to reduce myself to bawling, either.

I'd brought the pictures with me, and in the end, I decided they could do the talking. I'd hand them to him and limit my question to a succinct, "Why?"

The icy detachment that had settled over me like frost melted the moment I saw Dabria's Bugatti parked outside Patch's townhouse. I braked a half block away, swallowing hard. A knot of anger swelled in my throat, and I shoved out of the car.

I jammed my key into the house lock and marched in. The only light came from a lamp on an end table in the living room. Dabria was pacing the balcony window but stopped when she saw me.

"What are you doing here?" she asked, visibly startled.

I shook my head angrily. "Nope. That's my line. This is my boy-friend's house, which makes that my line, exclusively. Where is he?" I demanded, already striding to the hallway leading back to the master bedroom.

"Don't bother. He's not here."

I whirled around. I gave Dabria a look that was incredulity, disgust, and menace all wrapped into one. "Then what. Are. You. Doing. Here?" I enunciated each word. I could feel rage bubbling up inside me, and I didn't try to temper it. Dabria had this coming.

finale

"I'm in trouble, Nora." Her lip quivered.

"Couldn't have said it better myself." I flung the envelope of pictures at her. It landed near her feet. "How does it feel knowing you're a boyfriend stealer? Is that what makes you feel good, Dabria? Taking what doesn't belong to you? Or is it just the act of ripping apart a good thing that you enjoy?"

Dabria bent to retrieve the envelope, but she held my eyes the whole way. Her eyebrows furrowed with guarded uncertainty. I couldn't believe she had the audacity to act like she didn't know.

"Patch's truck," I raged. "You and him, some night earlier this week, together in his truck. You kissed him!"

She broke eye contact just long enough to peer inside the envelope. She set it on a sofa cushion. "You don't understand—"

"Oh, I think I do. You're not that hard to figure out. You have no sense of respect or dignity. You take what you want, forget everyone else. You wanted Patch, and it looks like you got him." Now my voice caught and my eyes burned. I tried to blink the tears away, but they were coming too fast.

"I'm in trouble because I made a mistake while doing a favor for Patch," Dabria said in a soft, worried voice, clearly oblivious to my accusations. "Patch told me Blakely is developing devilcraft for Dante, and that the lab needs to be destroyed. He said if I ever came across information that might lead him to Blakely, or the lab, I was to immediately tell him.

"A couple nights ago, very late, a group of Nephilim came

to me, wanting their fortunes told. I quickly learned they were employed as bodyguards in the Black Hand's army. Up until that night, they had served as guards for a very powerful and important Nephil named Blakely. They had my attention. They went on to tell me their work was tedious and uneventful, and the hours long. Earlier that night, they had agreed to play a game of poker to pass the time, even though games or distractions of any kind were forbidden.

"One of the men left his post to buy a deck of cards. They played only a few minutes before they were discovered by their commander. He immediately dismissed and dishonorably discharged them from the army. The leader of the dismissed soldiers, Hanoth, was desperate to get his job back. He has family here and worries about supporting them, and about their safety if they are punished or cast out for his crimes. He came to me, hoping I could tell him whether there was a chance he would get his job back.

"I told his fortune first. I felt a strong urge to tell Hanoth the truth: that his former commander sought to imprison and torture him, and he should leave town with his family immediately. But I also knew that if I told him that, I'd lose all hope of finding Blakely. So I lied. I lied for Patch.

"I told Hanoth he should resolve his concerns directly with Blakely. I told him if he begged forgiveness, Blakely would pardon him. I knew if Hanoth believed my prophecy, he would lead me to Blakely. I wanted to do this for Patch. After everything he has done for me, giving me a second chance when no one else would"—her teary eyes flickered to mine—"it was the least I could do. I love him," she stated simply, meeting my hard gaze without flinching. "I always will. He was my first love, and I won't forget him. But he loves you now." She gave a despondent sigh. "Maybe the day will come when the two of you aren't so serious, and I'll be waiting."

"Don't count on it," I said. "Keep talking. Get to the part where you explain those pictures." I glanced at the envelope on the sofa. It seemed to take up far too much space in the room. I wanted to rip up the pictures and fling the remains into the fireplace.

"Hanoth appeared to believe my lie. He left with his men, and I followed them. I took every precaution not to be detected. They outnumbered me, and if they caught me, I knew I would be in great danger.

"They left Coldwater, heading northwest. I followed them over an hour. I thought I must be getting close to Blakely. Towns had thinned and we were far out in the countryside. The Nephilim turned down a narrow road, and I followed.

"Right away, I knew something was wrong. They parked in the middle of the road. Four of the five had left the car. I sensed them fanning out, to my sides and behind me, creating a net in the darkness to surround me. I don't know how they figured out I'd followed them. I drove the whole way with my lights off and stayed back far enough that I nearly lost them several times. Fearing it was already too late, I did the only thing I could. I ran on foot toward the river.

"I called Patch, telling him everything in a message. Then I waded into the river's current, hoping the turbulence of the water would slow their ability to hear or sense me.

"They closed in on me many times. I had to leave the river and run through the woods. I couldn't tell which direction I was running. But even if I made it to a town, I knew I wasn't safe. If anyone witnessed Hanoth and his men attacking me, the Nephilim would just erase their memories. So I ran as fast and as far as I could.

"When Patch finally called back, I was hiding in an abandoned sawmill. I don't know how much longer I could have kept running. Not long." Tears sparkled in her eyes. "He came for me. He got me out of there. Even when I failed to find Blakely." She smoothed her hair behind her ears and sniffled. "He drove me to Portland and made sure I had a safe place to stay. Before I got out of his truck, I kissed him." Her eyes found mine. I couldn't tell if they blazed with challenge or apology. "I initiated it, and he immediately ended it. I know what it looks like in the pictures, but it was my way of thanking him. It was over before it began. He made sure of it."

Dabria jerked suddenly, as though yanked by an invisible hand. Her eyes rolled back to whites for a moment, then snapped back to their usual arctic blue. "If you don't believe me, ask him. He'll be here in less than a minute."

I'D NEVER BELIEVED DABRIA TRULY HAD THE GIFT OF foresight and prophecy—not after she'd fallen, anyway—but she was doing a good job lately of convincing me to change my opinion. Less than a minute later, Patch's garage door opened with a low hum, and he appeared at the top of the stairs. He looked a little worse for wear—tired lines etched his face, and his eyes held a jaded edge—and seeing Dabria and me standing in a face-off in his living room didn't appear to improve his mood.

He regarded us with dark, evaluating eyes. "This can't be good."

"I'll go first," Dabria began, sucking in a rattling breath.

"Not even close," I shot back. I faced Patch directly, cutting Dabria out of the conversation. "She kissed you! And Dante, who's been tailing you, by the way, caught it on camera. Imagine my surprise when *that's* what I got an eyeful of earlier tonight. Did you even think to tell me?"

"I told her I kissed you, and that you pushed me away," Dabria protested shrilly.

"What are you still doing here?" I exploded at Dabria. "This is between me and Patch. Leave already!"

"What *are* you doing here?" Patch echoed to Dabria, his tone sharpening.

"I—broke in," she sputtered. "I was scared. I couldn't sleep. I can't stop thinking about Hanoth and the other Nephilim."

"You have got to be kidding me," I said. I looked to Patch for corroboration, hoping he wasn't going to fall for her damsel-in-distress ploy. Dabria had come here tonight looking for one particular brand of comfort, and I didn't approve. Not one bit.

"Go back to the safe house," Patch ordered Dabria. "If you'd stay there, you'd be safe." Despite his exhaustion, his words adopted a harsh note. "This is the last time I'm going to tell you to keep your head down and stay out of trouble."

"For how long?" Dabria practically whimpered. "I'm lonely

there. Everyone else in the house is human. They look at me funny." Her eyes pleaded with him. "I can help you. This time I won't make any mistakes. If you let me stay here—"

"Go," Patch commanded her sharply. "You've stirred up enough trouble already. With Nora, and with the Nephilim you followed. We can't be sure what conclusions they've drawn, but one thing is certain. They know you're after Blakely. If they have any brains at all, they've also figured out that means you know why Blakely is vital to their operation, and what he's doing in that secret lab of his, wherever it is. I wouldn't be surprised if they've moved the whole operation. And we're back at square one, no closer to finding Blakely and disabling devilcraft," Patch added with frustration.

"I was only trying to help," Dabria whispered, her lips trembling. With one last look at Patch that resembled that of a scolded puppy, she saw herself out.

That left Patch and me alone. He strode across the room without hesitating, even though I was sure my expression was far from inviting. He rested his forehead against mine and shut his eyes. He exhaled, long and slow, as if weighed down by an invisible force.

"I'm sorry," he said quietly and with genuine remorse.

The bitter words, "Sorry about the kiss, or merely sorry I saw it?" balanced on the tip of my tongue, ready to spring, but I swallowed them back. I was tired of dragging around my own invisible weight—comprising jealousy and doubt.

Patch's regret was so sharp it was nearly tangible. As much as I disliked and distrusted Dabria, I couldn't blame him for saving her butt. He was a better man than he gave himself credit for. I suspected that years ago, a very different Patch would have responded to the situation in another way. He was giving Dabria a second chance—something he, too, fought for daily.

"I'm sorry too," I murmured into Patch's chest. His strong arms folded me into an embrace. "I saw the pictures, and I've never been so upset or scared. The thought of losing you was—unimaginable. I was so angry at her. I still am. She kissed you when she shouldn't have. For all I know, she'll try it again."

"She won't, because I'm going to make it very clear how things are to be between us from now on. She crossed a line, and I'll make her think twice about doing it again," Patch said with resolve. He tipped my chin up and kissed me, letting his lips linger when he spoke. "I wasn't expecting to come home to you, but now that you're here, I have no intention of letting you leave."

Hot, aching guilt swept through me. I couldn't be close to Patch and not feel my lies hanging between us. I'd lied to him about devilcraft. I was still lying. How could I have done it? Self-disgust boiled up in me, filled with shame and loathing. I wanted to confess everything, but where to start? I'd been so negligent, letting the lies blaze out of control.

I opened my mouth to tell him the truth, when icy hands seemed to slide up my neck and clench it. I couldn't speak. I could

finale

barely breathe. My throat filled with thick matter, like when I'd first taken devilcraft. A foreign voice crept into my mind and reasoned with me.

If I told Patch, he'd never trust me again. He'd never forgive me. I'd only cause him more pain if I told him. I just had to get through Cheshvan, and then I'd stop taking devilcraft. Just a little longer. Just a few more lies.

The cold hands relaxed. I drew a rocky breath.

"Busy night?" I asked Patch, wanting to move forward in our conversation—anything to forget my lies.

He sighed. "And no closer to pinning down Pepper's black-mailer. I keep thinking it's got to be someone I've looked into, but maybe I'm wrong. Maybe it's someone else. Someone off my radar. I've chased down every lead, even those that seemed like a stretch. Far as I can tell, everyone's clean."

"Is there a chance Pepper is making it up? Maybe he isn't really being blackmailed." It was the first time I'd considered it. All along I'd trusted his story, when he'd proven to be anything but trustworthy.

Patch frowned. "It's possible, but I don't think so. Why go to the trouble of making up such an elaborate story?"

"Because he needs an excuse to chain you in hell," I suggested quietly, just now thinking of it. "What if the archangels put him up to this? He said he's down here on Earth on an assignment from them. I didn't believe him at first, but what if he really is? What if the archangels gave him the task of chaining you in hell? It's no secret they want to."

"Legally, they'd need a reason to chain me in hell." Patch stroked his chin thoughtfully. "Unless they've gone so far off the deep end, they're not bothering to stay within the law anymore. I definitely think there are a few rotten eggs in the bunch, but I don't think the entire archangel population has been corrupted."

"If Pepper is on an errand from a small faction of archangels, and the others find out or suspect foul play, Pepper's employers have the perfect cover: They can claim he'd gone rogue. They'd rip his wings out before he could testify, and they'd be off the hook. It doesn't seem so far-fetched to me. In fact, it seems like the perfect crime."

Patch stared at me. The plausibility of my theory seemed to settle over us like a cold fog.

"You think Pepper is on assignment from a group of crooked archangels to get rid of me for good," he said slowly at last.

"Did you know Pepper before you fell? What was he like?"

Patch shook his head. "I knew him, but not well. More like I knew of him. He had a reputation as a hard-boiled liberal, especially loose on social issues. I'm not surprised he fell hard into gambling, but if I remember right, he was involved in my trial. He must have voted to banish me; strange, since it's at odds with his reputation."

"Do you think we can get Pepper to turn on the archangels? His double life might be part of his cover . . . then again, he might be enjoying his time down here just a little too much. If we apply the right kind of pressure, he might talk. If he tells us that a secret faction of archangels sent him here to chain you in hell, at least we'd know what we're up against."

A dangerous little smile tightened Patch's mouth. "I think it's time to find Pepper."

I nodded. "Fine. But you're going to play this one from the sidelines. I don't want you going anywhere near Pepper. For now, we have to assume he'd do anything to chain you in hell."

Patch's eyebrows drew together. "What are you proposing, Angel?"

"I'm meeting Pepper. And I'm taking Scott with me. Don't even think about arguing with me," I said warningly before he could veto the idea. "You've taken Dabria as backup on more occasions than I want to think about. You swore to me it was a tactical move and nothing more. Well, now it's my turn. I'm taking Scott, and that's final. As far as I know, Pepper isn't holding any one-way tickets to hell with Scott's name on them."

Patch's mouth thinned and his eyes darkened; I could practically feel his objection radiating off him. Patch held no warmth for Scott, but he knew he couldn't play that card; it would make him a hypocrite.

"You're going to need an airtight plan," he said at last. "I'm not letting you out of my sight if there's any chance things could go south."

There was always a chance things could go south. If I'd learned anything during my time with Patch, it was that. Patch knew this too, and I wondered if it was part of his plan to keep me from going. I suddenly felt like Cinderella, prevented from going to the ball on a small technicality.

"Scott is stronger than you give him credit for," I argued. "He's not going to let anything happen to me. I'll make sure he understands he can't tell a soul that you and I are still very much together."

Patch's black eyes simmered. "And I'll make sure he understands that if a single hair on your head is lost, he'll deal with me. If he's got any sense, that's a threat he'll take to heart."

I smiled tensely. "Then it's settled. All we need now is a plan."

The following night was Saturday. After telling my mom that I was staying at Vee's all weekend and we'd head to school together on Monday, Scott and I made a trip to the Devil's Handbag. We weren't interested in the music or drinks, rather in the basement level. I'd heard rumors about the basement, a burgeoning gambling haven, but had never actually stepped foot inside. Word had it Pepper couldn't say the same. Patch had supplied us with a list of Pepper's favorite haunts, and I hoped Scott and I would get lucky on our first try.

Trying to look both sophisticated and guileless, I followed Scott over to the bar. He was chewing gum, looking as relaxed and confident as ever. I, on the other hand, was sweating so bad I felt like I needed another shower.

I'd flat-ironed my hair for a sleek and mature look. Throw on some liquid eyeliner, lipstick, four-inch heels, and a high-end handbag on loan from Marcie, and I'd magically aged five years. Given Scott's fully developed and intimidating build, I didn't think he had to worry about getting carded. He wore tiny silver hoops in his ears, and while his brown hair was closely cropped, he still managed to look both tough *and* handsome. Scott and I were just friends, but I could easily appreciate what Vee saw in him. I linked my arm through his, a show of being his girlfriend, as he signaled the bartender over to talk.

"We're looking for Storky," Scott told the bartender, leaning close to keep his voice low.

The bartender, who I'd never seen before, eyed us shrewdly. I met his gaze, trying to keep my eyes impassive. *Don't look nervous*, I told myself. *And whatever you do, don't look like you've got something to hide.*

"Who's looking?" he asked gruffly at last.

"We heard there's a high-stakes game tonight," Scott said, flashing a stack of hundreds lined up neatly inside his wallet.

The bartender hiked his shoulders and went back to wiping the bar. "Don't know what you're talking about."

Scott laid one of the bills on the bar, covering it with his hand. He slid it toward the bartender. "That's too bad. You sure we can't convince you to rethink?"

The bartender eyed the hundred-dollar bill. "Have I seen you around?"

"I play bass for Serpentine. I've also played poker from Portland to Concord to Boston, and everywhere in between."

A nod of recognition. "That's it. I used to work nights at the Z Pool Hall in Springvale."

"Fond memories of the place," Scott said without missing a beat. "Won a lot of cash. Lost even more." He grinned as though sharing a private joke with the bartender.

Sliding his hand flush with Scott's, and looking around to be sure he wasn't under surveillance, the bartender pocketed the bill. "Got to frisk you first," he told us. "No weapons allowed downstairs."

"No problem," Scott answered easily.

I started to sweat even more. Patch had warned us they'd be on the lookout for guns, knives, and any other sharp object that could be used as a weapon. So we'd gotten creative. The belt holding up Scott's jeans, and hidden beneath his shirt, was in fact a whip enchanted with devilcraft. Scott had sworn up and down he wasn't ingesting devilcraft, and had never heard of the super-drink, but I figured we might as well make use of the enchanted whip he'd lifted from Dante's car on a whim. The whip glowed the telltale shade of iridescent blue, but as long as the bartender didn't raise Scott's shirt, we'd be safe.

At the bartender's invitation, Scott and I walked around the bar, stepped behind a privacy screen, and lifted our arms. I went first, enduring a brief, cursory pat-down. The bartender moved to Scott, brushing down his inseams and patting under his arms and

finale

across his back. It was dim behind the bar, and even though Scott had worn a thick cotton shirt, I thought I saw the whip glow faintly through it. The bartender seemed to see it too. His eyebrows pulled together, and he reached for Scott's shirt.

I dropped my handbag at his feet. Several hundred-dollar bills spilled out. Just like that, the bartender's attention was drawn to the money. "Oops," I said, feigning a flirty smile as I swept the bills back inside. "This cash is burning a hole. Ready to play, hot stuff?"

Hot stuff? Scott echoed to my thoughts. Nice. He grinned and leaned down to kiss me, hard, on the mouth. I was so surprised by this, I froze at his touch.

Relax, he spoke to my mind. We're almost in.

I gave a nearly imperceptible nod. "You're going to win big tonight, babe, I can feel it," I crooned.

The bartender unlocked a big steel door, and grasping Scott's hand, I followed him down a dark, uninviting staircase that smelled of mildew and standing water. At the bottom, we followed a hallway around several bends, until we came out in an open space sparsely decorated with poker tables. A single Mason-jar-turned-pendant hung above each table, shedding minimal light. No music, no drinks, no warm, friendly welcome.

One table was in use—four players—and I instantly spotted Pepper. He had his back to us, and he didn't turn at our approach. Not unusual. None of the other players glanced at us either. They were all tuned intently to the cards in their hands. Poker chips stood in neat towers at the center of the table. I had no idea how much money was involved, but I was betting those who lost would feel it, and deeply.

"We're looking for Pepper Friberg," Scott announced. He kept his tone light, but the way his muscles bulged when he crossed his arms sent a different message.

"Sorry, sweetheart, my dance card's full for the night," Pepper shot back cynically, brooding over the hand he'd been dealt. I studied him closely, thinking he was much too involved in the game for this to be a cover. In fact, he was so sucked in, he'd apparently completely missed that I stood beside Scott.

Scott snagged a chair from a nearby table and made room for it right next to Pepper. "I've got two left feet anyway. You'd be better off dancing with . . . Nora Grey."

Now Pepper reacted. He set his cards facedown, turning that round, full body of his to see me for himself.

"Hello, Pepper. It's been a while," I said. "The last time we met up, you tried to kidnap me, isn't that right?"

"Kidnapping is a federal offense for us Earth dwellers," Scott chimed in. "Something tells me it's frowned on in heaven, too."

"Keep your voice down," Pepper growled, nervously eyeing the other players.

I swept my eyebrows up, speaking directly to Pepper's thoughts. *You haven't told your human friends what you really are? Although I don't suppose they'd be too happy to learn that your poker*

finale   303

skills have a lot more to do with mind-compulsion than luck or skill.

"Let's take this outside," Pepper told me, folding from the game.

"Up you go," Scott said, hoisting him up by the elbow.

In the alley behind the Devil's Handbag, I spoke first. "We're going to make this simple for you, Pepper. As fun as it's been having you use me to get to Patch, I'm ready to move on. The way I figure it, that's only going to happen if I find out who's really blackmailing you," I said, testing him. I wanted to tell him my theory: that he was playing errand boy for a secret group of archangels and needed a half-decent excuse to send Patch to hell. But in the name of playing it safe, I decided to hold off and see how this shook out.

Pepper squinted at me, his features as disgruntled as they were skeptical. "What's this about?"

"Which is where we come in," Scott chimed in. "We're motivated to find your blackmailer."

Pepper narrowed his eyes further at Scott. "Who are you?"

"Think of me as the ticking bomb under your seat. If you don't make a decision to agree to Nora's terms, I'll make it for you." Scott started rolling up his sleeves.

"Are you threatening me?" Pepper asked incredulously.

"Here are my terms," I said. "We'll find your blackmailer, and we'll deliver them to you. What we want in return is simple. Swear an oath to leave Patch alone." I slapped a pointy toothpick into Pepper's fleshy palm. Since the bartender had frisked me, it was the best I could do. "A little blood and a few earnest words should do the trick." If I got him to swear an oath, he'd have to slink back to the archangels with his tail between his legs and confess failure. If he refused, it only gave more validity to my theory.

"Archangels don't swear blood vows," Pepper sneered.

Getting warmer, I thought.

"Do they shove fallen angels they've got a beef with into hell?" Scott asked.

Pepper looked at us as if we were insane. "What are you raving on about?"

"How does it feel to be the archangels' peon?" I asked.

"What'd they offer you in return?" Scott demanded.

"The archangels aren't down here," I said. "You're on your own. Do you really want to go up against Patch alone?" *C'mon, Pepper,* I thought. *Tell me what I want to hear. That this contrived story of blackmail is an excuse to fulfill your assignment from a rogue group of archangels to get rid of Patch.*

Pepper's expression of disbelief deepened, and I pounced on his silence. "You're going to swear that oath right now, Pepper."

Scott and I closed in on him.

"No oath!" Pepper squeaked. "But I'll leave Patch alone—I promise!"

"If only I could trust you to keep your word," I returned. "Trouble is, I don't think you're a very honest guy. In fact, I think this whole blackmailing business is a ruse."

Pepper's eyes widened with understanding. He sputtered in disbelief, his face turning a throttled pink. "Let me see if I've got this. You think I'm after Patch for blackmailing me?" he screeched at last.

"Yeah," Scott supplied. "Yeah, we do."

"That's why he's refused to meet me? Because he thinks I want to chain him in hell? I wasn't threatening him!" Pepper squealed, his round face growing more flushed by the moment. "I wanted to offer him a job! I've been trying to get that across all along!"

Scott and I spoke at the same time. "A job?" We shared a hasty, skeptical glance.

"You were telling the truth?" I asked Pepper. "You really have a job for Patch—and that's all?"

"Yes, yes, a job," Pepper snarled. "What did you think? Crikey, what a mess. Nothing has gone as it should."

"What's the job?" I quizzed him.

"Like I'd tell you! If you'd helped me reach Patch in time, I wouldn't be in a hot mess. This whole thing is your fault. My job offer is for Patch, and Patch alone!"

"Let me get this straight," I said. "You don't think Patch is blackmailing you?"

"Why would I think that when I already know who's blackmailing me?" he fired back, exasperated.

"You know who the blackmailer is?" Scott repeated.

Pepper shot me a look of disgust. "Get this Nephil out of my face. Do I know who's blackmailing me?" he snorted impatiently. "Yes! I'm supposed to meet them tonight. And you'll never guess who it is."

"Who?" I asked.

"Ha! It would be lovely if I could tell you, wouldn't it? Trouble is, my blackmailer made me swear an oath not to reveal their identity. Don't bother probing. My lips are sealed, literally. They said they'd call with the location of the meeting twenty minutes before I have to be there. If I don't cover up this mess soon, the archangels are going to sniff me out," he added, wringing his hands. I noted that his demeanor quickly switched to fearful at the mention of other archangels.

I tried to remain unfazed. This wasn't the move I'd expected him to make. I wondered if this was a tactic to throw us off his trail—or walk us into a trap. But the sweat beading his brow and the desperate look in his eyes seemed genuine. He wanted this over as badly as we did.

"My blackmailer wants me to enchant objects using the powers of heaven that all archangels possess." Pepper dabbed his pink forehead with a handkerchief. "That's why they're blackmailing me."

"What objects?" I asked.

Pepper shook his head. "They're going to bring them to the meeting. They said if I enchant them to their specifications, they'll leave me alone. They don't get it. Even if I enchant the objects, the powers of heaven can only be used for good. Whatever evil ideas they're entertaining, they won't work."

"Just the same, you're actually considering doing it?" I asked reprovingly.

"I need them off my back! The archangels can't know what I've been doing. I'll be banished. They'll rip out my wings and it'll all be over. I'll be stuck down here forever."

"We need a plan," Scott said. "Twenty minutes between the call and the meeting doesn't give us a lot of wiggle room."

"When your blackmailer calls, agree to the meeting," I instructed Pepper. "If they tell you to come alone, say you will. Sound as compliant and cooperative as you possibly can without going over the top."

"And then what?" Pepper asked, flapping his shoulders as if to air out his armpits. I tried not to stare. Never could I have guessed that the first archangel I'd meet would be such a sniveling, cowardly rat. So much for the archangels of my dreams—powerful, inescapable, all-knowing, and perhaps most important, exemplary.

I fixed my eyes on Pepper's. "And then Scott and I will go in your place, take the blackmailer down, and deliver them to you."

WHAT! YOU CAN'T DO THAT!" PEPPER SPAT the words vehemently. "They won't be happy, and they'll refuse to work with me. Worse, they might go straight to the archangels!"

"Your blackmailer doesn't work with you anymore. From now on, he or she deals directly with us," I said. "Scott and I are going to retrieve the objects they want enchanted, and we might need your cooperation in evaluating them. If you can tell us what you think they might have intended to use them for, the information could be valuable."

"How do I even know if I can trust you?" Pepper said in high-pitched protest.

"There's always a blood oath. . . ." I let the idea dangle. "I'll swear my intentions, and you'll swear to stay away from Patch. Unless, of course, you're still too good for an oath."

"This is awful," Pepper said, tugging at his collar like it was pinching him. "What a tangle."

"Scott and I will have a team in place. Nothing will go wrong," I reassured Pepper, then added a quick private instruction to Scott using mind-speak: *Keep him calm while I call Patch, will you?*

I walked to the end of the alley before placing the call. Dried leaves rustled past my feet, and I snuggled deeper into my coat for warmth. Of all the nights to be out, I'd chosen the coldest one yet. Frost bit into my skin and made my nose run. "It's me. We've got Pepper."

I heard Patch sigh in relief.

"I don't think the double life is an act," I went on. "He's got a genuine gambling problem. Nor do I think he's on a mission from the archangels to chain you in hell. He might have been down here on assignment originally, but he's given it up in favor of indulging in a human lifestyle. Now for the big news. He knows you aren't blackmailing him—all this time he's been trying to pencil you in for a job."

"What job?"

"He didn't say. I think he's dropped it. He's got bigger problems to fret over. He's scheduled to meet with the real blackmailer tonight." I didn't say the rest, but that didn't keep me from thinking it. I felt so confident Dabria was behind this, I would have bet my life on it. "We don't know the time or the meeting place yet. When the blackmailer calls Pepper, we're going to have a twenty-minute window. We'll need to move fast."

"Do you think it's a trap?"

"I think Pepper is a coward, and he's glad we're going in and he doesn't have to."

"I'm ready," Patch said grimly. "As soon as I know where we're heading, I'll meet you there. Do one last thing for me, Angel."

"Name it."

"I want to find you safe and sound when this is over."

The call came ten minutes before midnight. Pepper couldn't have given better answers if he'd rehearsed them. "Yes, I'll come alone." "Yes, I'll enchant the objects." "Yes, I can be at the cemetery in twenty minutes."

The instant he hung up, I said, "Which cemetery? Coldwater's?"

A nod. "Inside the mausoleum. I'm supposed to wait there for further instructions."

I turned to Scott. "There's only one mausoleum in the city cemetery. It's right by my dad's gravesite. We couldn't have picked a better spot ourselves. There are trees and headstones everywhere, and it will be dark. The blackmailer won't be able to tell it's you in the mausoleum, not Pepper, until it's too late."

Scott tugged the black hoodie he'd been carrying all night over his head, leaving the hood partly up to cover his face. "I'm a lot taller than Pepper," he said doubtfully.

"Walk hunched over. Your sweatshirt is baggy enough that they won't be able to tell the difference from a distance." I faced Pepper. "Give me your phone number. Keep the line open. I'll call you the minute we have your blackmailer."

"I have a bad feeling," Pepper said, wiping his palms on his slacks.

Scott lifted the hem of his hoodie, revealing to Pepper his unusual belt, which was glowing an unearthly blue. "We aren't going unprepared."

Pepper's lips pinched together, but not before a wail of disapproval escaped. "Devilcraft. The archangels can never know I was involved in this."

"Once Scott immobilizes your blackmailer, Patch and I will rush in. This is about as simple as it gets," I explained to Pepper.

"How do you know they won't have their own backup?" he challenged.

An image of Dabria flashed across my mind. She had only one friend, and even that was putting it kindly. Too bad that one friend would be instrumental in bringing her down tonight. I couldn't wait to see the look on her face when Patch jabbed a sharp, and hopefully rusty, object in her wing scars.

"If we're gonna do this, we gotta roll," Scott told me, glancing at his watch. "T-minus fifteen minutes."

I grabbed Pepper's sleeve before he could run off. "Don't forget your end of the bargain, Pepper. Once we have your blackmailer, you and Patch are done."

He nodded earnestly. "I'll leave Patch alone. You have my word." I didn't like the spark of mischief that seemed to flare momentarily at the backs of his eyes. "But I can't help it if he comes looking for me," he added cryptically.

CHAPTER

28

S COTT DROVE HIS BARRACUDA ACROSS TOWN, AND
I rode shotgun. He had the stereo turned low, playing
Radiohead. His hard, set features flashed in and out of sight
as we passed under cones of streetlight. He drove with both hands
on the steering wheel, at ten and two precisely.

"Nervous?" I asked.

"Don't insult me, Grey." He smiled, but it wasn't relaxed.

"So. What's up with you and Vee?" I asked, trying to keep our minds off what lay ahead. No need to overthink things, or start imagining worst-case scenarios. It was Patch, Scott, and me against Dabria. The take-down wouldn't last more than a couple of seconds.

"Don't get all girlie on me."

"It's a valid question."

Scott bumped the stereo up a few notches. "I don't kiss and tell."

"So you *have* kissed!" I waggled my eyebrows. "Anything else I should know?"

He almost smiled. "Absolutely not." The cemetery came into view around the next bend, and he tipped his head toward it. "Where do you want me to park?"

"Here. We'll walk the rest of the way."

Scott nodded. "Lots of trees. Easy to hide. You'll be in the upper parking lot?"

"Bird's-eye view. Patch will be stationed by the south gate. We won't let you out of our sight."

"You won't."

I didn't comment on the ongoing rivalry between Patch and Scott. Patch might hold Scott in the same regard as a snake underfoot, but if he said he'd be there, he would.

We swung out of the Barracuda. Scott tugged his hoodie down to hide his face, and slumped his shoulders. "How do I look?"

"Like Pepper's long-lost twin. Remember, the minute the blackmailer enters the mausoleum, handcuff them with the whip. I'll be waiting for your call."

finale

Scott gave me a fist bump—good luck, I supposed—then took off at a steady jog toward the cemetery gates. I watched him swing over them with ease and disappear into the darkness.

I called Patch. After several rings, it went to voice mail. Impatiently I told the recording, "Scott's gone in. I'm heading to my post. Call me the minute you get this. I need to know you're in position."

I hung up, shivering against the gusts of icy wind. It rattled branches that autumn had stripped bare with a hollow, clanging sound. I stuffed my hands under my arms to warm them. Something didn't feel right. It wasn't like Patch to ignore a call, especially one from me, during an urgent situation. I wanted to discuss this inopportune turn of events with Scott, but he was already out of sight. If I chased him now, I'd risk blowing the operation. Instead I hiked uphill toward the parking lot that sat on a ridge overlooking the cemetery.

Once in position, I gazed down at the crooked rows of headstones rising out of grass so dark it appeared black. Stone angels with chipped wings seemed to float in the air just above the ground. Clouds obscured the moon, and two of the five lights in the parking lot were out. Below, the white mausoleum radiated a faint ghostly luminescence.

Scott! I shouted in mind-speak, putting all my mental energy behind it. When only the whistle of wind sweeping over the hills answered, I assumed he was out of range. I didn't know how far mind-speak traveled, but it seemed Scott was too far away.

A rubble stone wall bordered the parking lot, and I crouched behind it, keeping my eyes trained on the mausoleum. A rangy black dog leaped suddenly over the wall, nearly causing me to fall back in fright. A pair of feral eyes gazed out from the ragtag animal's narrow face. The wild dog paced beside the wall, stopped to growl territorially at me, then bounded out of sight. *Thank goodness.*

My vision was better than it had been when I was human, but I was far enough away from the mausoleum that I couldn't make out nearly as many details as I would have liked. The door appeared shut, but that made sense; Scott would have closed it behind him.

I held my breath, waiting for Scott to emerge dragging Dabria, bound and helpless. Minutes ticked by. I shifted on my haunches, trying to get blood flow to my legs. I checked my cell phone. No missed calls. I could only assume Patch was sticking to the plan and patrolling the cemetery's lower gate.

A horrible thought struck me. What if Dabria saw through Scott's disguise? What if she suspected he'd brought backup? My stomach slid to my knees. What if she'd called Pepper with a revised meeting place after Scott and I had left the Devil's Handbag? Either way, Pepper would have known to call me. We'd traded numbers.

I was occupied with these troubling thoughts when the black dog returned, directing a menacing gnarl at me from the shadow of the wall. He flattened his ears against his head and arched his back threateningly.

finale

"Shoo!" I hissed back, gesturing with my hand.

This time he bared pointy white teeth, pawing the dirt ferociously. I was just about to move a safe distance down the wall, when—

A hot wire cut into my throat from behind, blocking my airway. I clawed at the wire, feeling it constrict tighter and tighter. I'd fallen back on my rear, my legs jerking. From my peripheral vision, I noted an eerie blue light emanating from the wire. It seemed to burn my skin like it had been dipped in acid. My fingers blistered with heat where they scratched at the wire, making it agonizing to grip.

My attacker jerked back on the wire, harder. Lights exploded across my vision. An ambush.

The black dog continued to bark and leap wildly in circles, but the image was quickly dissolving. I was losing consciousness. Summoning what little energy remained, I focused on the dog, urging it in mind-speak. Bite! Bite my attacker!

I was too weak to attempt a mind-trick on my attacker, knowing they'd feel me groping clumsily in their mind. Though I'd never attempted to mind-trick an animal, the dog was smaller than a Nephil or a fallen angel, and if it was possible to compel them, it made sense that a slightly smaller animal would require less effort. . . .

Attack! I thought at the dog again, feeling my mind slide down a dark, drowsy tunnel.

To my astonishment and disbelief, the dog raced forward and sank his jaws into my attacker's leg. I heard a sharp nip of teeth on bone, and a male's guttural curse. The familiarity of the voice stunned me. I knew that voice. I trusted that voice.

Propelled by betrayal and anger, I lunged into action. The dog's bite was just enough of a distraction for my attacker to loosen his grip on the wire. I closed my hands fully around it, ignoring the fiery burn long enough to yank it from my neck and fling it aside. The snakelike wire skittered over the gravel, and I recognized it in an instant.

Scott's whip.

CHAPTER

29

BUT IT WASN'T SCOTT ATTACKING ME.

Gagging and wheezing as I sucked air back into my lungs, I saw Dante move to attack, and immediately spun around and shoved my foot into his stomach. He flew back, tumbling to the ground, looking startled.

His eyes instantly hardened. So did mine. I pounced on him, straddling his chest, and mercilessly slammed his head repeatedly into the ground. Not enough to knock him out; I wanted him stunned, but still able to speak. I had plenty of questions I wanted answered *now*.

Bring me the whip, I ordered the dog, transmitting a picture of it to his mind so he'd understand my command.

The dog obediently trotted over, dragging the whip between his teeth, seemingly immune to the effects of devilcraft. Was it possible this prototype couldn't harm him? Either way, I couldn't believe it. I could *mind-speak* to animals. Or at least this one.

I rolled Dante onto his stomach and used the whip to hand-cuff his wrists. It burned my fingers, but I was too angry to care. He made a groan of protest.

Standing, I kicked his ribs to get him fully awake. "The first words out of your mouth had better be an explanation," I said.

With one cheek pressed into the gravel, his lips curved into a bullying smile. "I didn't know it was you," he said innocently, mocking me.

I crouched down, locking our gazes. "If you don't want to talk to me, I'll turn you over to Patch. You and I both know that road will be a lot more unpleasant."

"Patch." Dante chuckled. "Call him. Go ahead. See if he answers."

Icy fear fluttered in my chest. "What do you mean?"

"Unlock my hands and maybe I'll tell you, in great detail, what I did to him."

I slapped him across the face so hard my own hand stung. "Where is Patch?" I asked again, trying to keep the panic out of my voice, knowing it would only amuse Dante.

finale

"Do you want to know what I did to Patch . . . or to Patch *and* Scott?"

The ground seemed to tilt. We'd been ambushed all right. Dante had taken Patch and Scott out of the picture, and then come for me. But *why*?

I put the puzzle together on my own.

"You're blackmailing Pepper Friberg. That's what you're doing here at the graveyard, isn't it? Don't bother answering. It's the only explanation that makes sense." I'd thought it was Dabria. If I hadn't been so set on it, maybe I could have seen the bigger picture, maybe I could have been open to another possibility, maybe I could have picked up warning signs—

Dante stretched out a long, evasive sigh. "I'll talk after you untie my hands. Not the other way around."

I was so consumed by anger, I was surprised to find tears burning at the backs of my eyes. I'd trusted Dante. I'd let him train and advise me. I'd built a relationship with him. I'd come to regard him as one of my allies in the Nephilim world. Without his guidance, I wouldn't have made it half as far.

"Why did you do it? Why did you blackmail Pepper? Why?" I shouted when Dante merely blinked up at me in smug silence.

I couldn't bring myself to kick him again. I could hardly stand, I was so overcome with hot, aching betrayal. I leaned against the stone wall, breathing deeply to keep my head on straight. My knees shook. The back of my throat felt slippery and tight.

BECCA FITZPATRICK

"Untie my hands, Nora. I wasn't going to hurt you—not really. I needed to calm you down, that's all. I wanted to talk to you and explain what I'm doing and why." He spoke with calm assurance, but I wasn't going to fall for it.

"Are either Patch or Scott hurt?" I asked. Patch couldn't feel physical pain, but that didn't mean Dante wasn't employing some new devilcraft prototype to cause him harm.

"No. I tied them up the same way you've tied me. They're about as pissed off as I've ever seen them, but no one is in immediate danger. The devilcraft isn't good for them, but they can last awhile longer without negative side effects."

"Then I'm going to give you exactly three minutes to answer my questions before I go after them. If you haven't answered my questions to my satisfaction in that time, I'm calling out the coyotes. They've been a nuisance around these parts, eating domestic cats and small dogs, especially with winter coming on and food scarce. But I'm sure you watch the news."

Dante snorted. "What are you talking about?"

"I can mind-speak to animals, Dante. Hence the dog attacking you at exactly the moment I needed him. I'm sure the coyotes wouldn't mind an easy snack. I can't kill you, but that doesn't mean I can't make you regret crossing me. First question: Why are you blackmailing Pepper Friberg? Nephilim don't dance with archangels."

Dante winced as he tried unsuccessfully to roll onto his back.

finale

"Can't you untie the whip so we can have a civil talk?"

"You threw civility out the window the minute you tried to strangle me."

"I'll need a lot more than three minutes to tell you what's going on," Dante returned without sounding the least bit concerned by my threat. I decided it was time to show him just how serious I was.

Food, I told the black dog, which had hung around to watch the proceedings with interest. With his fur lying flat, I could tell he was scrawny and half-starved, and if I'd needed more evidence of his hunger, his anxious pacing and the routine licking of his lips would have been plenty. To clarify my command, I sent to his mind a picture of Dante's flesh, then stepped back, relinquishing my claim on Dante. The dog loped over and sank his teeth into the back of Dante's arm.

Dante cursed and attempted to squirm away. "I couldn't have Pepper muddling up my plans!" he spat finally. "Call off the dog!"

"What plans?"

Dante writhed, hitching up his shoulder to fend off the dog. "Pepper was sent down to Earth by the archangels to run a full-fledged investigation into me and Blakely."

I worked this scenario out in my head, then nodded. "Because the archangels suspect that devilcraft didn't disappear with Hank, and that you're still using it, but they want to know for sure before they act. Makes sense. Keep talking."

"So I needed a way to distract Pepper, all right? Get your dog off me!"

"You still haven't told me why you're blackmailing him."

Dante squirmed once again to avoid my new favorite dog's snapping jaws. "Give me a break here."

"The faster you talk, the sooner I give my new best friend here something else to snack on."

"Fallen angels need Pepper to enchant several objects using the powers of heaven. They know about devilcraft, and they know Blakely and I control it, so they want to harness the powers of heaven—they want to make sure Nephilim don't stand a chance at winning the war. They're blackmailing Pepper."

Okay. This also seemed plausible. There was just one thing that still didn't make sense. "How are you messed up in this?"

"I'm working for the fallen angels," he said so quietly I was sure I'd heard wrong.

I leaned closer. "Care to repeat that?"

"I'm a sellout, all right? The Nephilim aren't going to win this war," he added defensively. "Any way you size it up, when all is said and done, fallen angels are going to come out of this on top. And not just because they intend to harness the powers of heaven. The archangels are sympathetic to fallen angels. Old ties run deep. Not so for us. The archangels consider our race an abomination, always have. They want us gone, and if that means temporarily siding with fallen angels to accomplish it, they'll do it. Only those of us who form an alliance with fallen angels early on have any chance at survival."

I stared at Dante, unable to digest his words. Dante Matterazzi, in bed with the enemy. The same Dante who'd stood by the Black Hand's side. The same Dante who'd trained me so faithfully. I couldn't grasp it. "What about our Nephilim army?" I said, my anger surging.

"It's doomed. Deep down, you know it. There isn't a lot of time left before fallen angels make their move and we're thrust into war. I've agreed to give devilcraft to them. They'll have the powers of heaven *and* hell—and the backing of the archangels. The whole thing will be over in less than a day. If you help me get Pepper to enchant the objects, I'll vouch for you. I'll make sure some of the most influential fallen angels know you helped out and are loyal to the cause."

I took a step back, seeing Dante through new eyes. I didn't even know who he was. He couldn't have been more of a stranger to me at that moment. "I don't— This whole revolution— All lies?" I finally managed to choke out.

"Self-preservation," he said. "I did it to save myself."

"And the rest of the Nephilim race?" I sputtered.

His silence told me just how concerned he was about their well-being. A disinterested shrug couldn't have been more telling. Dante was in this for himself, end of story.

"They believe in you," I said with a sick feeling swelling in my heart. "They're counting on you."

"They're counting on you."

I flinched. The full impact of the responsibility weighing on my shoulders seemed to crush me at that moment. I was their leader. I was the face on this campaign. And now my most trusted adviser was defecting. If the army had been standing on weak legs before, one of those knees had just been kicked out.

"You can't do this to me," I said threateningly. "I'll expose you. I'll tell everyone what you're really up to. I don't know everything about Nephilim law, but I'm pretty sure they have a system to take care of traitors, and I somehow doubt it will be very judicial!"

"And who's going to believe you?" said Dante simply. "If I argue that you're the real traitor, who do you think they'll believe?"

He was right. Who would Nephilim believe? The young, inexperienced imposter placed in power by her dead father, or the strong, capable, and charismatic man who had both the looks and skill of a fabled Roman god?

"I have pictures," Dante said. "Of you with Patch. Of you with Pepper. Even some of you looking friendly with Dabria. I'll pin this on you, Nora. You're sympathetic to the fallen angel cause. That's how I'll frame it. They will destroy you."

"You can't do this," I said, rage sizzling in my chest.

"You're walking down a dead-end road. This is your last chance to turn around. Come with me. You're stronger than you think you are. We'd make an unstoppable team. I could use you—"

I gave a harsh laugh. "Oh, I'm quite finished with you using me!" I grabbed a large stone from the rubble wall, intending to smash it against Dante's skull, knock him unconscious, and recruit Patch's help in deciding what to do with him next, when a cruel and twisted smirk transformed Dante's dark features, making him appear decidedly more demon than fabled Roman god.

"What a waste of talent," he muttered in a chastising tone. His expression was too smug, given that I held him captive, and that was when an awful suspicion began to form in my mind. The whip binding his wrists wasn't causing his skin to blister the way it had mine. In fact, other than having his face planted in gravel, he didn't look uncomfortable.

The whip snapped free from Dante's wrists, and in an instant, he sprang to his feet.

"Did you really think I'd allow Blakely to create a weapon that could be used against me?" he jeered, his upper lip curling over his teeth. Commanding the whip, he cracked it at me. Scorching heat sliced across my body, pitching me off my feet. I landed hard, robbed of breath. Dizzy from the impact, I scuttled backward, trying to bring Dante into focus.

"You might like to know I have every intention of taking over your position as commander of the Nephilim army," Dante sneered. "I have the backing of the entire fallen angel race. I plan to lead the Nephilim right into the hands of fallen angels. They won't know what I've done until it's too late."

The only reason Dante would be telling me any of this was if he sincerely believed I had no chance at stopping him. But I wasn't throwing in the towel now, or ever. "You swore an oath to Hank to help me lead his army to freedom, you arrogant idiot. If you try to steal my title, we'll both see the consequences of having broken our oaths. Death, Dante. Not exactly a minor complication," I reminded him cynically.

Dante chuckled with derision. "About that oath. A complete and utter lie. When I said it, I thought it might convince you to trust me. Not that I needed to make the effort. The devilcraft prototypes I gave you have been doing a fine job of compelling you to trust me."

There was no time for his deception to fully sink in. The whip lashed fire through my clothes a second time. Urged to action solely out of self-preservation, I scrabbled over the wall, hearing the dog bark and attack behind me, and dropped to the opposite side. The steep hill, slick with dew, sent me rolling and skidding toward the gravestones far below.

30

AT THE BOTTOM OF THE HILL I LOOKED UP, BUT I didn't see Dante. The black dog bounded after me, circling me with what almost appeared to be concern. I pulled myself up to sitting. Thick clouds blotted the moon, and I shivered violently as frost nipped my skin. Suddenly acutely aware of my surroundings, I jumped to my feet and ran through the maze of graves toward the mausoleum. To my surprise, the dog raced ahead, peering back every few steps as though to make sure I was still following.

"Scott!" I called out, flinging open the mausoleum's door as I burst inside.

There were no windows. I couldn't see. Impatiently, I swept my hands out, trying to feel my surroundings. I tripped on a small object and heard it roll away. Patting my hands across the cold stone floor, I grasped the flashlight Scott had taken with him and obviously dropped, and switched it on.

There. In the corner. Scott was on his back, eyes open but dazed. I scrambled over, tugging at the blue-glowing whip scorching his wrists until it fell free. His skin blistered and oozed. He gave a pained moan.

"I think Dante is gone, but stay alert just the same," I told him. "There's a dog guarding the door—he's on our side. Stay here until I come back. I have to find Patch."

Scott groaned again, this time cursing Dante's name. "Didn't see it coming," he muttered.

That made two of us.

I rushed outside, sprinting across the cemetery, which had fallen into near-perfect darkness. I batted my way through a hedge of bushes, plowing my own shortcut to the parking lot. I leaped the wrought-iron fence and ran straight for the lone black truck parked in the lot.

I saw the eerie blue light glowing behind the windows when I was still several feet away. Wrenching the door open, I dragged Patch out, laid him on the pavement, and began the laborious process of uncoiling the whip, which snaked the width of his

finale

chest, pinning his arms at his sides like a torturous corset. His eyes were shut, his skin emanating a faint blue. At last I jerked the whip loose and flung it aside, oblivious to my burned fingers.

"Patch," I said, shaking him. Tears jumped to my eyes, and my throat clogged with emotion. "Wake up, Patch." I shook him harder. "You're going to be fine. Dante is gone, and I untied the whip. Please wake up." I pushed resolve into my voice. "You're going to be okay. We're together now. I need you to open your eyes. I need to know you can hear me."

His body felt feverish, heat pouring through his clothes, and I ripped open his shirt. I gasped at the bubbled skin, patterned where the whip had coiled. The worst wounds curled up like blackened, scorched paper. A blowtorch would have produced as much damage.

I knew he couldn't feel it, but *I* did. My jaw tightened with venomous hatred toward Dante even as tears streamed down my face. Dante had made a massive, unforgivable mistake. Patch was everything to me, and if the devilcraft left any lasting damage, I would see to it that Dante regretted this single assault as long as he lived, which if I had anything to say about it, wouldn't be long. But my seething rage was pushed aside by a consuming distress for Patch. Grief and guilt and ice-cold apprehension plummeted inside me.

"Please," I whispered, my voice rattling. "Please, Patch, wake up," I begged, kissing his mouth and wishing it would miraculously wake him. I gave my head a hard shake to dislodge the worst thoughts. I wouldn't allow them to form. Patch was a fallen angel.

He couldn't be hurt. Not this way. I didn't care how potent devil-craft was—it couldn't cause Patch permanent harm.

I felt Patch's fingers grip mine a moment before his low voice vibrated weakly in my mind. *Angel.*

At that one word, my heart soared with joy. *I'm here! I'm right here. I love you, Patch. I love you so much!* I sobbed back. Before I could restrain myself, I flung my mouth against his. I was strad-dling his hips, elbows planted on either side of his head, not want-ing to cause him any more damage, but unable to restrain myself from embracing him. Then, just like that, he hugged me in such a tight embrace, I collapsed on top of him.

"I'll injure you worse!" I shrieked, squirming to roll off him. "The devilcraft— Your skin—"

"You're just the thing to make me feel better, Angel," he mur-mured, finding my mouth and effectively cutting off my protest. His eyes were shut, lines of exhaustion and stress tightening his features, and yet the way he kissed me melted away every other worry. I relaxed my posture, sinking down on top of his long, lean form. His hand moved up the back of my shirt, feeling warm and solid as he held me close.

"I was terrified of what might have happened to you," I choked out.

"I was terrified thinking the same about you."

"The devilcraft—" I began.

Patch exhaled beneath me, and my body dipped with his. His breath carried relief and raw emotion. His eyes, stripped of everything but sincerity, found mine. "My skin can be replaced. But you can't, Angel. When Dante left, I thought it was over. I thought I'd failed you. I've never prayed so hard in my life."

I blinked back tears glittering on my lashes. "If he had taken you from me—" I was too choked up to finish the thought.

"He tried to take you from me, and that's reason enough for me to mark him a dead man. He's not getting away with this. I've forgiven him for several small trespasses in the name of trying to be civil and understanding about your role as leader of his predecessor's army, but tonight he threw out the old rules. He used devilcraft on me. I don't owe him any gestures of courtesy. Next time we meet, we'll play by my rules." Despite the exhaustion evident in every tense knot of muscle down his body, the decisiveness in his voice held no wavering or sympathy.

"He's working for fallen angels, Patch. They have him in their pocket."

I'd never seen Patch look as surprised as at that moment. His black eyes dilated, sorting out this news. "He told you that?"

I nodded soberly. "He said there's no way the Nephilim are going to come out of this war on top. Despite every convincing, contradictory, and hope-filled word he's been singing to the Nephilim," I added bitterly.

"Did he name specific fallen angels?"

"No. He's in this to save his own skin, Patch. He said when push comes to shove, the archangels will side with fallen angels.

After all, their history runs deep. It's hard to turn your back on blood, even if it is bad blood. There's more." I sucked in a sharp breath. "Dante's next move is to steal my title as leader of the Black Hand's army, and march the Nephilim straight into the hands of the fallen angels."

Patch lay in stunned silence, but I saw thoughts shooting rapid-fire behind his black eyes, which held a sharp edge. He knew, like I did, that if Dante succeeded in stripping me of my title, my oath to Hank would be broken. Failure meant only one thing: death.

"Dante is also Pepper's blackmailer," I said.

Patch gave a curt nod. "I made that assumption when he ambushed me. How did Scott fare?"

"He's in the mausoleum, with an incredibly smart stray dog watching over him."

Patch lifted his eyebrows. "Should I ask?"

"I think that dog is vying for your job as my guardian angel. He scared off Dante and is the only reason I got away."

Patch traced the curve of my cheekbone. "I'll have to thank him for saving my girl."

Despite the circumstances, I smiled. "You're going to love him. The two of you share the same fashion sense."

Two hours later I parked Patch's truck in his garage. Patch was slumped in the passenger seat, his complexion washed out, the same blue hue still radiating from his skin. He smiled his lazy smile when he spoke, but I could tell it took effort; it was a ploy to reassure me. The devilcraft had weakened him, but for how long was anyone's guess. I was grateful Dante had fled when he did. I imagined I had my new dog friend to thank for that. If Dante had hung around to finish what he'd started, we'd all have been in more danger than I suspected we could have escaped. Once again, I directed my gratitude toward the stray black dog. Scrappy and eerily smart. And loyal nearly to his own detriment.

Patch and I had stayed at the cemetery with Scott until he'd recovered enough strength to drive himself home. As for the black dog, despite several attempts to ditch him, including forcibly removing him from the bed of Patch's truck, he'd persistently leaped back inside. Giving up, we'd let him tag along. I'd take him to an animal shelter *after* I'd gotten enough sleep to start thinking clearly.

But as much as I wanted to collapse into Patch's bed the moment I stepped foot inside his townhouse, there was still work to be done. Dante was already two steps ahead. If we rested before taking countermeasures, we might as well start assembling a white flag of surrender.

I paced Patch's kitchen, clasping my hands behind my neck as though the gesture might squeeze out a brilliant next move. What was Dante thinking now? What was his next move? He'd threatened to destroy me if I accused him of treason, so he'd at least considered that I might go through with it. Which meant he was most likely busy doing one of two things. First, devising a watertight alibi. Or second, and far more troublesome, beating me to the punch by spreading news that I was the traitor. The thought froze me in my tracks.

"Start at the beginning," Patch said from the sofa. His voice was low with fatigue, but his eyes burned with wrath. He stuffed a pillow under his head and directed his full attention my way. "Tell me exactly what happened."

"When Dante told me he's working for fallen angels, I threatened to out him, but he only laughed, saying no one would believe me."

"They won't," Patch agreed bluntly.

I tipped my head against the wall, sighing in frustration. "Then he told me he plans on taking over as leader. Nephilim love him. They wish he were their leader. I can see it in their eyes. It won't matter how vehemently I try to warn them. They'll welcome him as their new leader with wide-open arms. I don't see a solution. He's got us beat."

Patch didn't answer right away. When he did, his voice was quiet. "If you publicly attack Dante, you'll give the Nephilim an excuse to rally against you, that's true. Tensions are high, and they're looking for an outlet for their uncertainty. Which is why publicly denouncing Dante is not the move we're going to make."

"Then what is?" I asked, turning to look at him straight on. He clearly had something in mind, but I couldn't guess what.

"We're going to let Pepper take care of Dante for us."

I carefully examined Patch's logic. "And Pepper will do it because he can't risk Dante ratting him out to the archangels? But then why hasn't Pepper already made Dante disappear?"

"Pepper isn't going to get his own hands dirty. He doesn't want to leave a trail leading back to him for the archangels to find." Patch's mouth hardened with a frown. "I'm starting to get an idea of what Pepper wanted from me."

"You think Pepper had hoped you'd make Dante disappear for him? Was that his so-called job offer?"

Patch's black eyes sliced into mine. "One way to find out."

"I have Pepper's number. I'll arrange the meeting right now," I said with disgust. And here I'd thought Pepper couldn't stoop any lower. Rather than man up to his own problems, the coward had tried to dump the risk on Patch.

"You know, Angel, he has something that could be useful to us," Patch added thoughtfully. "Something we might convince him to steal from heaven, if we play this right. I've tried to avoid war, but maybe it's time to fight. Let's end this. If you beat the fallen angels, your oath will be fulfilled." His eyes locked on mine. "And we'll be free. Together. No more war, no more Cheshvan."

I started to ask what he was thinking, when the obvious answer hit me. I couldn't believe I hadn't thought of it before. Yes, Pepper did have access to something that would give us bargaining power over fallen angels—and secure Nephilim faith in me. Then again, did we really want to go down that road? Was it our right to put the entire fallen angel population at grave risk?

"I don't know, Patch. . . ."

Patch stood and reached for his leather jacket. "Call Pepper. We're meeting him now."

The lot behind the gas station was empty. The sky was black, and so were the store's greasy windows. Patch parked his motorcycle, and we both swung off. A short, pudgy form waddled out of the shadows and, after looking apprehensively around, scurried over to us.

Pepper's eyes danced self-righteously at the sight of Patch. "Look a little worse for wear, old friend. I think it's fair to say life on Earth hasn't been kind."

Patch ignored the insult. "We know Dante is your blackmailer."

"Yes, yes, Dante. The dirty pig. Tell me something I don't know."

"I want to hear about your job offer."

Pepper drummed his fingertips together, his shrewd eyes never leaving Patch's. "I know you and your girlfriend here killed Hank Millar. I need someone ruthless like that."

"We had help. The archangels," Patch reminded him.

"I'm an archangel," Pepper said peevishly. "I want Dante dead, and I'll give you the tools to do it."

Patch nodded. "We'll do it. At the right price."

Pepper blinked, taken aback. I didn't think he'd expected to come to an agreement so easily. He cleared his throat. "What did you have in mind?"

finale

Patch glanced at me, and I inclined my head. Time to pull out the proverbial ace up the sleeve. With little time to consider, Patch and I had decided this was one card we couldn't afford not to play.

"We want access to every fallen angel feather being stored in heaven," I announced.

The pompous smirk drained from Pepper's eyes, and he gave a cold bark of laughter. "Are you out of your mind? I can't give you that. It would take a whole committee to release those feathers. And what are you planning to do? Burn the whole lot of them? You'd send every fallen angel on Earth to hell!"

"Would you really be that disappointed?" I asked him in all seriousness.

"Who cares what I think?" he growled. "There are rules. There are procedures. Only fallen angels who've committed a serious crime or breach of humanity are sent to hell."

"You're out of options," Patch stated coldly. "We both know you can get the feathers. You know where they're stored, and you know the procedure for releasing them. You have everything you need. Devise a plan and carry it out. Either that, or take your chances against Dante."

"One feather, possibly! But thousands? I'll never get away with it!" Pepper protested shrilly.

Patch stepped toward him, and Pepper shrank back in fear, his arms flying up to shield his face.

"Look around," Patch told him in a quiet, lethal voice. "This isn't a place you want to call home. You'll be the newest fallen angel, and they'll make you remember it. You won't last a week of initia-tion."

"I-i-initiation?"

Patch's black stare sent a shiver up my spine.

"W-w-what do I do?" Pepper wailed softly. "I can't go through initiation. I can't live on Earth full-time. I need to be able to go back to heaven when I want."

"Get the feathers."

"I can't d-d-do it." Pepper hiccuped.

"You don't have a choice. You're going to get those feathers, Pepper. And I'm going to kill Dante. Have you thought this plan through?"

A miserable nod. "I'll bring you a special dagger. It will kill Dante. If the archangels come after you, and you try to give them my name, you'll cut your own tongue out with the dagger. I've enchanted it. The dagger won't let you betray me."

"Fair enough."

"If we go through with this, you can't contact me. Not while I'm in heaven. All communication goes dark until I finish. If I can finish," he whimpered wretchedly. "I'll let you know when I have the feathers."

"We need them by tomorrow," I told Pepper.

"Tomorrow?" he fussed. "Do you realize what you're asking?"

"Monday at midnight at the latest," Patch said with no room for compromise.

finale

Pepper gave a queasy nod. "I'll get as many as I can."

"You need to clear out the inventory," I told him. "That's our deal."

Pepper swallowed. "Every last one of them?"

That was the idea, yes. If Pepper succeeded in getting the feathers, the Nephilim would have a way of winning the war with a single strike of a match. Since we couldn't chain fallen angels in hell ourselves, we'd let their Achilles' heels—their former angelic feathers—do it for us. Every fallen angel would be given a choice: release their Nephilim vassal from their oath and swear a new oath of peace, or make a new home for themselves in a place much hotter than Coldwater, Maine.

If our plan worked, it wouldn't matter if Dante accused me of treason. If I won the war, nothing else would matter to the Nephilim. And despite their lack of faith in me, I *wanted* to win this for them. It was the right thing to do.

I met Pepper's gaze, putting steel behind mine. "All of them."

CHAPTER

31

S COTT CALLED ME AS SOON AS PATCH AND I WERE BACK at the townhouse. It was now Sunday, just after three in the morning. Patch closed the front door behind us, and I put the phone on speaker.

"We might have a problem," Scott said. "I've gotten a handful of texts from friends saying Dante is making a public announcement to Nephilim later tonight at Delphic, after closing. After what happened tonight, anybody else find this odd?"

Patch swore.

I tried to stay calm, but black tinged the edges of my vision.

"Everyone's speculating, and the theories are all over the board," Scott continued. "Any idea what this is about? The prick pretended to be your boyfriend and then *wham*. Earlier tonight. And now this."

I braced my hand on the wall for support. My head spun and my knees shook. Patch took the phone from me.

"She'll call you back, Scott. Let us know if you hear anything else."

I sank into Patch's sofa. I stuck my head between my knees and drew several rapid breaths. "He's going to publicly accuse me of treason. Later tonight."

"Yes," Patch agreed quietly.

"They'll lock me in prison. They'll try to torture a confession out of me."

Patch knelt in front of me and placed his hands protectively on my hips. "Look at me, Angel."

My brain automatically switched into action. "We have to contact Pepper. We need the dagger sooner than we thought. We need to kill Dante before he can make his announcement." A rattled sob escaped my chest. "What if we don't get the dagger in time?"

Patch drew my head against his chest, gently kneading the muscles at the back of my neck that were clenched so tight I thought they'd snap. "Do you think I'm going to let them lay a

BECCA FITZPATRICK

single hand on you?" he said in that same soft voice.

"Oh, Patch!" I flung my arms around his neck, tears warming my face. "What are we going to do?"

He tilted my face to look at his. He brushed his thumbs under my eyes, drying my tears. "Pepper is going to come through. He's going to bring me the dagger, and I'm going to kill Dante. You're going to get the feathers and win the war. And then I'm taking you away. Someplace where we'll never hear the words 'Cheshvan' or 'war' again." He looked like he wanted to believe it, but his voice wavered just enough.

"Pepper promised us the feathers and dagger by Monday at midnight. But what about Dante's announcement tonight? We can't stop him. Pepper has to bring the dagger sooner. We have to find a way to contact him. We'll have to risk it."

Patch fell silent, rubbing his hand across his mouth in thought. At last he said, "Pepper can't solve the problem of tonight—we're going to have to do that ourselves." His eyes, unshaken and determined, flicked up to mine. "You're going to request an urgent and mandatory meeting with the most prominent Nephilim, schedule it for tonight, and steal Dante's thunder. Everyone is expecting you to launch an offensive, to catapult our races into war, and they'll think this is it—your first military move. Your announcement will trump Dante's. The Nephilim will come, and out of curiosity, so will Dante.

"In front of everyone, you'll make it very clear you're aware there are factions in favor of putting Dante in power. Then you'll tell them you're going to put their doubts to rest once and for all. Convince them you want to be their ruler, and that you believe you can do a better job than Dante. Then challenge him to a duel for power."

I stared at Patch, confused and dubious. "A duel? With Dante? I can't fight him—he'll win."

"If we can delay the duel until Pepper gets back, the duel will be nothing more than a gimmick to stall Dante and buy us time."

"And if we can't delay the duel?"

Patch's eyes cut sharply to mine, but he didn't answer my question. "We have to act now. If Dante finds out you've also got something to say tonight, he'll put his plans on hold until he knows what you're up to. He has nothing to lose. He knows if you publicly denounce him, he merely has to point a finger at you. Trust me, when he finds out you're challenging him to a duel, he'll break out the champagne. He's cocky, Nora. And egotistical. It will never cross his mind that you can win. He'll agree to duel, thinking you've just dropped a cake in his lap. A messy public pronouncement of your treason and a drawn-out trial . . . or stealing your power with a single shot from a pistol? He'll kick himself for not thinking of it first."

My joints felt as though they'd been replaced with rubber. "If the duel goes through, we'll fight with guns?"

"Or swords. Your preference, but I'd strongly suggest pistols. It will be easier for you to learn to shoot than to sword fight," Patch said calmly, clearly not hearing the distress in my voice.

I felt like throwing up. "Dante will agree to duel because he knows he can beat me. He's stronger than I am, Patch. Who knows how much devilcraft he's consumed? It won't be a fair fight."

Patch took my trembling hands and brushed a soothing kiss across my knuckles. "Dueling went out of fashion hundreds of years ago in human culture, but it's still socially acceptable to Nephilim. In their eyes, it's the fastest and most obvious way of solving a disagreement. Dante wants to be leader of the Nephilim army, and you're going to make him and every other Nephil believe you want it just as badly."

"Why don't we just tell prominent Nephilim about the feathers at the meeting?" My heart surged with hope. "They won't care about anything else when they know I have a surefire way of winning the war and restoring peace."

"If Pepper fails, they'll see it as your failure. Getting close won't count. Either they'll hail you as a savior for getting the feathers, or they'll crucify you for flopping. Until we know for sure Pepper has succeeded, we can't mention the feathers."

I raked my hands through my hair. "I can't do this."

Patch said, "If Dante is working for fallen angels, and if he gains power, the Nephilim race will be more deeply in bondage than ever before. I worry fallen angels will use devilcraft to make Nephilim slaves long after Cheshvan ends."

I shook my head miserably. "There's too much at stake. What if I fail?" And undoubtedly I would.

"There's more, Nora. Your oath to Hank."

Dread formed like chunks of ice in the pit of my stomach. Once again, I remembered every word I'd spoken to Hank Millar the night he'd pressured me to take up the reins of his doomed uprising. *I'll lead your army. If I break this promise, I understand my mom and I are both as good as dead.* Which didn't leave me much of a choice, did it? If I wanted to stay on Earth with Patch, and preserve my mom's life, I had to keep my title as leader of the Nephilim army. I couldn't let Dante steal it from me.

"A duel is a rare show, and throw in two high-profile Nephilim, such as you and Dante, and this will be an event not to be missed," Patch said. "I'm hoping for the best, that we'll be able to push out the duel, and that Pepper won't fail, but I think we should prepare for the worst. The duel might be your only way out."

"Just how large of an audience are we talking?"

Patch's gaze as it met mine was cool and confident. But for a moment, I saw sympathy flicker behind his eyes. "Hundreds."

I swallowed hard. "I can't do this."

"I'll train you, Angel. I'll be by your side every step of the way. You're far stronger than you were two weeks ago, and all that after a few hours of work with a trainer who was only doing enough to make you think he was invested. He wanted you to think he was training you, but I highly doubt he was doing much more than putting your muscles through the minimum resistance. I don't think you realize just how powerful you are. With true training, you can beat him."

Patch clasped the back of my neck, pulling our faces together. He looked at me with such confidence and trust it nearly shattered my heart. *You can do this. It's a task no one would envy, and I admire you even more for considering it,* he spoke to my mind.

"Isn't there some other way?" But I'd spent the past several moments frantically analyzing the circumstances from every possible angle. With Pepper's questionable chance at success, combined with the oath I swore to Hank, and the precarious situation of the entire Nephilim race, there was no other way. I had to go through with this.

"Patch, I'm scared," I whispered.

He pulled me into his arms. He kissed the top of my head and stroked my hair. He didn't need to say the words for me to know he was frightened too. "I'm not letting you lose this duel, Angel. I'm not letting you face Dante without knowing I control the outcome. The duel will appear fair, but it won't be. Dante sealed his fate the moment he turned on you. I'm not letting him off the hook." His murmured words hardened. "He won't come out of this alive."

"Can you rig the duel?"

The vengeance smoldering in his gaze told me all I needed to know.

"If anyone were to find out—" I began.

Patch kissed me, hard, but with an amused glint in his eye. "If I get caught, it'll mean the end of kissing you. Do you really think I'd risk that?" His face grew serious. "I know I can't feel your touch, but

finale   349

I feel your love, Nora. Inside me. It means everything to me. I wish I could feel you the same way you feel me, but I have your love. Nothing will ever outweigh that. Some people go their entire lives never feeling the emotions you've given me. There is no regret in that."

My chin quivered. "I'm scared of losing you. I'm scared of failing, and of what will happen to us. I don't want to do this," I protested, even though I knew there was no magic trapdoor to escape through. I couldn't run; I couldn't hide. The oath I'd sworn to Hank would find me, no matter how hard I tried to disappear. I had to stay in power. As long as the army existed, I had to see this through. I squeezed Patch's hands. "Promise you'll be with me the whole time. Promise you won't make me go through this alone."

Patch tipped my chin up. "If I could make this go away, I would. If I could stand in your place, I wouldn't hesitate. But I'm left with one choice, and that's to stand by your side through the end. I won't waver, Angel, I can promise you that." He ran his hands over my arms, unaware that his promise did more to warm me than the gesture. It nearly brought me to tears. "I'll start leaking news that you've called an urgent meeting for tonight. I'll call Scott first, and tell him to get the word out. It won't take long for news to spread. Dante will have heard your announcement before the end of the hour."

My stomach took a nauseating lurch. I chewed at the inside of my cheek, then forced myself to nod. I might as well accept the inevitable. The sooner I confronted what lay ahead, the sooner I could formulate a plan to conquer my fear.

"What can I do to help?" I asked.

Patch studied me, frowning slightly. He stroked his thumb over my lip, then across my cheek. "You're ice cold, Angel." He tilted his head toward the hallway leading deeper into the townhouse. "Let's get you into bed. I'll light the fireplace. What you need right now is warmth and rest. I'll draw a hot bath, too."

Sure enough, fierce shivers racked my body. It was as if, in an instant, all heat had been sucked from me. I supposed I was going into shock. My teeth chattered, and the tips of my fingers vibrated with a strange, involuntary tremor.

Patch scooped me up and carried me back to his bedroom. He nudged the door open with his shoulder, peeled back the duvet, and deposited me gently in his bed. "A drink?" he asked. "Herbal tea? Broth?"

Looking at his face, so earnest and anxious, guilt spiraled inside me. I knew right then that Patch would do anything for me. His promise to stay by my side was as good to him as a sworn oath. He was part of me, and I was part of him. He would do whatever—whatever—it took to keep me here with him.

I forced myself to open my mouth before I chickened out. "There's something I need to tell you," I said, my voice sounding thin and brittle. I hadn't planned on crying, but tears welled in my eyes. I was overcome with shame.

"Angel?" Patch said, his tone questioning.

I'd taken that first step, but now I froze. A voice of justification

finale

drifted across my mind, telling me I had no right to dump this on Patch. Not in his current weakened state. If I cared about him, I'd keep my mouth shut. His recovery was more important than getting a few white lies off my chest. Already I felt those same icy hands slide up my throat.

"I— It's nothing," I corrected. "I just need sleep. And you need to call Scott." I turned into the pillow so he wouldn't see me cry. The icy hands felt all too real, ready to close on my neck if I said too much, if I told my secret.

"I need to call him, that's true. But more than that, I need you to tell me what's going on," Patch said, just enough concern slipping into his tone to tell me I was past the point where I could use a simple distraction to get out of this.

The freezing hands curled around my throat. I was too scared to speak. Too scared of the hands, and how they would hurt me.

Patch clicked on a bedside lamp, pulling gently on my shoulder, trying to see my face, but I only twisted farther away. "I love you," I choked out. Shame ballooned inside me. How could I say those words and lie to him?

"I know. Just like I know you're holding something back. This isn't the time for secrets. We've come too far to turn down that road," Patch reminded me.

I nodded, feeling tears slide onto the pillowcase. He was right. I knew it, but it didn't make it any easier to come clean. And I didn't know if I could. Those wintry hands, closing off my throat, my voice . . .

Patch slipped into bed beside me, dragging me against him. I felt his breath on the back of my neck, the warmth of his skin touching mine. His knee fit perfectly in the crook of my own. He kissed my shoulder, his black hair falling over my ear.

I—lied—to—you, I confessed to his thoughts, feeling as though I had to push the words out through a brick wall. I tensed, waiting for the cold hands to seize me, but to my surprise, their grip seemed to weaken at my confession. Their chilly touch slipped and faltered. Buoyed by this small step forward, I pushed on. I lied to the one person whose trust means more to me than anything. I lied to you, Patch, and I don't know if I can forgive myself.

Rather than demand an explanation, Patch continued a trail of slow, steady kisses down my arm. It wasn't until he'd pressed a kiss into the inside of my wrist that he spoke. "Thank you for telling me," he said quietly.

I rolled over, blinking in astonishment. "Don't you want to know what I lied about?"

"I want to know what I can do to make you feel better." He rubbed my shoulders in tender circles, giving me a certain reassurance.

I wouldn't feel better until I came clean. It wasn't Patch's responsibility to lighten my burden—it was mine, and I felt every last pang of guilt as though they speared me with an iron blade.

"I've been taking—devilcraft." I hadn't thought my shame could grow, but it seemed to swell inside me by three sizes. "All this time I've been taking it. I never drank the antidote you got from Blakely. I kept it, telling myself I'd take it later, after Chesh-van, when I didn't need to be superhuman anymore, but it was an excuse. I never intended to take it. This whole time I've been rely-ing on devilcraft. I'm terrified I'm not strong enough without it. I know I have to stop, and I know it's wrong. But it gives me abilities I can't get on my own. I mind-tricked you into thinking I drank the antidote, and—I've never been more sorry in my life!"

I dropped my eyes, unable to bear the disappointment and disgust that would surely rise in Patch's face. It was awful enough knowing the truth, but hearing myself say it aloud cut to the core. Who was I anymore? I didn't recognize myself, and it was the worst feeling I'd ever experienced. Somewhere along the way, I'd lost myself. And as easy as it was to blame devilcraft, *I* had made the choice to steal that first bottle from Dante.

At last Patch spoke. His voice was so steady, so full of quiet admiration, it made me wonder if he could have known my secret all along. "Did you know, the first time I saw you, I thought: I've never seen anything more captivating and beautiful?"

"Why are you telling me this?" I said miserably.

"I saw you, and I wanted to be close to you. I wanted you to let me in. I wanted to know you in a way no one else did. I wanted you, all of you. That wanting nearly drove me mad." Patch paused, inhaling softly, as though breathing me in. "And now that I have you, the only thing that terrifies me is having to go back to that place. Having to want you all over again, with no hope of my desire ever being fulfilled. You're mine, Angel. Every last piece of you. I won't let anything change that."

I propped my weight on my elbow, staring at him. "I don't deserve you, Patch. I don't care what you say. It's the truth."

"You don't deserve me," he agreed. "You deserve better. But you're stuck with me, and you might as well get over it." Scooping me under him in one agile movement, he rolled on top of me, his black eyes all pirate. "I have no intention of letting you go easily, something to keep in mind. I don't care if it's another man, your mother, or the powers of hell trying to pry us apart, I'm not easing up and I'm not saying good-bye."

I blinked my wet lashes. "I'm not letting anything come between us either. Especially not devilcraft. I have the antidote in my purse. I'll take it right now. And, Patch?" I added with heartfelt emotion. "Thank you . . . for everything. I don't know what I'd do without you."

"Good thing," he murmured. "Because I'm not letting you get away."

I sank back on his bed, happy to oblige.

32

SURE ENOUGH, WORD OF MY REQUESTED MEETING with Nephilim higher-ups spread. By Sunday afternoon, Nephilim channels buzzed with anticipation and speculation. I was getting all the press, and news of Dante's announcement had fizzled. I'd stolen the show, and Dante hadn't put up any protest. I had no doubt Patch was right—Dante was putting his plans on hold until he could see my next move.

Scott called every hour with an update, which was usually to tell me the latest theories Nephilim were churning out in regard to my first combative strike against fallen angels. Ambush, destroying lines of communication, sending in spies, and kidnapping fallen angel commanders had all made the glorified list. As Patch had predicted, the Nephilim had quickly concluded that war was the only reason I'd call a meeting. I wondered if Dante had jumped to the same conclusion. I wished I could say yes, I had him fooled, but experience told me he was cunning enough to know better—he knew I was up to something.

"Big news," Scott said excitedly over the phone. "The big-wigs—high-powered Nephilim—have accepted your request for a meeting. They've determined the location, and it's not Delphic. Also, they are keeping things cozy. As might be expected, it's an invitation-only party. Twenty Nephilim at most. No leaks, lots of guards. Every Nephil invited will be screened before entering. Good news is, I'm on the guest list. Took some schmoozing, but I'll be there with you."

"Just tell me the location already," I said, trying not to sound nauseated.

"They want to meet at Hank Millar's old house."

My spine tingled. I would never be able to erase those arctic-blue eyes his name summoned to mind.

I pushed his ghost aside and focused. A classy Georgian colonial in a respected human neighborhood? It didn't seem shady enough for a covert Nephilim meeting. "Why there?"

"The higher-ups thought it showed a nod of respect to the Black Hand. Good call, I say. He started this whole mess," Scott added snidely.

"Keep talking like that, and they're going to boot you off the guest list."

"The meeting has been scheduled for ten tonight. Keep your cell phone close, in case I learn anything else. Don't forget to act surprised when they call with the details. Can't have them thinking they've got a spy problem already. One more thing. I'm sorry about Dante. I feel responsible. I introduced you. If I could, I'd dismember him. And then tie a brick to each of his limbs, take them to sea, and throw them overboard. Chin up. I've got your back."

I hung up and turned toward Patch, who'd been leaning against the wall and watching me carefully throughout the conversation.

"Meeting is tonight," I told him. "At the old Millar residence." I couldn't bring myself to finish the thought bearing down on my mind. A private home? Screenings? Guards? How on earth would Patch ever get in? To my great discouragement, it looked like I was going in without him tonight.

"That works," Patch said calmly. "I'll be there."

I admired his cool confidence, but I didn't see how he could possibly sneak in unnoticed. "The house will be highly guarded. The minute you set foot on the block, they'll know. Maybe if they'd selected a museum or the courthouse, but not this. The Millar house is big, but not that big. They'll have every square inch covered."

"Which is exactly what I planned for. I've already worked out the details. Scott is going to let me in."

"It won't work. They'll be expecting fallen angel spies, and even if Scott does unlock a window for you, they will have thought of it. Not only will they capture you, but they'll know Scott's a traitor—"

"I'm going to possess Scott's body."

I flinched. Slowly, his solution came together in my mind. Of course. It was Cheshvan. Patch would have no problem taking control of Scott's body. And from an outsider's perspective, there would be no way to tell the difference between the two. Patch would be welcomed into the meeting without a batted eye. It was the perfect disguise. Only one tiny little problem. "Scott will never agree to it."

"He already has."

I stared back in disbelief. "He has?"

"He's doing this for you."

My throat suddenly closed up. There was nothing in the world Scott fought harder for than to keep fallen angels from possessing him. I realized at that moment just how much my friendship must mean to him. For him to do this— The one thing he abhorred— There were no words. Just a deep, aching gratitude for Scott, and the determination not to fail him.

"Tonight, I need you to be careful," I said.

"I'll be careful. And I won't overstay my welcome. The minute you're out of the meeting safely, and I've stayed long enough to learn all I can, Scott will have his body back. I'll make sure nothing happens to him."

I squeezed Patch into a fierce hug. "Thank you," I whispered.

Later that night, an hour before ten, I departed Patch's home. I left alone, driving a rental car at the request of my Nephilim hosts. They'd dotted every i and crossed every t and weren't taking any chances of having me followed by nosy Nephilim, or worse, any fallen angel who might have caught wind of tonight's top secret meeting.

The streets were dark and slick under a film of fog. My headlights swept across the black ribbon of pavement that rolled over hills and around curves. I had the heater cranked, but it never quite cast out the chill dancing in my bones. I didn't know what to expect tonight, and that made it difficult to plan. I'd have to play things by ear, my least favorite way to go. I wanted to walk into the Millar house with something to hold on to besides my own instincts, but that's all I had. Finally I pulled up in front of Marcie's old house.

I sat in the car a moment, gazing at the white columns and black shutters. The lawn was lost under withered leaves. Brown twigs, the remnants of hydrangeas, jutted from twin terra-cotta pots flanking the porch. Newspapers in various states of decay littered the walkway. The house had been vacated after Hank's death and didn't look as inviting or elegant as I remembered. Marcie's mom had moved into a condo on the river, and Marcie, well, Marcie had taken the phrase mi casa es su casa to heart.

Faint lights glowed behind draped windows, and while they didn't reveal silhouettes, I knew several of the Nephilim world's most influential and powerful leaders sat just behind the front door, waiting to form judgments on the news I was about to deliver. I also knew Patch would be there, making sure no danger befell me.

Clinging to that thought, I drew a jagged breath and marched to the front door.

I knocked.

The front door opened, and I was ushered inside by a tall woman whose eyes lingered on me just long enough to confirm my identity. Her hair had been combed back in a tight braid, and there was nothing either remarkable or memorable about her face.

She murmured a polite but reserved, "Hello," and then, with a stiff sweep of her hand, directed me deeper into the house.

The tap of my shoes echoed down the dimly lit hallway. I passed portraits of the Millar family, smiling behind dusty glass. A vase of dead lilies sat on the entryway table. The whole house smelled bottled up. I followed the trail of lights toward the dining room.

As soon as I stepped through the French doors, the hushed conversation died. There were six men and five women seated on each side of a long, polished mahogany table. A few more Nephilim stood around the table, looking both fidgety and apprehensive. I almost did a double take when I saw Marcie's mom. I knew Susanna Millar was Nephilim, but it had always felt like an intangible thought drifting at the back of my mind. Seeing her here tonight, convening a secret meeting of immortals, made her suddenly feel . . . threatening. Marcie wasn't with her. Maybe Marcie hadn't wanted to come, but a more plausible explanation was that she hadn't been invited. Susanna seemed like the kind of mother who bent over backward to keep her daughter's life clear of even the tiniest complication.

I found Scott's face in the crowd. Knowing Patch was possessing him, the clanging in my stomach took a momentary reprieve. He caught my eye and inclined his head, a secret nod of encouragement. A deep feeling of assurance and security flooded me. I wasn't in this alone. Patch had my back. I should have known he'd find a way to be here, no matter the risk.

And then there was Dante. He sat at the head of the table, wearing a black cashmere turtleneck and a ponderous frown. His fingers were steepled over his mouth, and when his eyes locked with mine, his lips twitched with a sneer. His eyebrows lifted in discreet but unmistakable challenge. I looked away.

I turned my attention to the elderly woman in a purple cocktail dress and diamonds seated at the opposite end of the long table. Lisa Martin. Second to Hank, she was the most influential and respected Nephil I'd met. I didn't like or trust her. Feelings I was going to have to suppress for the next several minutes, if I wanted to get through this.

"We're so glad you instigated this meeting, Nora." Her warm, regal, and accepting voice slipped like honey into my ears. My racing heart slowed. If I could get her on my side, I was halfway there.

"Thank you," I managed at last.

She gestured at the empty seat beside her, beckoning me to sit.

I walked over to the chair, but I didn't sit. I was afraid I'd lose my nerve if I did. Leaning my hands on the table for support, I bypassed pleasantries and launched into the true meaning of my visit.

"I'm aware that not everyone in this room thinks I'm the best person to lead my father's army," I stated bluntly. The word "father" tasted like bile in my mouth, but I remembered Patch's admonition to attach myself to Hank any way I could tonight. Nephilim worshipped him, and if I could use his endorsement, even a backdoor endorsement, I should.

I made eye contact with everyone seated at the table, and a few standing behind it. I had to show them I had fortitude and courage, and most of all, that I was displeased with their lack of support. "I know some of you have already come up with a list of men and women better suited for the task." I paused again, turning the full weight of my gaze on Dante. He held my stare, but I saw hatred sizzle behind his brown eyes. "And I know Dante Matterazzi is at the top of that list."

A murmur circled the room. But no one disputed my claim.

"I didn't call you here tonight to discuss my first offensive strike in the war against fallen angels. I called you here because without a strong leader and your approval of that individual, there won't be a war. Fallen angels will tear us apart. We need unity and solidarity," I urged them with conviction. "I believe I am the best leader, and my father thought likewise. Clearly, I haven't convinced you. Which is why, tonight, I am challenging Dante Matterazzi to a duel. The winner leads this army once and for all."

Dante shot to his feet. "But we're dating!" His expression painted a perfect portrait of shock mingled with wounded pride. "How can you suggest dueling me?" he said, his voice sagging with humiliation.

I hadn't expected him to plead our utterly fake relationship, built on the weak foundation of my spoken agreement and never carried out—a relationship I had forgotten immediately, and that now soured in my bones, but it didn't startle me into silence. I said coolly, "I'm willing to take down anyone—that's what leading the Nephilim means to me. I hereby officially challenge you to a duel, Dante."

Not a single Nephil spoke. Surprise registered in their expressions, quickly followed by satisfaction. A duel. Winner take all. Patch had been right—Nephilim were still fully entrenched in an archaic world, ruled by Darwinian principles. They were pleased by this turn of events, and it was crystal clear from the adoring eyes they cast in Dante's direction that not one Nephil in the room doubted who the winner would be.

Dante tried to keep his face impassive, but I saw him smile

softly at my folly and his own good fortune. He thought I'd blundered, all right. But his eyes immediately narrowed with wariness. Apparently he wasn't going to lunge for the bait headlong.

"I can't do that," he announced. "It would be treason." His eyes swept the room, as if to gauge whether his gallant words had won him any further approval. "I've given my allegiance to Nora, and I couldn't think of doing any act that would contradict it."

"As your commander, I'm ordering you to duel," I retorted crisply. I was still leader of this army, damn it, and I wasn't going to let him undermine me with smooth words and flattery. "If you truly are the best leader, I'll step aside. I want what is best for my people." I had rehearsed the words a hundred times, and while I was giving a well-practiced speech, I meant every word. I thought of Scott, of Marcie, of thousands of Nephilim I'd never met, but still cared about because I knew they were good men and women who didn't deserve to be enslaved by fallen angels every year. They deserved a fair fight. And I was going to do my best to give them one.

I'd been wrong before—shamefully wrong. I'd avoided fighting for the Nephilim out of fear of the archangels. Even more reprehensible, I'd used war as an excuse to get more devilcraft. All this time I'd been more concerned with myself than the people I'd been charged with leading. That ended now. Hank had trusted me with this role, but I wasn't doing it for him. I was doing it because it was the moral thing to do.

"I think Nora has made a strong point," spoke Lisa Martin.

finale

"There is nothing more uninspiring than leadership propagating itself. Perhaps the Black Hand was right about her." A shrug. "Perhaps he made a mistake. We will take the matter into our own hands and settle it once and for all. Then we can go to war against our enemies, unified behind a strong leader."

I gave her a nod of appreciation. If I had her on my side, the others would step into line.

"I agree," a Nephil across the room spoke up.

"As do I."

More ratifying buzzed through the dining room.

"All in favor, make it known," said Lisa.

One by one, hands shot up. Patch locked eyes with me, then raised his arm. I knew it killed him to do it, but we were out of alternatives. If Dante swept me out of power, I would die. My only chance was to fight, and try my hardest to win.

"We have a majority," Lisa said. "The duel will take place at sunrise tomorrow, Monday. I will send word of the location, once it has been determined."

"Two days," Patch immediately interjected, speaking in Scott's voice. "Nora has never shot a pistol before. She'll need time to train."

I also needed to give Pepper time to return from heaven with his enchanted dagger, hopefully making the duel a moot point.

Lisa shook her head. "Too long. Fallen angels could come against us any day now. We have no idea why they've waited, but our luck might not hold."

"And I never said anything about pistols," Dante spoke up, eyeing Patch and me shrewdly as though trying to guess what we were up to. He watched my face for any hint of emotion. "I'd prefer sabers."

"It is Dante's call," Lisa stated. "The duel was not his idea. He reserves the right to choose the weapon. You've settled on sabers, then?"

"More ladylike," Dante explained, squeezing every last ounce of approval from his Nephilim peers.

I stiffened, resisting the urge to send Patch a plea for help.

"Nora has never touched a sword in her life," Patch argued, again speaking through Scott's voice. "It won't be a fair fight if she can't train. Give her until Tuesday morning."

No one was quick to support Patch's request. The disinterest in the room was so thick, I could have reached out and punched it. My training was the least of their concerns. In fact, the sooner Dante was in power, their impassive attitude said, the better.

"Are you taking it upon yourself to train her, Scott?" Lisa asked Patch.

"Unlike some of you, I haven't forgotten she's still our leader," Patch answered with a cold edge.

Lisa tilted her head as though to say, *Very well.* "Then it's decided. Two mornings from now. Until then, I wish you both the best."

I didn't hang around. With the duel rolling forward, and my part in this dangerous plan upheld, I let myself out. I knew Patch would have to stay a little longer, to gauge the room's reaction and possibly overhear vital information, but I found myself wishing he'd hurry.

This wasn't a night I wanted to be alone.

CHAPTER

33

KNOWING PATCH WOULD BE OCCUPIED UNTIL THE last of the Nephilim left the Millars' old house, I drove to Vee's. I was wearing my jean jacket with the tracking device and knew Patch would be able to find me if he needed to. In the meantime, there was something I needed to get off my chest.

I couldn't do this on my own anymore. I'd tried to keep Vee safe, but I needed my best friend.

I had to tell her everything.

Figuring the front door wasn't the best way to reach Vee at this time of night, I picked my way carefully through her yard, hopped the chain-link fence, and tapped on her bedroom window.

A moment later the curtains were flung aside and her face appeared behind the glass. Even though the hour was creeping up on midnight, she hadn't changed into pj's. She raised the window a few inches. "Boy, you picked a bad time to show up. I thought you were Scott. He's on his way over any minute now."

When I spoke, my voice sounded hoarse and shaky. "We need to talk."

Vee didn't miss a beat. "I'll call Scott and cancel." She slid the window all the way open to invite me in. "Tell me what's on your mind, babe."

To her credit, Vee didn't scream, sob hysterically, or flee from the room the moment I finished telling her the fantastical secrets I'd kept to myself the past six months. She'd flinched once when I'd explained that Nephilim were the progeny of humans and fallen angels, but other than that, her expression had remained free of horror and disbelief. She listened attentively as I described two warring races of immortals, Hank Millar's role in everything, and how he'd dumped his baggage in my lap. She even managed to smile slightly as I lifted the cloak on Patch and Scott's true identities.

When I finished, she merely cocked her head, scrutinizing me. After a moment, she said, "Well, that explains *a lot*."

It was my turn to blink. "Seriously? That's all you have to say? You aren't, I don't know . . . stunned? Confused? Bewildered? Hysterical?"

Vee tapped her chin contemplatively. "I knew Patch was way too hard-core to be human."

I was starting to wonder if she'd even heard me say that *I* wasn't human. "What about me? You're completely cool with the idea that not only am I Nephilim, but I'm supposed to be leading all the other Nephilim out there"—I thrust my finger at the window—"into war against fallen angels? *Fallen angels,* Vee. Like in the Bible. Heaven's banished evildoers."

"Actually, I think it's pretty incredible."

I scratched my eyebrow. "I can't believe you're being so calm about this. I expected some kind of reaction. I expected an outburst. Based on past experience, I anticipated flailing arms and a healthy dose of swearing, at the very least. I might as well be divulging this to a brick wall."

"Babe, you're making me sound like a diva."

That brought a quirk to my lips. "You said it, not me."

"I just think it's really weird that you said the easiest way to spot Nephilim is by their height, and you, my friend, aren't extraordinarily tall," said Vee. "Now take me, for instance. I'm tall."

"I'm average height because Hank—"

"Got it. You already explained that part about swearing an oath to become Nephilim while you were human, hence the

finale   371

average physique, but it still kind of sucks, right? I mean, what if the Changeover Vow had made you tall? What if it had made you as tall as me?"

I didn't know where Vee was going with this, but I felt like she was missing the point. This wasn't about how tall I was. This was about opening her mind to an immortal world that wasn't supposed to exist—and I'd just burst the secure little bubble she'd been living in.

"Does your body heal rapidly now that you're Nephilim?" Vee continued. "Because if you didn't get that perk, you really got shortchanged."

I stiffened. "Vee, I didn't tell you about our accelerated healing capabilities."

"Huh. I guess you didn't."

"How could you possibly know, then?" I stared at Vee, revisiting every word of our conversation. I had definitely not told her. My brain seemed to struggle forward in slow motion. And then, just like that, understanding came rushing at me much too fast to digest. I covered my mouth with my hand. "You . . . ?"

Vee smirked. "I told you I was keeping secrets from you."

"But— It can't be— It's not—"

"Possible? Yeah, that's what I thought at first too. I thought I was going through some kind of whacked-up second menstruation thing. These past couple weeks I've been tired and crampy and totally pissed off at the world. Then, a week ago, I cut my finger

BECCA FITZPATRICK

while slicing an apple. It healed so fast I almost thought I'd imagined seeing blood. More weird stuff happened after that. In PE, I served the volleyball so hard it hit the back wall on the opposite side of the court. During weights, I had no problem lifting what the bulkiest guys in the class were lifting. I hid it, of course, because I didn't want to draw attention to myself until I figured out what was happening to my body. Trust me, Nora. I am one hundred percent Nephilim. Scott caught on to it right away. He's been teaching me the ropes and helping me cope with the idea that seventeen years ago, my mom did the deed with a fallen angel. It's helped knowing Scott went through a similar physical change and realization about his own parents. Neither of us can believe it's taken you this long to figure it out." She punched my shoulder.

I felt my jaw hanging stupidly agape. "You. You're—really Nephilim." How could I not have seen it? I should have detected it in an instant—I could with any other Nephil, or fallen angel for that matter. Was it because Vee was my very best friend in the world, and had been for so long, that I couldn't view her any other way?

"What has Scott told you about the war?" I asked at last.

"That's one of the reasons he was coming over tonight, to bring me up to speed. 'Twould appear you're a big deal, Miss Queen Bee. Leader of the Black Hand's army?" Vee let out an appreciative whistle. "Dang, girl. Make sure to stick that on your résumé."

34

I WORE NOTHING BUT TENNIS SHOES, SHORTS, AND A tank top when I met Patch early the following morning on a rocky piece of coastline. It was Monday, Pepper's deadline. It was also a school day. But I couldn't worry about either of those things now. Train first, stress later.

I'd wrapped my hands in bandages, anticipating that Patch's version of training would put Dante's to shame. My hair was pulled back in a tight French braid, and my stomach was empty except for a glass of water. I hadn't ingested devilcraft since Friday, and it showed. I had a headache the size of Nebraska lodged in my head, and my vision seesawed in and out of focus when I turned my head too sharply. A jagged hunger clawed inside me. The pain was so fierce, I couldn't catch my breath.

Upholding my promise to Patch, I'd taken the antidote Saturday night directly after confessing my addiction, but apparently the medication took a while to run its course. Probably didn't help that I'd pumped large quantities of devilcraft into my system over the past week.

Patch wore black jeans and a matching T-shirt that hugged his form. He rested his hands on my shoulders, facing me. "Ready?"

Despite the grim mood, I smiled and cracked my knuckles. "Ready to wrestle with my gorgeous boyfriend? Oh, I'd say I'm ready for that."

Amusement softened his eyes.

"I'll try to control where I put my hands, but in the heat of things, who knows what could happen?" I added.

Patch grinned. "Sounds promising."

"All right, Trainer. Let's do this."

At my word, Patch's expression turned focused and business-like. "You haven't been trained in swordsmanship, and I'm guessing Dante has had more than his fair share of practice over the years. He's as old as Napoleon, and probably came out of his mother's womb waving a cuirassier's sword. Your best bet is to strip him of his sword early and move quickly into hand-to-hand combat."

"How am I going to do that?"

Patch picked up two sticks near his feet that he'd cut to approximately the length of a standard sword. He tossed one through the air, and I caught it. "Draw your sword before you begin fighting. It takes more time to draw a sword than it does to get struck."

I pretended to draw my sword from an invisible scabbard at my hip, and held it at the ready.

"Keep your feet shoulder-width apart at all times," Patch instructed, engaging me in a slow, relaxed parry. "You don't want to lose your balance and trip. Never move your feet close together, and always keep the blade close to your body. The more you lean or stretch, the easier it will be for Dante to knock you over."

We practiced footwork and balance for several minutes, the blunt clashing of our makeshift swords ringing out above low tide.

"Keep a close eye on Dante's movements," Patch said. "He'll settle into a pattern right away, and you'll start to learn when he's going to move for an attack. When he does, launch a preemptive strike."

"Right. Going to need a role play for that one."

Patch slid his feet forward rapidly, swinging his sword down on mine so forcibly, the stick vibrated in my hands. Before I could recover, he made a swift second blow, sending the sword sailing out of my grip.

I picked up my sword, wiped my brow, and said, "I'm not

BECCA FITZPATRICK

strong enough. I don't think I'll ever be able to do that to Dante."

"You will, once you've weakened him. The duel is set to take place at sunrise tomorrow. Following tradition, it will be outside, somewhere remote. You're going to force Dante into a position where the rising sun is in his eyes. Even if he tries to reverse your positions, he's tall enough that he'll shade the sun's rays from your vision. Use his height to your advantage. He's taller than you, and it will expose his legs. A hard strike to either knee will unbalance him. As soon as he loses his stance, attack."

This time I reenacted Patch's earlier move, forcing him off balance with a hit to his kneecap, followed by a rapid succession of strikes and blows. I didn't strip him of his sword, but I did thrust the tip of my own against his exposed midsection. If I could do that to Dante, it would be the turning point of the duel.

"Very good," Patch said. "The entire duel will most likely take less than thirty seconds. Every move counts. Be cautious and level-headed. Don't let Dante goad you into making a reckless mistake. Dodging and sidestepping are going to be your greatest defenses, especially in an open clearing. You'll have enough room to avoid his sword by sliding out of its path quickly."

"Dante knows he's, like, a zillion times better than me." I arched my eyebrows. "Any wise words of advice to cope with a complete and utter lack of confidence?"

"Let fear be your strategy. Pretend to be more frightened than you are to lull Dante into a false sense of superiority. Arrogance can be deadly." The corners of his mouth crept up. "But you didn't hear me say that."

I hung my mock sword over my shoulders like a baseball bat. "So, basically, the plan is to strip him of his sword, deliver a fatal blow, and claim my rightful position as leader of the Nephilim."

A nod. "Sweet and simple. Another ten hours of this, and you'll be a pro."

"If we're doing this for ten hours, I'm going to need a little incentive to stay motivated."

Patch hooked his elbow around my neck and dragged me into a kiss. "Every time you strip my sword, I owe you a kiss. How's that sound?"

I bit my lip to keep from giggling. "That sounds really dirty."

Patch waggled his brows. "Look whose mind just rolled into the gutter. Two kisses per strip. Any objections?"

I pulled on an innocent face. "None whatsoever."

Patch and I didn't stop dueling until sunset. We'd demolished five sets of swords, and stopped only for lunch and for me to receive my awarded kisses—some of which lasted long enough to draw the attention of beachcombers and a few joggers. I'm sure we looked insane, darting about on the craggy rocks while swinging wooden swords at each other hard enough to leave bruises and, very likely, a few cases of internal bleeding. Fortunately, my accelerated healing meant the worst of my injuries didn't interfere with our training.

By dusk, we were covered in sweat and I was thoroughly exhausted. In just over twelve hours, I would duel Dante for real. No makeshift swords, rather steel blades sharp enough to sever a limb. The thought was sobering enough to make my skin prickle.

"Well, you did it," I congratulated Patch. "I'm as trained as I'll ever be—a lean, mean sword-fighting machine. I should have made you my personal trainer from day one."

A rogue smile surfaced, slow and wicked. "No match for Patch."

"Mmm," I agreed, glancing up at him coyly.

"Why don't you head back to my place for a shower, and I'll pick up takeout from the Borderline?" Patch suggested as we trudged up the rocky embankment toward the parking lot.

He said it casually enough, but the words drew my eyes directly to his. Patch had worked as a busboy at the Borderline the first time we met. I couldn't drive past the restaurant now and not think of him. I was touched that he remembered, and to know that the restaurant held special memories for him, too. I forced myself to put all thought of tomorrow's duel, and Pepper's slim chance at success, out of my mind; tonight I wanted to enjoy Patch's company without worrying what would become of me—us—if I had to duel and Dante won.

"Can I put in a request for tacos?" I asked softly, remembering the first time Patch had taught me to make them.

"You read my mind, Angel."

• • •

I let myself into Patch's townhouse. In the bathroom, I stripped out of my clothes and untangled my braid. Patch's bathroom was magnificent. Deep blue tiles and black towels. A freestanding tub that would easily fit two. Bar soap that smelled like vanilla and cinnamon.

I stepped into the shower, letting the water beat over my skin. I thought of Patch standing in this same shower, arms braced against the wall as water poured over his shoulders. I thought of pearls of water clinging to his skin. I thought of him using the same towels I was about to wrap around my own body. I thought of his bed, just feet away. Of how the sheets would hold his scent—

A shadow slid across the bathroom mirror.

The bathroom door was cracked, light spilling in from the bedroom. I held my breath, waiting for another shadow, waiting for time to tell me I'd imagined seeing one. This was Patch's home. No one knew about it. Not Dante, not Pepper. I'd been careful—no one had followed me tonight.

Another dark cloud drifted over the mirror. The air crackled with supernatural energy.

I shut off the water and knotted a towel around my body. I looked for a weapon: I had a choice of a roll of toilet paper or a bottle of hand soap.

I hummed softly under my breath. No reason to let the intruder know I was onto them.

The intruder moved closer to the bathroom door; their power

BECCA FITZPATRICK

jolted my senses with electricity, the hairs on my arms standing alert like stiff flags. I continued to hum. From the corner of my eye, I saw the doorknob turn, and I was done waiting.

I shoved my bare foot against the door with a grunt of exertion. It splintered, breaking off the hinges as it flew outward, knocking over whoever was behind it. I lunged through the entrance, fists bared, ready to attack.

The man on the floor curled into a ball to protect his body. "Don't," he croaked. "Don't hurt me!"

Slowly, I lowered my fists. I cocked my head sideways for a better look.

"Blakely?"

35

"WHAT ARE YOU DOING HERE?" I DEMANDED, hitching up the bath towel to keep myself covered. "How did you find this place?"

Weapon. I needed one. My eyes scanned Patch's meticulous bedroom. Blakely might look compromised now, but he'd been manipulating devilcraft for months. I didn't trust him not to have something sharp and dangerous—and blue-tinted—hidden beneath his trench coat.

"I need your help," he said, raising his palms as he crawled to his feet.

"Don't move," I snapped. "On your knees. Keep your hands where I can see them."

"Dante tried to kill me."

"You're immortal, Blakely. You're also teammates with Dante."

"Not anymore. Now that I've developed enough devilcraft prototypes, he wants me gone. He wants to control devilcraft exclusively. He used a sword I enhanced specifically to kill you, and tried to use it against me. I barely got away."

"Dante ordered you to make a sword that would kill me?"

"For the duel."

I didn't yet know Blakely's endgame, but I didn't put Dante past using forbidden—and lethal—methods to win the duel. "Is it as good as you say? Will it kill me?"

Blakely looked me squarely in the eye. "Yes."

I tried to calmly process this information. I needed a way to disqualify Dante from using his sword. But first things first. "More."

"I suspect Dante is working for fallen angels."

I didn't bat an eye. "What makes you say that?"

"All these months, and he's never allowed me to make a weapon that will kill fallen angels. Rather, I've developed a whole host of prototypes that were supposedly aimed at killing you. And if they can kill you, they can kill any Nephil. Since fallen angels

finale

are the enemy, why have I been developing weapons that hurt Nephilim?"

I remembered my conversation with Dante at Rollerland, over a week ago. "Dante told me that with enough time, you'd be able to develop a prototype strong enough to kill a fallen angel."

"I wouldn't know. He's never given me the chance."

In a risky move, I decided to come clean with Blakely. I still didn't trust him, but if I gave a little, he might too. And right now, I needed to know everything he did. "You're right. Dante is working for fallen angels. I know this for a fact."

For a moment, he shut his eyes, taking the truth hard. "I never trusted Dante, not from the beginning. Bringing him on board was your father's idea. I couldn't convince Hank not to do it then, but I can avenge his name now. If Dante is a traitor, I owe it to your father to destroy him."

If nothing else, I had to give Hank credit for inspiring loyalty.

I said, "Tell me more about the devilcraft super-drink. Since Dante is working for fallen angels, why would he have you develop something that would aid our race?"

"He never distributed the drink to other Nephilim like he told me he would. It's only strengthening him. And now he has all the prototypes. The antidote, too." Blakely squeezed between his eyes. "Everything I worked for—he stole it."

My damp hair clung to my skin, and chilled water dripped down my back. Goose bumps stood out on my flesh, from cold and Blakely's words both. "Patch will be here any minute. Since you were apparently clever enough to find his home, I'm guessing you were looking for him."

"I want to ruin Dante." His voice vibrated with conviction.

"You mean you want Patch to ruin him for you." What was it with evildoers trying to hire my boyfriend as a mercenary? Granted, he'd worked as one in a past life, but this was starting to get ridiculous—and irritating. What happened to taking care of one's own problems? "What makes you think he'll do it?"

"I want Dante to spend the rest of his life in misery. Isolated from the world, tortured to the breaking point. Patch is the only one I trust to do it. Price isn't an issue."

"Patch doesn't need money—" I stopped, holding the thought. An idea had just come to me, and it was as devious as it was manipulative. I didn't want to take advantage of Blakely, but then again, he'd hardly been gracious to me in the past. I reminded myself that when push came to shove, he'd driven a knife enhanced with devilcraft deep inside me, introducing me to a toxic addiction. "Patch doesn't need your money, but he does need your testimony. If you agree to confess Dante's crimes at the duel tomorrow in front of Lisa Martin and other influential Nephilim, Patch will kill Dante for you." Just because Patch had already promised to kill Dante for Pepper didn't mean we couldn't take advantage of circumstances and position ourselves to gain something from Blakely as well. The expression "two

finale

birds with one stone" hadn't come from nowhere, after all.

"Dante can't be killed. Imprisoned eternally, yes, but not killed. None of the prototypes work against him. He's immune because his body—"

"This is a job Patch can handle," I fired back tersely. "If you want Dante dead, consider it done. You have your connections, and Patch has his."

Blakely studied me with a contemplative, discerning gaze. "He knows an archangel?" he guessed at last.

"You didn't hear it from me. One more thing, Blakely. This is important. Do you hold enough clout with Lisa Martin and other powerful Nephilim to turn them against Dante? Because if not, we're both going down tomorrow."

He only debated a minute. "Dante charmed your father, Lisa Martin, and several other Nephilim from the beginning, but he doesn't have the history with them that I do. If I call him a traitor, they'll listen." Blakely reached into his pocket and offered me a small card. "I need to retrieve a few important items from my home before I relocate to my safe house. This is my new address. Give me a head start, then bring Patch. We'll work out the details tonight."

Patch arrived minutes after Blakely left. The first words out of my mouth were, "You'll never believe who just stopped by." With that captivating hook, I launched into my story, relaying to Patch every word from my conversation with Blakely.

"What do you make of it?" Patch asked when I finished.

"I think Blakely is our last hope."

"You trust him?"

"No. But your enemy's enemy . . ."

"Did you make him swear an oath to testify tomorrow?"

My heart sank. I hadn't thought of it. It was an honest mistake, but it made me wonder if I'd ever be a worthy leader. I knew Patch didn't expect perfection from me, but I wanted to impress him just the same. An idiotic voice inside my head questioned whether Dabria would have made the same mistake. Doubtful. "When we meet him tonight, it will be the first thing I take care of."

"It makes sense that Dante would want to control devilcraft exclusively," Patch mused. "And if Dante thought Blakely suspected him of working for fallen angels, he would kill him to keep his secret safe."

I said, "Do you think Dante told me about devilcraft that day at Rollerland because he anticipated that I'd tell you, and you'd go after Blakely? I've always wondered why he told me. Looking back, it almost seems like he had a strategy: for you to snatch Blakely and bury him from the light of day, leaving Dante alone to control devilcraft."

"Which is exactly what I had planned. Until Marcie upset those plans."

"Dante has been undermining me from the start," I realized.

"Not anymore. We have Blakely's testimony."

finale

"Does that mean we're meeting him?"

Patch had set the keys to his motorcycle on the kitchen counter not five minutes ago, and he reached for them again. "Never a dull moment, Angel."

The address Blakely had given me took us to a single-story red-brick home in an older neighborhood. Two shaded windows flanked the front door. The sprawling property seemed to swallow the little cottage whole.

Patch drove around the block twice, eyes sharp, then parked down the street out of the reach of the streetlights. He gave the front door three solid raps. A light burned behind the living room window, but there were no other signs that someone was home.

"Stay here," Patch told me. "I'm going around back."

I waited on the stoop, glancing behind me at the street. It was too cold for the neighbors to be out walking the dog, and not a single car drove past.

The front door lock tumbled, and Patch opened the door from within. "Back door was wide open. Got a bad feeling," he said.

I stepped inside, shutting the door behind me. "Blakely?" I called out softly. The house was small enough to make raising my voice unnecessary.

"He's not on the first floor," Patch said. "But there are stairs leading to a basement."

We took the stairs and turned into a lit room. I sucked in a breath as my eyes focused on the trail of red liquid smeared across the carpet. Red handprints painted the wall and led in the same direction—to a dark bedroom straight ahead. In the grainy shadows, I could just make out the outline of a bed—and Blakely's body crumpled beside it.

Patch's arm immediately shot out, blocking me. "Go upstairs," he ordered.

Without thinking, I ducked under Patch's arm and rushed toward Blakely. "He's hurt!"

The whites of Blakely's eyes sizzled an ethereal blue. Blood trickled from his mouth, gurgling as he tried unsuccessfully to speak.

"Dante did this?" Patch asked him, following directly behind me.

I crouched down, checking Blakely's vital signs. His heartbeat thrummed weakly and erratically. Tears stung my eyes. I didn't know if I was crying for Blakely, or for what his death would mean for me, but I suspected, selfishly, it was the latter.

Blakely coughed blood, his voice threadbare. "Dante knows— fallen angels' feathers."

I gave Patch's hand a numbing squeeze. *How can Dante know about the feathers? Pepper wouldn't have told him. And we're the only other two who know.*

If Dante knows about the feathers, he'll try to intercept Pepper on his way back to Earth, Patch answered tensely. *We can't let him get the feathers.*

finale

"Lisa Martin—here—soon," Blakely rasped, each word a struggle.

"Where is the lab?" I asked Blakely. "How can we destroy Dante's supply of devilcraft?"

He gave his head a hard shake, as if I'd asked the wrong question. "His sword—he—doesn't know. Lied. Kill—him too," he choked hoarsely, more blood washing over his lips. The blood had turned from red to fiery blue.

"Okay, I understand," I said, patting his shoulder to console him. "The sword he's going to duel with tomorrow will kill him too, only he doesn't know it. This is good, Blakely. Now tell me where the lab is."

"Tried—tell—you," he croaked.

I shook Blakely's shoulders. "You didn't tell me. Where is the lab?" I didn't believe destroying the lab would change the outcome of tomorrow's duel—Dante would have plenty of devilcraft in his system when we fought, but no matter what happened to me, if Patch could destroy the lab, devilcraft would vanish once and for all. I felt personally responsible for putting the powers of hell back in, well, hell.

We have to go, Angel, Patch spoke to my thoughts. *Lisa can't see us here. It doesn't look good.*

I rattled Blakely harder. "Where is the lab?"

His balled hands relaxed. His eyes, glazed that chilling shade of blue, stared vacantly up at me.

"We can't waste any more time here," Patch told me. "We have to assume Dante is going after Pepper and the feathers."

I dried my eyes with the heels of my hands. "We're just going to leave Blakely here?"

The sound of a car pulling to a stop sounded on the street outside. "Lisa," Patch said. He shoved the bedroom window open, hoisted me into the window well, and leaped up beside me. "Any last respects to the dead have to be said now."

Casting a mournful look back at Blakely, I simply said, "Good luck in the next life."

I had a feeling he'd need it.

We sped off through the woodsy back roads on Patch's motorcycle. Cheshvan's new moon had started nearly two weeks ago, and now it hung like a ghostly orb high overhead, a wide, watchful eye we couldn't escape. I shivered and snuggled closer against Patch. He rocketed around the narrow bends so fast that tree branches began to blur into flashes of skeletal fingers reaching out to snare me.

Since yelling above the roar of wind was impractical, I resorted to mind-speak.

Who could have told Dante about the feathers? I asked Patch.

Pepper wouldn't risk it.

Neither would we.

If Dante knows, we can assume the fallen angels do too. They are going to do everything they can to keep us from getting those feathers, Angel. No course of action will be ruled out.

His warning came through all too clear: We weren't safe.

We have to warn Pepper, I said.

If we call him, and the archangels intercept it, we'll never get the feathers.

I glanced at the time on my cell phone. Eleven. We gave him until midnight. He's almost out of time.

If he doesn't call soon, Angel, we're going to have to assume the worst and come up with a new plan.

His hand dropped to my thigh, squeezing. I knew we were sharing the same thought. We'd exhausted every plan. Time was up. Either we got the feathers—

Or the Nephilim race would lose more than the war. They'd be in bondage to fallen angels for eternity.

CHAPTER 36

A MUTED JINGLE RANG FROM MY POCKET. PATCH immediately steered the motorcycle to the roadside, and I answered the call with a prayer in my heart.

"I have the f-f-feathers," Pepper said, his voice high and quivering.

I exhaled in relief and gave Patch a high five, curling my fingers between his, locking our hands together. We had the feathers. We had the dagger. Tomorrow morning's duel was no longer necessary—dead opponents didn't wield swords, enchanted or otherwise.

"Good work, Pepper," I said. "You're almost done. We need you to hand over the feathers and dagger, and then you can put this behind you. Patch will kill Dante as soon as he gets the dagger. But you need to know Dante is after the feathers too." There wasn't time to break it to him gently. "He wants them as badly as we do. He's looking for you, so don't let your guard down. And don't let him get the feathers, or the dagger."

Pepper sniffled. "I'm s-s-scared. How do I know Dante won't find me? And what if the archangels notice the feathers are missing?" His volume shot up to a screech. "What if they figure out it was me?"

"Calm down. Everything will be fine. We're going to make the transfer at Delphic Amusement Park. We can meet you in about forty-five minutes—"

"That's almost an hour! I can't hold the feathers that long! I have to dump them. That was the deal. You never said anything about babysitting them. And what about me? Dante is after me. If you want me to hang on to your feathers, then I want Patch to go after Dante and make sure he's not a threat to me!"

"I explained this," I said impatiently. "Patch will kill Dante as soon as we have the dagger."

"A whole lot of good that will do me if Dante finds me first! I watch Patch out there, this minute, going after Dante. In fact, I won't give you the dagger until I have proof that Patch has Dante!"

I pulled the phone away to save my eardrums from Pepper's hysterical shrieks. "He's cracking," I told Patch worriedly.

Patch took the phone from me. "Listen up, Pepper. Take the feathers and the dagger to Delphic Amusement Park. I'll have two fallen angels meet you at the gates. They'll make sure you get safely inside my studio. Just don't tell them what you're carrying."

Pepper's squeaked response crackled from the phone.

Patch said, "Put the feathers in my studio. Then stay put until we get there."

A loud wail.

"You aren't leaving the feathers unguarded," Patch argued, each word breathed with murderous intent. "You're going to sit on my sofa and make sure they're still there when we get there."

More frantic squawking.

"Stop blubbering. I'll hunt Dante down now, if that's what you want, then come get the dagger, which you're going to sit on until I meet you at the studio. Go to Delphic and do exactly as I told you. One more thing. Stop crying. You're giving archangels everywhere a bad name."

Patch hung up and handed the phone back to me. "Keep your fingers crossed that this works."

"Do you think Pepper will stay with the feathers?"

He dragged his hands down his face, a sound escaping his throat that sounded half harsh laugh, half groan. "We're going to have to split up, Angel. If we hunt down Dante together, we risk leaving the feathers unguarded."

"Go find Dante. I'll take care of Pepper and the feathers."

Patch studied me. "I know you will. But I still don't like the idea of leaving you alone."

"I'll be fine. I'll guard the feathers, and I'll call Lisa Martin right away. I tell her what I have, and she'll help me execute our plan. We're going to end the war and free Nephilim." I squeezed Patch's hand reassuringly. "This is it. The end's in sight."

Patch rubbed his jaw, clearly unhappy, thinking deeply. "For my own peace of mind, take Scott with you."

An ironic smile crept to my mouth. "You trust Scott?"

"I trust you," he answered in a husky voice that made me feel warm and slippery inside.

Patch backed me into a tree and kissed me, hard.

I regained my breath. "Boys everywhere take note: That was a kiss."

Patch didn't smile. His eyes darkened with something I couldn't name, but it put a weight in my stomach. His jaw locked, the muscles along his arms tensing just as visibly. "We're going to be together at the end of this." A cloud of uneasiness passed over his expression.

"If I have anything to say about it, yes."

"Whatever happens tonight, I love you."

"Don't talk that way, Patch," I whispered, emotion catching my voice. "You're scaring me. We are going to be together. You'll find Dante, then meet me at the studio, where we'll end this war together. Doesn't get any more straightforward."

He kissed me again, delicately on each eyelid, then each cheek, and at last, a soft seal across my lips. "I'll never be the same," he said in a gravelly tone. "You've transformed me."

I folded my arms around his neck and pressed my body hard to his. I clung to him, trying to cast out the chill that tapped in my bones. "Kiss me in a way I'll never forget." I drew his eyes toward mine. "Kiss me in a way that will stay with me until I see you again." *Because we will see each other soon.*

Patch's eyes grazed me with silent heat. My reflection swirled in them, red hair and lips aflame. I was connected to him by a force I couldn't control, a tiny thread that tethered my soul to his. With the moon at his back, shadows painted the faint hollows beneath his eyes and cheekbones, making him look breathtakingly handsome and equally diabolical.

His hands steadied my face, holding me still before him. The wind tangled my hair around his wrists, twining us together. His thumbs moved across my cheekbones in a slow, intimate caress. Despite the cold, a steady burn coiled up inside me, vulnerable to his touch. His fingers traced lower, lower, leaving behind a hot, delicious ache. I closed my eyes, my joints melting. He lit me up like a flame, light and heat burning at a depth I'd never fathomed.

His thumb stroked my lip, a soft, seductive tease. I gave a sharp sigh of pleasure.

Kiss you now? he asked.

I couldn't speak; a wilted nod was my reply.

His mouth, hot and daring, met mine. All play had left him, and he kissed me with his own black fire, deep and possessive, consuming my body, my soul, and laying waste to all past notions of what it meant to be kissed.

I HEARD SCOTT'S BARRACUDA RUMBLE DOWN THE road toward me long before the headlights flashed through the murky darkness. I flagged him down and swung into the passenger seat.

"Thanks for coming."

He shoved the car in reverse and floored it the same way he'd approached. "You kept your call short. Tell me what I need to know."

I explained the situation as quickly, yet comprehensively, as possible. When I finished, Scott let out a low whistle of astonishment. "Pepper's got every fallen angel feather, *ever*?"

"Surreal, right? He is supposed to meet us at Patch's studio. He'd better not leave the feathers unguarded," I muttered mostly to myself.

"I can get you safely beneath Delphic. The park gates are closed, so we'll go into the tunnels using the cargo elevators. After that, we'll have to use my map. I've never been to Patch's place."

The "tunnels" referred to an underground network of convoluted, mazelike passageways that operated like streets and neighborhoods beneath Delphic. I'd had no idea they existed until I met Patch. They served as the primary residence for fallen angels living in Maine, and until recently, Patch had lived among them.

Scott steered the Barracuda down an access road short of the park's main entrance. The road opened to a loading dock with truck ramps, and a warehouse. We entered the warehouse through a side door, crossed an open space stacked wall to wall with boxes, and at last reached the cargo elevators. Once inside, Scott ignored the normal buttons indicating floors one, two, and three, and pressed a small, unmarked yellow button at the bottom of the panel. I'd known there were entrances to the tunnels all over Delphic, but this was my first time using this particular one.

The elevator, which was almost as large as my bedroom, clanged lower and lower, at last grinding to a stop. The heavy steel door rose, and Scott and I walked out onto a loading dock. The ground and walls were dirt, and the only light came from the single bulb swinging like a pendulum overhead.

"Which way?" I asked, peering into the tunnel ahead.

I was grateful to have Scott as a guide through the underbelly of Delphic Amusement Park. It was immediately clear that he traversed the tunnels regularly; he led at a hurried pace, sweeping down the dank corridors as though they had long ago been committed to memory. We referenced the map, using it to make our way beneath the Archangel, Delphic's newest roller coaster. From there, I took over, glancing down corridors randomly, until at last we came to what I recognized as the entrance to Patch's old living quarters.

The door was locked from the inside.

I rapped on it. "Pepper, it's Nora Grey. Open up." I gave him a few moments, then tried again. "If you're not opening because you sense someone else, it's Scott. He's not going to beat you up. Now open the door."

"Is he alone?" Scott asked quietly.

I nodded. "Should be."

"I don't sense anybody," Scott said skeptically, bending his ear toward the door.

"Hurry up, Pepper," I called.

Still no response.

"We're going to have to break down the door," I told Scott. "On the count of three. One, two—three."

In unison, Scott and I landed forceful kicks to the door.

"Again," I grunted.

We continued to drive our soles into the wood, striking it until it splintered and the door slammed inward. I strode across the foyer and into the living room, looking for Pepper.

The sofa had been knifed multiple times, stuffing spewing from each incision. Picture frames that had once decorated the walls now lay shattered on the ground. The glass coffee table was tipped on its side, with an ominous crack down the center. Clothes from Patch's wardrobe had been dragged out and thrown like confetti. I didn't know if this was evidence of a recent struggle, or left over from Patch's hasty departure nearly two weeks ago, when Pepper had hired thugs to destroy the place.

"Can you call Pepper?" Scott suggested. "Do you have his number?"

I punched Pepper's number into my phone, but he didn't pick up. "Where is he?" I demanded angrily to no one in particular. Everything was riding on his end of the bargain. I needed those feathers, and I needed them now. "And what is that smell?" I asked, wrinkling my nose.

I walked deeper into the living room. Sure enough, I detected a noxious, acrid smell wafting in the air. A rotten smell. A smell almost like hot tar, but not quite.

Something was burning.

I ran from room to room, trying to find the feathers. They

weren't here. I shoved open the door to Patch's old bedroom and was immediately overwhelmed by the smell of burning organic material.

Without pausing to think, I ran to the far wall of the bedroom—the one that slid open to reveal a secret passageway. The moment I cracked the sliding door, a thunderhead of black smoke rolled into the room. The greasy, charred stench was unbearable.

Sealing my mouth and nose with the collar of my shirt, I called to Scott, "I'm going in."

He strode through the doorway behind me, batting the smoke with his hand.

I'd been down the passageway once before, when Patch had momentarily detained Hank Millar before I'd killed him, and I tried to remember the way. Dropping to my knees to avoid the worst of the smoke, I crawled quickly, coughing and gagging every time I drew breath. At last my hands struck a door. Fumbling for the ring pull, I jerked on it. The door swung slowly open, sending a fresh wave of smoke billowing into the corridor.

The light from a blazing fire flashed through the smoke, flames leaping and dancing like an exquisite magic show: brazen gold and molten orange and great plumes of black smoke. An awful crackling and snapping sounded in my ears as the flames devoured the massive hill of fuel beneath it. Scott vised my shoulders protectively, forcing his body in front of mine like a shield. The heat from the fire broiled our faces.

It only took me a moment to howl in terror.

finale

CHAPTER

38

I SHOT TO MY FEET FIRST. OBLIVIOUS TO THE HEAT, I charged the fire while sparks rained down like fireworks. I clawed at the towering hill of feathers, shrieking with panic. Only two of Patch's feathers from his days as an archangel remained. One feather we held for safekeeping. The other had been taken and meticulously stored by the archangels when they'd banished Patch from heaven. That feather was somewhere in the pile before me.

Patch's feather could be anywhere. Maybe already burned.

There were so many. And an even greater number of ash flecks floated like singed pieces of paper around the fire.

"Scott! Help me find Patch's feather!" Think. I had to think. Patch's feather. I'd seen it before. "It's black, all black," I blurted. "Start looking—I'll go get blankets to smother the fire!"

I raced back toward Patch's studio, the smoke forming a screen across my eyes. Suddenly I came up short, detecting another body in the tunnel, just ahead. I blinked against the smoke grinding into my eyes.

"It's too late," Marcie said. Her face was puffy from crying, and the tip of her nose glowed red. "You can't put out the fire."

"What have you done?" I yelled at her.

"I'm my dad's rightful heir. I should be leading the Nephilim."

"Rightful heir? Are you listening to yourself? Do you want this job? I don't—your dad forced it on me!"

Her lip wobbled. "He loved me more. He would have chosen me. You stole this from me."

I said, "You don't want this job, Marcie. Who put these ideas in your head?"

Tears tumbled down her cheeks, and her breathing became choppy. "It was my mom's idea for me to move in with you— she and her Nephilim friends wanted me to keep an eye on you. I agreed to do it because I thought you knew something about my dad's death that you weren't telling me. If I got close to you, I thought maybe—" For the first time, I noticed the pearly dagger in her hands. It shined a lustrous white, as if the sun's purest rays were trapped beneath the surface. It could only be Pepper's enchanted dagger. The nitwit hadn't been careful enough, and had allowed Marcie to follow him here. Then he'd dumped the feathers and the dagger and bolted, leaving them to fall into Marcie's possession.

I reached for her. "Marcie—"

"Don't touch me!" she shrieked. "Dante told me you killed my dad. How could you do it? How could you! I was sure it was Patch, but all along it was you!" she screeched hysterically.

Despite the heat, a shiver of fear whipped up my spine.

"I—can explain." But I didn't think I could. Marcie's wild, overwrought expression hinted that she was spiraling into shock. I doubted she'd care to know that her dad had forced my hand when he'd attempted to send Patch to hell. "Give me the dagger."

"Get away from me!" She scrabbled out of reach. "Dante and I are going to tell everyone. What will the Nephilim do to you once they know you murdered the Black Hand?"

I studied her carefully. Dante must have only just learned I'd killed Hank. Otherwise, he would have told the Nephilim long ago. Patch hadn't given up my secret, which left Pepper. Somehow, Dante had gotten to him.

"Dante was right," Marcie spat, cold rage bubbling up in her voice. "You stole the title from me. It was supposed to be mine. And now I've done what you couldn't—I freed the Nephilim. When that fire finishes, every fallen angel on Earth will be chained in hell."

"Dante is working for fallen angels," I said, frustration sharpening my tone.

"No," Marcie said. "You are."

She swiped Pepper's blade at me, and I jumped back, tripping. Smoke pressed down on me, fully obscuring my vision.

"Does Dante know you burned the feathers?" I yelled up at Marcie, but she gave no answer. She was gone.

Had Dante switched his strategy? After an unexpected windfall of every fallen angel feather, and therefore surefire victory for Nephilim, had he decided to side with his race after all?

There wasn't time to debate. I'd already wasted too much precious time. I had to help Scott find Patch's feather. Running back to the fiery chamber, I coughed and gagged my way into the entrance.

"They're all turning black from the ash," Scott hollered at me over his shoulder. "They all look the same." His cheeks glowed scarlet with heat. Embers whirled around him, threatening to ignite his hair, which had turned black with soot. "We have to get out of here. If we stay longer, we'll catch on fire."

I ran to him in a crouch, trying to avoid the heat, which blasted relentlessly. "First we find Patch's feather." I flung burning heaps of feathers behind me, shoveling deeper. Scott was right. A greasy black soot smeared every feather. I made a high sound of despair. "If we don't, he'll be sent to hell!"

I scattered handfuls of feathers, praying I would know his on sight. Praying it hadn't already burned. I wouldn't let my thoughts turn to the worst. Ignoring the smoke that scratched at my eyes and lungs, I sifted the feathers with more urgency. I couldn't lose Patch. I wouldn't lose Patch. Not like this. Not on my watch.

My eyes watered, tears brimming over. I couldn't see clearly. The air was too hot to breathe. The skin on my face seemed to melt, and my scalp felt like it was on fire. I plunged my hands into the hill of feathers, desperate to find a solid black feather.

"I'm not going to let you burn," Scott ground out above the crackling whoosh of flames. He rolled back on his knees, dragging me with him. I scratched ruthlessly at his hands. Not without Patch's feather.

The fire clamored in my ears, and my concentration was wilting without enough oxygen. I wiped the back of my hand across my eyes, only to rub in more soot. I groped at the feathers, my arms feeling as though they were attached to hundred-pound weights. My vision seesawed. But I refused to pass out until I had Patch's feather.

"Patch," I murmured, just as an ember landed on my shirt-sleeve, igniting the fabric. Before I could raise a hand to tamp it out, the flame shot to my elbow. Heat torched my skin, so bright and agonizing, I screamed and pitched sideways. It was then that I saw my jeans were also ablaze.

Scott bellowed orders behind me. Something about leaving the chamber. He wanted to close the door and trap the fire inside.

I couldn't let him. I had to save Patch's feather.

I lost my sense of direction, stumbling forward blindly. Bright, licking flames eclipsed my vision.

Scott's voice, so urgent, dissolved into nothing.

Even before I opened my eyes, I knew I was in a moving car. I felt the irregular bump of tires bouncing over potholes, and an engine growled in my ears. I sat slouched against the car door, my head propped on the window. There were two unfamiliar hands in my lap, and it startled me when they moved at my command. I turned them over slowly in the air, staring at the strange black paper curling off them.

Blackened flesh.

A hand squeezed my arm in consolation.

"It's okay," Scott said from the driver's seat of his Barracuda. "It will heal."

I shook my head, implying he'd misunderstood. I licked my parched lips. "We have to go back. Turn the car around. We have to save Patch."

Scott said nothing, just cast me a sidelong look of uncertainty.

No.

It was a lie. A deep, unimaginable fear swallowed me up. My throat felt thick and slippery and hot. It was a lie.

"I know you cared about him," Scott said quietly.

I love him! I'll always love him! I promised him we'd be together! I screamed inside my head, because the words were too jagged to push out. They scraped like nails in my throat.

I turned my attention out the window. I stared at the night, at the blur of trees and fields and fences, here one moment, gone the next. The words in my throat coiled into a scream, all sharp edges and icy pain. The scream hung there, swelling and hurting while my world unraveled and drifted out of orbit.

A pile of twisted metal blocked the road ahead.

Scott swerved to miss it, slowing as we passed. I didn't wait for the car to stop; I threw myself out, running. Patch's motorcycle. Beaten and battered. I gaped at it, blinking over and over, trying to see a different picture. The demolished metal, twisted over on itself, appeared as though the driver had raced at top speed—then jumped through a hole in the wind.

I ground my palms into my eyes, waiting for the awful picture to clear. I searched the road, thinking he must have crashed. In the impact, his body must have been thrown a distance. I ran farther, a little farther, searching the ditch, the weeds, the shadows off in the trees. He could be just ahead. I called his name. I paced up and down the roadside, my hands shaking as I plowed them through my hair.

I didn't hear Scott come up behind me. I hardly felt his arms around my shoulders. Grief and anguish rattled me, a living presence, so real and frightening. It filled me with such cold, it hurt to draw breath.

"I'm sorry," he said hoarsely.

"Don't tell me he's gone," I snapped. "He crashed his motorcycle and kept on walking. He said he'd meet me at the studio. He wouldn't break his promise." I said the words because I had to hear them.

"You're shivering. Let me take you back to my house, your house, his place—wherever you want."

"No," I barked. "We're going back to the studio. He's there. You'll see." I shoved out of his embrace, but I felt unsteady. My legs shuffled one numb step after another. A wild, unforgivable thought gripped me. What if Patch was gone?

My feet drifted back to the motorcycle.

"Patch!" I cried out, dropping to my knees. I stretched my body over his motorcycle, strange, powerful sobs erupting from deep in my chest. I was slipping, sliding into the lie.

Patch.

I thought his name, waiting, waiting. I sobbed his name, hearing myself make uncontrollable noises of anguish and despair.

Tears rolled down my face. My heart hung by a thread. The hope I'd clung to untethered, drifting out of reach. I felt my soul shatter, irreparable pieces of me flying outward.

What little light was left inside me flickered out.

CHAPTER

39

I GAVE MYSELF UP TO SLEEP. DREAMS WERE THE only place I could reach Patch. Holding on to a phantom memory of him was better than living without him. Curled up in his bed, surrounded by a smell that was distinctly his, I summoned his memory to haunt me.

I never should have trusted Pepper to get the feathers. I should have known he'd screw up. I should not have underestimated Dante. I knew Patch would dismiss my guilt at once, but I felt responsible for what had happened to him. If only I'd arrived at his studio ten minutes earlier. If only I'd stopped Marcie from lighting the match . . .

"Wake up, Nora."

Vee leaned over me, her voice hurried and charged. "You have to get ready for the duel. Scott told me everything. One of Lisa Martin's messengers came by while you were asleep. The duel is at sunrise in the cemetery. You have to go kick Dante's butt to Jupiter. He took Patch away from you, and now he's out for your blood. I'll tell you what I think about that. Hell, no. Not if we have anything to say about it."

Duel? The idea seemed almost laughable. Dante didn't need to clash swords with me to steal my title; he had more than enough ammunition to blow apart my credibility and reputation. Every last fallen angel had been chained in hell. The Nephilim had won the war. Dante and Marcie would take credit, explaining how they'd bullied an archangel into giving them the feathers, and how they relished every moment of watching them burn.

The thought of Patch imprisoned in hell slashed a fresh wave of pain through me. I didn't know how I would hold my emotions in check as the Nephilim cheered wildly over their triumph. They would never know that up until the last moment, Dante had been helping fallen angels. Nephilim would sweep him into power. I didn't yet know what it meant for me. If the army was abolished, would it matter that I lost control of leading it? In retrospect, my oath had been too vague. I hadn't planned for this.

finale

But I had to assume Dante had plans for me. Like me, he knew the moment I failed to lead the army, my life was over. But in the name of covering his bases, he'd likely arrest me for the Black Hand's murder. Before the day was out, I'd either be executed for treason, or at best, imprisoned.

I was betting executed.

"It's almost sunrise. Get up," Vee said. "You aren't letting Dante get away with this."

I hugged Patch's pillow to me, breathing in the lingering smell of him before it was gone forever. I memorized the contours of his bed and nestled into the imprint of his body. I shut my eyes and imagined he was there. Beside me. Touching me. I imagined his black eyes softening as he caressed my cheek, his hands warm and sturdy and real.

"Nora," Vee warned.

I ignored her, choosing to stay with Patch. The mattress dipped as he scooted closer. He smiled and slid his hands beneath me, rolling me on top of him. *You're cold, Angel. Let me warm you.*

I thought I'd lost you, Patch.

I'm right here. I promised we'd be together, didn't I?

But your feather—

Shh, he soothed. His finger sealed my lips. *I want to be with you, Angel. Stay here with me. Forget about Dante and the duel. I won't let him hurt you. I'll keep you safe.*

Tears burned at the backs of my eyes. *Take me away. Like you promised. Take me far away, just the two of us.*

BECCA FITZPATRICK

"Patch would hate to see you like this," Vee chided, clearly trying to appeal to my conscience.

I pulled the covers up to form a secret canopy above Patch and me, and giggled in his ear. *She doesn't know you're here.*

Our secret trick, he agreed.

I won't leave you, Patch.

I won't let you. In one swift movement, he reversed our positions, pinning me to the mattress. He bent over me. *Try and escape now.*

I frowned at the glimpse of icy blue that seemed to lurk under the surface of his eyes. I blinked to clear my vision, but when my eyes came into focus, I was very aware of the sizzling blue that ringed his irises.

Swallowing, I said, *I need to get a drink of water.*

I'll get it for you, Patch insisted. *Don't move. Stay in the bed.*

I'll only be a second, I argued, trying to wiggle out from beneath him.

Patch seized my wrists. *You said you wouldn't leave.*

I'm only getting a drink, I demurred.

I won't let you leave, Nora. The words resonated like a growl. His features contorted, twisting and morphing, until I saw flashes of another man. Dante's olive skin, cleft chin, and those hooded eyes that at one time I'd actually believed were handsome appeared before me. I rolled away, but not fast enough. Dante's fingers dug painfully into my shoulders, shoving me back under him. His breath felt hot on my cheek.

finale

It's over. Give up. I've won.

"Get away from me," I hissed.

His touch dissolved, his face hovering briefly over mine like a blue haze before it disappeared.

Ice-cold water struck my face, and I bolted upright with a gasp. The dream shattered; Vee stood an arm's reach away, holding an empty pitcher.

"Time to go," she said, clutching the pitcher as if preparing to use it as a weapon of defense if she had to.

"I don't want to," I croaked, too miserable to get angry over the water. My throat tightened, and I feared I was going to cry. I only wanted one thing, and he was gone. Patch wasn't coming back. Nothing I did could change that. The things I'd thought were worth fighting for, the things that burned and raged inside me, even beating Dante and destroying devilcraft, had lost their fire without him.

"And Patch?" Vee demanded. "You've given up on yourself, but have you given up on him, too?"

"Patch is gone." I pressed my fingers into my eyes until I'd ground out the urge to cry.

"Gone, not dead."

"I can't do this without Patch," I said, my breath catching.

"Then find a way to get him back."

"He's in hell," I snapped.

"Better that than in the grave."

I drew my knees up and bowed my head against them. "I killed Hank Millar, Vee. Patch and I did it together. Dante knows, and he's going to arrest me at the duel. He's going to execute me for treason." My mind conjured up a very real portrait. Dante would make my humiliation as public as possible. As his guards dragged me from the duel, I'd be spit on and called a myriad of vile names. As for the execution, how he would go about ending my life—

He would use his sword. The one Blakely had enhanced with devilcraft to kill me.

"That's why I can't go to the duel," I finished.

Vee's silence stretched out. "It's Dante's word against yours," she said at last.

"That's what I'm worried about."

"You're still leader of the Nephilim. You've got some street cred. If he tries to arrest you, challenge him." Conviction flashed in her eyes. "Fight him to the end. You can make it easy for him, or you can dig in your heels and make him work for it."

I sniffled, wiping my nose on the back of my hand. "I'm scared, Vee. So very scared."

"I know, babe. But I also know that if anyone can do this, it's you. I don't tell you this often, and maybe I've never told you, but when I grow up, I want to be just like you. Now for the last time, get out of bed before I drench you again. You're going to the cemetery. And you're going to give Dante the fight of his life."

• • •

finale

The worst of my burns had healed, but I felt drained and weakened nonetheless. I hadn't been a Nephil long enough to know the mechanics behind my rapid healing, but I imagined I'd unwittingly expended a lot of energy in the process. I hadn't checked the mirror before leaving Patch's place, but I had a pretty good idea of how miserable and downtrodden I looked. One glance at me, and Dante would call his own victory.

As Vee and I pulled into the gravel parking lot overlooking the cemetery, I reviewed my plan. After Dante announced he'd banished fallen angels to hell and won the war, he would most likely accuse me of murdering Hank and proclaim himself as my replacement. At that point, I would not step aside and relinquish my title. Vee was right; I would fight. Against all odds, I would fight. Dante would lead the Nephilim over my dead body—literally.

Vee's hand closed over mine. "Go secure your title. We'll figure out the rest later."

I swallowed back a disbelieving laugh. Later? I didn't care what happened after this. I felt a cold detachment toward my future. I didn't want to think about an hour from now. I didn't want to think about tomorrow. With each passing moment, my life veered further away from the path Patch and I had walked together. I didn't want to press forward. I wanted to go back. Where I could be with Patch again.

"Scott and I will be down there, in the crowd," Vee stated firmly. "Just . . . be careful, Nora."

Tears welled in my eyes. Those were Patch's words. I needed him here now, assuring me I could do this.

The sky was still dark, the moon washing white light over the ghostly landscape. A heavy frost made the grass crunch beneath my feet as I walked slowly downhill to the cemetery, giving Vee a head start. The grave markers seemed to float on the mist, white stone crosses and slender obelisks. An angel with chipped wings stretched two broken arms toward me. A ragged sob clamped in my throat. I shut my eyes, conjuring up Patch's strong, handsome features. It hurt to picture him, knowing I'd never see him again. *Don't you dare cry now*, I berated myself. I looked away, afraid I wouldn't get through this if I allowed any emotion other than icy determination into my heart.

Hundreds of Nephilim gathered in the cemetery below. The sheer size of their numbers caused my stride to catch. Since Nephilim stopped aging the day they swore fealty, most were young, within ten years of me, but I saw a handful of elderly men and women grouped among them. Their faces were bright with expectation. Children dodged in circles around their parents' legs, playing tag, before they were wrestled by the shoulders and pinned still. Children. As if this morning's event were family entertainment: a circus or a ball game.

As I drew closer, I noticed that twelve Nephilim wore ankle-length black robes, hoods drawn up. They had to be the same powerful Nephilim I'd met the morning following Hank's death. As leader of the Nephilim, I should have known what the robes signified. Lisa Martin and her cohorts should have told me. But they had never welcomed me into their circle. They'd never wanted me in the first place. I was sure the robes signified position and power, but I'd had to figure it out on my own.

One of the Nephilim pushed her hood back. Lisa Martin herself. Her expression was solemn, her eyes tense with anticipation. She handed me a black robe, as though it were more a matter of obligation than a sign of acceptance. The robe was heavier than I expected, made of thick velvet that felt slippery in my hands. "Have you seen Dante?" she asked me in an undertone.

I slipped the robe over my shoulders but didn't answer.

My eyes fell on Scott and Vee, and my chest loosened. I drew my first deep breath since leaving Patch's townhouse. Then I saw that they were holding hands, and a strange loneliness washed over me. My own empty hand tingled in the breeze. I worked my fist to keep it from shaking. Patch wasn't coming. Never again would he thread his fingers through mine, and a soft moan escaped my throat at the realization.

Sunrise.

A band of gold illuminated the gray horizon. Within minutes, rays of light would filter through the trees and burn off the fog. Dante would come, and the Nephilim would learn of their victory. The fear of swearing fealty and the dread of Cheshvan would become stories written in history. They would rejoice, cheering

BECCA FITZPATRICK

wildly and hailing Dante as their savior. They would carry him on their shoulders and chant his name. And then, when he had their unanimous approval, he would call me up out of the crowd. . . .

Lisa walked to the center of the gathering. She amplified her voice to say, "I'm sure Dante will arrive shortly. He knows the duel is strictly set for sunrise. It isn't like him to be late, but in any case, we may have to delay a few—"

Her remark was cut short by a rumbling that seemed to ripple across the ground. It vibrated through the soles of my feet, growing stronger. An instant uneasiness clamped like a fist in my stomach. Someone was coming. And not just someone, but several someones.

"Fallen angels," a Nephil whispered, fear threading her voice.

She was right. Their perceptible power, even from a distance, made every nerve ending in my body tingle. My hairs stood on end, stiff with aversion. I guessed their numbers to be hundreds. But how? Marcie had burned their feathers—I'd watched her.

"How did they find us?" another Nephil asked, dread rattling her familiar voice. I glanced sideways sharply, seeing Susanna Millar's mouth pucker with bewilderment beneath the folds of her hood.

"So they've come at last," Lisa hissed, a bright thirst for blood gleaming in her eyes. "Quick! Hide your children and gather your weapons. We will go against them, with or without Dante. The final battle ends here."

Her command spread through the crowd, followed by calls for order. Nephilim staggered and jostled into hurried, disorganized ranks. Some had knives, but those who didn't picked up rocks, broken bottles, and any other debris they could find to arm themselves. I ran to Vee and Scott. Without wasting breath, I directed my first words at Scott.

"Get Vee out of here. Go somewhere safe. I'll find you both when this is over."

"You're insane if you think we're leaving without you," Vee stated firmly. "Tell her, Scott. Pick her up and carry her out of here if you have to."

"How are fallen angels here?" Scott asked me, searching my face for an explanation. We'd watched the feathers burn together.

"I don't know. But I plan on finding out."

"You think Patch is out there. That's what this is about, isn't it?" Vee said, looking in the direction of the distant rumble that made the ground beneath us quake.

I met her eyes. "Scott and I watched the feathers burn. Either we were tricked, or someone has opened the gates of hell. Instinct tells me the latter is a better bet. If fallen angels are escaping hell, I have to make sure Patch gets out. And then I have to shut the gates before it's too late. If I don't end this now, there isn't going to be another chance. It's the last day fallen angels can possess Nephilim bodies, but I no longer think that means anything to fallen angels." I thought of devilcraft. Of its power. "I believe they have the means to enslave us indefinitely—that is, if they don't kill us first."

Vee nodded slowly, digesting the full weight of my words.

BECCA FITZPATRICK

"Then we'll help you. We're in this together. This is as much Scott's and my fight as it is yours."

"Vee—" I began warningly.

"If this really is the fight of my life, you know I'm gonna be there. Whether you say so or not. I didn't pass up those last few doughnuts to get here on time, just to turn around and leave," Vee told me, but there was something almost tender in the way she said it. She meant every word. We were in this together.

I was too choked up to speak. "All right," I said at last. "Let's go slam shut the gates of hell once and for all."

CHAPTER

40

THE SUN CRESTED ABOVE THE HORIZON, BACK-
lighting the seemingly endless silhouette of fallen angels
charging across the cemetery grounds. In the early,
slanted light, their shadows emitted an incandescent blue, like a
great ocean wave roaring toward shore. One man—a Nephil—ran
at the front of the army, wielding a blue-gleaming sword. A sword
created to kill me. Even from this distance, Dante's eyes seemed to
cut through all distraction, hunting for me.

I'd wondered how the gates of hell had been opened, and now I had my answer. The dark-blue halo hovering above the fallen angels told me Dante had employed devilcraft.

But why he'd allowed Marcie to burn the feathers, only to free fallen angels—that I didn't know.

"I need to get Dante alone," I told Scott and Vee. "He's looking for me, too. If you can, lead him to the parking lot above the cemetery."

"You don't have a weapon," Scott said.

I pointed ahead, at the surging army. Every fallen angel carried a sword that seemed to shoot from their hand like a shining blue flame. "No, but they do. I just have to convince one of them to make a donation."

"They're spreading out," Scott said. "They're going to kill every Nephil in this cemetery, and then invade Coldwater."

I grasped his hands, then Vee's. For one moment, we formed an unbreakable circle, and it gave me strength. I'd be alone when I faced Dante, but Vee and Scott would not be far away—I would remember that. "Whatever happens, I'll never forget our friendship."

Scott dragged my head against his chest, holding me fervently, then kissed my forehead tenderly. Vee flung her arms around me, embracing me long enough that I feared I might shed more tears than I already had.

Pulling away, I ran.

finale

The terrain of the cemetery offered multiple hiding places, and I climbed swiftly into the branches of an evergreen tree growing out of the hill leading up to the parking lot. From here, I had an unobstructed view, watching as unarmed Nephilim men and women, outnumbered twenty to one, charged at the wall of fallen angels. In a matter of seconds, fallen angels descended over them like a cloud, chopping them down as if they were nothing more than weeds.

At the bottom of the hill, Susanna Millar was locked in a wrestling match with a fallen angel whose pale blond hair whipped about her shoulders as the two women thrashed for control. Susanna flung a knife from the hidden folds of her cloak and launched it into Dabria's breastbone. With a high growl of rage, Dabria two-handed her sword, skidding over the wet grass as she swung it in retaliation. Their fight carried them behind the maze of tombstones and out of sight.

Farther away, Scott and Vee fought back to back, using tree branches to fend off four fallen angels who had them surrounded. Despite their numerical advantage, the fallen angels receded from Scott, whose sheer strength and size gave him the upper hand. He knocked them over with the tree branch, then used it as a sledgehammer to pummel them senseless.

I scanned the cemetery for Marcie. If she was out there, I couldn't see her. It wasn't a wild guess to believe she'd deliberately avoided the battle and chosen safety over honor. Blood painted

BECCA FITZPATRICK

the cemetery grass. Nephilim and fallen angels alike skidded on it—some of the blood was pure red, much of it tainted blue with devilcraft.

Lisa Martin and her robed friends ran along the perimeter of the cemetery, black smoke billowing from the torches they carried. At a hurried pace, they moved from one tree and shrub to the next, lighting them on fire. Flames erupted, consuming the foliage and narrowing the battlefield, forming a barrier around the fallen angels. The smoke, hazy and thick, stretched across the cemetery like the shadow of nightfall. Lisa couldn't burn fallen angels to death, but she had bought the Nephilim extra coverage.

One fallen angel emerged from the smoke, trudging up the hillside, eyes alert. I had to believe he sensed me. His sword radiated blue fire, but the way he held it concealed his face. Still, I could plainly see he was gangly, an easier match for me.

He crept toward the tree, eyeing the dark spaces nestled between branches cautiously. In five seconds, he'd be directly below me.

Four, three, two—

I dropped from the tree. I slammed into him from behind, the weight of my impact shoving him forward. His sword flew from his hand before I could steal it. We rolled several feet, but I had the advantage of surprise. Scrabbling upright quickly, I stood over his back, landing several crushing blows to his wing scars before he shoved his foot back, sweeping my legs out from under me. I rolled away, missing the downward drill of a knife he'd extracted from his boot.

finale

"Rixon?" I said, shocked to recognize the pale face and hawkish features of Patch's former best friend glaring at me. Patch had personally chained Rixon in hell after he'd attempted to sacrifice me to get a human body.

"You," he said.

We faced each other, knees bent, ready to spring. "Where's Patch?" I dared ask.

His beady eyes clung to mine, narrowed and cold. "That name means nothing to me. The man is dead to me."

Since he didn't surge at me with the knife, I risked asking another question. "Why are fallen angels letting Dante lead you?"

"He forced us to swear an oath of loyalty to him," he said, his eyes narrowing into twin slits. "It was that, or stay in hell. Not many stayed."

Patch wouldn't stay behind. Not if there was a way back to me. He'd swear the oath to Dante, as much as he'd rather rip out the Nephil's neck, and then repeat the procedure with every other square inch of his body.

"I'm going after Dante," I told Rixon.

He laughed, a hiss between his teeth. "I claim a prize for every Nephil body I drag back to Dante. I failed to kill ye before, and now I'll do it properly."

At the same time, we dived for his sword, several feet away. Rixon reached it first, rolling agilely onto his knees and slicing the sword crosswise at me. I ducked, hurtling myself at his

BECCA FITZPATRICK

midsection before he could swing again. I slammed him back against the ground on his wing scars. Taking advantage of his brief immobility, I disarmed him; I plucked the sword from his left hand, and the knife from his right.

Then I kicked his body over and plunged the knife deep into his wing scars. "You killed my dad," I told him. "I haven't forgotten."

I hustled uphill toward the parking lot, glancing back to see that I wasn't being followed. I had a sword, but I needed a better one. Recalling my training with Patch, I replayed every sword-stripping maneuver we had practiced together. When Dante met me in the parking lot, I would steal his sword. And I would kill him with it.

When I rounded the hill, Dante was waiting. He watched me, sliding his finger indolently back and forth over the tip of his sword.

"Nice sword," I said. "I heard you had it made especially for me."

His bottom lip curled marginally. "Only the best for you."

"You murdered Blakely. A pretty cold way of saying thank you for all the prototypes he developed for you."

"And you murdered Hank. Your own flesh and blood. A bit like calling the kettle black, isn't it?" he quipped. "I spent months infiltrating Hank's secret blood society and gaining his trust. I have to tell you, I raised a toast to my good fortune the day he died. It would have been far harder to dethrone him than you."

I shrugged. "I'm used to being underestimated."

"I trained you. I know exactly what you're capable of."

finale

"Why'd you free fallen angels?" I asked bluntly, since he seemed amenable to sharing secrets. "You had them in hell. You could have defected and ruled the Nephilim. They never would have known the truth about your shifting loyalties."

Dante smiled, his teeth sharp and white. He looked more animal than man, a swarthy, savage beast. "I've risen above both races," he said in a voice so practical it was hard to think he didn't truly believe it. "I will give Nephilim who survive my army's attack this morning a similar choice to the one I gave fallen angels: swear loyalty to me or die. One ruler. Indivisible. With power and judgment over all. Wish you'd thought of it first?"

I held Rixon's sword close to my body, shifting on the balls of my feet. "Oh, there are several things I'm wishing right now, but that's not one of them. Why haven't fallen angels possessed Nephilim this Cheshvan? I'm guessing you know, and don't take that as a compliment."

"I ordered them not to. Until I killed Blakely, I didn't want him superseding my orders and distributing the devilcraft super-drink to Nephilim. He would have, if fallen angels had come against Nephilim." Again, spoken so practically. So superior. He feared nothing.

"Where's Patch?"

"In hell. I made certain his face never passed through the gates. He'll stay in hell. And only when I feel like brutally abusing and tormenting something will he get a visitor."

I lunged for him, swinging my sword lethally at his head. He sprang from its swath, countering with several explosive blows of his own. With each defensive block, my sword vibrated up to my shoulders. I gritted my teeth to battle the pain. He was too strong; I couldn't fend off his powerful strokes forever. I had to find a way to strip his sword and puncture his heart.

"When was the last time you took devilcraft?" Dante asked, using his sword like a machete to hack at me.

"I'm done with devilcraft." I blocked his strikes, but if I didn't stop playing defense soon, he'd back me into the fence. Aggressively, I lunged to stab his thigh. He sidestepped, my sword driving into air and nearly unbalancing me.

The more you lean or stretch, the easier it will be for Dante to knock you over. Patch's caution sounded in my head as clearly as he'd spoken it yesterday. I nodded to myself. *That's it, Patch. Keep talking to me.*

"It shows," Dante said. "I'd hoped you'd take enough of the poisonous prototype I gave you to rot your brain."

So that had been his initial plan: get me addicted to devilcraft and let it quietly kill me. "Where are you storing the rest of the prototypes?"

"Where I can harness their power whenever I want," he returned smugly.

"Hope you hid them well, because if there's one thing I'm doing before I die, it's destroying your lab."

"The new lab is inside me. The prototypes are there, Nora,

finale

replicating over and over. *I* am devilcraft. Do you have any idea what it feels like to be the most powerful man on the planet?"

I ducked just in time to miss a chop at my neck. Quickening my steps and plunging my sword forward, I aimed for his stomach, but he danced sideways again, and the blade nipped the flesh above his hip instead. Blue liquid oozed from the wound, blooming across his white shirt.

With a guttural growl, Dante flew at me. I ran, jumping the stone wall encasing the parking lot.

Dew beaded the grass, and my balance faltered; I slipped and slid downhill. Just in time I scrabbled behind a gravestone; Dante's sword speared the grass where I'd landed. He chased me through the headstones, swinging his sword at every chance, the steel ringing out as it clanged against marble and stone.

I ran behind the first tree I saw, putting it between us. It was on fire, popping and crackling as the flames devoured it. Ignoring the heat blasting my face, I faked left, but Dante wasn't in the mood for games. He chased around the tree, holding his sword over his head as though he intended to slice me in half, skull to toes. I fled again, hearing Patch in my head.

Use his height to your advantage. Expose his legs. A hard strike to either knee, then steal his sword.

I ducked behind the mausoleum, flattening myself against the wall. The moment Dante moved into my line of vision, I stepped out from my hiding place, driving my sword into the flesh of his thigh. Watery blue blood spurted from the wound. He'd consumed so much devilcraft, his veins literally flowed with it.

Before I could retract my sword, Dante swung at me. I cleared his sword, but in doing so, had to leave my own buried in his leg. The emptiness in my hands suddenly felt very real, and I swallowed down panic.

"Forgot something," Dante jeered, clenching his teeth as he pulled the blade out of his leg. He hurled my sword onto the mausoleum's roof.

I dashed away, knowing his leg wound would slow him—until it healed. I hadn't made it far before agonizing heat ripped into my left shoulder blade and spread down my arm. I stumbled to my knees with a cry. I glanced back, just able to see Pepper's pearly-white dagger deeply lodged in my shoulder. Marcie must have given it to Dante last night. He limped up behind me.

The whites of his eyes sizzled blue with devilcraft. Blue sweat popped from his brow. Devilcraft trickled from his wound. The prototypes he'd stolen from Blakely were inside him. He'd consumed them all, and somehow had transformed his body into a devilcraft factory. A brilliant plan, except for one small detail. If I could kill him, every prototype on Earth would go with him.

If I could kill him.

"Your fat archangel friend confessed to enchanting that dagger specifically to kill me," he said. "He failed, and Patch did too." His lips curled in a nasty smile.

finale

I ripped a marble headstone from the earth and hurled it at him, but he batted it away as though I'd flung a baseball.

I inched backward, relying on my good arm to drag me. Too slow.

I attempted a hurried mind-trick. *Drop the sword and freeze!* I shouted into Dante's subconscious.

Pain splintered across my cheekbone. The blunt edge of his sword had lashed out so hard, I tasted blood.

"You'd dare mind-trick me?" Before I could recoil, he lifted me by the scruff of my neck and flung me savagely against a tree. The impact cast a fog over my vision and stole my breath. I tried to balance on my knees, but the ground rocked.

"Let her go."

Scott's voice. What was he doing here? My dazed apprehension lasted only a moment. I saw the sword in his hands, and sheer anxiety shot to every corner of my body.

"Scott," I warned. "Get out of here *now*."

His steady hands encircled the hilt. "I swore an oath to your father to protect you," he said, never lowering his evaluating gaze from Dante.

Dante tipped his head back, laughing. "An oath to a dead man? How does that work?"

"If you touch Nora again, you're as good as dead. That's my oath to you."

"Step aside, Scott," Dante barked. "This isn't about you."

"That's where you're wrong."

Scott charged at Dante, the two battling in a blur of rapid strokes. Scott relaxed his shoulders, relying on his powerful build and athletic grace to make up for Dante's experience and devilcraft-enhanced skill. Scott held the offense, while Dante skirted agilely to the side. A brutal arc from Scott's sword severed the lower half of Dante's left arm. Scott skewered the limb and held it up. "As many pieces as it takes."

Dante cursed, sloppily slashing his sword at Scott with his usable arm. The ringing collision of their blades cracked the morning air, seeming to deafen me. Dante forced Scott back toward a towering stone cross, and I shouted my warning in mind-speak.

Headstone directly behind!

Scott skipped sideways, easily avoiding a fall while simultaneously blocking an attack. Dante's pores leaked blue sweat, but if he noticed, he didn't show it. He shook his damp hair from his eyes and continued to hack and chop, his good arm visibly tiring. His thrashing strokes turned desperate. I saw my chance to circle behind him, trapping him between Scott and me, where one of us could finish him off.

A grunted cry stopped me in my tracks. I turned just as Scott slipped on wet grass, falling onto one knee. His legs spread awkwardly as he tried to regain his stance. He rolled safely away from Dante's plunged sword, but he didn't have time to climb to his feet before Dante pounced again, this time driving the sword deeply into Scott's chest.

finale

Scott's hands curled weakly around Dante's sword, impaled in his heart, trying unsuccessfully to dislodge it. Fiery blue devil-craft pumped from the sword into his body; his skin darkened to a ghastly blue. He feebly croaked my name. *Nora?*

I screamed. Paralyzed by shock and grief, I watched as Dante finished his attack with a clean twist of the blade, cleaving Scott's heart.

I shifted my full attention to Dante, trembling with a hatred like I'd never known before. A wave of violent loathing rippled through me. Poison filled my veins. My hands curled into fists of rock, and a voice of fury and vengeance screamed in my head.

Fueled by this deep, abiding anger, I drew on my inner power. Not halfheartedly or hurried, or with a lack of confidence. I summoned every drop of courage and determination I possessed and unleashed it at him. I would not let him win. Not this way. Not with devilcraft. Not by killing Scott.

With all the strength of my mental conviction, I invaded his mind and shredded the impulses firing to and from his brain. Just as quickly, I plugged in an unyielding command: *Drop the sword. Drop the sword, you worthless, cunning, twisted man.*

I heard the chink of steel on marble.

I glared nails at Dante. His dazed expression stared into distant space, as though he was looking for something lost.

"Ironic, isn't it, that it was you who pointed out my greatest strength?" I said, every word dripping abhorrence.

I'd sworn I would never use devilcraft again, but this was one circumstance where I'd gladly bend the rules. If I killed Dante, devilcraft went too.

The temptation to steal devilcraft for my own flickered across my mind, but I flushed the idea away. I was stronger than Hank, stronger than Dante. Stronger, even, than devilcraft. I would send it back to hell for Scott, who'd given his life to save mine. I'd just picked up Dante's sword when his leg bucked up, kicking it from my hands.

Dante catapulted himself on top of me, his hands vising my neck. I raked my fingernails at his eyes. I clawed his face.

I opened my mouth. No air.

His cold stare gleamed with triumph.

My jaw opened and closed uselessly. Dante's ruthless face turned grainy, like an old TV picture. Over his shoulder, a stone angel watched me with interest.

I wanted to laugh. I wanted to cry. So this was what it meant to die. To give in.

I didn't want to give in.

Dante pinched my airway with his knee, stretching sideways to pick up his sword. The tip centered over my heart.

Possess him, the stone angel seemed to calmly command me. *Possess him and kill him.*

Patch? I wondered almost dreamily.

Clinging to the strength that came from believing Patch

was near, watching over me, I stopped resisting Dante. I lowered my scratching fingers and relaxed my legs. I succumbed to him, even though it felt like a cowardly, conceding thing. I focused my thoughts on gravitating toward him.

A foreign coldness rippled over my body.

I blinked, staring at the world through Dante's eyes. I looked down. His sword was in my hands. Somewhere buried inside me, I knew Dante was grinding his teeth, uttering blood-chilling noises, howling like a miserable animal.

I turned the sword to face me. I pointed it at my heart. And then I did a surprising thing.

I fell on the blade.

CHAPTER

ANTE'S BODY EXPELLED MINE SO FAST, I
felt like I'd been flung from a moving car. My
hands snatched at grass, searching for something
solid in a world that spun, tipping and turning over itself. As
the dizziness faded, I looked around for Dante. I smelled him
before I saw him.

His skin had deepened to the color of a bruise, and his body
began to bloat. His corpse purged its fluids, his devilcraft blood

seeping into the earth like something living, something that burrowed away from sunlight. Flesh fell away, deteriorating into dust. After only a handful of seconds, all that remained of Dante were sucked-dry bones.

He was dead. Devilcraft was gone.

Slowly I pushed to my feet. My jeans were tattered and stained, streaks of grass rubbed across the knees. I licked the crack of my mouth, tasting blood and the salty tang of sweat. I walked to Scott, each step heavy, tears hot on my face, my hands hovering uselessly over his rapidly decaying body. I shut my eyes, forcing myself to recall his lopsided grin. Not his vacant eyes. In my mind, I played back his teasing laugh. Not the gurgling, gasping sounds he'd made right before dying. I remembered his warmth in accidental touches and playful jabs, knowing his body was rotting even as I clung to the memory.

"Thank you," I choked out, telling myself that somewhere nearby, he could still hear my voice. "You saved my life. Good-bye, Scott. I'll never forget you, that's my oath to you. Never," I vowed.

The fog hanging over the cemetery burned gold and gray as the sun's rays sliced through it. Ignoring the fire clawing my shoulder as I drew out Pepper's dagger, I staggered out of the cluster of headstones and into the open cemetery.

Strange lumps littered the grass, and as I came closer, I saw them for what they really were: corpses. Fallen angels, from what I could tell of what remained of them. Just like Dante, their flesh fell away in seconds. Blue fluid wept from their carcasses and was immediately sucked up by the earth.

"You did it."

I spun around, instinctively hardening my grip on the dagger. Detective Basso tucked his hands in his pockets, a grim little smile playing at his mouth. The black dog who'd saved my life just a few short days ago sat stalwartly at his ankles. The dog's feral yellow eyes stared up at me contemplatively. Basso bent down, rubbing the mangy fur between his ears.

"He's a good dog," Basso said. "Once I'm gone, he'll need a good home."

I took a cautious step backward. "What's going on here?"

"You did it," he repeated. "Devilcraft is eradicated."

"Tell me I'm dreaming."

"I'm an archangel." The corners of his mouth crooked, almost, but not quite, sheepishly.

"I don't know what I'm supposed to say."

"I've been on Earth for months, working undercover. We suspected that Chauncey Langeais and Hank Millar were summoning devilcraft, and it was my job to keep a close eye on Hank, his dealings, and his family—including you."

Basso. Archangel. Working undercover. I shook my head. "I'm still not sure what is happening here."

"You did what I've been trying to do. Get rid of devilcraft."

I digested this in silence. After what I'd seen these past few weeks, it took a lot to surprise me. But this certainly did. Good to know I wasn't entirely jaded yet.

"Fallen angels are gone. It won't last forever, but enjoy it while we can, right?" he grunted. "I'm closing this case and heading home. Congratulations."

My brain hardly heard him. Fallen angels, gone. *Gone*. The word yawned inside me like an endless hole.

"Good work, Nora. Oh, and you might like to know we've got Pepper in custody and we're dealing with him. He claims you put him up to stealing the feathers, but I'm going to pretend I didn't hear it. One last thing. Consider this a thank-you of sorts: Go for a nice, clean cut through the middle of the mark on your wrist," he said, sawing his own wrist with the side of his hand in demonstration.

"What?"

A knowing smile. "For once, just trust me."

And he was gone.

I leaned back against a tree, trying to slow the world long enough to make sense of it. Dante, dead. Devilcraft, demolished. The war, nonexistent. My oath, fulfilled. And Scott. Oh, Scott. How would I tell Vee? How would I help her get through the loss, the heartache, the despair? Down the road, how would I encourage her to move on, when I had no such plans for myself? Trying to replace Patch—even trying to find happiness, however small, with someone else—would be a lie. I was Nephilim now, blessed to live forever, cursed to do so without Patch.

Footsteps rustled ahead, cutting through the grass, a familiar sound. I stiffened, poised to attack, as a dark outline emerged through the fog. The figure's eyes raked the ground, clearly hunting for something. He crouched at every body, inspecting it with a hurried fervor, then kicked it aside with an impatient curse.

"Patch?"

Hunched over a decaying body, he froze. His head whipped up, his eyes narrowing, as if disbelieving what he'd heard. His gaze locked with mine, and something undecipherable moved in his black eyes. Relief? Solace? Deliverance.

I ran in a frenzy the last several feet separating us and threw myself into his embrace, digging my fingers into his shirt, burying my face into his neck. "Let this be real. Let this be you. Don't let me go. Don't ever let me go." I started crying freely. "I fought Dante. I killed him. But I couldn't save Scott. He's dead. Devilcraft is gone, but I failed Scott."

Patch murmured soft sounds in my ear, but his hands shook where they held me. He guided me to sit on a stone bench, but he never released me, holding me as though he were afraid I'd drain through his fingers like sand. His eyes, weary and red, told me he'd been crying.

Keep talking, I told myself. Keep the dream going. Anything to keep Patch here.

"I saw Rixon."

"He's dead," Patch said bluntly. "So are the rest of them. Dante released us from hell, but not before taking our oaths of loyalty and injecting us with a devilcraft prototype. It was the only way out. We left hell with it swimming in our veins, our lifeblood. When you destroyed devilcraft, every fallen angel being sustained by it died."

It can't be a dream. It must be, and at the same time, it's too real. His touch, so familiar, caused my heartbeat to soar and my blood to melt— I couldn't fabricate such a forceful response to him in a dream.

"How did you survive?"

"I didn't swear an oath to Dante, and I didn't let him inject me with devilcraft. I possessed Rixon just long enough to escape hell. I didn't trust Dante or devilcraft. I trusted you to finish them both off."

"Oh, Patch," I said, my voice trembling. "You were gone. I saw your motorcycle. You never came back. I thought—" My heart twisted, a deep ache expanding to fill my chest. "When I didn't save your feather—" The loss and devastation crept inside me like a winter chill, relentless and numbing. I snuggled closer to Patch, fearing that he might vanish through my hands. I climbed onto his lap, sobbing into his chest.

Patch cradled me in his arms, rocking me. *Angel,* he murmured to my mind. *I'm right here. We're together. It's over, and we have each other.*

Each other. Together. He'd come back to me; everything that mattered was right here. Patch was right here.

Drying my eyes with my sleeves, I pushed onto my knees and

straddled his hips. I combed my fingers through his dark hair, locking his curls between my fingers and drawing him close.

"I want to be with you," I said. "I need you close, Patch. I need all of you."

I kissed him, frantic and bold, my mouth crushing forcefully to his. I pressed deeper, drowning in his taste. His hands tightened around my back, pulling me closer. I shaped my palms to his shoulders, to his arms, to his thighs, feeling his muscles work, so real and strong and alive. His mouth ground against mine, bright, needy pressure.

"I want to wake up with you every morning and fall asleep beside you each night," Patch told me gravely. "I want to take care of you, cherish you, and love you in a way no other man ever could. I want to spoil you—every kiss, every touch, every thought, they all belong to you. I'll make you happy. Every day, I'll make you happy." The antique, almost primitive band he held between his fingers caught the sunlight, glinting silver. "I found this ring shortly after I was banished from heaven. I kept it to remind myself of how endless my sentence was, how eternal one small choice can be. I've kept it a long time. I want you to have it. You broke my suffering. You've given me a new eternity. Be my girl, Nora. Be my everything."

I bit my lip, snagging a smile that threatened to split my face. I checked the ground to make sure I wasn't floating. "Patch?"

He scraped the rough edge of the ring on his palm, raising a thin trail of blood. "I swear to you, Nora Grey, on this day, from now and forever, to give myself to you. I am yours. My love, my body, my soul—I place in your possession and protection." He held out the ring, a single offering, a binding promise.

"Patch," I whispered.

"If I fail my covenant, my own misery and regret will be my endless punishment." His eyes pinned mine, a stripped sincerity clear in his gaze. *But I won't fail, Angel. I won't fail you.*

I accepted the ring, about to slice the edge across my palm the same way Patch had done. And then I remembered Basso's cryptic admonition. Sliding the ring higher, I slashed the pencil-like marking on the inside of my wrist, which I'd been born with—a mark of my Nephilim heritage. Bright red blood smeared my skin. I fit my incision snugly against Patch's hand, feeling a warm pins-and-needles sensation where our blood mingled.

"I swear to you, Patch, to take your love and cherish it. And in return, to give you my body and my heart—everything I possess, I give to you. I am yours. Wholly and completely. Love me. Protect me. Fulfill me. And I promise to do the same."

He pushed the ring onto my finger.

Patch jerked unexpectedly, as though powerful voltage had coursed through his body. "My hand," he said, low. "My hand is—"

His eyes locked with mine. A slow burn of confusion filled his expression. "My hand is tingling where you mixed our blood."

"You feel it," I said, too scared to believe it might be true.

Scared of raising my hopes. Terrified that the trick would fade, and his body would once again shut mine out.

No. This was Basso's gift to me.

Patch, a fallen angel, could feel. All my kisses, every touch. My warmth, the depth of my response to him.

He made a sound that was trapped between a laugh and a groan. Amazement lit his eyes. "I feel you." His hands roved up my arms, hastily exploring my skin, catching my face. He kissed me, hard. He shuddered with pleasure.

Patch scooped me into his arms, and I shrieked with joy. "Let's get out of here," he murmured, his eyes blazing with desire.

I wrapped my arms around his neck and nestled my head on the curve of his shoulder. His body was solid assurance, a warm counterpoint. And now he could feel me, too. A flush of anticipation burned under my skin.

This was it. Together. Forever. As we left it all behind, the sun warmed my back, lighting the way before us.

I knew of no better omen.

EPILOGUE

THREE YEARS LATER
THE HODDER VALLEY, LANCASHIRE, ENGLAND

O KAY, YOU WIN," I BREATHED, PUSHING OUT OF my chair and staring at Vee with admiration as she entered the church's vestry, carrying the hem of her floor-length pewter silk gown. Light from the stained-glass window seemed to set the fabric aflame with glittering, metallic color. "I know I told you to stick with traditional white, but I was wrong. Vee, you are stunning."

She twirled, showing off combat boots I hadn't seen since high school. "Something old," Vee said.

I bit my lip. "I think I'm going to cry."

"You're gonna catch my bouquet, right? And then give it back to me when no one is watching so I can have it professionally dried and framed—and then you can mock me for the rest of my life for being such a sap?"

"I'm Nephilim. I'll have those flowers in my hands before the brains of your other friends have registered that you've tossed them."

Vee gave a happy sigh. "Babe, I'm so glad you came."

"It would've taken a lot more than three thousand miles to keep me from my best friend's wedding." I smiled suggestively. "Where are you honeymooning?"

"Gavin won't tell. It's his big secret. He's got the whole thing planned out. I told him I only had one request: a hotel with dough-nuts on the room-service menu. We're gone ten days. When we get back, we'll both start looking for jobs."

"Do you ever think of moving back?"

"To Coldwater? Heck, no. England suits me fine. These Brits love my accent. The first time Gavin asked me out it was just to hear me talk. Lucky for him, it's one of the things I do best." All teasing left her eyes. "Too many memories back home. Can't drive down the street without thinking I see Scott in the crowd. Do you think there's an afterlife? Do you think he's happy?"

My throat grew slippery, too raw to speak. Not one day had

finale

passed since Scott's death that I hadn't taken a small, quiet moment to send up gratitude for his sacrifice.

"He should be here. I wish like hell he was," Vee said, bowing her head and chipping at her freshly painted nails.

"Me too." I squeezed her hands.

"Your mom told me Marcie died a couple months ago."

"She lived longer than anyone expected."

"A rotten apple to the end?"

"My mom went to her funeral. Five people total, including Marcie's mom."

Vee shrugged, unsympathetic. "Karma, alive and well."

The arched oak door across the room opened, and my mom poked her head in. She had flown out a week ago to play wedding coplanner alongside Vee's mom, and I think she was secretly reveling in the role. She'd finally accepted that Patch and I—a pairing she'd gradually warmed to over the years— had sworn our vows under heaven, sealed in blood, and were never doing the big, white wedding thing, and this was her chance. The irony of it all. Who would have guessed Vee would go a more traditional path than me?

My mom beamed at us. "Dry those eyes, my darling girls, it's almost time."

I fussed over Vee's bun, teasing loose a few more strands to frame her face, and pinned fragrant stephanotis flowers at the crown. After I finished, Vee flung her arms around me, rocking

BECCA FITZPATRICK

me back and forth in an animated hug, when we both heard a seam rip.

"Dang it ALL," Vee said, twisting around to examine the ripped seam on her dress. "I ordered a size smaller, planning to lose ten pounds for the wedding. I wouldn't call myself fat, but I could stand to lose a little Nephilim bulk. Trouble was, there was never a shortage of Twinkies in my cupboard."

I couldn't help it; I burst into a fit of giggles.

"I see how it is. I'm gonna have to walk in front of all those people with my undies waving in the air, and you don't even care," Vee said, but she, too, was grinning. She took a Band-Aid from her purse and slapped it over the torn fabric.

We laughed so hard we turned red in the face, gasping for air.

The door opened a second time. "Places! Hurry!" my mom said, ushering me out. Organ music drifted in from the chapel. I shuffled to the back of the line of bridesmaids, who all wore identical yellow taffeta mermaid dresses, and accepted my bouquet of white lilies from Vee's brother, Mike. Vee took her place beside me and sucked in a long breath.

"Ready?" I asked.

She winked. "And willing."

Attendants stationed on either side of the massive, engraved doors pulled them open. Arm in arm, Vee and I walked inside the chapel.

• • •

finale

After the wedding, we took pictures outside. A bright afternoon sun spilled light over green pastures with picturesque sheep grazing in the distance. Through it all, Vee glowed, looking more serene and radiant than I'd ever seen her. Gavin held her hand, caressed her cheek, whispered in her ear. Vee hadn't told me he was human, but I knew right away. Since Vee hadn't sworn fealty, they'd grow old together. I didn't know exactly how her aging, or mine for that matter, would work, since up until now, it was unheard of for a Nephil to live indefinitely without being forced to swear fealty. Either way, she was immortal. Someday Gavin would die, never knowing his wife wouldn't follow him into the next world. I didn't hold Vee's omission against her; I admired her for carving out happy memories, period. I hadn't met Gavin before today, but his adoration and love for her was obvious, and really, what more could I ask for?

The reception, too, was outside, under a large white tent. With the camera's flash still popping behind my eyes, I made my way over to the bar and asked for sparkling water. Couples were dancing to the live orchestra, but I hardly noticed them. My focus turned singularly on Patch.

He'd cleaned up for the wedding, wearing a tailored black tux and his best depraved smile. The tux framed his athletic build, and the smile put a shot of adrenaline into my heartbeat. He saw me, too, his black eyes warming with affection and desire. A flush of anticipation burned under my skin. I'd been separated from him most of the day, and now I wanted him. Badly.

Patch made his way over, sipping from a wineglass. His tuxedo jacket was slung over his shoulder, his hair curling rakishly from the humidity. "There's an inn just down the road. A barn behind those trees over there, if you're feeling frisky," he said, clearly having no doubts as to the direction of my thoughts.

"Did you just say 'frisky'?"

Patch's hands fell on my hips, pulling me close. "Yeah. Need a demonstration?" He kissed me once. Then again, drawing it out with a few inventive maneuvers of his tongue. "I love you."

"Words I'll never grow tired of hearing."

He brushed my curls back off my face. "I never pictured my life so complete. I never thought I'd have everything I want. You're everything to me, Angel."

His words filled my heart to the brim. I loved him in a way I'd never be able to express in words. He was part of me. And I was part of him. Tethered together for the rest of eternity. I leaned in and kissed him. "I just might take you up on your offer. A quaint countryside inn, you say?"

Cadillac is parked out front, or I've got a motorcycle out back, Patch spoke to my thoughts. Traditional departure or escape?

I, personally, had had enough tradition for one day. Escape.

Patch scooped me into his arms, and I shrieked with joy as he carted me toward the back of the church. We swung onto his motorcycle and rocketed up the road, flying over the green hills toward the inn.

finale

Inside our cozy, private room, I reached up and tugged on his silk necktie, undoing the knot. "You dress to impress," I said approvingly.

"No, Angel." He leaned in, his teeth softly grazing my ear. "I undress to impress."

ACKNOWLEDGMENTS

My heart is filled with gratitude for the people who have made writing the Hush, Hush series possible. First, to my family for their unfailing support. Every day I am amazed to be surrounded by people who love me so unconditionally.

Many thanks to my agent, Catherine Drayton, for her leap of faith.

I consider myself lucky to work with some of the industry's finest: Courtney Bongiolotti, Julia Maguire, Zareen Jaffery, Justin Chanda, Anne Zafian, Jenica Nasworthy, Lucille Rettino, Elke Villa, Chrissy Noh, Jon Anderson, and Valerie Shea.

Thanks are owed to Anna McKean and Paul Crichton for many, many hours of work behind the scenes—and for taking such great care of me while I'm on the road.

I'm grateful for the friendships I've made during this journey, particularly with Jenn Martin and Rebecca Sutton, the savvy sisters behind FallenArchangel.com. Keep calm and call Patch!

Lyndsey Blessing, Charlie Olsen, and the rest of the team at InkWell Management—thanks for having my back.

I love my books' covers, and applaud James Porto and Lucy Ruth Cummins for their artwork and creativity.

Thanks to Lisa Martin, fan extraordinaire, who bid on a character name to benefit Kids Need to Read—your generosity is appreciated, and now you're immortalized in this book!

To the many booksellers and librarians working on the front lines: If you've ever shared Hush, Hush with a reader, I owe you a high five. In the meantime, consider this thank-you just for you.

Since Hush, Hush was published, I've had the amazing opportunity to travel abroad and meet readers all over the world. None of this would have been possible without my international publishers. Special thanks to my friends at Simon & Schuster UK, Simon & Schuster Australia, Simon & Schuster Canada, Piemme Freeway, and Lattès.

Finally, a note to my readers. What an amazing three years! Thank you for being such a fun audience to write for. Thank you for your letters of support, for coming to my events, and for falling in love with Patch, Nora, Vee, and Scott. I look forward to writing for you in the future.